THE BURNING WOMAN

PATRICIA MARQUES

First published in Great Britain in 2025 by Hodder & Stoughton Limited
An Hachette UK company

This paperback edition published in 2025

The authorised representative in the EEA is Hachette Ireland, 8 Castlecourt Centre, Dublin 15, D15 XTP3, Ireland (email: info@hbgi.ie)

1

A CIP catalogue record for this title is available from the British Library

Paperback ISBN 978 1 399 70734 3
ebook ISBN 978 1 399 70733 6

Typeset in Sabon MT Std by Manipal Technologies Limited

Printed and bound in Great Britain by Clays Ltd, Elcograf S.p.A.

Hodder & Stoughton policy is to use papers that are natural, renewable and recyclable products and made from wood grown in sustainable forests. The logging and manufacturing processes are expected to conform to the environmental regulations of the country of origin.

Hodder & Stoughton Limited
Carmelite House
50 Victoria Embankment
London EC4Y 0DZ

www.hodder.co.uk

Praise for *The Burning Woman*
and the Inspector Reis series

'Beautifully told, with great verve, this is sharp, taut storytelling'

Daily Mail

'An original clever, inventive and suspenseful thriller. I loved being back in Inspector Reis's world'

Nadine Matheson

'A brilliant read and a stunning addition to the Isabel Reis series . . . Patricia Marques is an author with a gift'

Steven Powell

'Assured writing, engaging characters and a brilliant speculative concept . . . a fantastic contribution to the contemporary crime genre'

Philippa East

'Breathtakingly original, and a captivating sense of place'

Val McDermid

'A brilliantly inventive and twisty tale'

Claire McGowan

'A distinctive, intriguing, immersive debut'

Mari Hannah

'Marques sets Lisbon alight with this beautifully drawn thriller . . . original and compelling, unique and fascinating. A story that'll leave you red-eyed and sleep deprived'

Helen Fields

Half-Angolan and half-Portuguese, Patricia was born in Portugal but moved to England when she was eight. As well as the MA in Creative Writing from City, she holds a BA in Creative Writing from Roehampton. She lives in London. *The Colours of Death* was her first novel and book one in the Inspector Reis series. *The Burning Woman* is the final book in the series.

Also by Patricia Marques

The Colours of Death
House of Silence
Broken Oaths

To yesterday me who worked so hard. Well done, I'm proud of you.

To future me who will be doing it all over again. You've got this, I believe in you.

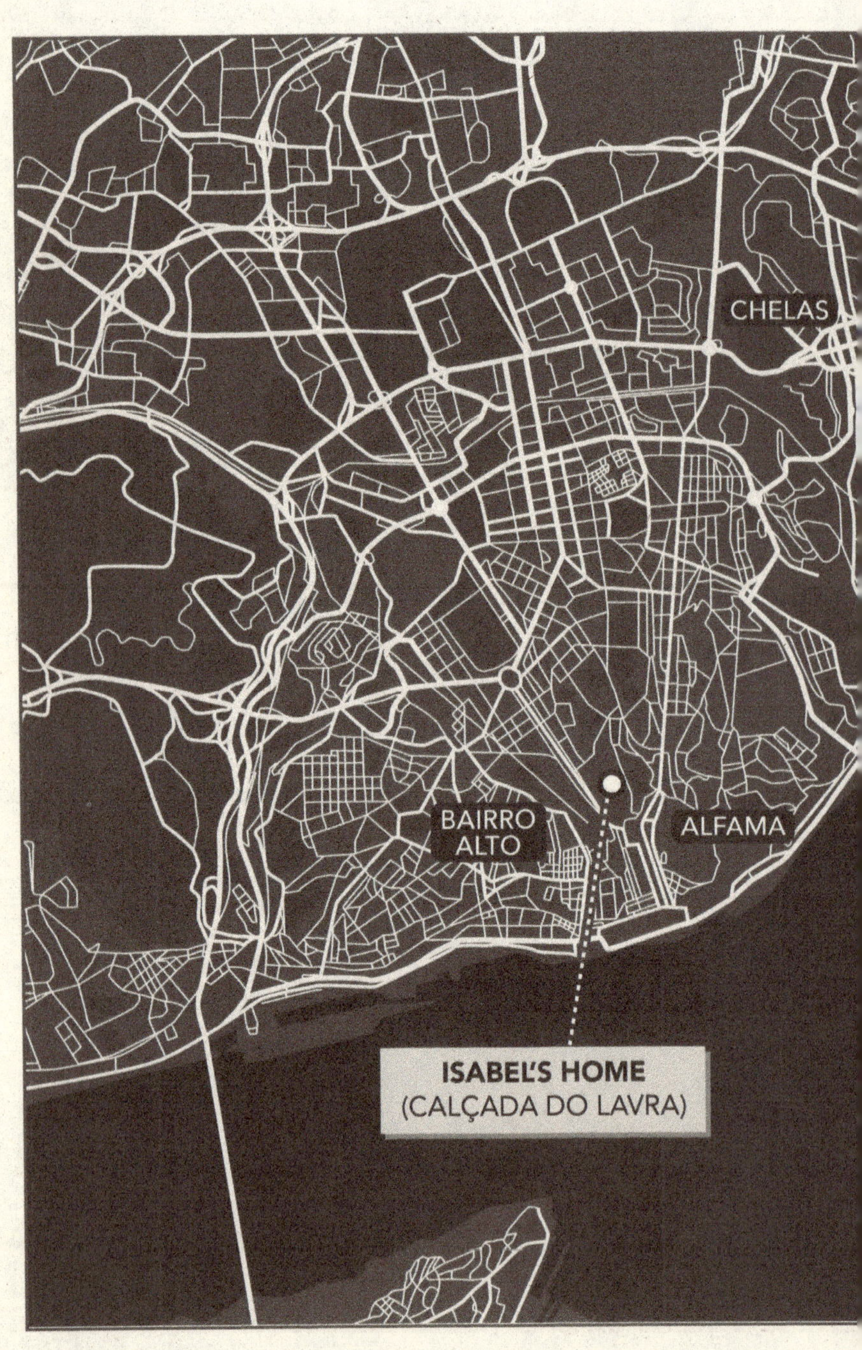
CHELAS
BAIRRO ALTO
ALFAMA
ISABEL'S HOME
(CALÇADA DO LAVRA)

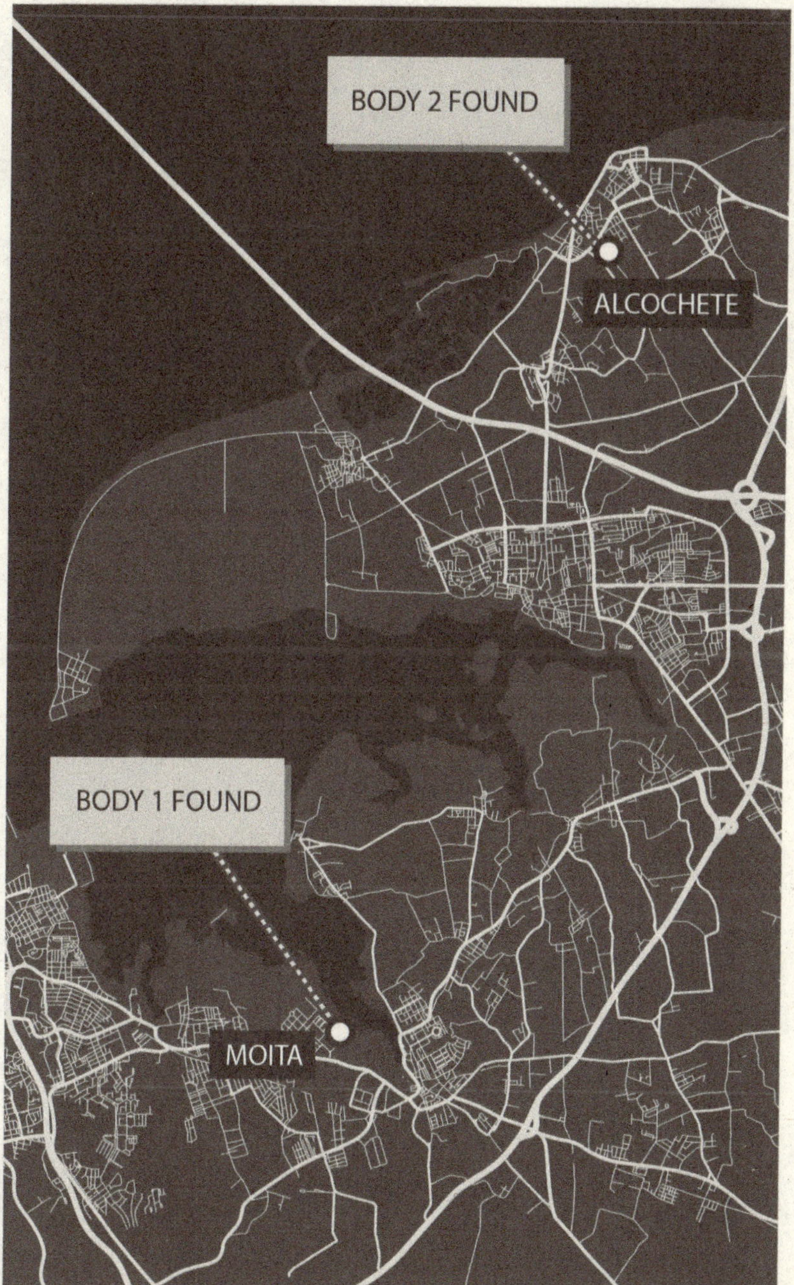

BODY 2 FOUND

ALCOCHETE

BODY 1 FOUND

MOITA

I

It's 4.50 a.m. on Wednesday morning and the air is thick with heat as Isabel opens the door, trying to make as little sound as possible to avoid waking her brother.

She'd landed in Lisbon late from her US trip and stayed at her brother's. By the time they'd finished talking and gone to sleep, it had been edging closer to two in the morning.

Isabel turns with a rueful smile at the sound of her dogs walking over, the clack of their nails and gentle snuffles preceding them. The slower, low wag of their tails gives away their drowsiness. She crouches down to run her hand over their soft coats.

'Sorry,' she says, keeping her voice as low as possible, 'I know I just got home. I won't take so long again, hmm?'

The lights come on behind her and she winces at the sudden brightness.

Sighing, she looks up at her brother who is standing there in a T-shirt and shorts, covering a yawn behind his hand.

'Sorry, mano,' she sighs, giving the dogs one last pat and standing, 'I didn't want to wake you.'

Sebastião rubs at his eyes and shakes his head. 'Work?'

'Yeah. Chief wants me at a crime scene.'

'Thought you weren't supposed to be back until tomorrow.'

'I know.'

He falls silent, a seriousness falling over his face. Eventually he nods, scratching absently at the scruff on his chin.

'Will you be all right?' he asks.

'Of course.' She steps up to give him a hug before pecking his cheek. 'I don't want you to worry, hmm?'

He smiles back but she can tell his heart isn't in it. 'Make sure you don't forget them, then. The pills.'

She pats his cheek. 'I've got them. Get back to sleep. I'll call you later.'

'Okay. Be safe.'

She nods and hurries to the door, the dogs, Tigre and Branca, trying to sniff their way after her but listening to Sebastião when he calls out to them.

The sky is still that sinking blue of night, no clouds, all stars.

Slinging her bag over her shoulder, she steps down on to the thin strip of pavement before heading across the narrow cobbled street to her partner, Inspector Aleksandr Voronov's, car. The headlights are on, two bright spotlights on the far end of the street that catch the curling tail of a cat as it disappears into a small alley.

The street is quiet at this time of night; just the sound of chirping birds, her steps and the running of the car engine.

Not too long ago, even in the quietest of nights, there would have been sounds that would be heard by her and no one else.

As a Gifted individual, and one with a telepathic affinity, Isabel's world had rarely ever been one of complete silence. It wasn't the same for all Gifted. In fact, she suspected this was something that those with a telekinetic affinity never had to concern themselves with. Then again, she didn't think lower-level telepathic Gifted had to concern themselves with it either. For her, there had always been stray thoughts spilling from alert minds or floating into the air around her from those dreaming.

It had only been in the last couple of months that she had finally learned what total silence is like. Now, there were no thoughts crowding around her, no dreams or nightmares seeping out into the early morning for her to block off. Not unless she chose to reach for them.

It's still new, and she wonders how long it'll take for her to stop feeling caught off-guard by the silence.

Her hair is still wet, and she feels rivulets of water slipping down her neck and sinking into the back of her top.

She peers through the windshield as she rounds the front of the car and sees Voronov dipping his head to peer back out at her.

Isabel opens the passenger door, and the steady drone of the radio news station spills out for the few seconds it takes her to slide into the passenger seat. She pulls the door shut, sealing them inside. The blast of cold air-con is instantly soothing over the heated skin of her neck and arms though she knows from experience that the relief won't last long before it becomes too much. She hates air-con, for the most part.

Throwing her bag into the footwell, she settles in her seat with a heavy sigh, head resting back. She turns her head without lifting it and looks at him in the shadowed interior.

It feels like she hasn't seen him in too long.

Towards the end of last year, she and Voronov had been called in to assist with a case at the Portuguese embassy in London. The case involved the US military and a renowned expert on research into the deterioration of the brain in Gifted individuals like Isabel, those born with a telekinetic or telepathic affinity. It wasn't Isabel's first involvement in a case that directly affected people like her but its tragic end had left an impression on her.

It hadn't been the only thing. During that entire case, she'd been dealing with an additional complication.

Gabriel Bernardo, a perpetrator from Isabel's first-ever case with Voronov and like her a Gifted person, had escaped from prison. He had developed a fixation on her, infiltrating her life. Her mind. He had made it personal: he touched her family. It compromised her, left her unsure of her ability to remain in her job. Thankfully, when she'd spoken to the chief, Bautista had pushed for her to take extended leave instead of resigning. It coincided well with the trial in America related to the London case.

Both Isabel and Voronov, alongside the two British detectives they had worked with then, went to America to testify. But an opportunity had opened there for her; she had ended up staying longer than intended with the research team and made some useful contacts elsewhere too. A trip that was supposed to last a month at most had stretched into two, then three.

Despite speaking on the phone almost every night, she and Voronov haven't seen each other in two months. It has been disconcerting to say the least after being used to seeing him almost every day. It also makes for a less-than-ideal start to the newer, romantic, aspect of their relationship. She thinks they've managed okay though.

He's watching her too, quiet, waiting, hands on his lap and looking as much as she is.

When Isabel lifts her hand to card her fingers through his hair, his mouth curves a little and when her hand slides to his cheek, he leans his face into it. The gesture warms her.

'You need a haircut,' she says.

He huffs out a quiet laugh. Then, twisting in his seat and with one arm resting on the wheel, he leans over and kisses her. Nothing more than a lingering peck, and Isabel holds him there a little longer. She's missed this. He smells good.

When he eases back, he seems a little more relaxed. 'Hi,' he says.

'Hi,' she says right back.

Then he's focusing on the rearview mirror and reversing the car.

Isabel buckles in. She wants to close her eyes and doze for a little longer but she enjoys looking at him so she ignores the sting of fatigue and does just that.

'Did you tell Sebastião you were leaving?' Voronov asks.

She shakes her head. 'Yeah, I tried not to but ended up waking him when I was leaving. Wasn't expecting that the chief would be calling me the day before I'm due back,' she says, tone wry.

Right as the skin on her arms is starting to pebble, Voronov turns down the air-con because of course he does. He's always like this. Always in tune with the people around him. If she didn't know any better, she'd wonder if he was Gifted too.

Voronov tilts his head in acknowledgement. 'That's the chief. Did you manage to get any sleep?'

'I managed a few hours on the plane,' she offers, sighing. 'Does that count?'

He gives her a look and then pulls the car out.

'I didn't think so either.'

2

By the time they reach the municipality in the district of Setúbal, the sky is inching out of the deep blue of night and turning pink around the edges.

It's a little after 5.30 a.m. when they drive over the small river bridge, past the large human-sized red letters that spell out MOITA, the stand they're mounted on welcoming visitors in a black cursive and embellished with a red flower painted in such a way that the start of the word *bem-vindos* cuts into one of the petals.

The streets here are small and winding, weaving through old buildings, with their shopfronts on the ground-floor levels and old apartments above those. Washing lines run along the upper floors like unique banners, broken only by the odd sealed windows or gutted insides of long-abandoned buildings.

Most of the shops are closed, though illuminated window displays cast their brightness out on to uneven cobblestones and the lights are on inside the small cafés and eateries they pass, places of business getting ready for their day, some already open to catch the earliest of customers – mostly people wanting to sneak in a quick bica before hurrying to catch the bus to work.

They drive past the town centre, with its benches and fountain, before finding themselves back by the riverside.

Here there are three large car parks, side by side, most of them with small alleys leading into the town centre and surrounded by low two-storey buildings that eventually give way to a newer section of town. A semicircular block of flats, painted in seashell pink and probably only a couple of years old, overlooks the river and its newness stands in sharp contrast to the white church beside it, only half its height. Its whole ground floor is dedicated entirely to commercial and community spaces; a strip of road and recreational grounds running alongside the length of it separate it from the riverside.

The moment they turn into that road, the crime scene comes into their line of sight.

Bright yellow crime-scene tapes are cutting off a chunk of the road. The tapes are secured from the river's fence to the lampposts on the same side of the road as the block of apartments.

Within the taped-off space, a fire engine is parked on the road directly in front of the building. Next to it is a familiar van with the logo for the forensic department of the Polícia Judiciária on its white surface. It belongs to Jacinta Cacho, their lead forensic investigator, a long-time colleague and friend. Isabel also spots two of Jacinta's people decked out in full protective gear on the rec strip, stepping carefully, the spotlight of their torches moving slowly over the ground.

The smell of smoke seeps into the car as they approach the crime scene, and a column of smoke rises into the air, not as prominent as it had probably been a little while ago but not entirely dissipated either. It hovers over a misshapen wooden zip line beam that is clearly a part of the children's playground section of the rec area. Isabel can just about make out something else that looks odd but it's still not bright enough for her to see that clearly from a distance.

What she doesn't miss is the small group of people gathered by a pavement bench. A couple of uniformed police officers are with them. She leans closer to the car window and peers up at the building. There are quite a few windows with the lights on inside. There are even more that remain dark. Those are probably the people who don't feel comfortable being as blatant about seeing what's going on as the others. She'd bet good money that everyone with a window facing the river has at least looked out to watch a slice of the action.

The headlights from Voronov's car light on Jacinta's familiar figure. She's got her protective gear shoved down to her waist; her white vest exposed. Her hair is pulled back into a large, neat bun that must have felt annoying in the hood of the suit. She's holding a clipboard in her hand and speaking to an older man standing next to her with a dog at his feet. Isabel doesn't recognise him.

A team of firefighters in their gear, six of them clustered together by the fire engine, are packing up, their moves practised. One of them is already out of their gear and she wonders how long they've been at the scene.

Voronov eases the car to a stop a small distance away from the taped-off section of road.

The smell of smoke intensifies as soon as they step out of the car, and the artificial coolness of the air-con is instantly replaced by the thick packing of heat on her skin. The car shakes with the force of Voronov shutting the door on his side.

'One second,' Isabel calls out and grabs her bag, quickly unzipping it. The bottle rattles when she makes contact with it. The cold, hard, round plastic fits perfectly into the cup of her hand as she pulls it out.

It's a plain white pill bottle. Her name is printed on the label, just above the instructions, in neat black, block letters: REIS, ISABEL.

She unscrews the top, spills two pills into the palm of her hand. They're minuscule, easily lost if dropped, and dwarfed by her fingers. She pops them on to her tongue and washes them down with the bottle of water she'd thrown into her bag as well.

Isabel fishes her ID out and shoves it into the back pocket of her jeans before following suit.

Voronov is looking at her, head tilted as if in question, and there's a small furrow between his eyebrows.

She gives a short shake of her head. 'Don't worry,' she says, 'I'm good.' It's also not a conversation for right now, though it's something that she will have to take the time to explain, later.

'All right,' Voronov says, and they start to walk towards Jacinta.

She's still in the same spot talking to that man Isabel doesn't recognise.

'Daniel and Carla on their way?' Isabel asks as they approach Jacinta.

Daniel Verde and Carla Muniz are both inspectors from the Anjos precinct, the same as Isabel and Voronov. Like Isabel and Voronov, they'd been paired together a few years back when it had become mandatory for Gifted individuals in the police to work with a designated Regular partner. They've all worked on more than one case together, and Daniel goes a long way back with both Isabel and Jacinta, all three of them having joined the force around the same time.

'They shouldn't be too far behind us,' Voronov says.

There's a breeze here but it brings no relief. She can hear the sound of the rippling river and the distant rhythmic song of grasshoppers hiding in the tall grass covering a large spread of land further down along the river. Gnats flit around in the beam of the streetlights.

Jacinta notices their approach and gives them a short nod of acknowledgement. She says a few more words to the man and gestures for him to wait.

Approaching them, she gives a tired-looking smile. 'I had a feeling the chief would be dragging you in early for this one. Well, it's good to have you back.' She looks in the direction of the children's zip line, indicating it with her chin. 'It's a gruesome one. Come on.'

As they walk closer, the details of the crime scene sharpen.

Jacinta is right. It is gruesome.

Up close, what Isabel hadn't been able to see clearly from the car is stark in its horror.

Arms stretched up above their head, the victim had been tied to the children's zip line beam and set alight. The surrounding space is splattered with patches of white where the foam extinguishers were used.

It's impossible to make out any features but the expression on the deceased's face is unmistakable.

The surface of the skin looks sticky and charred, no way to tell what the colour had previously been. Isabel can make out the areas where the eyes would be, the slight roundedness there, and the slope and peak of a nose.

The mouth is the clearest thing; it's stretched in an unnatural way, wide and showing teeth. The shape of their skull is clearly delineated, if any hair had been present it had burned off long ago.

Isabel can see all the places on their throat and chest, along their shoulders and arms, on their thighs, where the skin has split to reveal the tissue beneath.

Her eyes feel dry and sensitive and she's not sure if it's from the lingering smoke in the air or from the effort of forcing herself not to look away from the body in front of her.

That expression on their face, one of unspeakable agony, tells Isabel that this person was conscious when they started to burn.

Despite the severe disfigurement of the body, it's clearly that of a naked female.

Up close, the smell of the smoke is different. It becomes something more akin to charcoal, and there's another layer to it – a pork-like scent that makes Isabel want to stop breathing. She's experienced worse. But it's the knowledge of *what* she's smelling.

'She was burned alive?' Voronov asks.

'I'll be able to tell more after I get her on my table,' Jacinta says. 'We've already photographed the body.' Jacinta points at her team members who are crouching now, torches carefully held as they set an L-shaped ruler down by something Isabel can't make out, placing a numbered marker next to it and snapping a picture. 'We're cataloguing the rest; it took us a little longer to gain access to the scene.'

'Fire investigator?' Isabel asks.

'Yes. He's a grouchy arsehole but he was fast. Here, I'll introduce you before you start doing your thing.'

She guides them over to the firefighting team who have joined the man they'd seen her talking to earlier, all of them near the destroyed beam. The dog is still quietly at his feet, tail gently sweeping the ground in contained excitement.

They stop speaking at their approach, the group spreading out to look them over. The team is made up of four men and two women.

Their faces have a sticky sheen that comes from having been up close and personal with extreme heat and there are traces of soot on their skin. Most have just pushed their overalls down to their waist. One of the team who is out of uniform, not the person Jacinta had been speaking with, is standing a little way from the group, phone pressed to his ear, talking in hushed but agitated tones.

'Sorry to interrupt,' Jacinta says, 'these are Inspectors Reis and Voronov. And this is Fire Investigator Cardoso and Setúbal's team three fire squad who were called to attend today.'

Cardoso is a thin but sturdy-looking older man, maybe early sixties, the stubble on his cheeks and chin mostly white and grey, bristly. His hair colour looks like a steel-grey in the limited lighting and is combed back. He has an unlit cigarette between his lips. He's in a neat pale-blue short-sleeved button shirt, the top two buttons undone to show a small glimpse of the white vest beneath. They're tucked into his belted grey trousers and his shoes, though smart, are creased and worn. A thick gold watch adorns the wrist of his left hand, in which he holds the lead of a very happy-looking dog that isn't looking anywhere but at the man's face.

It's a big dog with a liver-and-white coat, sitting upright, nose pointed right up.

'Station dog?' Isabel asks, as Cardoso eyes them both up, eyes squinted and a severely unimpressed look on his face.

Cardoso harrumphs and extends a hand to Voronov first to shake. 'Arson dog.' He holds out his hand to Isabel. 'His name is Kuma.'

Isabel glances down at his outstretched hand for no more than a split second, nothing anyone who isn't watching for it would notice, and then she reaches out and takes it, giving his hand a strong shake. Out of the corner of her eye, she catches both Voronov's and Jacinta's double take. There will be time for explanations later. It feels almost surreal – she's spent so much of her life bracing against any kind of skin contact, always poised to counteract the barrage of people's thoughts and emotions as a result of her Gift.

The man who's also out of uniform finishes his call and joins them too. His expression is tired but more welcoming than Cardoso's. He reaches his hand out to shake theirs. There's a tattoo of a flower on the back of it. His hair is shaved close to his head and his beard is neatly trimmed.

'Sorry,' he says, phone still in hand. 'I had an urgent call.'

'This is Captain Horta,' Jacinta says, gesturing to the newcomer, 'he heads this team.'

Isabel shakes his hand, notes the extra whiteness to his fingers squeezing around the phone, and an exhausted fatigue peeling off him. 'Inspector Reis,' she says, and steps back so Voronov can introduce himself too.

She turns back to Cardoso.

'Did Kuma find anything?' At the sound of his name, the dog flicks a look at her before immediately going back to stare at Cardoso. When Horta crouches down beside them though, the dog ditches Cardoso in a heartbeat, losing all sense of composure and leaping at him to lick at his face and making the team crack reluctant tired smiles.

Cardoso makes that grunting sound again. 'Confirmed an accelerant was used. The point of origin was here.' He points down at the blue rubber ground-covering material at the base of the vertical beam. Isabel follows the direction of Cardoso's finger and can just about make out the way the soot black spreads outwards from where the victim's feet touch down, some of it partially covered by the white foam.

The rubber around the beam is charred where it's burned, with sharp lines between it and the rest of the surface. It's easy to spot where forensics have already taken samples, small squares methodically cut. Surprisingly, the beam hasn't burned completely, and the worst parts are where the victim is in direct contact with it.

Isabel glances at him in question. 'Did they pour accelerant around her?' She can't think of any other reason for the difference in the intensity of the burns on the beam.

Cardoso plucks the cigarette from his lips and tucks it behind his ear, folding his arms across his chest. 'Her feet.'

The feet?

'And it travelled all the way up. Without forensic testing, I can't confirm right away but I'm pretty sure. By the smell and the severity of the burns.' He circles to the back and Isabel and Voronov follow. He flicks his finger up, indicating the length of the beam. 'You can see where the accelerant was also present on the beam. Accidental, probably. It's in better shape than she is.'

Jacinta steps in. 'We'll be working together with Investigator Cardoso to properly determine the cause of the fire. We're almost done documenting. Cardoso has already had a word with the witness.' She looks in the direction of the small crowd Isabel had glimpsed on arrival. They're still there, gathered and flanked by police.

Sitting on one of the benches that look out at the river and slightly behind the bulk of the fire engine are a young woman and a girl. They seem oddly apart from the small group. Despite the heat, the young woman is wrapped up in a robe and the girl has an emergency blanket over her shoulders. A uniformed officer stands nearby.

The sky is beginning to lighten at a faster pace, the blue turning purple now, and with it, out of place given the scene in front of them, comes birdsong.

The young woman is wrapping her arm around the girl and bringing her closer, rubbing her shoulder and pressing her chin to the girl's head, murmuring.

Up close, the young woman is younger than Isabel had first thought. Isabel would put her at sixteen, maybe seventeen. Her face has a vulnerability that hadn't been noticeable from far away. Her long blond hair is pulled back from her face in a messy ponytail and she has big, round eyes. She's cradling the girl in her arms and trying her best to look calm but it's there in how wide her eyes are and the not-quite-normal breathing. She's wearing flip-flops and her robe is skewed like she'd pulled it on in a hurry.

The little girl clings to her waist, head tucked under the older girl's chin and chest – but her eyes, so similar to the older girl's, are staring in the direction of the recreational area. They have a spooked glaze to them. Her hair is a slightly darker blond, thick and tucked into a plait that is starting to come undone, the rest of it completely dishevelled on the top of her head as if she had just now rolled out of bed. She looks like she's around eight years of age.

'Hi,' Isabel says, stopping in front of them, 'I'm Inspector Reis and this is Inspector Voronov. How are you both feeling?' she asks.

The older girl visibly swallows and hugs the other one a little tighter. 'We're tired,' she says, her voice deeper than Isabel expected. 'My sister has school, and we haven't really got any rest. When can we head back inside?'

Isabel squats down so she's at eye level with them. 'I understand and we'll get you home as soon as we can.' She gives them both a reassuring nod. 'Can you tell me your names?'

'I'm Savana,' she says, 'and this is Sara.' She pulls the younger girl even closer, her protectiveness instinctive.

'Thank you. I know you've already spoken with Fire Investigator Cardoso. Investigator Cardoso's job and ours are a little different so we'd like to ask you some questions too. Please be a little patient with us, okay?' Isabel looks from one of them to the other. 'Do you mind me asking where your parents are?'

Both girls are out here in the early hours of the morning and none of the other adults present seem to be with them.

'Our mother is at work,' Savana says. 'She works night shifts at a hotel in Lisbon. She'll be home in a few hours.'

Isabel nods. 'Was it just you and Sara at home tonight?'

'Yes,' Savana says, 'it's like that most days.'

'Okay. Has anyone called your mum yet?'

Savana shakes her head.

'Do you mind giving me her number? I think it would be a good idea to have her come home early. Inspector Voronov here will help us call her.'

Savana looks between Isabel and Voronov. She looks uncomfortable and reluctant as if she doesn't want to disturb her mother.

It's a look Isabel recognises. Trepidation.

Inwardly, Isabel nips the thought in the bud. The last thing she needs to be doing here is projecting.

'Savana,' Isabel says gently, 'something very serious has happened here tonight and if I were your parent, I'd want to know. Inspector Voronov can explain the situation to her.'

Savana gnaws at the inside of her cheek for a moment, her forehead scrunching as she debates with herself. Eventually she pulls her phone out from her pocket, quickly scrolling through her contacts list before reading the number out to Voronov in a low voice.

'Thank you,' Voronov says, giving them both a small smile which has Sara peering up at him from the circle of her sister's arms. 'I'll call her now.' He steps back to make the call.

'Thanks, Aleks,' Isabel says as he walks past her. She turns back to the two girls in front of her. 'I heard you were the ones who called the emergency services for the fire. Can you tell me about that?'

'I saw there was a fire!' Sara pipes up suddenly. She pulls at her sister's arm but doesn't attempt to extricate herself. She wraps thin arms around her sister's forearm and clinging to her that way instead.

'You did?' Isabel asks. 'Were you at home when you saw it?'

'Hm-hm.' She nods her head fast, making Isabel think of those little dolls with wobbly heads that will bop continuously if you nudge them. Sara clumsily tucks some stray strands behind her ear and sits up straighter. 'I saw it when I climbed down from my bunk bed. I couldn't close the curtains properly so I could see outside a little bit and that's when I saw the park was on fire!'

She talks fast, barely drawing breath, and her words end on a higher note. Despite the rush of words and her eagerness to get them out, her face has a pallor to it that is a little worrying and her fingers dig into her sister's arm hard enough that Savana yelps.

'Sara!' Savana cries out, slapping a hand on top of her sister's to still it.

'Oh, oh,' Sara stops, looking startled, and immediately rubs the part where she hurt her. 'Desculpa, Savana.'

Savana shakes her head. 'It's okay.' She looks up at Isabel. 'She woke me up because it scared her, she wanted to sleep in my room. I thought she was maybe dreaming or something like that.' She sighs. 'I tried to go back to sleep but she wouldn't let me, so I went out to look. I saw the fire but . . .' She blinks several times in quick succession and wets her lips. 'Then I noticed someone was in there, it looked like . . . like they were still moving.' Her voice wobbles and she pulls in a shaky breath, her eyes staring at a fixed point on the ground somewhere at Isabel's feet.

'Go on,' Isabel encourages.

'I threw on a robe and ran downstairs. The lifts are out of service, so it took me a little bit of time, I dialled one-one-two – I didn't know what I was going to do. I yelled for help as I was going down. A few people heard me and ran down with me but there was nothing we – any of us – could do. Senhor Mario tried to get close, but the flames were too hot.' She looks at Isabel. 'The person, they . . . they stopped moving soon after we got downstairs. By the time the firefighters arrived the fire was even stronger.'

Isabel touches a hand to her shoulder, wanting to comfort. 'Savana, you said you came downstairs. What floor do you live on?'

'We're on the fifth floor.'

'Did you notice anything odd when you got downstairs, or on your way down? Anyone downstairs or any voices, something else that caught your attention?'

Savana shakes her head.

'Yes,' Sara says.

Isabel glances over at her. She doesn't miss the way Savana stiffens and tightens her grip on the little girl.

'No, you didn't,' Savana says. Her voice is stern and she stares at Sara, mouth turned down at the corners.

Sara looks up at her sister, face setting into stubborn lines. 'Yes, I did! I told you! And you shouldn't lie to the police!'

'Sara—'

'I'd like to hear what Sara has to say,' Isabel says, cutting Savana off.

'She didn't see anything though!' Savana is sitting up now. She puts her arm out, attempting to push Sara further back.

Isabel narrows her eyes. 'Maybe . . . but I still want to hear what your sister has to say.'

Sara shoves her sister away and her jaw juts out, stubborn. 'See? She believes me—'

'You shouldn't—'

Isabel stands and takes a seat next to Sara. She rests her arms on her knees and smiles at her in encouragement. 'I'll listen, Sara.'

Savana's mouth snaps shut, her jaw locking tight. She can't quite hide the fear though. Isabel can see her hands clenching and unclenching and she's bouncing her leg.

'What is it that you want to tell me, Sara?'

Sara twists in her seat, hitches one leg on to it and leans forward to rest her hands on the bench. 'When we got down here I saw the red smoke,' she says, voice spilling with excited eagerness, the earlier quietness fading into the background as if having someone willing to listen to her overrode the rest of the night and the fatigue of it all.

'From the fire?' Isabel asks.

Sara shakes her head so hard her plait whips back and forth. 'No. From there. Behind the tree.'

Isabel follows her line of sight. Aligned with the strip of the recreation grounds and just past the community gym is a row of trees planted over some shinier-looking seating with a view upriver. But Isabel can see no hint of any fire. If there had been, the firefighters would have been there too and Jacinta would have said something.

'See?' Savana says, too eager to dismiss what Sara has said. 'I told you she didn't see anything. She's tired and confused.'

Isabel doesn't have the heart to tell her she's being way too transparent to be in any way convincing.

'Sara,' Isabel says, 'I'm not sure what you mean. Can you explain a little more?'

Honestly, if it weren't for how desperate Savana is to have Isabel dismiss her sister's words, Isabel would be agreeing with her that Sara is just tired. In fact, she still might be. It wouldn't be surprising if Savana was just eager to get away from the police and go home. Isabel is sure this isn't what Savana expected when she'd rushed downstairs with the intent of helping someone in need.

'His smoke was red,' Sara says. 'I could see it behind the tree. No one else saw it. I tried to tell them, but they didn't see it.'

That gives Isabel pause.

Savana's face pales even more than before and she looks like she's going to be physically ill.

Isabel tilts her head. Ah. Could it be?

'Sara,' Isabel says, 'do you have a Gift?'

It's like the little girl lights up, eyes opening wide, excitement adding a touch of colour to her cheeks. The heat from the fire combined with the temperature has dampened her skin and wisps of hair catch on her round cheeks. She shoves at them impatiently. 'Yes! My affinity is telepathy! Savana and Mum don't like me talking about it, but you said *did you notice anything* and I did!' She's brimming with pride.

Yeah, Savana's panic makes a little more sense now.

'That's right,' Isabel says, and she gives the little girl a gentle smile, 'well done. Have you had your testing yet?' Isabel asks, though she knows it's unlikely.

The National Testing Institute oversees the yearly examinations that take place at testing centres all over the country to determine whether an individual is Gifted, and if so, their affinity. It tends to take place around ages twelve to thirteen, though sometimes tests happen as early as eleven or as late as eighteen. She doubts that Sara will have already been tested. Though if these are the kinds of impressions she's getting at her age then her level is likely to be something that will give her mother even greater concern.

Being classed a higher-level Gifted can be a dangerous thing.

Being classed as a Gifted at all is already enough of a burden. Society in general has never welcomed what it doesn't entirely understand. More often than not, being known as a Gifted individual will earn you passive-aggressive hostility at best.

'Not yet! Mãe says I have to wait a few more years,' she says excitedly and despite the situation, Isabel feels a pang, a bittersweetness.

Seeing the way Savana is casting furtive glances at the people milling around that they are neighbours with, a worried crease to her brow, clearly worried that they'll overhear, shows how far society still has to go in its perception of Gifted people.

She hopes Sara will have a different view of what being Gifted means. She hopes it won't take her as long to come to terms with it as it did her.

'Can you tell me, Sara, what you think the smoke felt like?'

Savana snaps round to look at Isabel, surprised.

That gives Sara pause and she stares for a moment before her face scrunches in concentration, trying hard to remember.

Then the excitement slowly drains from her and she says, 'Hungry.'

This time her tone is laced with fear. She drops her gaze and, like her sister had done only seconds ago, her hands curl into tight fists where they rest on her thighs.

'I see. Thank you, Sara. That's very helpful.' Isabel dips her head low to catch Sara's eye. 'Want to know something?' she asks.

Kids and curiosity. That gets her to peer up at Isabel almost right away.

Isabel lowers her voice to a whisper. 'I'm telepathic Gifted too.'

That brings out a proper smile, which Isabel returns before standing up and ruffling her hair under her sister's wide gaze.

'An officer will escort you both back home, okay? We'll contact your mum if we need anything else.' She gives them both a wave.

Voronov, having finished the call, has remained some distance away, waiting. He's watching the rest of the neighbours who are clustered together, dotted around the surrounding area, the others who must also have come down after hearing Savana's calls for help.

More lights have already come on in some of the nearby cafés and, at some point, staff have begun to ready for the day, carrying out stacked chairs and tables for the early-morning rush. The church has also opened its doors wide, the light spilling out from them. Their day starts early.

'Their mother is on her way,' Voronov says, 'she has my number. I've told her to call when she arrives.'

Isabel hears the sound of a car driving up and sees Daniel's car slowing down by Voronov's parked vehicle. 'Good, they're here. We need to speak to the rest of these people.' But she heads in the opposite direction. 'The younger sister, Sara, says she saw red smoke coming from here.'

'Another fire?' He frowns.

Isabel shakes her head. 'No,' she replies as she glances at him, 'she's Gifted. And she said *his* smoke was red.'

The tree is an older one, roots buried deep in grass and trunk twisted and wide, shooting straight up. Its large leaves rustle gently in the barely-there breeze that brings no relief.

Isabel filters easily through the presences scattered around her. It takes her only a moment, her mind soaking them all in first, gauging the distance, gauging who's visible, and then allowing all of them to drop away. It's like looking into the dark and searching for the one silhouette. Just the one. One she hasn't seen yet.

In the last few months, it's not so much that her Gift has sharpened – it hasn't got any stronger. Rather, her use of it, her handling of it, her perception of it is what has got better. And it's as if what felt like a full-body suit of cement attempting to drag her down to the seabed has finally cracked to let her escape.

It makes it all . . . so effortless.

'Do you sense anything?' Voronov asks.

He knows her well enough to know exactly what she would do. Even after months spent apart.

'No.' She slows down as they reach the tree, looking around at the closest buildings, trying to look beyond the bright spotlights of the streetlights and into the dark pockets swallowing all the shapes behind them. 'If she really did sense someone, then that person isn't here now.' And even if there had been, it doesn't mean that this person is related to the incident. It could have just been someone from one of the other buildings who had also seen the fire and come down to try to do something about it.

Except . . .

Hungry.

They stop by the tree.

It's as if the trickle of the river is louder here, away from the sounds of the crime-scene investigators diligently searching every inch of space around the site of the fire.

'All right, let's head back—'

It catches her attention at the same time Voronov reaches for her shoulder. 'Look.'

At the base of the tree trunk is a neatly folded pile of clothes. In front of it is a pair of worn, strappy gold sandals. Leaning on the tree is a purse, black and bulky, the zip of it strained and a few bank cards peeking out of their slots. A keyring with two keys attached and a thin gold necklace with a small simple crucifix rest on the clothes.

'We need to get—'

She doesn't get to finish her sentence before barks erupt elsewhere, ripping into the silence.

'We found something!'

3

The car sits alone just past the bridge that Voronov had driven them over.

It's a bright yellow Peugeot 108. It looks out of place with its cheerful colour where it's parked on the gravel-filled edge of the road.

Jacinta and one of her assistants circle the car, torches in place while Cardoso stands back with the dog. Isabel and Voronov join him. This time, the cigarette on his lips is lit, which makes Isabel give him a side-eye.

The man has been around accelerants for most of the night, they are all over the place, and he's here smoking a cigarette. And people wonder how fires catch so easily over here when one of the people working in a fire department doesn't seem to be doing any better.

He catches her looking and his expression barely changes. 'Do you have something to say, menina?' He takes a drag of it, never looking away from her as if trying to make a point.

Isabel suppresses an eyeroll. 'Inspector will do, thanks,' she says, deadpan, 'and no. As long as you don't accidentally set our evidence on fire.'

To her surprise he only scoffs. She thought he might get puffed up with indignation and give her a few choice words. Men of his age that speak to women the way he just did tend not to like being told about themselves. No hint of that though. If anything it looks like he just found her comment cheeky.

He doesn't put out the cigarette though.

Isabel sighs and refocuses. 'So. What are we thinking? If the accelerant leads all the way here?'

Cardoso takes another pull of his cigarette. He's careful to stay further back than the rest. Isabel supposes that's something. She watches the discarded ashes with narrowed eyes. She's tempted to just snatch the stupid thing from his hand but doesn't think that would go down very well.

'Most likely it leaked out of whatever they used to carry the gasoline,' Cardoso says.

Isabel takes in the distance from the car to the site of the murder. 'Meaning maybe they arrived in this car, carried what they needed with them and parked here out of the way. That's a long way to walk.'

Gutsy or reckless. Or simply arrogant. Anyone could have seen them at any time. This was probably on someone's jogging route and there are plenty of people who like to get their run in early in the morning. Earlier still when the heat is this bad. Though with the timing of the call Isabel doubts someone would have been out exercising before 4.30 in the morning, even if she herself does it every now and then.

'If they did use the car,' Voronov says, 'how did they get her over there?' He takes a few steps forward, roughly retracing the same steps that the dog had taken to guide them here. 'Unless they snatched her here, they would have had to get her over there somehow. There are no signs of someone having struggled though.'

They had taken care walking over, minding their steps, trying to disturb the gravel as little as possible, but Voronov is right. If she had fought against being taken to the zip line area, then there would be signs. Especially if they were carrying the accelerant as well. They would have been dragging her along.

So, either she was too scared and following them obediently or they'd made two trips to the car. One for the gasoline. One for her. Maybe they carried her over there. Kuma had detected traces of accelerant on the items left by the tree before tracing directly back to the zip line, lending weight to the latter option.

Jacinta straightens up from peering into the car. 'We've already bagged samples of the gravel.'

The morning light is spreading now, the sky suffused with the soft pink of early sunrise. The weather reports are forecasting another day of thirty degrees Celsius. Abnormally high for spring in Portugal, it means they have to make quick work of moving the body before it's further affected by the heat. They're doing it now, Jacinta's team carefully zipping up the corpse into a white plastic body bag and lifting it on to the gurney to wheel over to the van.

Although they're standing quite far away from the recreation ground, Isabel can see it all perfectly clearly, which means that whoever put her there and lit her up had been able to do the same from here. They could have done the same from the tree too.

Isabel wonders if they took their time. If they stood and watched.

They quickly brief Daniel and Carla.

'We'll have to do door-to-door,' Voronov says, 'there may be others who saw something but didn't come down. The first officers on the scene have already taken statements from the people who did come down.' If Savana and Sara had seen and alerted their neighbours, it's likely that others had seen too. Not everyone would want to make themselves known to police though.

Daniel nods. He's in a bright blue T-shirt and jeans, and his face and close-shaven head have an extra sheen from sweat. His trainers scrunch the tiny little stones of grey and white gravel.

Looking around, Isabel can see all the lights that have now come on in the building. There are more of them than there had been when they'd arrived. People who had woken up from the commotion now, perhaps.

'We'll join you in doorstepping when we're done here,' Isabel says. 'We'll have to comb through the front-facing businesses as well, check if any of them have CCTV that caught something.'

'Isabel,' Carla says, joining them, her phone in hand. 'I've just called in the number plates. They're running them now; I'll update you when they get back to me.'

Unlike her partner and the rest of them, even in the midst of the heat, Carla is as perfectly turned out as usual. She's in a short-sleeved white button shirt tucked into black trousers, chin-length dark hair tucked behind one ear, revealing the glint of a diamond stud. Even her trainers are spotless. Isabel really doesn't know how she does it.

'Thanks,' Isabel says, 'okay, we'll join you guys in a bit.'

Investigator Cardoso pats Kuma's head, praising him in a voice that Isabel isn't sure comes off as praise at all, but the dog seems to believe it because he's grinning from ear to ear, tail swinging low on the ground.

Isabel dabs at her forehead with her wrist. She can feel the sweat prickling at her skin along the hairline. The heat feels as if it's only getting worse. 'The car?' she prompts.

'The dog followed a trail here,' Jacinta says.

'Person who set the fire wasn't as careful as he should have been,' Cardoso says, 'accelerant led the mutt right here. Starting to think we got lucky that we weren't facing a bigger fire.' Cardoso waves a hand to catch Horta's attention and Horta splits himself from the fire team, hurrying over. When he reaches them, Cardoso hands the dog over to him.

'He's done well. Make sure to give him a nice treat today.'

'Yes, Senhor Cardoso,' Horta says. He has the tone of a man who is used to humouring people.

'Wish we were meeting under better circumstances, Inspectors,' Horta says, hunkering down and petting Kuma's head, attempting – and failing – to dodge a well-aimed lick at his face, 'my team are off the next forty-eight, so if you need to send your people over to speak with us, have someone get the addresses from our station. It'll be better to find them at home.'

'Thanks,' Isabel says, 'we appreciate it.'

'No problem.' He looks to Cardoso. 'Paulo, see you at the station.' He leads the dog and the rest of his crew to the fire engine.

Cardoso turns to them all. 'Let me know if you find anything in the car and when the autopsy is done. I'll be in touch later today,' he says and then takes his leave.

Isabel and Voronov accept the torches Jacinta hands over to them having completed her own check of the car.

'Anything?' Isabel asks and steps closer to the vehicle. She shines the light on the doors first, scanning for anything that looks out of the ordinary before moving on to peer into the dark interior.

'Nothing immediately obvious,' Jacinta says, 'but we'll be able to take a closer look once I have it in the lab. Dust it for prints, check the interior.' She steps back and shrugs back out of the top half of her suit, huffing out a breath in relief at being rid of the additional warmth. 'These things are the worst in weather like this,' she mutters and then looks over her shoulder towards the scene of the crime. 'That poor woman.'

Isabel is torn between hoping the woman had been alive but unconscious or her not being alive at all before being set alight. It's not as if murder is ever anything but gruesome. But this . . .

What a horrific way to go.

4

Isabel accepts the coffee Voronov hands over to her and hums in relief when the scalding hit of caffeine makes contact with her tongue.

'Needed that,' she says and takes a bite of the pão com chouriço in her other hand. The paper bag crackles around it as she tightens her grip to get another bite.

The four of them are clustered outside the café steps, refuelling after spending the last couple of hours going from floor to floor in the buildings where they think people might have seen something.

What they'd got back from speaking to the other neighbours fell into two categories. Category one: they didn't hear anything, they didn't see anything, they were asleep. Category two: by the time they noticed anything was amiss, the police were already on the scene.

Morning activity is in full swing: cars on the road, people driving to work, kids walking in groups, bags on their shoulders and textbooks in their arms, chatting away as they hurry to make it to school before their first class.

Carla, sitting next to Isabel, sighs in agreement. 'Me too. Didn't get much sleep with this heat so I was craving this.' Unlike Isabel, she's only having the coffee. Isabel never understands how Carla doesn't need more fuel on a regular basis, especially when using her Gift.

Carla, like Isabel, was a telepathic Gifted. They'd split up and ensured that either Isabel or Carla were present when speaking to each person, just to feel out anything that seemed potentially off. Especially after Sara, only a little girl, had identified such a clear marker of someone being present at the scene.

Whilst Carla's gift was on a lower level than Isabel's, she could easily pick out and identify strong emotions, something she used as an indicator of whether someone warranted further scrutiny. But that's as far as her Gift went, so usually there was no need for her to identify herself as Gifted to the people she spoke to. There was nothing that she would be submitting as evidence to the court, not even by way of providing context on a case being tried. This was not the case for Isabel's Gift. Isabel's level of telepathy was significantly higher, and she could, at will, use her Gift to access someone's memories or hear their thoughts. If an individual consented to Isabel accessing their mind, then Isabel would be able to submit a statement in court, detailing what she had seen, though it would never be submitted as evidence, only to provide additional information. She'd had no offers this morning from the neighbours she'd spoken to, to allow her to view what they'd experienced through their eyes.

It wasn't surprising, but it certainly made Savana and her mother's fear of her sister outing herself as Gifted to a stranger, and one with the police at that, even more understandable than it would otherwise have been. Isabel didn't have to wonder too much about the rhetoric those girls had probably had to hear. She'd been there herself.

Isabel thinks now about Savana's protective arm around her sister. She can't speak for the mother, but at least she knows Sara has one person fighting in her corner.

It makes her think about her own brother and sister. About her mother.

She cuts the thoughts off there and refocuses. She doesn't have time for that right now.

The quiet that had been in place when they'd arrived hours ago is gone.

The community has come out in its numbers to gawk at the crime scene, and officers have been attempting to field their questions while at the same time instructing everyone to go about their day. Not one of the people trying to get a look – just so they can gossip about it later – has come forward with any information of value.

Isabel sips from her coffee. 'Any luck with surveillance?' she asks Daniel. Her phone vibrates where it's shoved into the pocket of her jeans, and she leans to one side of the chair to pull it out.

Daniel had gone along to the businesses one by one as they'd opened, while Voronov, Carla and Isabel had carried out the door-to-door in the residential building overlooking the crime scene.

The name on the screen gives Isabel pause but she quickly swipes through to access the message written in English:

Isabel, I hope you landed safely. Thank you for the assistance and keep us posted on your progress with Gabriel Bernardo. The job offer stands. C. Matthews

She locks her phone and shoves it back into her pocket. She'll have time to reply later.

'Not anything of help,' Daniel says, answering Isabel's question. 'The ones that had surveillance, their cameras don't face the rec park, but I've requested their footage anyway, will look through it once we're back in the precinct.'

Voronov is staring down at the ground, forehead lined with concentration as he ponders something. 'Let's check with emergency services. See if there were any other calls they received around the same time as Savana's call.'

True. Calling 112 meant that people could remain anonymous when reporting, less intimidating than having to relate something to a police officer face to face.

Carla's phone buzzes and she puts down her coffee to fish it out of her pocket.

'Okay,' Isabel says, chewing slowly around the bite in her mouth, 'let's get back to the precinct. See if Jacinta has anything for us.'

'They've just sent me through the information on the plates,' Carla says, looking up at them from her phone. She flips it over so they can see.

Isabel is somewhat familiar with the name of the bairro on it and it's the same municipality as the one they're in right now.

'It's registered to a Carmo Vilar,' Carla says.

Isabel straightens and takes her own phone back out, typing the address into the search engine one-handed. When the little map comes up, she pauses. She looks up at the others. 'This is just on the other side of the river. A five- to ten-minute drive at most.'

Daniel knocks back the rest of his coffee and rises up from the crouch he was eating in. He balls up the paper bag from his sandwich. 'All right. I want to tap a few of the other businesses further down, see if we can catch anything there. Killer had to run somewhere, could be there's something further back that picked something up. Does that work for you?'

Isabel looks at Voronov and gets a nod of his head. 'Good with us. Meet us there when you're done here.' She gets up, rubs a hand over her sore eyes. 'And let's hope no one blabs to the media. Something like this will get their attention in no time.'

As the map said, without traffic, it takes just under ten minutes to reach the address the car is registered to.

They drive through into the bairro past a large roundabout that has tall grass sprouting from it. No other signage though.

At a glance it seems to be made up of eight or so buildings. They're squat and stocky with sets of open stairs with painted iron guardrails indicating a middle entry point into the buildings in addition to the entryways at the front.

The shops here are already fully open. There's a school across the road from the residential area, and Isabel can see past the fences to the windows, where children sit at their desks, school day underway.

Old men walking quietly along, some with dogs in tow, newspapers tucked under their arms. Others sitting outside their favourite café or having a morning smoke with their neighbours. Women huddle around the fruit stalls outside one particular grocery shop, their morning conversations loud enough that Isabel is able to hear them even from inside the car.

Most of the windows have their shutters down to protect their houses from heating any further under the sun that has emerged in full force.

They follow the instructions of the robotic female sat nav voice to the building at the very opposite end of where they'd entered through the roundabout.

There are enough parking spaces available that they don't have to struggle for a spot.

'Block M,' Isabel says, getting out of the car and eyeing it up.

A woman is half out of the window, plucking pegs from a little basket balanced on the windowsill and hanging her washing on the lines. She casts Isabel a suspicious look when she sees her looking up.

'Bom dia,' Isabel says obligingly.

'Bom dia,' the woman says back, not even attempting to hide her disapproving look.

Isabel ignores her and looks around as Voronov gets out of the car. She walks a few paces to look around the corner of the building.

This end of the bairro is nestled into a corner created by the small river they'd just driven back over and a series of low sprawling buildings that go all the way from this side of the river to the high road they'd taken to get here. They look industrial, though Isabel can't really tell what kind. Up at the top, where they end, there's a petrol station and a chain supermarket.

The space between the bairro and the autoestrada is made up of what looks like a maze of smaller roads that make no sense to Isabel and dry weeds and grass that are probably crawling with green snakes. There's a lone person riding a bike on one of those roads now, weaving their way slowly closer to the bairro.

She turns her attention back to the other side, leading down to the river. That land is being made use of as well. Allotments it seems like, disappearing beyond the back of the building that Isabel can't see from this vantage point.

The woman finishes hanging up her washing and ducks inside. Her shutters slam down in a series of loud clacks.

'Let's go up,' Voronov says.

Isabel turns to follow him.

The address leads them to the second floor. It's an open building that acts like a hollowed-out square. The corridors are open and from within, they can see all the other corridors and their doors, both on the upper and lower floors.

Plants line the walls between doors, some huge, some small, some thriving and some very much dead. One house has a birdcage next to the window, containing two parakeets, one yellow and one green, flitting around, chirruping.

'Cute,' Isabel murmurs as they walk past.

Door number nine.

It's almost at the very end and it sits under the shadows of the connecting part of the building, unlike the other doors which face directly towards the outside. They stop in front of it.

It's cooler here, where the sun doesn't touch.

The door is a sturdy, thick, wooden one. The number nine is a small silver metal plate stuck to it.

'Should be this one.' Inside, it's still. No sounds at all coming through. She glances at Voronov, who's also leaning closer, trying to see if he can pick up anything. 'Doesn't sound like anyone is in,' she says.

'I'm not hearing anything,' he agrees.

Isabel raps her knuckles on the door. 'Senhora Vilar,' she calls out, 'we're from the Polícia Judiciária. We need to speak with you.'

No movement. No sounds.

Isabel knocks again.

'Senhora Vilar?'

There's a small rectangular window high up, next to the door, typically the type of window used for bathrooms when they're in this kind of position in an apartment. The window is one that slides open, allowing for ventilation. It's wide enough that, at a squeeze, someone slight could probably climb through. It's open a few inches.

Voronov steps closer and easily fits his hand to the edge of the sliding panel. He pushes it open the rest of the way and leans in to peer through.

'Anything?' Isabel asks.

'Nothing. The bathroom door is open, and I can see a bit of what's probably the entryway, but can't see anything else,' he says.

Isabel's mouth flattens into a grim line.

Doesn't bode well.

The sound of a door opening to their left has them both stepping back and looking.

A young woman, barefoot and in shorts and a T-shirt, steps out, bouncing a baby on her hip. Her hair is covered in a scarf and she's peering at them curiously.

'Are you looking for tia Carmo?' she asks.

'Senhora Vilar is your aunty?' asks Isabel.

The woman shakes her head. 'It's just what we all call her.'

'I see. Have you seen her today? We need to speak with her but it seems she's not home.'

'Oh, yeah, Tiago's been waiting for you guys, but he thought you'd be meeting him at the shop.'

Isabel and Voronov share a look. 'Who is Tiago?' Isabel asks. 'Someone placed a call to the police?'

The baby spits out its dummy and it falls, trapped against her chest. The woman pauses to pick it up and return it to the baby's mouth before hitching the baby up higher on her waist, smoothing a hand over the baby's head. It gurgles in response.

'Yes. That's not why you're here? Tiago is her son. He was going around this morning checking if anyone had seen tia Carmo. The door to her shop was left open this morning but she wasn't there. Her car isn't there and no one's seen her today.'

Well.

'Where is her shop?'

5

Tiago Vilar is a tall white man with a handsome face and a big, soft body. His jeans are worn and stained with paint; the red T-shirt he's sporting fares little better. His trainers are even worse than his jeans. He's clutching his phone in his hand and pacing up and down outside his mother's shop on the lower ground floor in Block O, three buildings down from Senhora Vilar's address.

His wife, Eugénia, stands beside him, resting her hand on his shoulder and squeezing the straps of her bag with the other. Her dark eyes watch them from a pale face. Her pitch-black hair, loose around her shoulders, emphasises the pallidness, making her seem ill.

'When did the call come through to you, Tiago?' Isabel asks.

'It was around five thirty in the morning,' he says; the hand not holding his phone keeps flexing into a fist and flexing out and then repeating. 'I was already in the van and on my way to work.'

'That's early.'

He nods several times in rapid succession. 'I'm in construction. The project we're working on right now is in Lisbon, and it takes time to get there. We've been starting earlier to avoid the worst of the heat.'

'Was anyone with you at the time you received the call?' Isabel asks.

'Yeah. My boss. I usually catch a lift with him. But I don't understand, you found her car in Moita?'

'Yes, early on this morning,' Isabel tells him, though she doesn't share beyond this, doesn't want to panic him further, not when they know so little. 'Do you live here too?'

He shakes his head. 'No. I live in Barreiro.'

Twenty minutes away by public transport, Isabel thinks, less by car.

'Do you have a recent photo of your mother?' Voronov asks. 'We'd like to share it with the other teams in the municipality.'

Eugénia takes out her phone before her husband can respond. 'I'm sure I have some on my phone, I can send one to you right away.'

'Thank you,' Voronov says.

They had already got hold of a picture of Carmo Vilar which had been attached to the records they'd pulled from her number plate. The passport-style picture showed a middle-aged woman, greyed black hair scraped back and glasses in place. She had been unsmiling in the photo, her features blanched under harsh lighting.

Isabel casts an eye out for prying ears. There are a few nosy people around, but at the moment they're keeping their distance. Probably because Voronov has drawn himself to his full height and levelled a pretty menacing glare when a man wandered out of the café nearby asking why the police were here, beer bottle in hand despite the hour. He'd quickly piped down after.

'Who was it that called you, Tiago?' Isabel asks.

Tiago rubs an agitated hand over his face. 'Dona Lurdes, next door.' He gestures with his hand at the grocery shop beside his mother's. It's the one Isabel had noticed with the fruit stall when they'd driven in.

As if to make his point, an older lady with curly white hair in a wraparound blue floral apron is standing next to the fruit stall, her arms hugging herself and her face creased with concern.

'And what did she say?'

'That the door to my mother's shop was open but no one was there and neither was her car. That never happens. Never. My mother is very particular about these things. So I asked my boss to bring me here, checked to see if her car was outside her block but it wasn't, she never parks anywhere else and it's her spot. Knocked on her door, she's not there either. I used my key to check inside. It's not normal. No one's seen her. That's when I started calling you guys, but you took forever to get here and she could be hurt somewhere or—'

He stops and buries his face in both his hands. His entire body is heaving. He yells into his hands.

'Hey, hey,' Isabel says stepping forward and laying a hand on his arm, 'come on. I think we should talk somewhere else.' The pent-up emotions he's probably been keeping leashed since receiving the phone call about his mother are bursting at the seams and Isabel feels as if she's breathing them in. 'Why don't you go with Inspector Voronov for a moment while I check your mother's shop, hmm?'

Tiago stiffens and glances at the shop an odd emotion touching his face. Like he's repelled.

She hadn't thought it was possible for him to get any more tense, but she was wrong. For a moment she gets the impression he's going to protest.

After a moment, he steps back, turning his back on them completely.

Isabel glances at Voronov who moves closer so that they won't be overheard.

'I'll find somewhere quieter for us to talk to him,' Voronov says.

'Okay,' Isabel nods.

Voronov gives her one last look before turning his attention back to Tiago and his wife, walking them away.

Isabel looks at the wide-open door of the shop.

The light inside is on.

From the outside looking in, the shop radiates an odd emptiness.

Something about this place clearly makes Tiago deeply uncomfortable.

The space she steps into is spotless.

The door itself is a heavy steel door. Sturdy. An odd choice for a bairro like this.

In fact the small square of room, which is just big enough for about four people to stand comfortably, has nothing inside at all, apart from a counter with an ancient cash machine and, completely out of place next to it, a much sleeker card machine. Both seem to be hooked up to something behind the counter. There's a wide bowl on the edge of the counter and it's filled to the brim with chocolates. Nothing fancy, but familiar ones, in shiny wrapping that Isabel associates with Christmas. She always digs through to find the caramel ones.

It smells like lavender. Nothing too overpowering, but enough that Isabel knows that when she walks back out of the shop, the smell of it is going to cling to her clothes and hair.

The floor is made up of sterile white tile. Easy to clean and good for balancing the temperature in the room. The walls are painted a terracotta colour. The light that hangs above her head is a warm yellow.

Curiously, to her left, instead of a door is an arched entryway with beaded curtains hanging down. The beads are in shades of red and pink and Isabel can vaguely see darkness beyond it. She glances around this side of things just once more and walks the few steps to the curtains and parts them.

When she goes through and lifts her head she stops, eyebrows furrowing.

A little bit of light leaks through into the space from behind her, enough for her to be able to make out the shelves. This room is much bigger than the immediate entrance and Isabel's footsteps echo within it. There's an entire shelf packed with labelled jars. She can't really tell what type of food they hold. The rest of the shelves hold other things she can't quite see properly either.

The smell of lavender is much stronger here.

'I need some light,' she murmurs and looks at the wall behind her to locate a light switch. She eventually finds it near the corner.

The light that flicks on is so incredibly low that Isabel wonders what the point is of having the light at all. It might as well not be there.

Her eyes adjust well enough though, and what she finds gives her pause.

There is a round table in the middle of the room. Its surface is covered in a soft purple tablecloth and a candelabra sits atop it, three white candles in its holders, all burned down to different lengths, pearls of wax dripping down their sides and on to the arms of the metal holders.

Isabel walks closer.

To the side of the candelabra is a wide heavy bowl with patterns carved on to its side, and to the other side of it is something rectangular wrapped in white cloth that is tied into place in a neat little bow. The wrapping looks like silk. There are three chairs set around the table, nothing fancy, simple foldout chairs, but like everything else in this room they look pristine.

There are two walls filled with shelves. One of them is the shelf holding all the jars. It's filled with them, and what she'd at first thought was food seems like something else entirely. None of them are labelled, though they seem to be in rows of the same thing judging by the colour; odd-coloured thick pastes and liquids, some of them pure white. Everything shiny and clean, just unidentifiable.

The other shelves holds other things. Tools, probably. Candles. Crystals. Stones. Boxes of what seem like every herb under the sun and rows and rows of little shiny bottles of oils. There are other things she doesn't really recognise but it's hard not to notice what look to be ceremonial knives and daggers, neatly nestled on black silk pillows in boxes.

If she had to hazard a guess, she'd say that she was standing in front of a tarot table.

Isabel walks to the far end of the room where there is another set of beaded curtains. These, when she parts them, reveal a door. She pulls her sleeve over her hand before reaching for it. The door handle twists easily under her grip and the light switch is right there.

Another room. This one is about the same size as the shop entrance. There's a tiny square desk in one corner, some pens and an A4 pad open on it, and an ergonomic chair at odds with the rest of this place. There's a glasses case resting on the seat of the chair, like someone had put it there for a second and then forgotten to take it with them. There's a footstool beneath it too. A small fridge that only comes to about waist height hums in the corner, a small potted plant sits on a crocheted circular mat in baby blue and there's additional lighting coming from a small window at the top. It's above Isabel's head and only partially opened. She'd have to go up on tiptoe to open or close it.

Isabel sighs.

No sign that a struggle or any other foul play took place. Maybe forensics will render better results.

Isabel heads back out.

Looks like Dona Vilar runs the type of business that not too far back in human history would have got her burned at the stake.

6

'Tiago, tell us about your mother's shop,' Isabel says.

Without any private places, Voronov had brought Tiago and Eugénia to their car. They sat in the front passenger seat and the back passenger seat, respectively, their feet planted outside the car, separated by the open back door. Voronov had fetched them both a cup of coffee while Isabel had been inside Vilar's shop. It was not the most ideal place, but they were parked away from the front of the shops and there was no one walking nearby. It was enough for them to get some questions out of the way.

Now, both Isabel and Voronov stand outside the car, looking down at the two people related to the one person connected to the crime so far.

Tiago shrugs, his gaze on the cup of coffee in his hands.

'It looks like an occult shop,' Isabel says. 'Is that what it is?'

The muscles of his jaw work beneath the skin as Tiago grinds his teeth together. Eugénia glances at him, forehead lined with concern.

'It's true, my mother-in-law's business is a little unusual. She . . . she helps people,' Eugénia says.

'Helps people how?'

Tiago keeps his face turned away from them and still doesn't respond, leaving his wife to try again. Eugénia clears her throat. 'She sells card readings . . .' She pauses there before forcing herself to go on, repeatedly flicking quick glances at her husband's face, as if worried that he might censure her. 'Healing . . . spells.'

Isabel glances over at the shop that they've locked back up, keeping it clear whilst they wait for forensics.

Having seen inside the shop Isabel isn't so surprised by what Eugénia is telling her but there's still a touch of incredulity. This kind of business? In a place like this? Sure, people do things through back doors, in each other's kitchens maybe. There are always people who are susceptible to these types of cons, but to have it as a business so openly?

'Is Senhora Vilar Gifted?' Voronov asks. Like Isabel, he too is probably sceptical about the truth of Carmo Vilar's psychic/healer business.

Eugénia's explanation seems to have nudged her husband out of his stubborn silence. 'I don't know.'

'She didn't tell you?'

'No, she didn't hide anything from me. You think if she was scared of being found out as Gifted she'd own a bruxaria business? She just never tested.'

Voronov looks at Isabel, surprised.

Isabel shrugs. 'It's possible.' The system has never been entirely foolproof and she's probably from a time where being branded as Gifted at a young age wouldn't have been safe for her or her family, never mind what her level of comfort is now. Back then there were ways of avoiding the testing. Most of them came down to either money or knowing someone who worked at the National Testing Institute. And it's not like they don't have examples of that still happening now.

Just have to look at me, Isabel thinks. Or Gabriel.

Isabel catches the quick look Voronov sends her way and understands what he's thinking.

Given what Carmo does for a living and the manner of death of their still-unidentified victim, and given that her car was found at the scene, there's a strong possibility that the deceased is Carmo Vilar. They need everything Tiago and Eugénia can tell them.

'Senhor Vilar,' Voronov says, 'we were called to an incident this morning where a woman was found dead due to a serious fire. We're in charge of that investigation and we don't yet have the identity of the deceased.'

Tiago falls still. He stares at Voronov.

'Your mother's car was discovered close enough to the location that there's a strong possibility your mother's disappearance is connected,' Voronov says the next words gently, 'and there's a possibility that the woman found this morning could be your mother.'

'Tiago,' Isabel says, and waits for him to meet her eyes. There's a touch of disconnection in his gaze, like he's not entirely there with them right now. 'I sincerely hope that it isn't your mother. And if isn't then my team and I are going to be looking for her. Our investigating team are out there as we speak trying to find answers for you as quickly as they can, but in the meantime, we need you to answer our questions to the best of your ability.'

'And we'll also need your permission to secure some of your mother's personal effects. It will help us determine whether the person found this morning is your mother,' Voronov adds.

Eugénia chokes out a sob, rounding the door over to Tiago's side. She hunkers down, resting her hand on his leg and leaning against his side.

'What were Carmo's working hours? Did any problems ever arise with clients in relation to her services?' Isabel asks.

Tiago takes a deep breath but still seems out of it. 'Her shop hours are twelve a.m. to three thirty a.m., Monday to Friday. Unless she is sick, which is rare. Her clients come to her for everything, but when their life doesn't magically change, they like to talk behind her back, call her all sorts of things. Then they go and snitch to the head priest. He always gives them what they want, entire sermons on the devil and letting it into your home.'

Okay.

'Head priest?' Isabel asks.

'Yeah. Everyone goes to him. He oversees the congregations for the Extremadura de Setúbal. He makes personal visits to the churches nearby whenever there's a new complaint about my mother.'

Seems a bit extreme. It's a lot of effort for just one woman. 'That's big interest in a woman with a small business.'

Eugénia shakes her head. 'She didn't only see clients from here. She has a reputation for being the real deal. She's well known and her name gets passed around all the time.'

'The rent for this place is cheap,' Tiago says, 'but do you think my mother can survive on working so few hours a day on what people like her typically make? My mother keeps her rates cheap for the locals, but outsiders? She charges them as high as eight hundred euros, sometimes more. Do you know how desperate people must be to pay such a ridiculous fee?' Tiago looks at them both. 'Not per service. Per hour.'

If you're willing to pay that much for this kind of service then you have to be desperate. Desperate people and high amounts of money don't make for the best combination.

'The head priest you mentioned, does he have a specific history with your mother?'

'When I was little we attended Padre Lopes's sermons. Despite her business, my mother is a practising Catholic, you see,' he says, lips twisting into a humourless quirk. 'We only stopped going after my mother decided to start her business once she was on her own.'

'Was your mother with someone at the time? Your father?'

'He passed away. Heart attack. She remortgaged the house and opened her shop. I was fifteen at the time.'

'And once she started her business, she stopped attending his service?'

'Not right away. But Padre Lopes told her she was no longer welcome. She still insisted I attend, so I went alone.' He sneers. 'He always asked me how my mother was.'

Isabel lifts an eyebrow.

'Do you still attend his service?' Voronov asks.

'At Christmas. It's the service Eugénia's parents go to so we always join them.'

'Has he said anything about your mother?' Isabel asks.

He meets Isabel's gaze, eyes red-rimmed and shining. 'He asks about her every time.'

7

Chief Bautista is standing and drinking in a rush from a coffee cup when Isabel walks into her office.

She's in a suit, which is unusual for her, and her hair has been pulled tight. Smart shoes and perfume, all of which are somewhat ruined by the cigarette smell that always surrounds her, not helped by the fan on her desk that is whirring away in an effort to ease the heat but only really seems to be pushing that same smell around the room.

Isabel gives a low whistle. 'Chief, you didn't have to get dressed up just for me.'

Chief Bautista pauses mid-sip and stares her down. 'If you have come back with a sense of humour I suggest you kill it now.'

Isabel snorts tiredly and shakes her head. She pulls the door closed behind her.

'What are you doing in here? Forgot how to do your job? You've been gone long enough. I heard you've been making friends in high places. Make it quick, I have a meeting at the centre in half an hour.' She mutters under her breath about having to catch a damn taxi as she digs out her bag from behind her desk.

Isabel leans back against the closed door, folding her arms. 'I was just coming to check in,' she says. 'if I hadn't, you'd be cursing me out.'

Chief harrumphs. She sets the coffee down and snags a bottle of water, unscrewing the lid and taking a drink. 'If I remember correctly I told you to take extended leave, not to go out and get yourself another job.' At Isabel's incredulous look Bautista snorts and sits back on the edge of her desk. 'What? You didn't think it would reach me?'

Isabel shakes her head. 'Is it a job if I don't get paid? Who told you?' she asks.

'Interpol have been in touch with me. Wanted my opinion.'

Soon after arriving in America for the London case trial, Isabel had met Carina Matthews, the Interpol agent in charge of overseeing the Gabriel Bernardo case. As an international fugitive, his case had been handed over to the Interpol branch that dealt with international Gifted crime. She'd also taken an interest in the London case because it had touched on three different countries and dealt with Gifted crime. She'd approached Isabel after Isabel took the stand to testify against Dr Cross.

She hadn't taken a job with them, but she had spent some time with their team, both in regard to Gabriel, but also in order to learn about the team's function.

'I don't appreciate them trying to poach my staff. Especially one who was meant to be on extended leave.'

Isabel shakes her head and crosses her arms in front of her.

'Well. Did you sort your mess out?'

Isabel thinks about it. Allows herself to feel the pure silence in her own mind. No intruding voices. Nothing that she doesn't want in there until she does. Well. Apart from one thing. But she'll get to that. She *is* getting to that. She's patient. Can afford to be now, which is ironic, considering that's one thing she now knows she won't have forever.

In answer to Bautista's question, she nods. 'I'll file all the updated records once I get home. Didn't really get the chance,' she scratches at the back of her neck, 'but I have to let you know that as of now, I've officially been assigned to a Monitoring agent.'

Monitoring is a government organisation that works in affiliation with NTI, the National Testing Institute. They're there to keep tabs on higher-level Gifted, those who may pose a threat to society at large. They'd had Isabel in their sights as a result of the Gabriel Bernardo case and she'd managed to dodge them for long enough.

However, during her time in America and with the research team there focusing on their work with higher-level Gifted, it had become clear that avoiding them would no longer be an option.

It's a talk she'll need to have with Voronov. She's already told her brother and Voronov is the next person she wants to know. The only other person she feels needs and *deserves* to know.

Chief Bautista considers her words. 'I see.' She straightens up and comes closer, slinging her bag over her shoulder. It's so weird seeing her like this. She looks like a smartly dressed head of a criminal enterprise of old who is about to make mincemeat out of some idiots. 'You don't seem worried.'

That gives Isabel pause. She thinks about it. 'I'm not.' Because there was a difference in having Monitoring trying to force themselves into her life versus contacting them herself and negotiating her own terms.

Chief Bautista inclines her head. 'Good. I have to go. Walk with me. What's happening with the case?'

Isabel opens the door for her and follows her out. 'I'll bring you up to speed.'

8

'It's good to have you back,' Daniel says and smacks Isabel's shoulder hard enough that she frowns and retaliates by shoving him halfway across the room.

They've taken over one of the empty case rooms on the same floor as their office and are waiting for Voronov and Carla who are coming back with food. They'd said they were at the entrance to the precinct and would be here any moment now.

'If that's how you treat me when I'm back I'm not sure I believe you.'

'No. Seriously.' And this time it's sincere, his voice pleased.

Isabel, Daniel and Jacinta had all started around the same time, had worked their way up together and had stayed close. If Isabel imagined working here without either of them she couldn't quite picture it. It didn't feel right. Despite that, she knows everything changes eventually. It's just the way life goes.

Voronov and Carla walk in, bags of food and drinks in hand. Isabel snags a prego sandwich and a Coke and sits herself on the edge of the table. Carla grabs a seat, notebook and pen out, lays out her food neatly in front of her with Daniel dragging a chair out to sit next to her. Voronov stands next to Isabel, carefully unwrapping his sandwich.

'All right, what are we thinking?' Isabel asks around a mouth full of sandwich. She's missed old man Días's food. She'll have to stop by to say hi at some point.

'Body is with Jacinta and she's prioritising that so she can check it against the personal matter we bagged at her place,' Daniel says.

After getting permission from her son, they'd gone back to Carmo Vilar's flat and taken a hairbrush and toothbrush to have something for Jacinta to work with.

'Okay, knowing Jacinta we'll probably have that in a day or two,' Isabel says.

'She's got her team working on the car. And we have the clothes.'

Isabel pushes away from the table. She pulls out the picture she's printed of Carmo Vilar and pins it up, then she grabs the red marker on the portable whiteboard. As soon as she starts writing the squeaking noise made by the marker and its weak colour tell her it won't be lasting much longer. She kisses her teeth in annoyance and keeps writing.

Body. Car. Clothes. Accelerant.

'Anything else from the fire investigator?'

Voronov turns and leans back on the table, just as she'd been doing. 'Not yet, and Jacinta has said she'll also get in touch with us right away if he goes to her directly.'

Hmm. That will have to do. She's not precious about it as long as he gets any information over to one of them and he keeps them up to date.

'The car belongs to Carmo Vilar, who was reported missing early this morning. Not at her house, not at her shop,' Isabel says, the pen squealing faster across the board as she goes. 'Normally her business hours are twelve a.m. to three thirty a.m.' She stands back from what they have so far. 'If Vilar does turn out to be our victim, and at this point that's looking very likely, then we may have a few people to look at for this. The way the son and daughter-in-law talked about it, sounds like Vilar was given more than one reason to be hypervigilant over her shop. I didn't see any graffiti or anything on the door but that's easily cleaned off . . .' She caps the pen and turns to look at them all. 'I just get the feeling maybe something's been done to the shop a few times.' She looks at Voronov. 'Did you see the door she has on that place? Every other business has a regular door. Hers weighs a tonne.'

'It's possible,' Voronov agrees, 'Tiago and Eugénia seemed convinced that not every person she saw was happy with the results and when that happened, they were vocal about it.'

'Let's start there. Think we have to spend some more time there, seeing what's what. And,' Isabel says, 'if she's not our victim then she's linked to the crime and we'll have to figure out in what capacity. There's the priest too. He's certainly an interesting one.'

Daniel shrugs a shoulder as he takes a huge bite of his sandwich. 'Well, if she's into bruxaria it's not that much of a stretch, right? They used to burn people over that kind of stuff back in the day.'

Carla gives him a sombre look. 'No. They used to burn *us,*' she says quietly. 'Midwives, healers, Gifted. Those were the women accused of witchcraft back in the day.'

It's true. And in all likelihood, if there was any accuracy at all to what Carmo Vilar did under the guise of a bruxa it was most likely because she was Gifted, and for her line of work, she would most likely be a telepathic Gifted.

Looking a little guilty, Daniel squeezes Carla's shoulder. 'You know what I meant,' he says quietly.

'I know,' Carla says and gives his hand a comforting pat, which is amusing, but then she seems to think of something else, 'although, if we look at it from another angle, if Vilar isn't the victim, the same holds true. Traditionally witchcraft has many of its roots in rituals; it's always been connected to the occult. Fire itself is often linked to purification. And,' she checks her notes, 'they've talked about the curing of illnesses. We don't have to go very far to see examples of that even in modern life, even from respected religious factions. It wouldn't be so farfetched for it to have been some kind of purification or healing ritual gone wrong.'

It's true.

How many times has it been on the news? So many documentaries now, telling the story of religions that are more cults than anything, religious leaders killing and raping, all in the name of whatever deity they worship and all under the guise of blessings and/or healings or divine punishments.

In this case they have a woman burned at the stake and they also have word of a head priest being fixated on her.

Isabel looks at the board.

After a moment she adds Carla's suggestions on there too.

'So at the moment, Carmo Vilar is both our suspected victim, and failing that, if she's not a match . . . then it looks like she's also our primary suspect.'

'Could be worse,' Daniel says.

'Oh?'

'We could have no suspected victim nor a primary suspect.'

He's not wrong.

Isabel sighs. 'Okay. So.' She checks her watch. It's going on close to six p.m. Most of them have been up since four in the morning if not earlier. 'I don't think we'll get anything else from Jacinta's team tonight, they're probably packing up soon, if they haven't started already. Now's a good time for us to catch some people at home though. I say we go back and speak with the shopkeeper next door who made the call to Tiago and speak with her properly, just in case there's anything we need to act on now. Then tomorrow we're at that town first thing and start talking to all of Carmo's neighbours.'

Isabel looks at Voronov to get his take. 'Thoughts?'

He stands. 'Sounds good. You want us to take it and then I can drop you off at your brother's?'

Isabel catches the little looks fired their way by Daniel and Carla as they get up and pretend very badly not to be paying attention.

Seems like they've clocked on already. Not that Voronov dropping her off anywhere is something new and would mean anything specific so it wouldn't have been based on that.

Well. It would be more embarrassing if they hadn't caught on, considering they're inspectors.

She ignores Daniel and Carla. 'Yeah, let's do that.'

9

Dona Lurdes holds the door and stares up at Isabel and Voronov from inside her home. 'I saw you both this morning, you were with Carmo's son.'

She lives in the same block as her shop, two floors up; however, whereas her shop is at the front of the building facing the road that welcomes people into the bairro, her apartment is on the other side of the block, with her home overseeing the same river dividing up the two neighbourhoods they'd spent time in today.

Like with Vilar's home, they can see all the doors to the other homes in the buildings from here, including the upper floors, and they can see down into the community square that's at the centre of the block, with its benches, playground and trees. Right now, it's mostly empty, with people just crossing it on a walk with friends on the way to someone's house or heading to one of the cafés. There's one couple nestled up close on one of the benches, heads together.

Isabel can hear the sounds of the evening all around them: pans moving here and there, families talking, televisions on and kids chatting away loudly. These types of houses and buildings are never particularly well soundproofed. It's probably why gossip is always so lively. Everyone hears everything there is to hear. If it's not the neighbour on the left blabbing, then it's the neighbour on the right or the neighbour above or below. Always someone.

'Good evening, Dona Lurdes,' Voronov says, offering a hand and keeping his distance so that he isn't looming over her. Up close, she's a very small lady. She's probably in her late sixties or early seventies though she looks to be in very good health. 'Yes, I'm Inspector Voronov and this is Inspector Reis. We're with the Polícia Judiciária. We were speaking with Tiago about his mother this morning. We were hoping to speak with you today about the call you made. I promise we won't take up too much of your time, I know it's late in the day.'

Although she's changed, she's wearing another wraparound apron over a pink T-shirt and a grey skirt that falls below her knees, and she's got on a pair of slippers. The smell of something cooking drifts out through the open door.

'No of course, of course, please come in.' She steps back and opens the door wider, 'I'm just getting dinner ready. My daughter will be home soon from work. Can I get either of you anything?' she asks as they come in. 'Just through here,' she says, gesturing to the first door that's only a few steps from the entrance, 'have a seat, have a seat.'

The kitchen is painted a warm yellow. It's not a particularly big room, not like the one they'd seen this morning belonging to Carmo Vilar, but it's cosy. There's a square table in one corner just beneath the window and two chairs tucked into the available sides. Next to it by the wall is a three-tiered storage basket. The lower one is filled with onions, the middle one is filled with potatoes and at the very top are tomatoes. All the vegetables are of various shapes and sizes and look fresh.

Dona Lurdes pulls out the chairs for them and urges them to sit before going over to the stove on the other side of the room. She's got a pot bubbling away and a frying pan that she immediately goes back to stirring. Isabel can smell the familiar scent of onion and tomato cooking together.

There's an open package of minced meat on the counter bought from the butcher's, probably a mixture of different kinds of meat by the looks of it.

'Water?' Dona Lurdes asks as she continues to stir. 'Or a coffee or tea?'

'No, thank you, Dona Lurdes, I'm fine,' Isabel says and Voronov also politely declines.

'Okay but if you change your mind, please let me know,' she says. As she talks she doesn't stop moving, opening cupboards and taking out spices, going back to the stove and stirring, tasting as she goes.

'Dona Lurdes, Tiago told us you called him very early in the morning to let him know Carmo Vilar's shop had been left wide open.'

'Yes, yes.' She scoots over to the sink to quickly wash her hands after tasting her sauce and grabs a dishtowel to dry them. 'It's so unusual. Normally by the time I get there, she's packing up. Carmo always closes her shop on time, three thirty and no more customers. The rest is her winding down and she leaves at four, sometimes a few minutes earlier or later but that's about it. I get there early myself because I always go to the bakery on the other side of the bairro to collect my morning bread. I like to get fresh batches because we always have the youngsters from Moita coming over after they finish clubbing and they eat like horses after a bit of drinking and dancing; sometimes they sit outside making a bag of noise and waking up all the neighbours. Anyway. I like to get my bread before they come in, have myself some breakfast and work on cakes. People put in a lot of orders with me, you see. I make birthday cakes, and other such things, to order. Always make them fresh the same day. They're not too complicated, I don't sleep much you see. Always up early, might as well work and make a little bit of extra cash on top of everything else. I like having some spending money.'

Woman sounds like she's savvier with money than I've ever been, Isabel thinks, impressed.

Dona Lurdes pulls some cups out of the cupboard and reaches for the filtered water sitting next to the biscuit tin on the counter. She pours two glasses and then sets one each in front of Isabel and Voronov on the table.

Clearly a woman who really needs her guests to be looked after considering they'd both said they were fine.

Isabel thanks her anyway, amused, and obligingly takes a drink. It is pretty hot, even warmer in here despite Dona Lurdes having her window open because of the pots on the stove.

'Anyway,' Dona Lurdes says, going back to her cooking. She scoops up the package with the meat and returns to the stove. 'When I got there, the door was wide open. The light was still on and I just peered inside. Didn't go in.' She looks at them then, as if to emphasise the truth of her words, like it's important they understand this part. 'I really like Carmo and she does a lot of good things for the people in this bairro. She's important to our community.'

Ah. Okay. Clearly there's a 'but' coming here.

Voronov gives her his full attention, all gentle speaking and attentive. The older ladies love it. Want to pat him on the head and feed him like he's their son. Some of it is because it's Voronov and he's a good-looking man with a charming smile, but a lot of it is because these women will never grow out of babying the male gender. Isabel is very used to it by now.

'You can tell us, Dona Lurdes, anything that you say to us is confidential and we're just here to listen to anything you might want to share with us. Your talking to us is much appreciated and very helpful to our investigation.'

She looks between him and Isabel. Then she transfers the meat into the frying pan, the sizzling sound loud in the small space as she uses the wooden spoon to break it up into smaller pieces.

'I heard about what happened in Moita this morning. Some woman was found burning to death by a little girl, isn't that right? Then you two showed up here right after.'

Isabel isn't surprised the story has made it over already. They were expecting it, and she bets it started doing the rounds soon after they got to speak with Tiago in Barreiro.

'There was an incident there,' Voronov confirms, 'and we are also looking into it.'

No point denying anything here; this woman is not stupid, and it might potentially put them on the wrong side of her good graces, which isn't where they want to be right now.

'It sounded like you were reluctant to check if Carmo was inside the shop, Dona Lurdes,' Voronov says.

'Hmm,' she says, 'I didn't want to go in there. I'm Catholic. I go to church every Saturday morning. I don't judge, I know everyone is different and people have their own beliefs and I try to mind my business no matter what I think of someone's lifestyle choice or what they do but . . .' she shakes her head, 'crossing over into that kind of space isn't something I feel comfortable doing. So I always keep my distance. But don't get me wrong, she comes into my shop for a cup of tea sometimes, or keeps me company or sometimes even comes up here for a chat. We get along well. She's a nice lady. I wish she didn't . . .' She sighs and shakes her head, 'I don't know. But if I'm honest, I'm surprised trouble didn't come knocking at her door a lot earlier.'

Isabel glances at Voronov from the corner of her eye.

'Why do you say that, Dona Lurdes?' he asks.

'She messes around with things that shouldn't be messed around with. It's unnatural, what she does.'

'Do you mean her prediction services and the healing?'

Dona Lurdes shakes her head. 'No, no I'm not talking about the other stuff – although that too. What kind of promises is she making to be able to have those kinds of abilities? She's not making them to God, I'm telling you that now.'

'If it's not those kinds of services, then what are the others?'

She switches off the burner on the stove. 'Her son didn't tell you?' At their blank looks she sighs. 'Well, I'm not surprised. That's why he and his wife moved to Barreiro a couple of years ago. Tiago doesn't like what his mum does and I can't blame him. There's always a price to pay. But I don't mean the healing and whatnot. I'm talking about the love spells.'

'I'm sorry,' Isabel asks, unable to help herself, 'love spells?'

'Yes. And there's been trouble over it too. Very ugly trouble. It's what I'm saying. You shouldn't mess with these things and it's only a matter of time before trouble comes knocking on your door.'

'What do you mean?'

Dona Lurdes sighs. She walks closer, reaching for her dishtowel again, an absent-minded gesture, as if she needs something to do with her hands now that she doesn't have the cooking to keep her busy anymore.

'You speak to anyone from here and you'll see just how much Carmo is loved. She looks after the people in this place. She's about community.'

'Even though she's a bruxa?' Isabel asks.

'That doesn't matter. She's kind. She takes care of her own and she's always giving. The rest of what she does is not for us to judge. That's between her and God. But still . . . there are lines you shouldn't cross. As much as she is loved here by all of us, she's caused a lot of heartbreak around these parts and worse in some cases. My mother always said there are things that you should stay out of in other people's lives: one is money and the other is love. Carmo interfered in both. A lot of bad things happened because of people going to her for that kind of thing and whenever it went wrong, people don't look at themselves, do they? Who do you think they blamed?'

'When you say people blamed her,' Isabel says, 'what did people do? Was it just talk?'

Dona Lurdes shakes her head. 'There were break-ins at her shop, it got smashed up. They had to call the police over it. There was talk too, of course there was – not that it stopped people still coming to her.'

That might explain the fortified door on the shop. Interesting though, that, despite the fact there had been no cameras installed in or around the shop and that neither Tiago nor Eugénia had mentioned the incident with the vandalism.

'Did the police find out who vandalised it?'

She shrugs. 'I didn't hear anything about that.'

Just everything else then, Isabel thinks.

'That wasn't even the worst one.'

Isabel glances at Voronov, giving him a subtle look so that he can contribute to moving this along. He's clearly the target audience here. Every time Dona Lurdes opens her mouth to answer their questions her gaze is glued to Voronov.

To his credit – and Isabel will never understand how his poker face is so good – not a hint of humour shows on his face. He responds to Dona Lurdes as patiently and respectfully as he always does.

'What else happened, Dona Lurdes?' he asks.

'Well.' She folds her arms across her chest and walks over so she's standing closer to them and her voice drops low like she's expecting someone else to overhear them. 'People were saying Carmo was getting regular visits from Thelma's husband, João.'

Before they can ask her if she knows what exactly João was visiting Carmo for, she saves them the trouble. Her hushed and hurried words carry the excitement of knowing she's sharing something exciting, made even better by the fact that she shouldn't know any of this in the first place.

'People were saying that he was planning on leaving Thelma for a younger woman. Said he was going to Carmo for help with it. You know,' she waves her hand, 'asking her to do all that unholy stuff.'

'The love spells?' Voronov asks.

'Bah.' She waves it away like she doesn't want to discuss it.

'And was she?' Isabel asks. 'Was Carmo helping him with that?'

'How should I know?' she says. 'One afternoon all you hear is a load of noise and this awful crashing sound. I was in my shop next door and rushed out to see what was happening. My heart was beating a mile a minute, and what do I see? Thelma's car on the pavement driven right up on there and right into one of the pillars. Thelma's hanging out the window of the car, head bleeding everywhere.' Her voice has gone soft at the end. The initial excitement at having something to share dissipates and she falls quiet. She lifts a hand to her face, resting it against her cheek. 'It was a terrible sight.'

She seems lost in the memory of the incident. And she really is; Isabel feels the vacantness of thought and emotion where there wasn't any before, like a pocket of air.

'Why did she do that?' Voronov asks after the quiet drags on for a little while.

Dona Lurdes sighs. 'She was after Carmo. God knows why. You might not agree with what she does but it's her husband that was going there for the help, wasn't it? But you drive people to the edge and they lose their minds. Thelma crashed because she was trying to hit Carmo.' She shakes her head. 'You should have seen Carmo's face, white as a ghost. She just stood there, frozen, looking at Thelma bleeding all over the car.'

Damn.

'She didn't move a muscle. Not even when that poor excuse for a man ran out of the shop and started losing his mind when he saw what his wife was done. What a useless man.'

10

Isabel walks out of her bedroom, hair dragged back up, the coolness of the cold shower still lingering on her skin. It won't last long. The heat shows no signs of abating and it's the kind of night where everyone will be sleeping with sheets kicked off.

She doesn't even bother to leave the bedside light on like she sometimes does, more than happy to leave the pretty silver envelope with her sister's wedding invitation under shadow where she'd chucked it on the nightstand earlier.

She comes back into her small living room having changed into comfortable loose shorts and a tank top. The smell of cheese, tomato and peppers fills the warm air, and Isabel becomes even more aware of what feels like a hole in her stomach. She's starving.

Voronov glances up from where he's sitting on the floor, an unopened box of pizza and two cans of Coke on the coffee table in front of him, both of her dogs trying their best to climb on to his lap, two tennis balls forgotten by his outstretched legs.

He looks up as she pads over on bare feet and sinks on to the sofa with a groan. Immediately the dogs abandon him for her.

'Tired?'

'Yes. Feels like I haven't stopped once since I got on the flight back.' She sighs and brings her legs up on to the sofa too to sit cross-legged. She reaches out to run her fingers through his hair. 'Thanks for coming with me and dropping us off.'

They'd left Dona Lurdes setting the table for dinner with her daughter and thanked her for speaking with them. She'd seen them out with a: 'I hope you find Carmo safe and sound. Good night, Inspectors.'

After that they'd left for Sebastião's house to pick up the dogs. Isabel's car was still at the precinct and exhaustion was fast sinking in. She wanted her dogs, food and her own bed.

Voronov passes one of the cans back to her and Isabel pops the tab open and guzzles half of it down, ignoring the fizzy burn of it and appreciating the cold sugar–caffeine combo.

She accepts the wedge of pizza he hands over with equal enthusiasm and almost sobs in pleasure as she takes a bite of the hot slice, the simplicity of the cheese, tomato, and onion combination perfect for her tired brain and hungry mouth.

'So good,' she manages around the mouthful as she falls back against the sofa.

Voronov shifts his position on the floor, sitting sideways between the table and the sofa so that he's facing her and still keeping an eye on the pizza where Tigre and Branca are showing a little too much interest. He sets his drink on the floor and takes a bite of his own slice. 'Hell of a case to come home to,' he says.

Isabel shakes her head. 'Yeah.' She demolishes her slice and scoots forward, leaning over him to grab another one. 'A self-proclaimed bruxa burned at the stake,' she murmurs, 'just . . . no words.'

'Hmm. When we were talking to her family and the neighbour you didn't seem particularly impressed by that part.'

She sighs. 'No? I guess not. You heard what Carla said. What people used to call witchcraft was never anything more than women practising medicine or women using their Gifts. Predicting the future? Romance spells? I don't believe in that type of thing. As much as everyone feels that Carmo was a kind woman, I think the reality is that she was a *smart* woman. I think she was Gifted and that she learned how to monetise that.' Psychic readings, all of those things, were always the result of someone getting in your head, learning about you and your life in ways you didn't even understand were happening, and then using that to make informed guesses about what people would face in the future.

As for the love spells . . . Yeah. No.

'I'm not saying she wasn't kind either,' she says, 'people are built in greys. I'm sure she could have found a way to contribute to her community and still con them into thinking her services were legit. Why?' she asks, looking down at him. 'Do you believe in all that stuff?'

'No more or less than anyone else,' he says.

'What do you mean? Like superstition?'

'I suppose. Every culture has its folklore and things that come with it that we can't quite shake. When I was growing up superstition was a big part of our lives. Russian culture is steeped in it so it's hard to escape it entirely.'

Makes sense. Isabel's tia Simone still throws salt over her shoulder every time she spills something.

'I agree with Dona Lurdes, though,' she says, 'money and love, she said. The two things guaranteed to make people irrational and desperate, and Carmo Vilar was dealing in both those things. The way she was killed . . . I'm worried about the ritualistic nature of it.'

Voronov hitches himself up to sit beside her. 'I don't like it either. Learning about her business and then looking at the way she was killed suggests maybe the killer knew who she was. The method feels too specific. We'll be all over it tomorrow; we can put it aside for today.'

'I'm not going to argue with that,' she says. She scoots around to face him, pressing her back to the arm rest.

'Listen,' she says, 'about the pills this morning . . .'

In the process of grabbing another slice of pizza, Voronov sets the box back down. 'Something wrong?'

Her response is something between a wince and a smile. 'Remember the research Anabel Pereira was working on before she fled to the Portuguese embassy in London?' Dr Anabel Pereira and her sister, Teresa Pereira, had been at the heart of the case Isabel and Voronov had been sent to investigate in London. She had been a research scientist of Portuguese heritage working for the American military specialising in Gifted research. Some of her research had looked at optimising Gifted individuals in combat, which involved a lot of research around higher-level Gifted and erosion.

Gifted individuals classed as levels seven to ten are at risk of erosion – in fact it is almost guaranteed. It's why higher-level Gifted require monitoring. The Gift begins to corrode parts of the brain, impacting the amygdala. Empathy and memory become affected, which can lead to a dangerous lack of empathy and less willingness to control oneself.

Years ago, when Isabel's level had shown clear signs of escalating, she had started taking a drug called S3, a heavy suppressant aimed at keeping the Gift's level steady. The effects it had on her were less than ideal. What started out as small headaches here and there escalated to her living with full-blown migraines every day, constantly feeling as if her head were about to crack open in two. It had been so debilitating. And then when her body had had enough, she'd been thrown into freefall, her Gift all over the place, overwhelmed and drowning in the emotions and thoughts of everyone around her. She'd come a long way since then.

'Yes. Focusing on Gifted in the military?'

Isabel nods. 'They've made some progress on the erosion process. They've had some success stories, and their testing methods are more advanced than the ones we use here at the NTI. I think it's more down to the fact that they test Gifted individuals in their care multiple times after the first test. So while I was there, I got curious.'

Voronov looks at her. 'You allowed them to test you.'

She shrugs. 'Like I said, I was curious. My level changed so suddenly. I wondered if there had been changes since my retesting and their processes were a little more in-depth as part of their research.'

'And?' he asks.

'The good news is it's the same.'

The sound of the ascending tram fills the room. It's probably the last one of the night.

'And the bad news?'

Isabel takes a deep breath, rocks a little in place before meeting his eyes. 'My Gift is teetering on the edge of ten.'

He stares at her.

Isabel lets out a breath and reaches to take his hand. 'But I know you already had an idea of how high up I was on the scale.'

He slides his fingers between hers, his face serious. He makes an affirmative sound.

'There's more,' she says.

His gaze flicks back up to her face. She can see the lines of his jaw tightening. 'What is it?'

She takes a deep breath, remembering how her brother had sat in silence just staring at her without any words when the first thing she had done on her return was to sit him down to tell him.

'They've identified early signs of erosion,' she says calmly.

And she is calm.

It had once been her biggest fear. It still was, but being told that the process was underway hadn't driven her to panic; instead it had filled her with an unexpected peace. Oh, she'd felt scared in the immediate aftermath of the news. Had sat in her hotel room, head in her hands, eyes sore from tears she had tried to hold back with the mounds of her palms and a chest that felt like it was burning.

Eventually, though, it passed and that odd sense of peace settled.

There was no more wondering *what if*? It's as if the news had snapped the fear that had a chokehold on her when it came to her Gift.

The saying goes that when you fear something it controls you. She'd gone her entire life fearing her Gift.

It's so much easier to be in control of something when it no longer holds a question mark over your head.

Even if, eventually, she'll lose to it.

But just because she's had time to process it and come to terms with it, the people closest to her haven't.

Her brother had been shaking and barely consolable.

Right now, Voronov is staring at her face and his hold on her hand is so tight she can see the veins protruding on the back of his own hand.

'Hey,' she murmurs, and lays her other hand on top of his, 'I'm all right.'

His grip eases, but he doesn't say anything.

She shuffles closer to him. 'We've known each other for a long time now. But this side of things is new for us,' she says. 'I wanted to tell you because you've become someone important to me. I also wanted to tell you because I want you to understand what you'd be signing up for, if you want to continue with . . . this. Us. Together.'

He nods tightly, like he understands, but his jaw just clamps together harder.

'The pills aren't like the S Three. No major side effects. They're proven in their trials to slow down the erosion. I'm okay to use my Gift but it will help if I don't take it to extremes.'

'What's taking it to an extreme?' he asks.

'Being switched on all the time,' she pauses, 'getting inside someone's head and almost walking them off a cliff.'

The former won't be an issue, not anymore. She's got really good at locking up her Gift. Nothing but sensing of emotions and no more than that, unless she actively wants to.

The latter – well.

She still needs to find Gabriel Bernardo. She's pretty sure that whatever she needs to do there will cross over into what is considered extreme.

Like he knows what she's thinking, Voronov slides an arm around her shoulders and brings her close so she's resting her head on his shoulder. 'What about Gabriel? Were Interpol any help?'

Isabel scoffs. 'Some. But I think they're counting on me more than I'm counting on them.'

He sighs and Isabel feels the soft pressure of the kiss he presses to her head.

She likes this. She likes that she can be soft with him.

'They offered me a job,' she says.

He lets out a low whistle. 'You *have* been busy. Anything else?'

Isabel makes herself more comfortable, ignoring how the heat makes it less than ideal for her to be glued to his side.

'No. I think that's enough for now.'

Voronov sighs. 'Good.'

11

Isabel heaves her breaths in and out, head between her knees, open bottle of water in her hand. Her legs feel shaky, the burn taking its time to fade.

The concrete of the steps she's sitting on is a little cool, but that will change once the sun is fully in the sky.

In front of her, her dogs play in the cool water of the river, happily splashing around and running.

Isabel had rolled out of bed at 5.30 a.m. The time difference between Lisbon and Massachusetts is five hours and she doesn't do too well with the readjustment. The best way to handle it, she'd reasoned, was to pick her routine back up and get to it.

Voronov had left late last night, and she'd fallen asleep on her sofa instead of the bed. She'd felt too full of pizza and exhaustion-weighed bones to have got up again.

Throwing on her gear as soon as her alarm had gone off, she'd whistled for the dogs and they'd set out at an easy pace, the temperature too hot to go full throttle or for as long as on one of her usual runs.

She drinks from the bottle of water, eyes drifting along the waterline. The ferries are already hard at work crossing from one side of the river to the other.

The city is still quiet at this time, though there are plenty of people out, making their way to work. Some stand at the café kiosks, knocking back strong shots of bica to wake themselves up before heading either in the direction of the train station or the opposite way towards the ferries.

She loves this type of quiet.

As her breathing calms, she sits up straighter and lets her legs splay outwards.

Grounded by the aches in her body from the satisfying run and the peace around her, Isabel turns her attention inwards.

She's not planning on doing much. She just wants to check in.

At some point during their interactions when Isabel had been investigating his case, Gabriel Bernardo had found a way to sneak into her mind and he had stayed there. And then a little over three months ago, he'd found Isabel's mother and he'd used his Gift to change something in her. Something important.

Isabel will have to go and see her soon.

She doesn't want to. Isn't quite ready to face her mother again. Or her sister for that matter. Isabel's relationships with them both are a tangled mess and she's not looking forward to dealing with it.

Pushing that aside for now, she focuses.

There, tucked away in her mind, like a small inky black mass, is his connection to her. Still. But very present. Alert. She's spent a lot of time during her stay in America learning how to approach the connection between them without giving her intention away. With the same guide she'd worked with when she'd been learning how to navigate her Gift as a young teen, she'd perfected her block, keeping him confined to just that small corner.

Gabriel Bernardo could no longer see anything – either inside her mind or through her own eyes – that she did not want him to.

Each time she'd been able to get closer and closer.

'I'll find you soon,' she murmurs.

She turns away, letting her surroundings fall back into place around her – just in time to feel Branca's tongue swiping over her cheek.

She laughs and jerks back before wrapping her arms around both her dogs and pulling them in tight.

'I missed you both,' she sighs, then kisses them both on the head and stands. 'Come on, let's go home.'

With Daniel and Carla making an early start with locating Thelma and João Frade, Isabel and Voronov's first stop is Jacinta.

Isabel signs in with her name at the front and stands back to allow Voronov to do the same. 'I think once Carla and Daniel are done with the neighbours, we should be able to reliably map things out from the time that Carmo was last seen and the operating times for her shop.'

Hopefully that's something they'll be able to ascertain today. The café owners near her shop might be able to tell them if they saw her open the shop. Most stay open until one in the morning, or later, depending on the season. It was a weeknight, however, so it is possible that they'd closed earlier. But surely someone, one of the attendants or a customer, would have seen her arriving to open up?

At the very least they know the shop was unlocked. She'd been there at midnight, which gives them a window of time. Whatever happened to Carmo, it would have taken place between midnight and the time that Savana and Sara's call had gone through to 112.

'Yes,' Voronov says, setting the pen down and thanking the attendant on reception.

They start walking to the double doors in the back where they'll find Jacinta.

At least here, unlike everywhere else in the city, it's blissfully cool, in a good way that you don't seem to get with air-con. Isabel doesn't even mind that it comes with the offensively strong smell of antiseptic.

'Daniel said the surveillance videos from the businesses in Moita are unlikely to have picked anything up because of the angles they were set up for,' Voronov says, 'but I think he's on the right track; maybe those are the most likely to have caught something and we should get what we can from the businesses in the bairro as well. We should speak to all of them and see if they have surveillance too.

Most of them face the road and all the cars are parked directly in front of the businesses there unlike in Moita.'

Isabel fishes out her phone and types a quick message to Daniel and Carla. 'I think they're probably already on it but I'll drop them a message just in case.'

Voronov stops to open up one of the doors and gesture her through.

Jacinta looks up from where she's standing at one of the workspaces, shoulder to shoulder with Fire Investigator Cardoso.

'Bom dia,' Isabel says, and masking her surprise.

'Hey,' Jacinta says.

Cardoso grunts at them in return. Must be his trademark.

At least he's not smoking in here.

'How is the investigation going?' Jacinta asks.

'It's going,' Isabel says. 'Found out our victim owned an occult shop and liked selling spells and predictions of the future, certainly a new one for us.' The truth is that if it isn't solved in the first twenty-four hours then they all know it's going to be one that might drag on. It's either an easy solve or it's a resource-drainer. There never seems to be an in-between, at least not from Isabel's perspective. 'What about you both, any luck?' She turns to Cardoso. 'No Kuma today?'

Cardoso rocks back on the heels of his feet. 'He's with his owner.'

Isabel blinks. 'I assumed he was yours.'

Cardoso shakes his head and surprisingly keeps going. 'No. I took him in as a puppy, couple wanted to get rid of him, but I couldn't keep him. Captain Horta wanted a dog for his daughter.'

Isabel remembers him handing off the dog to the captain of the firefighter squad from yesterday.

'Ah. I see. How did he become an arson dog?'

He frowns at her. 'You like dogs or something?'

Isabel huffs out an amused breath. 'I do actually. Just left my two at home just now.'

She isn't sure if it's because of her response but he answers her question. 'Dog was at the fire station all the time. Thought I might as well. Trained him myself.'

Isabel nods. That's probably the best interaction she's going to get out of this man so she's happy to leave it there.

She looks at Jacinta and him expectantly.

Jacinta gestures them over. 'I do actually have something, well – a couple of things. Thanks for getting over Carmo's personal matter, that sped things along quite a bit.'

Isabel and Voronov approach and find A4 prints of photos from the crime scene from yesterday. Pictures of the burnt body as it had first been found, of the burn patterns on the rubber surfacing, of the clothes where they'd been found and the car, along with a few others.

Isabel's eyebrows shoot up in surprise. 'You're done with the body?'

'Yes, late yesterday, as usual we're pushed for time and have more bodies coming in so the sooner we process one, the sooner we can process the next poor soul,' Jacinta says. 'We were able to match the DNA to Carmo Vilar.'

'We'll have to go and inform her son and daughter-in-law,' Isabel says. Delivering the news that a loved one is dead to family members still remains one of the hardest parts of her job. She doesn't think that will ever change.

'The cause of death was immolation.'

Jesus. What a way to go.

'We've found traces of the accelerant on the body as well as the clothes and the car, though we're still processing that.'

Cardoso, who is standing there with his arms crossed, says, 'It was gasoline. Which means it was carried, most likely from the car over to the point of origin of the fire.'

'Her feet,' Isabel says, remembering what he said yesterday.

'That's right.'

'There's more. The clothes we found, and the shoes.' Jacinta leans forward and drags one of the photos closer to them all. This one isn't of the crime scene but Carmo Vilar on the slab, or, more accurately, her feet.

'See that?' Jacinta asks. She points at the soles of Carmo's feet.

The skin is split open and there are dried fluids on them, the toes misshapen and blackened. But when they look at what Jacinta's pointing at Isabel's still able to make it out. 'Gravel?' Isabel asks, glancing up at Jacinta.

'We compared it to the gravel that was present where the car was found parked and it matches,' Jacinta says. 'Now, I don't know if she was stripped there or at the burning site, but I'd say based on the amount of gravel embedded in her feet and other abrasions on the bottom of the feet, she was barefoot on the walk from the car to the playground area.'

So, she hadn't been carried. She'd been made to walk.

Which means that Carmo Vilar had been alive and conscious.

'This confirms they burned her alive,' Isabel says slowly, looking at the grim understanding on the faces of those with her in the room. 'She was conscious when they set her on fire.' She shakes her head. 'There's no way that not one person in those buildings didn't hear this woman scream.'

Jacinta sighs. 'She couldn't.' She walks over to another station and Isabel shifts to look at what she's doing. It's the clothes that she'd found at the base of the tree, neatly laid out. 'Notice anything missing?'

Isabel and Voronov go over to Jacinta and Isabel looks at what's set out. A flowy white skirt, a short-sleeved white top, the strappy pair of worn gold sandals and the delicate gold chain with its simple crucifix.

When she realises, her stomach rolls.

'No underwear,' Voronov murmurs.

Jesus. Isabel wipes a hand over her mouth and leaves it there when she looks at Jacinta. 'You're saying that's what they gagged her with.'

'Yes. We pulled them out of her mouth. They were held in place with tape, which wasn't immediately obvious to us at the crime scene because of the fire. By the time we got there it had fused with the skin due to the temperature she was exposed to.'

This hadn't started out as a typical murder to begin with, if any murder could be referred to as typical. But this was stepping it up to another level entirely. There was deep cruelty in these actions.

'Okay,' Isabel says, 'okay. Is there anything else?'

'There is,' Cardoso says, and he reaches for an envelope near the edge of the workstation. It's A4 too and he pulls out what looks to be a sketch of the crime scene. Cardoso nudges it to the centre of the workstation.

He taps the place on the sketch that marks the beam their victim had been tied to. 'This is where she was found. Now, as I already showed you at the crime scene, besides the point of origin where the body was, we found traces of the accelerant on the clothes,' he taps the sketch where the clothes were found, marked by a tree on the sketch, 'and on the car.'

'Right,' Isabel says.

'But there are two separate routes that Kuma sniffed out at the scene of the crime. You see these lines I've drawn on here?' he asks, twirling his finger over the arrows that arch across the page. One goes from the car to the point of origin. The other goes from the point of origin to the tree. The final one points back again, arching all the way from the tree to the car.

'So, they stop at the zip line beams, they tie her up, start the fire, and then take her clothes to the tree,' Voronov says.

Cardoso nods. 'Based on what we have here that's what I believe. The highest amount of gasoline is found at the base of the beam. The rest of the traces must have been either on their shoes or leaking from a container.'

'They would have needed a container to pour that much there,' Isabel murmurs. 'And if it's the shoes, then we would have had additional traces walking away from the scene.'

'Not necessarily,' Voronov says, 'they could have had a change of shoes. They wouldn't have had to carry them if they went back to the car. It's possible he could have had something to change into there.' He shrugs. 'But that would have been an inconvenience.'

It's true. From what she's seeing, the murderer had planned this out effectively.

'Going by the information we have, Carmo used her car to take supplies to work in the morning. Her son said that the neighbours all let her have the same spot because they knew she has a problem with one of her knees. He also said apart from him, no one else has keys to the shop. Her shop was open and that's most likely where she was taken. Then they use her car to get them both to Moita.'

'Snatching her from in front of her shop is risky,' Jacinta says.

'Less risky than taking her from her house and then going to her place of business with her in the car. This woman has a routine and is well known. They'd remember someone opening up the shop in her place. It would have been unusual since it almost never happens. According to the son and the daughter-in-law, if Carmo was sick then she didn't go to work. That was it. Which means no one else opening that shop for her.'

So this person was walking around, taking the time to set down Carmo's clothes neat and tidy, all of this as if she wasn't there burning to death right in front of them.

Isabel narrows her eyes and looks at Voronov.

'Sara said that when she looked outside, she saw that Carmo was still moving,' she says.

Voronov locks eyes with her. 'That's right.'

'That couldn't have been very long after the killer tied her up, meaning it's possible that when Sara looked outside, they were still there.'

Voronov steps back from the workstation. 'Sara said *he* was hungry and that she saw his red smoke from behind the tree.'

Cardoso frowns. 'There were no other fires.'

'Not literal smoke,' Isabel says, glancing at him and Jacinta, 'Sara is a telepathic Gifted. A very strong one by the sounds of it. She sensed that there was someone there. That's why I checked the tree in the first place, because that's where she described that his sense was coming from.'

Cardoso doesn't look convinced but at least doesn't follow it up with a bigoted comment and Isabel is forced to admit that she's probably stereotyping him.

'All of those people who followed her down there . . . I would have thought they would notice someone trying to skulk around but I suppose when there's someone burning to death in front of you, you might not really notice much else,' Isabel says.

'Okay. So, either he managed to hide very well,' Voronov says, 'or he's a local and they wouldn't have thought anything of him being there either.'

Fuck.

'We're going to have to re-interview everyone we spoke to from those buildings yesterday,' Isabel says, 'and that includes Sara. We need to know if she saw anything else when she looked out of that window.'

At Voronov's look, she gives him a grim smile.

'If there's anything else there, I'll see it.'

'All right,' Jacinta says, 'we're still working on the car. I'll get back to you when we find more.'

'Okay, thank you.' Isabel looks over at Cardoso. 'Both of you.'

12

'You're saying she's dead.'

Tiago's words are muffled against his hands.

He's in a T-shirt and shorts and his eyes have the kind of haze that you see on the face of someone who has only just rolled out of bed although it's past midday.

The living-room curtains are wide open, but the shutters are down. Sunlight filters in through the little holes that dot each slat, stamping a pattern of distorted white circles on the floor and the wall opposite.

'Yes,' Voronov confirms.

Tiago lifts his head with a sharp intake of breath through his nose. His eyes when he looks up are red-rimmed. No tears. The red veins stand out against the whites of his eyes.

'Where is Eugénia, Tiago?' Isabel asks.

'She's at work. We can't both afford to be out at the same time.'

'I see, is her workplace far from here?' Isabel asks.

'No. She works in Baixa da Banheira, at the sports clothing factory.'

Isabel tucks her hands into her pockets. 'Tiago,' she says, quietly, 'would you like us to call Eugénia and ask her to come home?'

Slowly, Tiago looks up at her, face blank. 'Are you sure?' he asks quietly.

'We used the items taken from her home to match via DNA,' Voronov explains, 'I'm afraid there's no mistake.'

He stares at Isabel, hard. 'People have been on the phone to me all of last night and this morning, asking me where my mother is, telling me someone was tied up and burned to death. How long have you known it was her? Did you know yesterday? Did you?'

'No, Tiago.' Isabel takes a seat next to him. 'We didn't know then. Right now, we're putting all our efforts into finding out what happened to your mother. I know this might not feel like the best time but we have some questions we need your help with. Can you do that for us, Tiago?' she asks.

He's agitated. Even like this, with her Gift in check and just a couple of feelers out to gauge the emotion of those around her, she can feel it without any problem. The agitation is twisted up with other things: shock, grief, like the intertwined roots of a tree that go deeper than she can see from this vantage point.

'We spoke to Dona Lurdes, yesterday,' Isabel says, keeps her tone low, soothing, 'she told us about some of the incidents that happened related to your mum. She told us that in addition to the services you and Eugénia talked to us about, she also provided a type of service for people's love lives.' She can't quite bring herself to use the term 'love spell'. One, because it's bullshit and two, because it sounds even more ridiculous when she says it out loud. 'She told us this led to quite a few people taking issue with your mother, and that led to some vandalism and a woman called Thelma attempting to hit your mother with her car. I need you to tell us more about those.'

For a moment Tiago doesn't respond. He sinks his face into his hands and just stays that way, expression hidden from view, shoulders rising and falling with each agitated breath that he takes.

Voronov gives Isabel a jerk of the head, indicating the kitchen, and when she nods, he leaves the room. Isabel listens to his steps as she waits Tiago out. She hears the running of the kitchen tap.

Here, in this room, Tiago's emotions continue to bubble, becoming stronger despite him trying to pull them back in. She can see the battle raging on inside him.

Voronov comes back into the room with a glass of water. 'Tiago,' he says, standing over him and holding the water out.

Tiago lifts his head and looks up. His face has an angry pink tinge to it, the veins next to his eyes and in his neck prominent. His jaw is clenched tight. He stares at the water Voronov is holding out. Slowly, he reaches out and takes the glass. His swallowing is audible in the silence. He doesn't stop until he's drained the glass and when he's finished he very carefully sets it on the coffee table, not letting go right away, his eyebrows creasing down and the line of his mouth unsteady.

He keeps his eyes on the now-empty glass and, holding the glass from the top, starts to twist it in increments. He clears his throat. Twist, pause, twist. 'Yes,' he says, his voice is hoarse. 'She did do . . .' He clears his throat again. 'She said she had the ability to help people but how people chose to use that was up to them.' His words come out thick, swollen with emotion, and it's clear that he's having trouble getting them out.

He pauses. Twist, pause, twist.

'She didn't know what she was getting into with these people. She was too naïve.' He shakes his head.

Isabel can feel the memories, pushing at the edges of his mind; these aren't new frustrations and thoughts, they move too quickly for that. Like flashes. She takes a small peek, enough to see, for the first time in something other than a picture, the woman that was Carmo.

In this memory she's sitting at the table they had seen in her shop. There's a crystal cup filled with what Isabel assumes is tea in front of her. Her hands are curled around it. The scent of chamomile, not lavender, is stamped on to the memory.

She isn't dressed in the way Isabel had expected someone in her line of work to dress – and that's probably a stereotype she needs to nip in the bud right now – but she's just surprised by how ordinary Carmo looks.

She's in a black top, red cardigan and dark-blue jeans. Her feet are in black flip-flops. Her hair, thick and a strong silver-grey that doesn't seem to age her one bit, is swept into a clip at the back of her head. No make-up. Clean-cut, plain nails with just a coating of gloss. And there's a delicate pendant with a cross around her neck.

It's the same as the one they had found with her clothes at the base of the tree in Moita.

Carmo has a gentle expression on her face, but there's stubbornness on it too as she looks up at Tiago. Whatever her son is asking of her, she's not giving in. It's clear in the set of her mouth that she's not going to.

Isabel gently pulls out of the glimpse of the memory.

'Regarding the relationship services your mother offered, do you know what kind of things people asked her for?' Isabel asks.

He takes a deep breath. He pulls his hand back and interlocks his fingers. He drops his head, letting it hang over his hands. 'I know some of it,' he says, 'I didn't want to know. It was . . . I don't think what she did was right. I don't know how she could say she was a woman of God and do all those things.'

Isabel thinks of the crucifix amongst Carmo's belongings.

'She told Eugénia. Eugénia is . . .' He swallows and clamps his hands tight together, lifting his head to stare straight ahead, jaw working. '*Was* always happy to listen to her. Even if she didn't agree either. I'll say one thing: my mother knew how to keep her mouth shut about what went on at her shop.' He looks at Isabel. 'That's why no matter what people said, even if they were angry, most of them would go back there. She was private. What went on inside, if people ever found out, it was never from her. It was gossip, or the people who went there themselves would open their mouths. These people,' he says, practically spitting the words, 'they are always out there, sharing every detail of their lives. No sense of shame.'

'So you didn't know what kind of things she dealt with?' Isabel nudges, trying to keep him on track.

'I heard it from others. How she was breaking up marriages. People going to her to ask for help with getting someone to fall in love with them. Crazy, all of them.'

'Dona Lurdes mentioned a married couple, João and Thelma. What do you know about that incident?'

'My mother didn't open her mouth even then. Not even to the police,' he says, shaking his head in disbelief, 'can you believe that? That woman tried to run her over. I heard she woke up in the hospital still cursing my mother out. Blamed my mother for breaking up their marriage.'

'Because your mother was helping him get with someone else by using her . . . services?' Isabel asks.

Tiago stills. And then he murmurs, 'She was never helping him get someone else.'

'Was Thelma wrong?'

He laughs and shakes his head. 'No. She wasn't wrong.' He looks at them, eyes brimming with resentment. 'João wasn't going there for my mother's help. He was going there because he was having an affair with my mother.'

Well that certainly paints things in a different light.

'Was the attack a shock to your mother? Had she been expecting it?' she asks.

'I don't know. It was only after Thelma's attack that my mother told me and Eugénia about the affair. When I said my mother was good at privacy I didn't mean just with work. If there was something she didn't want me to know then I wouldn't know.' He rubs his hands over her eyes. 'She knew I would never approve.'

'And did you?'

'No. My mother was a very attractive woman. She never stopped getting attention, did she really have to break up a marriage? It wasn't bad enough that she was doing that kind of work, she had to add adultery to that too? And all for what? After the accident they didn't even last long anyway. My mother left him a month later.'

'When was this?' Isabel asks.

'Last year, just before Christmas.'

So almost four months ago.

'Did she say why she ended it?'

'She didn't really talk about it. But I know he was showing up near her shop for a while after, rumours get around. He wasn't leaving her alone, constantly calling her – he wanted her to take him back.'

'How did your mother feel about that?'

'I don't know. Maybe she kept it to herself out of guilt or . . . We only found out he was following her because Eugénia heard about it when she went to the bairro for her hair appointment.'

'So your mother never mentioned him again?'

Tiago shakes his head.

Outside, there's the sound of a loud car beeping and then of a couple of shouted expletives – another neighbour yelling for them to tone it down.

'The last time we spoke you mentioned the priest,' Voronov says, 'what can you tell us about him?'

'Like what?' Tiago asks.

'You told us he was the reason your mother no longer attended church. It also sounded as if he was keeping tabs on your mother's business, what she did or didn't do. Do you know if she'd crossed paths with him recently?' Voronov checks back in his notes. 'Padre Lopes, correct?'

It seems it's just occurring to Tiago that they're asking about these things in relation to his mother's death. That the people they are discussing may have done something to his mother. That his mother didn't just die. That this is something someone *did* to her.

Isabel sees it on his face as the puzzle pieces slot into place.

'He's a priest . . .' Tiago says, almost as if speaking to himself, frowning.

'We're at the information-gathering stage of this investigation,' Isabel says, 'that's all. But if you think that there is someone who had any reason to hurt your mother, then we'd like to speak with them.'

'There were always people who were upset with my mother.'

'*Did* she cross paths with Padre Lopes again? Or mention anything about him?' Voronov tries again.

'Not that she told me.'

'Do you know why your mother didn't file charges regarding the vandalism?' Isabel asks.

He shakes his head. 'She said she didn't want to cause a fuss.'

'Do you think that was out of fear of retaliation?' she asks.

'No.' The answer is decisive. 'My mother wasn't afraid of anyone or anything.'

Isabel remembers Carmo's burnt corpse tied to that beam. The clothes. The walk she had been forced to make from the car.

She's sure that on that dark early morning, Carmo Vilar had been very afraid.

13

The Igreja de São Martinho in Alhos Vedros is a half-hour drive from the precinct give or take a few minutes, and it makes for a pretty sight.

It sits in the middle of the sprawling neighbourhood, surrounded by a spacious courtyard. The path leading up to the church steps runs down the middle of two sprawling seating areas set within a pretty mosaic-patterned square, each with three of their corners full-stopped by short stocky palm trees that gave the church a touch of the exotic, especially against a hot blue sky like today.

Isabel and Voronov exit the car into a quietly busy road. The town seniors are sitting on the public benches, hats on; a few more of them are at the couple of local stone chess tables, dogs at their feet in the shadow cast by the chairs and board, napping as their owners play a calm, well-thought-out game. A few of them glance up as Isabel and Voronov walk past, heads turning in curiosity to watch them making their way down the centre path to the short number of steps leading up to the church entrance.

She's curious to see how this meeting with Padre Lopes is going to go. She wants to see how this man who had such an unusual interest in their victim's life will react to their presence.

Before they're even anywhere near the building itself, Isabel hears the intimidating notes of the organ, its imposing sound pushing past the church walls to vibrate in the air around it.

'Sounds like they're in the middle of a service,' Isabel says. She really isn't a fan of churches. Doesn't matter that her brother is a man of God. The only exception she makes is for him.

The thought reminds her of the wedding invitation still on her nightstand.

Her sister's wedding is taking place in four days' time.

Despite her previous threats and assertions, she'd still sent Isabel an invitation to her wedding.

A while ago, Isabel had found out that her sister, Rita, had got engaged to Isabel's ex-boyfriend Michael, who at that time had also still been Isabel's personal doctor. Apparently they'd been seeing each other for some time but neither had thought it might be an important detail to tell her.

Although it hadn't worked out, Isabel's relationship with Michael had been a long-term and serious one. Their problems had stemmed largely from Michael's discomfort with Isabel's Gift.

Not many men – or people in general – felt comfortable being with someone who could take a peek into their mind whenever they wanted. Even if that was something she never would have done.

They'd parted in a respectful way. And then, at a time when Isabel had been struggling with her Gift and unable to access S3, Michael was the person who had stepped up and helped her as her doctor. It had made for awkward interactions, their failed relationship a constant elephant in the room.

Finding out that he and Rita were seeing each other had been a shock and Isabel had even felt resentful, though that had been more about being kept in the dark and the assumption made by her sister and her mother that Isabel would just accept it and move on. At least Michael had had the presence of mind to feel some shame. Not much, though.

In the end, Isabel had let it go. They were broken up. Her sister was in love with him. What else was there to do?

Except her sister had been the one to change, becoming upset about Isabel and Michael's interactions as patient and doctor. Rita had become hostile towards her in a way she had never previously been, not even when their mother had been at her worst, constantly putting Isabel down or outright ignoring her. She'd even started to adopt some of those mannerisms.

More than the engagement and being kept in the dark, her sister's hostility was what ended up hurting the most.

Isabel had had no plans to attend the wedding from the start, but the invitation had been in her post box along with a less-than-genuine text from Rita asking her to be there for her as a sister. That text message had little to do with her sister wanting her at the wedding and more to do with their mother's newfound love for her eldest daughter. This was something neither Isabel nor her sister would have seen coming prior to Isabel's return from London. Then again it hadn't come about as a result of any personal reflection.

Gabriel Bernardo had got to her mother and her softening towards Isabel was due to whatever mess he'd made of her head using his telepathic Gift.

One more reason for Isabel to make sure she finds him.

A lot of things have happened since the awful dinner where Rita and Michael announced their engagement. Isabel has tried her best since to wrap her head around it all. She hasn't been all that successful.

They reach the church doors and Isabel smooths the frown away from her expression.

It's all floor varnish and clean and cool air. Some might even say cleansing. Isabel didn't belong to that 'some'.

She pauses inside the entryway. It's a wide room; its varnished flooring gleams in the sun. There's a table and a couple of seats to her left. The table is covered in a pristine cloth and contains a number of leaflets and schedules. A woman who looks to be about Isabel's age in a neat, pearl-buttoned shirt and a straight navy-blue skirt sits behind it. She smiles at Isabel and Voronov.

Inside the music stops, the lingering notes seeming to hang in the ceiling, and Isabel hears the sound of several people rising from their seats as one.

The priest's voice rings out as he talks them through what seems to be the end of the service. His voice has the same strength as the organ had.

'Boa tarde,' the woman says, and Isabel marvels at how much her smile resembles the smile of a salesman.

If her brother could hear her thoughts Isabel would be in for a scolding look.

'Welcome to Igreja de São Martinho, my name is Alicia. Our service is just coming to an end but you're free to go inside if you like! Our late-afternoon service will take place in ninety minutes.'

Isabel smiles back politely. 'Thank you. My partner here and I are with the Polícia Judiciária, and we'd like to speak with Padre Lopes if he's around.' She leans forward to peer past the double wooden and glass doors, sees a man in white and gold robes at the altar and sparsely filled benches. 'Is he leading the current service?'

At the mention of police, the woman's expression falters briefly, that familiar gleam of curiosity peering through the confident sales-pitch persona. 'Yes, he is. If you'd like you can go ahead and speak to him once the service finishes.' She glances briefly at her slim gold watch. 'He will be finishing in the next five minutes.' Her eyes flick over to Voronov and the smile immediately becomes more genuine.

Inwardly, Isabel sighs. 'Thank you. We'll do that.'

She hears Voronov thanking her before joining Isabel by the doors.

Isabel opens the doors as quietly as possible but it seems the hinges on the door aren't as well taken care of as the floor because the squeaking of the doors opening is loud enough to draw attention away from the padre's words and, as if of one mind, every person turns to look at who has just walked in.

Padre Lopes, who is presumably the priest at the front, also glances over. To his credit he doesn't stop his words but does give Isabel a kindly smile as he continues.

He's sort of what Isabel imagines most priests to look like: older, grey-haired, white. His eyebrows are thick and dark-brown still and lend a heaviness to his face. He's maybe in his late fifties with a lean face and a slight hook to his nose. There's certainly a sense of confidence around him that makes it easy to see how he holds attention.

Isabel and Voronov tuck themselves into one of the back benches, settling in to wait out the last few minutes of the service.

It's always an odd experience for Isabel, being inside a church, and has been ever since she tested as Gifted.

It's cool in here and the ceiling stretches high over their heads. Scenes from the Bible are painted on it with impressive skill, in pastel shades; they draw the eye even when certain expressions on the faces of those depicted look a little intense. It feels a lot like being stared at by judgemental eyes.

Isabel doesn't like it. It makes her feel on edge. Reminds her a little too much of the time after she'd lost her father and found herself rejected by her mother. But, more than that, what really makes her skin crawl is the uniformity of the people within the building. Especially in the middle of a service. It's a good thing their thoughts don't make it into her head. It's easy enough to keep them from getting anywhere near her shields. But she can still feel how they swell with the same emotions, pushed into it by Padre Lopes's strong guiding words. It feels like she's surrounded by a hive mind.

True to Alicia's word, the service is brought to an end a few minutes after they sit down, and Alicia pops her head through as if to double-check before she props the doors open for those leaving.

They watch as the majority of the parishioners file their way out, the low murmur of conversation a quiet chorus whereas before there had been only ringing silence enveloping the padre's words.

A few people linger, heading to the front to speak with Padre Lopes. He takes his time with them, sometimes reassuringly patting someone's shoulder or holding a hand with a sympathetic expression.

It's not until the last woman heads out after speaking with him that Padre Lopes turns his attention to the two of them who have remained seated throughout the farewells.

'Good afternoon,' he says, heading over, unhurried, that same calm and considered smile on his face as he stops at their row, fingers steepled together.

Behind him, at the altar, the assistants begin to tidy up, some coming up with brooms and cleaning wipes to begin going over the floor and the benches. Padre Lopes pays them no mind.

'Were you intending to attend the service?' he asks. 'Our late-afternoon service begins in an hour and a half if you would like to wait?'

They stand and shuffle the few steps over to the end of their row.

Voronov reaches out a hand in greeting. 'Padre Lopes?'

'Yes,' he says, glancing from him to Isabel.

'My name is Inspector Voronov, this is Inspector Reis.' He pulls his ID out from his back pocket to show him, and Isabel does the same.

She's not expecting the priest to inspect them as closely as he does and refrains from raising an eyebrow at him.

It's easy to see when he notices the Gifted tag on her ID because she feels the hiccup in that calm he exudes. Outwardly though, he just hums and stands back to give them space to come out of the row.

Isabel waits for Voronov to take the lead. She wants to pay extra attention to this one.

'Are you here to speak with me, Inspectors?' he asks.

'Yes,' Voronov says, 'we found a woman dead, yesterday, in Moita. Carmo Vilar.'

Another hiccup. The polite smile on his face slips. A stony look enters his eyes, but his voice remains composed. 'I'm sorry to hear that. I've known Senhora Vilar many years. She's very valued by her community.'

'Hmm.' Voronov is a head taller than the other man, and despite his friendly openness, just the fact that he's looking down at him evokes a certain sense of power over the other. 'We've heard from many people who seem to agree with you. Unfortunately, Senhora Vilar's death was not a natural or an accidental one. Inspector Reis and I are investigating her case, which is why we're here to speak with you today.'

Padre Lopes nods along. 'I see. Then how may I help you, Inspectors?' He flicks a look at Isabel but she merely gives him a polite quirk of the lips and doesn't say anything.

'We've heard from some of Senhora Vilar's neighbours and her son that you had particular views on what she did for a living and that at one point she used to attend your services. They also said you made a point of checking on what she was doing and following up with her clients. It sounded like your relationship wasn't a friendly one,' Voronov says.

Lopes blinks at him. That calm holier-than-thou attitude he's been emanating seems to dissipate and he drops his hands to his side. Indignation is pretty quick to show through. 'I'm sorry?'

'We'd like to hear from you your thoughts on Senhora Vilar and what issues you may have had with her,' Voronov clarifies, unperturbed by Lopes's reaction.

'Why is that something you'd need to discuss with me?' he asks. 'Shouldn't you be out there questioning people who may be involved in whatever happened?'

Voronov doesn't immediately reply and stares him down.

'As I said,' he says politely, after a time when Padre Lopes has snapped his hanging mouth back shut and switched to watching them with narrowed eyes, 'if you could tell us about your interactions with Carmo Vilar and any disagreements you may have had with her, we would greatly appreciate it.'

'There's nothing to tell.'

Isabel can't resist. She looks around them, gaze encompassing the entirety of the church. 'I thought you were supposed to tell the truth in this place,' she murmurs. When she looks at him again, he's glaring daggers at her.

Such a temper for a man of God.

'We know you didn't like Carmo Vilar,' Isabel says, 'my partner is more polite than I am. So why don't we start there. Why did she stop coming to your service? Were you harassing her because of what she did for a living?'

'There's no starting anything, Inspector,' he says, standing straighter and drawing his composure back into place. He smooths out his expression to resemble the man they'd seen when they'd first arrived. 'Senhora Vilar employed practices that I didn't approve of.'

'That's all?' Isabel says. 'It sounded to us like you went out of your way to let everyone know just how much you didn't approve of those practices. Not a fan of live and let live? Or were you trying to discredit her?'

'I did speak to a few members of our church but only when it was brought up in conversation. Many people considered employing Senhora Vilar's services. I simply cautioned them against involving themselves with that kind of . . . work.'

'It would help us out if you could tell us the names of those you spoke to,' Voronov says.

'I can't do that.'

'Why not?'

'They told me in confidence,' he says. 'I can't betray the trust of our community in that way.'

'You just said yourself that your community really valued Senhora Vilar. Would they really consider it a betrayal, or would they see it as an upstanding leader of their community trying his best to help right a grievous wrong that has been committed against a fellow member of said community?' Isabel asks. 'You'd look very accepting of your differences, it would paint you in a good light.'

He comes dangerously close to sneering. 'You're very cynical, Inspector.'

'Yes,' Isabel answers mildly. 'If you were in our line of work, you might be too. Where were you Wednesday morning, between midnight and three a.m.?'

That throws him and he reels. 'Excuse me?'

'Where were you, Padre Lopes, between midnight and three in the morning yesterday?'

His mouth opens and closes a few times, producing a few choked sounds that don't quite turn into words. 'At home.'

'Anyone who can vouch for you?' Isabel asks.

'I live alone.'

'I see,' Isabel says and lets her eyes bore into him without saying anything else. 'Where is home?'

He closes his mouth then and refolds his hands together, clutching tightly.

'Padre?' Voronov prompts.

'Moita.'

The same town where Carmo Vilar was burned alive.

That is a really unfortunate coincidence for him. If it is a coincidence.

He's unsettled, the blanket of calm and self-assuredness gone, but Isabel can see the constant struggle as he tries and fails to drag it back into place.

What captures her attention though, is his anger.

She can see the way it falls off him like spores ready to infect anyone who comes into contact with them; they stand out in a bright angry red that easily catches the eye.

Sara had seen red the night Carmo had died.

Unfortunately, that isn't enough. Emotions and how they manifest aren't the same from Gifted to Gifted. It'll often depend on their affinity and their level and how they perceive things. Besides, it could be that Sara just sees the colour red for everything when it comes to seeing others' emotions.

Isabel wonders how Carla sees them and wonders too if she'd mind Isabel asking.

She tilts her head, feigning curiosity. 'Why are you angry, Padre?' she asks.

He stiffens. The look he sends her way lets her know that if she were to be burned at the stake he wouldn't think it was undeserving.

'I don't appreciate you using your Gift without my consent, Inspector.'

'I didn't. It's not like I read your mind, Padre. Unless you'd like me to?'

He doesn't respond.

'Did Carmo Vilar make you angry?' she asks.

'Are you trying to provoke me, Inspector? As I said, I simply didn't approve of what she did.'

'Hmm.'

Voronov pulls out his notebook and a pen. 'Padre, I need you to talk me through your whereabouts Tuesday evening and yesterday. If you can include times that would be helpful also.'

Padre Lopes's eyes widen, sending those thick eyebrows almost crashing into his hairline. He relents however when Voronov waits him out.

Grudgingly he gives them a rough summary of his day.

Early wake-up call, 5.00 a.m. on the dot, shower and breakfast. At the church for 7.00 a.m. He was on the 6.00 a.m. bus from Moita to Alhos Vedros. He talks them through the schedule for his sermons, confessionals and lunch that day and the evening marriage counselling sessions he offered. He provides names for those, though it's clear he is reluctant to do so. 'These people trust me to be discreet. What are you planning to do with those names?' he asks.

'We'll just check in with them to corroborate what you've shared with us, Padre,' Voronov says, 'nothing more.'

He nods but still looks tense.

'You said you take a bus?' Isabel asks.

'That's right.'

'No car?'

'I do, but the bus is more convenient for work.'

First time she's heard that. Here, if you have a car, you drive your car. That's it, end of. Unless there's something wrong with it.

'We'll be needing your number plate,' Isabel says, 'Padre, when was the last time you spoke to Carmo Vilar?'

He shifts on his feet, glances at the watch on his wrist. 'Inspectors, I have to get ready for my next service.'

'You have time,' Voronov says calmly.

Lopes swallows and must realise the quickest way to get Voronov to leave him alone is through giving them what they want. 'I guess... the last time would have been at last month's feira.'

'What day and where?'

'It's the communal fair, it takes place on the third Saturday of every month,' he says.

'And you were there in what capacity?'

'We have our under-twenty-one groups with a stall, going out and speaking to the youth, inviting them to our youth activities. A lot of families attend together so it's a good space for us to connect with the community and check in with our members in a different setting. I'm always there in case we get some more complicated questions, though when I can't attend, Alicia usually covers for me.'

'What about Carmo?'

He stiffens. 'She attended every fair. It's the only time she was seen working in the daytime.'

He's even familiar with her business hours. Does he not realise how that comes across?

Disapproval is stamped loud and clear on his words and his disgust is plain to see now too. He's trying to paint their acquaintanceship as civil but his dislike for her pushes at his calm edges and spills over without much incentive from them. He couldn't stand Carmo. Just talking about her clearly agitates him.

'Did you speak with her?'

'No. There was no need for me to. Besides, there was a commotion that day, the fair ended up getting closed early, there were even police on the scene. I'm sure you could verify all this if you wanted to. They were speaking to everyone there who witnessed it.'

'What kind of commotion?'

He frowns, clearly disapproving. 'Someone from the fair arguing with a member of the public. It got physical, I even stepped in to try to calm things but left it to the authorities when it continued to escalate. Unpleasant business, people airing their problems in public. Many people really don't have a sense of shame anymore. It's a disgrace to our community.'

Considering Carmo's line of work, Isabel wonders if there is a connection. 'Were any of the people involved there to see Carmo Vilar?'

This time, he doesn't bother to hold the sneer in. 'It wouldn't have surprised me. But I don't believe so. I'm sure the police who were present on the scene or the fair organisers can give you better information than I can.' He pointedly glances at his watch again. 'Is that all, Inspectors? I think your time could be better spent speaking with her customers,' he says.

'We will be speaking with them,' Voronov assures him, tucking his notebook away.

'Right, well,' he settles back into the confidence that had been there earlier, 'I hope this was helpful. If you see Tiago, please do give him my condolences and do let him know that if he and Eugénia need to speak with anyone, I'm here to provide support.'

First-name basis with Carmo's son and her daughter-in-law? Tiago did say they attend his service every Christmas. 'I didn't get the impression you had a familiar relationship with them, Padre,' Isabel says.

'I don't. But they still attend my service every now and then. Tiago has always been very steadfast in his faith. He wasn't happy with his mother's line of business, which is to be expected.'

'Oh?' Isabel crosses her arms. 'Did he talk to you about it?'

'Tiago is a loyal son. He didn't like to speak ill of his mother.'

'And yet . . . here you are, telling us that he wasn't happy with her line of business. Means he was happy to speak ill of her to *someone*,' Isabel points out.

'That's different. I'm here to listen without judgement.'

'Right.' Isabel says, crossing her arms, 'the same way you didn't pass any judgement on Carmo Vilar?'

'If Senhora Vilar had come to me to speak of her troubles, I would have welcomed her the same way I welcome anyone else.'

I bet you would, creep, she thinks. 'As we mentioned earlier, that's not what we heard. I wonder if you saw her as competition,' Isabel says. 'Instead of coming to you, maybe your precious parishioners were going to her in your place. They did, didn't they?'

'Some did and that is their prerogative but all who did returned to the trust and safety of this church. Every week, without fail.'

He doesn't seem to realise that as he says those words, he comes across exactly as someone who has won something. That arrogance of having come out on top.

Isabel eyes him and steps closer to him. 'You know what's odd, Padre?' she asks.

He doesn't seem to notice that he's leaning slightly away from her, as if the very air she breathes is contagious. It tells her a lot about this man's views on Gifted.

'What's that, Inspector?' he asks.

'You really don't seem all that sorry that she's dead.'

His face pales a little at that.

'Thank you for your time. We'll be in touch if we have any more questions. And Padre, if you remember anything else you'd like to share, please make sure you get in touch.'

She gives him her card before Voronov can offer his, taking a perverse pleasure in how he delicately takes it from her with the tips of his fingers.

Holding the card exactly like that he meets her gaze. 'I will, Inspector.'

14

'That man is an obsessed creep,' Isabel mutters as they get back in the car.

'Hmm, and possessive of her,' Voronov says, resting back in his seat.

Obsessed and possessive enough to burn her at the stake? Isabel wouldn't put it past him. Men are capable of a lot of horrors when faced with rejection from a woman they want.

She sighs. 'What do you think, find out what the fair organisers have to say about what went down there? See if Padre Lopes isn't keeping anything a little more interesting from us?'

Voronov agrees. 'Sounds like a plan. I think while we're at it we should go to his house while he's still out. Check the distance from his place to the crime scene.'

'Yeah, okay.' Isabel agrees.

Before he can start the car, Isabel's phone goes off.

She sees Carla's name on display and puts it on loudspeaker. 'Hey,' Isabel says.

'Hey, we're on our way back, heading to Moita to finish up with Carmo's neighbours,' Carla says.

'We've just finished with Padre Lopes, too. He talked about Carmo Vilar very . . . diplomatically.'

'So he played it down?' Carla asks.

'Made it all sound very civil, meanwhile he could barely stand to touch the business card I gave him. He's definitely a bigot and saying he didn't like Carmo is an understatement; his emotions were too strong for someone who simply doesn't like someone, but beyond that,' she shrugs, 'there's no reason yet to doubt what he's said. We'll check with the couples he was providing counselling for that day. The timings he gave us don't immediately eliminate him from our persons of interest according to our timeline for the murder. He also lives in Moita. Once we know how close his house is to the location of the murder that should help us out a bit.'

'Did you get anywhere with Thelma and João?' Isabel asks, leaning back in her seat and resting a hand on her stomach. She's starting to feel hungry.

'João has moved from the address we had on file,' Carla says, 'we need to track down his new address. Thelma almost broke Daniel's nose trying to slam the door in his face,' there's a small note of amusement there that earns her a snort from her partner, 'but she says she hasn't gone near Carmo since the car crash incident, and she was at her sister's house looking after her niece and nephew. We're lucky we caught her; she was only there for a change of clothes, but we still have to just confirm with the sister. She wasn't lying though,' Carla says.

Isabel sighs. 'Right.'

On paper, a lot of people had reasons to go after Carmo and cause her real harm.

Still, the kind of people she associated with aren't the type to commit a crime in this manner. This feels carefully planned. The way she was killed was intended to make the victim suffer as much as possible. Most of these people could have committed a crime of passion at best, a loss of temper, something in that vein – still bad, but involving a lot more messiness, more clumsiness.

Or maybe she's being too dismissive. There are plenty of people in history whose family and friends would swear they would never hurt a fly yet who have gone on to commit the most horrible crimes. Some, she's sure, have even got away with it.

Then there's Padre Lopes. She doesn't like this fixation he had on Carmo. That's the type of thing that could lead to a nastier outcome, like the fate Carmo had suffered.

Obsession is a scary thing.

Which also makes her want to have that conversation with João Frade and as soon as they can too.

'All right. Let us know if you get anything else. Voronov and I are going into Moita to speak to the municipality about the fair and then we're checking out the padre's place. See how close he lives to the scene.'

'Got it,' Carla says.

Isabel hangs up and drags her seatbelt into place. 'All right, let's go.'

15

The municipal building is a circular structure, with columns surrounding it, and painted in a burgundy colour that immediately makes it stand out from every other building around it. It sits in the middle of a lush town garden with some benches around it, though all of them are unoccupied at the moment. The area itself is quiet, looking a little deserted.

Voronov holds the door open for Isabel.

It used to give her pause every time, but over the last couple of years, she's got used to his random little chivalrous gestures.

'Thanks,' she says, going on ahead.

Ah. Appropriately programmed air-con is great.

The inside is all marble floors and grand columns, with windows that look out on to the garden outside, adding green beyond the dark interior of the building. A plaque on the wall guides visitors to the service they're looking for. Passports and ID one way, tax and benefits another, etc., etc.

The guy on reception peers up at them from above the counter when they approach. He's got a slightly put-out expression on his thin face.

'Bom dia.' The name tag on his chest reads Tomás.

'Bom dia, my partner and I are from the Polícia Judiciária and we need to speak to the person in charge of organising the community fairs,' Isabel says, taking out her police ID and showing it to him. 'We need to speak with someone who works on the community fairs,' she repeats, deadpan.

He blinks at her ID and then up at them. 'That would be the municipal planning department. They're on the second floor and first on the left but they're not here today.'

Isabel leans her arms on the counter, 'We're on a time crunch, are you able to help us?'

'I can give you the names of the organisers?' he offers uncertainly.

'Thanks, and their numbers as well. What type of businesses are allowed to participate in the fair?'

'Places are reserved for local businesses, and they have to pay a fee to rent out a stall. We have our regulars, like our emergency services; they don't pay anything and also don't have to book in. They're part of the municipal service to the community and must attend all fairs.'

'So, no outside businesses allowed?' Isabel asks.

'No, though for entertainment, bands and performing groups they do make exceptions. They still try to keep it local.'

'What happens if there's an incident at one of the fairs? We know there was one at the last fair and the police got called in.'

'The planning department would keep records of it if any incidents involved attending businesses. But apart from that, there wouldn't be much else. They'd just let the police deal with it.'

Isabel processes that.

Padre Lopes said the police were called. 'You said that emergency services are a part of the fairs, would the police have been there already?'

'That's right.'

In that case it's odd that the police had been called. Unless Padre Lopes had misunderstood and not realised the incident was dealt with by the police already there as part of the fair. It's possible, especially if he hadn't been paying it too much attention.

'Okay,' she says, 'there was an altercation at the last fair. Would you have any details of that?'

There's a flicker of annoyance on the clerk's face, as if he doesn't understand why they are still asking questions. 'I think the police would probably be your best source of information for that.'

Voronov's sharp tap on the counter and the way he leans over it to stare down at him makes that expression go away.

'You don't have a representative present at each fair overseeing the logistics on the day?' Voronov asks quietly.

'Uh – yes.'

'If an altercation takes place, is it not their responsibility to ensure it is dealt with and ensure the health and safety of the other businesses and people partaking in the fair?'

His eyes flit away from Voronov's face, clearly nervous about the way he's being stared down like he's under a microscope. 'Yes, sir.'

'Then answer my partner's question. Who dealt with the altercation on the day?'

Tomás shuts his mouth so tightly that little dimples appear on his chin. 'Senhora Santiago is the one who is always present on fair days.'

'Is she one of the organisers not in today?' Isabel asks.

'That's right.'

'Okay, then just get us her details and we'll be out of your hair.'

He quickly focuses his attention on his computer to find the information. 'We're not supposed to share personal staff information for health and safety,' he says with a sniff. 'I'll have to let my superiors know that I've shared this with you.' He scribbles down on a pale-blue Post-it and holds it out to them.

Voronov takes it from him and places his card on the counter. 'That's fine. If they have any questions they can reach us on this number.'

On the way to Moita Isabel calls Senhora Santiago, the organiser whose number they were given. She tries to reach her twice on the drive over to Padre Lopes's house, but no one picks up. She ends up leaving a message with the precinct's number.

Padre Lopes lives about a thirty-minute walk from the municipal building in Gaio-Rosário, a civil parish in the municipality of Moita. It takes them just a little under ten minutes to reach it by car though.

When Voronov pulls up the car in front of the address they have for him, Isabel is surprised by the lovely two-storey home painted in a cheerful yellow. It's surrounded by similar homes, all with front gardens and gates and pretty, sloped roofs.

Compared with the part of Moita where Carmo had been found, this area is more remote. The streets are quieter, even the cafés they'd driven by on the way here were emptier. They passed along entire stretches of road that ran adjacent to empty plots of land on one side, trees and the river on the other. Isabel had glimpsed a clear path on the side of the river, though, running from the centre of Moita to Gaio-Rosário. It had been semi-hidden by tall grass and punctuated by rickety-looking bridges over cracked banks of mud where the river had receded due to low tide.

Padre Lopes's house has parking inside double gates and when they get out, it's easy to spot the small, old green car sitting behind them.

Isabel walks up to the gate. The pavement outside the house is a thin strip, barely there. Over the shoulder-height black iron gate, she snaps a picture of the car, making sure to get the licence plate.

She steps back from it, scanning the windows of the upper floor as Voronov joins her.

'It's big for one person, don't you think?' she asks.

He nods and glances towards the opposite end of the street where they'd driven in from. The road takes a left turn. From here, Isabel can see a glimpse of the river. It runs behind the house.

Isabel glances at him. 'You think there's another way down to Moita on that side?'

He looks around them, considering. 'Probably.'

'Not that he would need it if he wanted to sneak there and back. I didn't see many traffic cameras on our way here and you saw that path that runs along the river too, didn't you?' she asks.

'I saw.'

Eyes squinting against the glare of the sun, she glances up at the sky. It's the brilliant, eye-watering blue of a scorching day.

Seriously. This is not normal March weather.

She cannot think of anything she wants less than a long walk in this heat.

'Let's see if there's also a way to connect to the centre on the other side,' she says.

They walk together to the turn in the road, and about five minutes later they come to an area that looks over the river, with a sloping road down to a small cluster of restaurants and cafés and then a stretch of beach that is mostly empty save for one lone sunbather in the distance.

Isabel looks at Voronov. 'Should we split up? One of us takes the path adjacent to our drive and the other tries this back way, and we meet up at the scene?'

Voronov nods. 'All right, I'll take the back way.'

'See you there.'

They split up. Isabel goes back the way they came.

As she predicted, it's a long walk, though at least it's not uphill. She notes the cafés she passes, dips inside every time she comes across one to ask if they have cameras. She gets a no from everyone and continues on, cursing herself for not at least having brought some water with her. She'll have to buy a bottle at the next café she comes across.

Mostly she walks alongside the road. Even during this time of day, not many cars drive past and the space between properties gradually becomes greater as she goes, until she's just walking alongside unoccupied land.

Even when she veers off the road and on to the path closest to the river, she doesn't pass a single soul.

The sounds of water and crickets chirping in the tall grass slowly envelop the silence. There are certainly no cameras on this side.

The path has no guardrails up and runs right along the water, though now the river tide is at its lowest. There's a part where the path acts like a bridge and at high tide it would become bracketed by the river. This part, she thinks, could be a little more treacherous at nighttime, but someone familiar with it could make the trek without difficulty.

If Padre Lopes had been the one to murder Carmo, this part of his getaway would have been the simplest thing. No eyes and no ears. He would easily have reached his house undetected.

It takes her roughly thirty-six minutes from the moment she'd split from Voronov to reach the still cordoned-off crime scene. She's there for about ten minutes before she spots Voronov approaching her.

She steps out of the shade of the apartment building that Sara and Savana live in and waves at him.

As he nears her, she holds out the cold bottle of water she'd bought from the nearby café. He's got a thin film of sweat on his forehead.

'Thanks,' he says, taking it from her. They retreat into the shade.

Isabel folds her arms and looks out at the quiet bustle of the afternoon. 'He could have made that walk on the night of the murder,' she says. 'I think he could have avoided any notice quite easily.'

Voronov nods as he gulps down the water. 'It took me a little longer; the path at the back runs along a few more residential back streets but it took me to to the same river path that leads here. Those streets were quiet,' he says, 'some of the houses are completely shuttered, like no one lives there.'

Padre Lopes had had issues with their victim, including a worrying fixation on her. He lived close enough to the scene and would have been able to get clean away without being noticed. Throw his self-righteousness into the mix, the method of killing reminiscent of old church witch-hunts against a woman who practised what some would consider bruxaria . . .

It wasn't looking good for Padre Lopes.

Except . . .

'Even if he looks suspicious, we don't have any hard evidence linking him to the murder,' Isabel says.

It wouldn't even be enough to get them a warrant to search his house.

Voronov sighs. 'And we can't get tunnel vision on this.' Then he takes out his phone and shows her the screen. 'Got a call from the precinct on the way here.'

Isabel peers down at it. She sees the name João Frade, followed by a phone number and an address. She looks up at him.

'News about Carmo Vilar's death has reached Senhor Frade,' Voronov says, 'and he's insisting on our presence at his house.'

Isabel glances back down at the address. 'But this address—'

Voronov nods. 'It's a five-minute drive from where Carmo Vilar's shop and home are.'

Not alarming at all.

She hands his phone back.

'We'd better not keep Senhor Frade waiting then.'

16

João Frade's street is as quiet as the woods it backs on to.

It's a tight squeeze finding any kind of parking.

Voronov ends up having to drive all the way back to the top of the street when they don't find anything.

It's nearing ten in the morning so it's a little odd that this out-of-the-way cul-de-sac with its two-floor summer-yellow houses with terracotta roofs is so full when most people are at work at this time of day. This area is definitely more upscale than where Carmo had lived, even though it's just about a five-minute drive away.

'Interesting contrast in living situation, no?' Isabel says as Voronov manoeuvres the car into a parking space.

Her phone starts vibrating in her pocket. Shifting her weight on to her left hip, Isabel fishes it out and sees her aunty's name on the screen.

It's unusual for her to call while she's working. She takes the call as they get out of the car.

Isabel grimaces as the heat descends on them. 'Boa tarde tia, tudo bem?'

'Amor, when are you coming to see me?'

Isabel chuckles, and Voronov looks over. He locks the car and they start walking.

'Sorry tia, I'm coming to see you, I promise. I got thrown into a case as soon as my feet touched Lisbon,' she says with a sigh. 'And it's a grim one.'

'Your whole job is grim,' tia Simone mutters, 'and I know, your brother already told me. Stop by tonight for some dinner.'

Isabel considers it as she reaches back into the car to grab her sunglasses. She slides them on to her face, at least getting some relief from the light bearing down on them.

They'll probably be done on time but there's always the possibility that they might come across information on the case that will keep her longer.

'Yes tia, I can come by, I think I might finish on time tonight but if something comes up you know I have to stay behind. Should be able to get to yours by eight otherwise.'

'It's fine, it's fine. Gives your brother time to finish his service then so he'll be here, too,'

'Okay tia, I'll see you both then. I missed you.'

'Missed you too, amor. Oh. And bring your boyfriend. About time I met him.'

She hangs up before Isabel even has a chance to respond, leaving her blinking at her phone.

'Everything okay?' Voronov asks, putting on his own pair of sunglasses as they start walking.

Isabel sighs. She tucks her hair back behind her ear. 'Tia Simone has invited us both over for dinner tonight.' An unexpected request, especially seeing as she hadn't told her she was seeing someone. Sebastião must have let it slip.

Still. The surprise request – or ambush – has given her a warm feeling. It's been so long since she's been with someone in this way. She'd forgotten the things that go along with it. It feels . . . nice.

He gives her a surprised look.

'She wants to meet you,' Isabel says with a shrug.

His expression softens and he nods. 'I can come.'

She smiles at him. The walk down to number nineteen doesn't take long.

'This is a very different neighbourhood from where Carmo lives,' she says.

'Maybe he comes from money, or has a decent paying job. Or, he is recently divorced,' he says, 'you never know, he may have seen some money from that.'

'If he met Carmo as a customer, he would have needed a good amount of disposable income to actually be able to afford her services,' she says.

An old man watches them walk by with a craggy expression.

'Boa tarde,' Isabel calls out, with a wave of her hand.

He grunts at them and nods their way, grudgingly. He makes a decent show of continuing to water his front garden, the water spilling over the stone slabs and out on to the cobblestone pavement, but he doesn't take his eyes off them for a moment.

When they reach João Frade's house, the gate is actually ajar, which is lucky because there's no doorbell there.

Voronov pushes the gate all the way open, its hinges protesting the motion loudly.

João Frade's front garden isn't as abundant as his elderly neighbour's, but it has one tall palm tree that is about level with the house. Right underneath it is a white plastic chair and a small table. The table has an old ashtray on it and a beer bottle, long since empty. There's a small old-school black radio next to the table legs, its antennae tucked into the slot at the top.

They walk up the path to the door. Frade's house has a metal gate in front of the flimsier-looking white door though, like the outer gate, this smaller protective gate isn't locked either.

Voronov opens that up too and knocks on the door.

'Senhor Frade,' he calls out, 'Polícia Judiciária.'

It doesn't take all that long. They hear the tell-tale slap of flip-flops on the floor and then, a moment later, the sound of the lock going and the door swings open.

So this is the type of man Carmo had wrapped around her little finger.

He's an athletic-looking man, maybe in his mid- to late fifties, in a navy polo and smart shorts. Grey and brown hair is neatly combed back from his face. There's not an inch of spare fat on him and despite the lines of age on his tanned face, his hazel-green eyes are sharp, and his jaw chiselled.

No sign of any tears though.

'From the police? You received my call about Carmo.'

'Yes, we did,' Voronov says, 'I'm Inspector Voronov and this is Inspector Reis. We're investigating Senhora Vilar's death.'

'Thank you for coming. Come in.' He leaves the door open behind him and strides back inside, expecting them to follow.

They're instantly enveloped in the cold current of air-con and there's only relief for a moment before Isabel's skin pebbles under what is clearly extreme cold. She's immediately irritated. She'll never understand why people don't use air-con just to regulate the temperature; why do they always have to turn it up to arctic levels? What's the point?

She sucks it up and prepares to freeze her arse off for the duration of their meeting with Frade.

Voronov, knowing exactly how she feels but looking too at home for her liking, gives her an amused look over his shoulder as he follows Frade into an open-plan living room and dining room overlooking an even more impressive garden seen through sliding glass doors.

The television is set on a low table in the corner of the room and the sofas are in a soft yellow leather. There are boxes of things pushed to the edges of the room, some open, some still closed and stacked on top of others. The white walls are bare and there aren't any pictures visible.

'This is a lovely home, did you recently move in?' Isabel asks.

'Yes. A month or so ago.'

Isabel nods, making a show of looking around. 'What is it that you do, Senhor Frade?'

'I own my own construction company,' he says, then goes on, 'thank you for coming. Tiago didn't even tell me, I had to hear it through the grapevine.' He runs his fingers through his hair, leaving new parting lines in it as he turns to look at them. He doesn't invite them to sit down.

'Maybe as you were no longer together, they didn't think it was necessary.' Isabel suggests.

He throws a sharp look her way, deeply unimpressed, and crosses his arms over his chest, settling into a wide stance. 'We were talking.'

'We heard she broke things off and wanted you to leave her alone.'

'No, no,' he says, pointing, 'it wasn't like that. She was upset. She hadn't been the same ever since Thelma lost her mind and tried to drive her car into the shop.' He looks at both of them. 'Have you already spoken to Thelma?'

He looks strong, Isabel thinks, easily capable of subduing a woman like Carmo.

'Yes, we've spoken to Thelma. We currently have no reason to believe she was involved if that's what you're concerned about, Senhor Frade,' Voronov says. 'We wanted to speak with you about your relationship with Carmo Vilar and your whereabouts on the night she was killed.'

Frade starts pacing back and forth in front of the sofa, his sliders slap-slap-slapping on the cream tiled floor. 'I knew it. I knew this was coming. It's why I got in touch with you as soon as I heard what happened. I don't know what Tiago told you, but I would never have hurt Carmo. She was the love of my life, do you understand?'

Isabel narrows her eyes. The grief isn't pouring off him. In fact, she isn't getting much from him at all. He feels as cold as the room they're in.

As she peeks in further, she comes up against a natural barrier.

Most people have an instinctive barrier in place around their minds. Nothing to do with whether they're Gifted or not, it's more dependent on the type of person they are – their mind reflecting their levels of guardedness. Voronov, for instance, is a natural, with sturdy barriers in place that take a little more of a push from someone like Isabel to be able to peer at his emotions. João Frade's barrier is different. His feels deliberate. Like that of someone who's had practice and knows a little bit of what they're doing.

It would be easy enough for her to push Frade's barriers aside. She doesn't. Instead, she asks him. 'Are you Gifted, Senhor Frade?'

That stops him in his tracks, and he looks at her, startled, then at Voronov. He turns back to her, and answers her, his tone cautious. 'Yes.'

Isabel nods. 'And your affinity?'

'Telepathy. Low-level,' he says. 'Why?'

'We've heard a lot about Senhora Vilar's services but as you know, she was never tested. For all intents and purposes, she was considered a Regular. What did you think? As a Gifted individual yourself.'

He sighs and rubs at his temples like the very question is bringing on a headache. 'She didn't like to talk about it.' He sits down on the edge of the sofa.

'Which means you *did* talk about it.'

He directs his gaze away from them and at the garden.

From here, Isabel can see the towering trees of the woodland there. She thinks of the fires being reported on the news. They'd go up very fast if someone got a lit match anywhere near them. Especially in this heat.

'Yes. I tried. Her business drew a lot of attention, some people called her a fake, said she was a telepathic Gifted trying to scam people into thinking she could see the future, that she was doing what any other con artist did.'

'And what did you think, Senhor Frade?'

He sighs. 'I think she was Gifted. I don't know what level. She—but she always had to touch someone when doing prediction work. And that's common practice for telepathic people using their Gift. I think maybe she was a five, even a six. Higher than me. I could never catch her out. Just talking about it got her back up, I don't know why.'

'You don't know why?' Isabel asks, incredulous. Around the time someone of Carmo and Frade's age would have been tested, hate for the Gifted had been at an all-time peak. It's not a stretch to think that if Carmo was Gifted, then she would have wanted nothing to do with it, or at least nothing to do with admitting it. Too many negative memories were attached to it. Better to just market herself as a psychic who was taken seriously by her customers and not taken seriously by everyone else. Safer that way.

Although in the end, maybe not so safe.

'Look, I didn't care. I just wanted her to be honest with me. I left my wife for her,' he says, and his voice shakes, 'I gave her everything I had. I would have given her more. But with Carmo it was as if she always kept part of herself back. Like it would be some great sin for her to trust me.'

Isabel tilts her head, curious. 'Well, cheating on your wife isn't exactly a fantastic endorsement of trustworthiness, don't you think? Maybe she wondered what would stop you from doing the same thing to her.'

'I would never!'

'I'm sure you once felt that way about Thelma too; after all, you did marry her,' Isabel points out.

'Look!' He shoots to his feet. 'Believe what you want. I don't care what you think of me as long as you find whoever hurt her. What have you found out? Do you have someone you're looking at?'

We're looking at one of them right now, she refrains from saying.

'I'm afraid that any developments in the case will be shared with Tiago Vilar first, not you. Why did Carmo break off her relationship with you, Senhor Frade?' Voronov asks.

He clenches his mouth together, chin jutting out. 'I told you we were still talking.'

'But broken up,' Isabel interjects. When he doesn't respond she tries a different tack. 'Isn't it better to tell us yourself? I'm sure you know people in Carmo's circle well enough that you might not want their version of the story to be the one we hear first, hmm?'

He glances at her quickly out of the corner of his eye, fingers tapping against his thigh, and then he's sitting back down again. 'Carmo . . . Carmo told me I was too much.'

'Too much how?' Isabel asks. She walks over to the sofa opposite and takes a seat, giving him room but coming down to his level, removing some of the implied hostility of having both her and Voronov standing over him. Voronov remains standing some distance away, watching him patiently.

Frade starts bouncing his feet on the floor and flings his hands up in frustration. 'I don't know. I got divorced, it was finally done! We were free to do what we wanted. I just wanted to give her all the things I could. I wanted her to move in with me, preferably somewhere far from that pathetic bairro with those small-minded idiots, but she didn't want to. Fine. I said we could find somewhere nearby. She liked her community. I understood that. I could compromise. Except she didn't want that either. Said she liked her space. And then there were the awful hours she kept at her shop. It's dangerous for a woman! I told her so many times. Why couldn't she just move it to daytime?'

Isabel refrains from pointing out that all he'd done with his attempts was make himself a major inconvenience to Carmo. She was a businesswoman, someone with her own house and with full control of her own life. She'd clearly been happy with the status quo. Not to mention that having Thelma try to run her down had probably gone a long way to souring things. Isabel isn't surprised that she hadn't wanted to change her life in that way for this man. Maybe any man.

'I didn't like that,' Frade says, 'it was like she didn't want us to get any closer. And I'd left Thelma for her. I expected her to—' He trails off there and falls silent. His breathing has picked up throughout his frustrated outpouring and now he tries to calm it down.

'Expected her to make the same sacrifices you made?'

He scoffs. 'What? You don't think she owed it to me?'

Interesting word choice.

'Did Carmo ask you to leave Thelma?' Isabel asks.

That seems to shut him up.

'So, were your demands the reason why she ended it?'

When he continues, his voice is quieter, more measured. He folds his hands together and very carefully doesn't look at either of them. 'I became frustrated. She started to answer my calls less and less. We weren't seeing each other as often and when we did, she always cut it short. I didn't like it. I thought maybe she might be seeing someone else.'

And there it is. Projection.

'Sometimes I'd show up at the end of her shifts to help her pack up. She didn't like that. She said I was interrupting her routine, that she needed to think about her customers. I didn't like that she was there at all hours, sometimes locked inside that stupid shop with them. When it was women, it was fine, but when it was men . . .' He shakes his head. 'She's . . . she *was* such an attractive woman. It was magnetic, you know? Even that bastard priest looked at her.'

Isabel raises an eyebrow at that and looks over at Voronov. Well, well.

'And then . . . I started looking at her phone.' He drops his gaze to the floor and shrugs his shoulders. 'She caught me looking one day. That was it. She didn't even ask me to explain. Didn't give me a chance to either. She ended it then.' He looks up at them, spreads his hands as if in supplication. 'I couldn't let it go. I just wanted to apologise. Because I knew I could make her happy, she just didn't want to let me. But I knew I could convince her.'

'And how did you try to do that? By stalking her?' Isabel asks.

'No! No. It's not like I had to sneak around. I knew where she worked, and she knew that as well. I'd go by her house sometimes, when I knew she'd be home, try to get her to come out for a coffee. I even bought this place,' he gestures around him, 'close enough for her to get to work. I wanted to show her I was committed and that I understood what she wanted.'

Clearly, you didn't, Isabel thinks.

'And now . . .' He blows out a long breath and digs his thumbs into his temples, squeezing his eyes shut.

Voronov walks closer to him. 'Senhor Frade, where were you in the early hours of Wednesday morning?'

'Asleep,' he snaps, and throws himself against the back of the sofa, arms folded across his chest. Face turned away.

'Was she in touch with you at all that day or any day leading up to her death? Did you try contacting her again?'

He shakes his head. 'I'm sure you heard about the restraining order.'

Isabel shares a look with Voronov. Tiago hadn't mentioned a restraining order. This means he hadn't stopped. Carmo just hadn't told her son. 'When did she file a restraining order against you?' Isabel asks.

'It came through in mid-February,' he says, looking at his hands, 'I didn't see it coming.'

'Didn't you? You were showing up at her home and her workplace after being asked to stop, Senhor Frade,' Isabel says, 'or did you think that because you weren't doing anything physically violent then it wasn't a problem?'

And this time, there's some evidence of his emotions. There's a gleam to his eyes he doesn't want them to see, and they look slightly reddened as he chews on the inside of his cheek and bounces his left leg in agitation.

'I wouldn't hurt her. I'm telling you I wouldn't hurt her.'

'Is there anyone who can corroborate that you were at home Tuesday night into Wednesday morning?' Voronov asks.

'No.'

'Is that your car outside? The silver Citroën?'

'Yes. Why?' He snaps his head back around to glare at them. 'You want to check it? Check it then! I have nothing to hide. You can check this whole house too. You won't find anything. All you'll be doing is wasting your time instead of putting it to good use, like finding the person who killed Carmo!'

Isabel stares him down.

She waits for him to become calmer.

'You mentioned a priest. Could you tell us what you meant when you said he looked at her? Who was he?'

'What? You haven't heard already? That arsehole who was always checking what she was up to. Padre Lopes. Self-righteous bastard. She used to attend his services before she started her business. He liked to talk shit about her, but he was there every Saturday market, watching her.'

Padre Lopes had mentioned the market as well, but he'd made it sound like he only went every now and then.

'You're saying he was there for every Saturday market?' Isabel asks.

'At least for the ones I went to with her, he was.'

'Did you ever see him do anything more than look? Or did Senhora Vilar ever mention anything about him to you?'

'No. He kept his distance when I was there and Carmo didn't talk to me about it. When I asked her why he was always watching her the only thing she said was for me to leave it alone.' He scoffs. 'She never let me do anything for her. I don't think she ever let me in. I just wanted her to let me in.'

Voronov glances over at Isabel and indicates the front door.

Yeah. She doesn't think they'll get much more from him today.

'All right. Thank you for your time, Senhor Frade. We'll be in touch if we have any more questions and if you think of anything else that could be helpful to our investigation, please get in touch with us right away.

He turns his face away from them.

'Just get out.'

17

Isabel takes a bite of the ham and cheese croissant. The cheese is still hot and stringy, and she has to suck in air through her teeth whilst chewing to avoid burning her tongue and lips on it at the same time. It gets her an arched eyebrow from Daniel, who is sitting on the other side of the room with his own lunch spread out in front of him next to Carla, who is typing away on her laptop. Isabel flips him off.

'According to Tiago, his mother and João Frade dated for some time after the incident with João's ex-wife Thelma,' Voronov says. He's next to Isabel, leafing through his notebook as he checks against his notes. 'From what his mother told him; they broke up around the end of December.'

'Who broke it off?' Daniel asks.

'Tiago says she did,' Isabel says, after a pause to swallow her food. She shifts in her seat, trying to catch some more of that useless warm air the fan is pushing her way, even if the effect it has is minimal.

Voronov reaches for his bottle of water. 'He wasn't impressed at João's persistence. He says his mother was struggling because João was calling her constantly, coming to her door at all hours. Apparently, it went on for a while. He doesn't know if and when it stopped but Carmo never went to the police.'

'I'm not entirely surprised by that,' Isabel says, thinking about it, 'her job and the things she did . . . that raises eyebrows. From what we've heard she was a smart woman. I think she knows the police might not necessarily have done their all to help her.'

'What?' Daniel says. 'You don't believe in magic?'

Isabel looks surprised. 'Hardly. But in this case, I'm referring to her meddling in relationships and, from the sounds of it, having an affair with a married man. Anyway, we do know from Frade that she eventually did file a restraining order against him.'

'She was meddling in others' love problems for money and having an affair of her own,' Carla says and shakes her head. 'It's a recipe for disaster. But we have something that might help.' She crosses to where she'd dropped a big black backpack when she'd arrived. 'Jacinta called for us to pick these up on the way. Her people finished combing through Carmo's shop and her home. You said her son and daughter-in-law told you she wasn't into tech?'

Isabel nods and straightens up, craning her neck to try and see what Carla is retrieving. She hears plastic crinkling. 'That's what they said.'

Carla comes back to the table carrying three sealed plastic bags. Each one contains a number of what looks like leather notebooks bound together by rubber bands. 'They're done processing these. They've only found one set of prints on them which Jacinta says they're fairly certain belong to Carmo. Without a computer it makes sense that she'd have to have some kind of system for her customers, right?'

Voronov nods slowly. 'One thing that Tiago got across strongly was Carmo's business sense. I found it odd that a woman like her wouldn't have a system of some sort for business costs and appointments.'

'You're right,' Carla says and unseals the bags one by one, and then sets the worn notebooks on the table in front of them all. 'Look at the labels.'

Each one has a carefully placed sticker on the top left-hand corner. Even the placement of the stickers says a lot about her. They're perfectly aligned and the writing on them is meticulous. There are six notebooks in total.

'These are all the ones that they found,' Carla says, bracing herself with one hand on the table to lean forward and tap two of the notebooks, 'and these are the most recent. Accounts for this year, and appointments for this year. The two other sets are for the two years before that. We'll look into when she actually opened her business, see if there's anything missing.'

Isabel sets down her food and wipes her hands on the napkins before ripping into a cleansing wipe packet. She inhales the sharply pleasant artificial scent of lemons as she cleans them, then reaches for the notebook marked as accounts for this year.

Just the first page of the accounts startles her. She gives a low whistle. 'I mean we know she was making money. But if the rest of this book is anything like the first page, then she wasn't just making money. She was making *money*.' Some of the figures are way above the fees Tiago and Eugénia had quoted.

Love is big business it seems.

Isabel presses the notebook open on the table and slides it forward for the others to see.

It's all very neatly annotated. Names, dates, amounts paid, deposit dates.

'There was a very basic receipt book with her stuff too,' Carla says after going back to her bag one more time, 'you know the kind. Write in the name, the amount, date, rip it off and you're left with the slip on the bottom.'

'Very old school,' Isabel murmurs, accepting the bag and looking at the receipt book that is about half used. 'She didn't use tech, but she was thorough.'

'It looks that way,' Carla says.

'Hmm,' Voronov says, 'it seems she was just as thorough with her clients.' He flips the notebook he'd been looking through so that they can all see it. Isabel leans closer and Daniel and Carla gather round the table to look it over better.

Isabel blinks in surprise. 'Are these case notes?' There are different coloured dividers splitting up sections of the notebook, which is the only difference between it and the accounting ones. Instead of it being by appointment, it looks to be by client, with dates written in of last visits and brief sentences detailing the type of appointment, the service provided and then what look like follow-up notes, noting down improvements, etc.

Very thorough indeed.

'Well. At least no one can say she was messing around,' Isabel says. She's surprised herself, even if it was all a con. But this explains a lot about why Carmo had been so successful at it.

The people they'd all spoken to so far all liked her. The reports they had of people not happy with her all came from others. Combine a naturally charming individual, a head for business and this kind of dedication to clients, how could it not work?

Isabel sighs. 'That's a lot of clients but maybe these will help us decide who deserves extra scrutiny. Let's ask Sansão and Felipe to get in touch with the clients she's got recorded in these, see if there's anything there.'

Sansão and Felipe are two junior officers in their precinct who they often work with. Isabel has liked them from the start. Both have proven themselves smart and trustworthy in the past and free of any biases towards Gifted people. Things like that always earn Isabel's respect.

She looks at Daniel and Carla. 'You guys managed to get through all the neighbours?'

Daniel shrugs. 'Some were at work, so we'll have to go back and knock on some doors, but we got a good majority. The cafés were fountains of information.'

'Fountains of gossip you mean.'

'She was well liked, even by the local churchgoers. Thought she was lovely but misguided, they didn't like what she got up to but even that didn't seem to put them off her.' He shakes his head, looking bemused, 'I've never seen anything like it.'

Carla sits on the edge of the desk. 'We got similar information to what you heard from Dona Lurdes, the shopkeeper next to Carmo's, but what did come up with the older residents who were regulars at the church was that the head priest was not a fan. She was well known to him, had previously attended his sermons until he found out what she did.'

Isabel picks her croissant back up and finishes it in two bites. 'That ties in with what Tiago told us. Let us guess, Padre Lopes?'

Daniel nods.

'I wasn't sure the cross pendant we found meant much, nowadays a lot of people wear them for the aesthetic, but it seems as though she genuinely believed in God. Enough to be a Catholic and still try to maintain ties to that community. Seems Padre Lopes didn't want her doing that though.'

Someone knocks on the door and then opens it.

Sansão pokes his head through. 'Sorry to interrupt, there's someone for you in reception, her name is Julia Garcia. She wants to talk to you about the Moita case.'

Isabel stands. 'I can take it, you guys have been talking to people all day,' she says and looks over at Voronov, who is already standing to follow her out.

'Can you do me a favour and look into the incident reports on file for the vandalism? Carmo Vilar didn't want to file charges but there should still be something on the system from the officers that attended the scene, oh and check if anything was reported from the community fair,' she says. 'We've reached out to the organiser but she hasn't got back to us. The good padre says there was an altercation there and the police stepped in, though we think they may have been local officers who had a stall. Just want to see if anything was logged.'

Daniel salutes her in acknowledgement.

'Clown,' she says, rolls her eyes and heads out with Voronov.

18

The woman Isabel and Voronov find waiting for them in interview room number two looks tired. Not just a little tired, but fall-down, face-planting-on-the-table kind of tired.

Her eyebags are dark and thick, her eyes look bloodshot and the hair she's scraped back from her face in a neat bun is oily. She's dressed in a loose black graphic T-shirt, worn-looking jeans and trainers and there's a beat-up and bulky grey bag at her feet.

When they enter the room, she stands up quickly, nearly spilling the coffee she'd been cupping in her two hands.

'Inspectors?' she queries, holding out a hand. Her forehead is creased, and Isabel is instantly buffeted by guilt and worry so strong it leaves an acrid taste on her tongue.

'Yes, I'm Inspector Reis,' Isabel says, holding out her hand and finds her hand gripped tight in a calloused and somewhat damp handshake. 'This is my partner.'

'Inspector Voronov,' Voronov says, also shaking her hand.

'Julia, yes?' Isabel asks, gesturing for her to sit down again and when she does, she and Voronov sit down themselves. 'I see you have a drink, but can we get you anything? A water or something else?'

Julia waves her concern away. 'No, no, thank you. I have some water in my bag and this is my fifth coffee of the day, I'm ready to collapse to be honest with you. I do a lot of early-morning shift work and then as soon as I get home I only have time to sleep for a couple of hours before my next job and it's always the way. Barely get some rest. I'm so sorry, if I had known I would have come to see you yesterday.'

Isabel nods and links her hands together, giving her a small smile to show her understanding. 'That's okay, Julia. Thank you for coming in. You wanted to speak with us regarding Carmo Vilar?'

Julia takes a deep breath and her eyes drop to the table. She nods in confirmation. 'Yes. I only heard a couple of hours ago that Carmo went missing.'

So the news that she's dead hasn't fully got around yet. 'That's right.'

Julia scoots to the edge of her chair, resting her hands on the table. 'Look, I don't know if this will be of any help but I think I saw something? I don't know. I don't know if it's actually anything,' she says. 'And I'm sorry if I'm wasting your time.'

'You're not wasting our time,' Isabel reassures her, 'what did you see?'

Julia nods convulsively at that and gulps down some more coffee. There's a shakiness to her hands which might be from the overload of caffeine, might be nerves from being in here, or might be something else.

Isabel sees the fatigue surrounding her like a cloak.

'I was running late for my shift – well – it was a last-minute call in, I wasn't meant to be working yesterday but one of my colleagues went home sick so they needed someone to finish her rooms. I'm a cleaner. Usually I just do commercial buildings but I'm with an agency too. Sometimes they call me for cover and this hotel is one of my regular temps. Anyway, I barely even had time to eat something before I left the house. I normally cycle when I have the midnight shifts because there aren't any buses at that time. I live at the back of Block O so I always pass near Carmo's shop on my way.' She pauses and runs her fingers over her hair a couple of times. 'It was only for a second, I was just checking for cars, you know. But the door to Carmo's shop was open. The light was on, I remember that clearly.'

'What time was this?'

'I think close to one a.m.?'

According to Tiago and Eugénia, Carmo opened her store at midnight.

'I didn't think anything of it, she usually only closes it if she has a client inside, otherwise I know she leaves it open for walk-ins, so

I wasn't thinking much of it, but I saw Carmo outside by her car. And she was talking to someone? I mean – it was a glimpse. I think it was a man.' She shrugs and looks from Isabel to Voronov like she's doubting herself. 'It looked like a man. But their back was to the road. I didn't recognise them.' She falls quiet and keeps looking at them both, like she's worried they're about to reprimand her.

'Julia, did you notice anything else?'

She lifts her hands helplessly. 'I was in a rush, at the time I wasn't really paying attention, just trying to get to work.'

'What about voices? Did you hear anything?'

'I had my music on,' she says, 'I'm sorry.' She twists her hands together, folding her lips together and shaking her head. 'That's all I remember. I'm sorry.'

Isabel gives her a reassuring touch on the shoulder. 'This is helpful, Julia, thank you. We appreciate you coming to see us.'

Julia nods. Even though she's only spoken to them for a little amount of time, she looks even more exhausted now than she did before she walked in.

'Did you know Carmo well?' Isabel asks.

'I've known her since my parents moved to the bairro,' she says, 'I always say hello when I see her, she asks after my mum, that's pretty much it, but everyone knows her. She's a really kind woman. Doesn't judge. Doesn't gossip. Never seen her say a mean word to anyone.'

Isabel sighs. 'Julia, I have to tell you, Senhora Vilar was identified as deceased this morning. Her body was found yesterday. I'm sorry.'

Julia stares at Isabel, mouth falling open but no words coming out. She looks at Voronov as if seeking confirmation and when he doesn't contradict Isabel, she sinks back in her chair. 'I didn't stop,' she murmurs, 'I should have stopped.'

Isabel gives her shoulder a squeeze. 'We're still investigating what happened. And there is nothing you could have done. Julia, can you tell us anything else about this person? Height, what he was wearing, anything that stood out to you at all.'

'I uh – I—' She blinks several times but doesn't say anything else. She closes her eyes, then squeezes them shut. 'I—' She shakes her head. 'I don't. I'm sorry. It was too dark.'

Isabel considers for a moment. 'Julia, I'm a telepathic Gifted. Would you consent to sharing that memory with me?'

She catches the look Voronov throws her way and knows he's thinking about what she'd shared with him the previous night.

Julia looks at her, startled. 'You mean, look inside my head?'

'Yes, but I'd only be looking at what you witnessed that night, I promise. Sometimes, when we're in shock it could be that we miss some things that we saw. In a sense I'm a fresh pair of eyes, I might be able notice something that maybe hasn't occurred to you.'

Julia is silent for a long time. Her hands twist together even harder and then she clenches them together and meets Isabel's eyes, determined. 'Yes. I consent.'

Isabel smiles at her. 'I promise this won't take long.' Then she steps into Julia's mind. The memory is at surface level, there's no need to search for it.

Isabel feels the pedals, the movement in her legs. She recognises the song playing in her ears. It's not playing the way it should, not following the proper sequence. Like a scratched record. It's stuck on the chorus. It happens sometimes, a moment in a memory pinned to a particular beat or lyric of whatever song the person was listening to at the time.

Isabel pushes the sounds to the back of her mind. She focuses, slowing it down. The song replays again in her head. She feels the force Julia's using to pedal, feels the strain on her calves and thighs, the seat unforgiving beneath her. She recognises the glimpse of the main road and the corner where Dona Lurdes's shop is. The streets are empty. It's hot. Her body feels uncomfortable in the clothes she's wearing. The speed of the bike pushes her hair back from her face but there's no relief in it. There aren't any buses or cars or people in her frame of vision. She veers her bike to the left.

Julia hadn't been lying. It's quick. Very quick. She clocks the open door, bright against the darkness of the rest of the building. There, just shy of the streetlights and too far from the brightness spilling out from the door, is a car. Even then, it's too dark and the moment too quick for Isabel to compare it to the one found at the crime scene or to catch the licence plate.

She sees Carmo. Not her face, but her hair stands out, thick and voluminous. Isabel can just make her out behind the man's frame. He is a silhouette at most. The shoulders look wide but she's not sure how much of what she's seeing is the play of light and shadow. It's merely a snapshot.

Isabel turns away from the memory and back into the room.

Julia is staring at her wide-eyed. She's shaking a little. 'Is it done? Did you see? Did it help?'

Isabel sits back. 'You've been very helpful, Julia. Thank you.'

'Julia saw enough to help us narrow down the timeline further. I agree with her, it was a short glimpse but it looked like a male. She really was telling us everything she saw,' Isabel says. 'It does support our male suspect theory.'

She walks with Voronov back to the case room.

Despite it being so early, many of the desks are empty. The whirring of fans dominates the silence in the room, making pieces of paper flutter in their current. Most of the lights have been left off – not that they need them with the sun blasting in through the windows. It's still cooler than it is outside. The few people at their desks have their heads down, working away, some filing paperwork without any real enthusiasm for it – not that there ever is enthusiasm for paperwork.

Must be a slow day.

Good.

'The timing,' Voronov says, wiping at his brow with the back of his arm, 'I think it's odd that no one else saw anything. The cafés close late, especially with weather like this. One in the morning—'

'Roughly,' Isabel interjects.

He inclines his head, acknowledging. 'Roughly. The car was at the scene, which means he got her in that car. If she had gone with him willingly then he probably would have let her close her shop, lull her into a false sense of security. But everything was left open.'

Isabel nods.

'It's unfortunate that Julia didn't hear anything. No way to know if they were having a casual conversation or if she was shouting.'

Isabel thinks of Julia's memory. That split-second loop, almost like a still frame enshrouded in shadows. The set of shoulders. She thinks of the distance between the suspect and Carmo. 'It didn't look aggressive,' she says, frowning, 'at least not at a glance like that. I can't be too sure but even the proximity . . . they were standing very close but there was nothing in what Julia saw to suggest aggression.' Then she sighs. 'Then again, as much as memories can be helpful, they can also be skewed by a person's state of mind, and by time. For Julia it was still fresh; but if we'd spoken to her right away, before she'd found out Carmo was missing, then it may have rendered a better result.' After finding out that she'd potentially been a witness to the crime, Isabel's sure Julia has been playing that memory in her mind on repeat. But that just means that the constant re-remembering has just sharpened things that Julia was specifically looking for and smudged the rest. It's what everyone does, even though they don't realise it. Eventually, years from now, when recalling the memory, she probably won't even remember as much as she did this morning. She might only remember the open door and that glimpse of Carmo's white hair.

They'd let Julia go with reassurances that they'd be in touch if they had any follow-up questions. She'd still been shaking as she'd accepted Isabel's contact card and tucked it away with utmost care.

Up ahead, they see Carla pop her head out of the case room, eyes briefly sweeping the room but quickly spotting Isabel and Voronov returning.

'All good?' Isabel asks.

'Yes,' Carla says, 'we were able to pull the records on the previous police reports filed in relation to Carmo Vilar. We've got the names of the kids who vandalised her place. We were thinking to pay them a visit this afternoon?'

Isabel stops just outside the room, leaning her shoulder against the doorframe. 'All right.' She peers into the room and Daniel is approaching the doorway to better hear what they're saying. Isabel hands over the form and signed statement completed by Julia. 'Witness saw Carmo speaking with someone outside her shop at approximately one in the morning. Carmo had already opened her shop, the door was open, and the lights were on inside. She saw the victim next to what she thinks was the victim's vehicle; the person she was with looked like a man. She wasn't able to get much more than that. We're lucky she even saw that much to be fair,' Isabel says, and has to shake her head again as the song that Julia had been listening to returns to her head, as if now that she'd heard it on a loop together with that haunting memory, it was there to stay.

Carla takes the form, skimming the information. 'I'll log it before we head out,' she says.

'Thanks.' Isabel rubs at her eyes. 'I think we should have another talk with the priest. We've heard from multiple people now that he wasn't too keen on Carmo, and if that many people are saying it then I'm thinking he was overly vocal about it. And if he doesn't know anything else, you never know what he might have heard in a confessional,' Isabel says.

'Are you hoping he'll be sharing that with you?' Daniel asks. 'Isn't Sebastião a priest? Shouldn't you know how confessionals work?'

Isabel flips him off. 'Yes. I know how they work, arsehole. But if he's heard anything incriminating it might spook him into loosening his tongue. It's worth a try.'

Daniel looks at them. 'Doubtful, but good luck.'

19

As Isabel raps her knuckles on the glass panels of tia Simone's door, she inhales the warm scent of bolinhos secos, an almost permanent smell when it comes to her aunty's house.

They're a little later than planned, having left the precinct shortly after seven thirty in the evening.

The kitchen window is open as usual, and she can hear the sound of the radio drifting out over the clang of pans being moved around. That window is open all year round, whether the weather is frost-edged or melting like it is right now.

'Who is it?' Her aunt's voice comes from deeper in the house so the person in the kitchen moving things around is probably her brother.

'It's me, tia,' she calls out and turns to look over at Voronov, who is looking unruffled as always. She reaches out a hand to adjust the neckline of his T-shirt where it's slightly skewed and arcs an eyebrow at him. 'If you're going to be this calm it'll make me wonder how many times you've done this.'

His mouth quirks at the side. 'I've already met your brother, so it isn't as scary.' He leans down and pecks her on the lips.

She snorts out a laugh. 'It's the women in my family that are scary, but you cling to that false sense of security.'

The door opens and she turns back, the smile still on her face.

She has a hard time keeping it there when she comes face to face with her mother's expectant expression. Her initial greeting dies in her throat.

'You're both right on time.' Her gaze jumps from Isabel's frozen expression to Voronov just behind her, and then she turns to call out over her shoulder, 'They're here! Rita, you can finish setting the table.'

Her heart sinks and the light buoyant feeling that had pleasantly accompanied her on their way here deflates as if it had never been.

Her mother reaches for her shoulders – Isabel just about manages to keep herself from flinching back – and kisses her on both cheeks. 'Então filha, come inside.'

Isabel nods, the motion stiff, and steps inside. She introduces Voronov as he follows her in. 'Mãe, this is Aleks,' she says, 'Aleks, this is my mother, Maria.'

To look at him no one would ever think anything was wrong. Voronov greets her mother with two kisses and a polite smile, telling her it's lovely to meet her.

'My goodness, you're tall. Come, come, everyone is excited to meet you.'

Isabel closes her eyes briefly, calming herself. When she opens them again, she sees her brother and tia Simone standing at the end of the corridor where it opens out on to the open-plan area. They're standing side by side next to the dining table, looking strained, reflecting Isabel's own feelings.

She knows they never would have sprung this on her and their expressions tell her this is as much of an awkward moment for them as it is for her.

Behind them, Isabel glimpses her sister, diligently laying out the plates on the large dining table. And next to her is her sister's soon-to-be-husband, Michael.

Isabel's ex.

Perfect.

'I'm sorry, I would've given you a heads up, but I didn't know,' her brother says, tone hushed.

They're both standing in the kitchen, dishing up the molotof her mother had apparently brought for dessert as a contribution to this impromptu family gathering.

Dinner had been everything Isabel hadn't wanted it to be. Forced conversation over her aunt's wonderful food with her sister and her fiancé sitting at one end, barely opening their mouths.

Voronov had been fine, had sat back, relaxed, taking it all in his stride. But she knows he'd understood right away that this was less than ideal. Still, having him sit next to her, arm around the back of her chair as they'd wrapped up the main meal, had made the situation a little more bearable.

'Is that right?' she says, setting another bowl aside and dropping a small spoon inside.

She stops when Sebastião reaches out and touches her shoulder.

She looks at him.

'Come on,' he says, and there's a note of censure in his tone, 'you know I'd never ambush you like that and neither would tia.'

Isabel leans back against the counter, lets her head fall back and lets out a heavy sigh. 'I know. I'm just . . . this is not how it was supposed to go.'

'Sebastião.'

They look to the kitchen entrance to see her mother standing there.

Maria Reis has remained a very attractive woman throughout her years and that hasn't changed in the few months Isabel has been away. She's dressed in an elegant black top with a square neckline and no sleeves, tucked into a black skirt that reaches below the knees. Her thick hair is styled up into a thick bun. She hasn't worn colour in all the years since Isabel's father died.

'Sim, tia?' Sebastião says. Although he is their father's son from his first marriage, his relationship with Isabel and Rita's mother has always been an affectionate one. It had made it difficult for Sebastião to reconcile Maria's treatment of him with the way she'd turned on Isabel after learning she was Gifted.

Maria steps into the room, clasping her hands together and giving him a smile. 'Can I talk to Isabel alone for a moment?'

Sebastião glances at Isabel. 'Of course, I'll take these to the table,' he says and takes the tray loaded with dessert before slipping out of the kitchen with a final apologetic look over his shoulder.

Her mother wraps her arms around herself, rubbing her hands over her arms. 'I didn't want to catch you off guard. I was on the phone to your aunty, and she mentioned you were coming by for dinner. It's been a while since we've all been together, and I thought it would be nice.' She shrugs and gives Isabel a tentative smile. 'And I wanted to meet your boyfriend as well. He seems like a nice man.'

Isabel realises that she's unconsciously mirrored her mother's body language, arms wrapped around herself, hands shifting over her biceps.

'It's okay,' she says, 'it was a nice idea.'

The smile her mother gives her tells her she knows that's a lie. 'I just wanted to see you. And I know you didn't plan to come visit any time soon.'

There's nothing Isabel can say to refute that.

Being around her mother as she is now puts her on edge almost as much as when her mother had treated her with contempt. She's not used to having her mother's warmth focused on her, of having her care, of having her want to see her.

None of it is real.

'Will Aleksandr be attending the wedding with you?'

'What's this about my wedding?' Rita pops up behind their mother, Michael in tow. Her gaze, when she meets Isabel's eyes over their mother's shoulder, isn't a friendly one.

Isabel meets her eyes briefly and though she can feel Michael's stare boring into her, she avoids looking at him altogether and answers her mother. 'Yes. He's coming with me. I was actually planning on introducing him to you all then.'

'Dessert is on the table!' her aunty's voice rings out through the apartment.

Rita threads her arm through their mother's and tugs gently. 'Anda mãe, it's been a while since you've made molotof, we all want to dig in.'

Her mother nods with a laugh. 'Okay, okay, come on.' But she doesn't leave right away, and instead holds out her hand, reaching out to Isabel.

Isabel sees the hopeful expression on her face.

Resigned, she takes it.

20

Isabel finishes wiping her hands and sets the dishtowel aside. 'You want anything else to drink?' she calls out. Her bare feet are silent on the kitchen floor as she peers out at where Voronov is entertaining her dogs.

Like her, he's kicked off his shoes. He's sitting right next to the swivelling fan and every time it swings his way, it blows the short strands of his hair.

The shutters on her windows are still down, but the windows themselves are open. The heat isn't as bad now so she'd decided to take a chance on airing out the house. She's got the lights off, leaving only the light by the door to illuminate the living room and kitchen. She's left the bedside table lamp on too.

The coolness that had been insulated in her unused apartment has disappeared in just the two days she's been back and she's in damage control mode. She hopes it's a better night of sleep tonight.

Well. Or something like that.

Voronov glances up at her, still stroking her dogs who are doing their best to vie for his attention. 'I still have my water.'

She nods and pads over. He gently nudges the dogs aside to look up at her, resting back against the sofa and making room for her to stand between his legs.

'So,' she says, 'today wasn't really what I had in mind.'

Voronov shrugs. 'The food was good.'

She snorts and shakes her head.

He smiles.

He'd come home with her after dinner at tia Simone's house.

For all of Isabel's sins, the visit hadn't ended with dinner and had dragged on into post-dinner coffee, her aunty bringing out her prized bolinhos to accompany the coffee as the focus had shifted to the final arrangements for her sister's wedding.

Rita had just about been civil every time she had to say any kind of word in Isabel's direction. Michael hadn't tried to contribute to the happy family reunion, keeping mostly quiet and breaking silence only when his input was needed or when her aunty or her mother had asked him questions directly. Although it hadn't helped the situation, Isabel had been grateful for the silence.

At least Voronov handled it all with his usual calm, relaxed and talking comfortably with Sebastião. Unsurprisingly, her aunty and her mother had both fallen for his charm.

She still doesn't understand how he manages it every time.

That part had been nice. Something she hadn't known she needed. To know that he was accepted and liked by those who matter to her. It's driven home just how important he's become in her life.

Eventually, they'd escaped and since they'd taken public transport over to her aunt's house, they'd hadn't rushed on their way home, winding their way through the city to work off all the food they ate and taking the time to browse some of the local shops that were open late.

Slowly, the tension from the unexpected ambush at her aunt's house had slipped away until it had just been them, enjoying a quiet walk.

Thinking back on it, it was their first time having any time to themselves like this.

It's nice.

Now it's just ticking past half-past midnight and they're still here, a little mellow from the beer but still too alert for people who need to be up in the early hours to get into work.

She cups Voronov's face in her hands even as she feels his arms slide around her waist and pull her closer.

She smiles at him and there isn't much she can do about the bittersweet edge to it. Which he notices. Because he always notices.

His brow furrows and he rests his chin on her stomach, neck probably at a really uncomfortable angle so he can keep looking up at her like this. She brushes her thumbs over the corners of his eyes, enjoying looking down at his face. He's always been very easy on the eye.

'What about you? Are you okay?' he asks.

She considers her answer. 'Yes and no. Still don't like the crap they pulled but,' she shrugs, 'I like what we did after it. And I suppose it could have been worse. Everyone behaved themselves, at least.' More or less, anyway.

'Your mother's still the same,' he says.

'Yeah,' she says, 'I don't know how to handle her. It's weird, I always thought if my mother ever changed, I'd be so relieved. I'd have my mother back. Even when I got used to it and accepted that it would never happen . . . you can't help but dream, you know?'

'Hmm.'

'But she's only being this way because someone got in her head and made her love me again.' She laughs, the sound hollow. 'I still can't believe it.'

'Does she understand?' he asks. 'What's happened?'

Isabel swallows, her jaw tightening. She shakes her head. 'I don't know how to tell her.'

Part of the reason why she's been keeping her distance from her mother isn't just because she doesn't know how to handle her like this. It's the guilt.

Guilt that despite everything, she hasn't told her mother the truth. That she hasn't told her mother there's a treatment that can return her to who she really is.

As much as she doesn't want this falseness, this fabricated loving woman who takes the time to worry about her, to seek her out, to take an interest in her life, she isn't quite ready to face the reality of who her mother really is again.

She shakes her head, as if by doing so she can banish those thoughts.

She tightens her hold on his hands and drags him up until he's towering over her and puts his arms back around her again.

'Listen,' she says. 'I wasn't ready for us to go beyond this before.' She wraps her arms around his neck. 'I know you've always understood and never really judged me and what my Gift can do. I've always been grateful for that. But before, you know, with Michael . . .' She clears her throat, feeling awkward bringing up her ex when she's with a current partner and especially in this context, but determined to forge on, 'I wanted to make sure that when you and I crossed that line that it wasn't going to be the same. Because I want us to both enjoy it.'

Voronov tightens his arms around her pulling her closer so that she has to tilt her head up even more. 'I know and I can wait.'

She groans and buries her head in his chest. He's so annoyingly good with these things that sometimes she doesn't know what to do with herself. It's why she's got to this stage. This man probably doesn't realise how much he's got her wrapped around his finger. Not that she'll ever let him know. Okay. Maybe she'll let him know a little.

'I know you can,' she says, her voice muffled by his chest. 'And that's great.' She stops there and takes a deep breath, suddenly nervous in a way she hadn't expected but still sure. She pulls back so she can meet his eyes. 'Want to cross that line tonight?'

And this, this is what she likes even more about him.

He trusts her word. He doesn't ask if she's sure, doesn't second-guess the choice she's made here.

No. He just takes a step forward, nudging her back. And another. And another. Not looking away from her as he steadily moves them towards her bedroom.

They're just at the entrance and he's lowering his mouth to hers when Isabel's phone goes off. And his goes off too.

The odds on them both going off at the same time for something unrelated to work are remote.

Isabel groans again and this time, it's more heartfelt. 'Because of course. Of course.'

Normally Voronov would be amused too, and there are traces of that, but when he steps away from her, their hands still locked together, he has his head tilted up to the ceiling and his eyes closed as if praying for patience.

That makes her feel a little better.

When he finally looks at her again, there's an aggrieved curve to his lips. 'Maybe it isn't work.'

Isabel snorts, shoves away from him and makes her way around him to grab her phone up from where she'd left it on the sofa earlier. It's still ringing, and the number is from the precinct.

She picks up even as she hears Voronov greeting the person on the other end of the line on his phone.

'Inspector Reis, we've received a report of someone restrained and on fire. Emergency services are on their way to the scene, and they've requested you attend.'

Isabel freezes.

Restrained and on fire. She glances over at the clock.

It's nearing one a.m.

Shit. Isabel rubs a hand over her face and turns to face Voronov, who is looking at her with the same grim expression on his face, phone pressed to his ear.

'Where?'

'Alcochete.'

'Send me the address. I'm on my way.'

21

This time, they arrive on the scene second only to the firefighters, and the audience is growing.

Word has clearly got around a lot faster than the last time and there are people standing around, kept at bay by the officers who have responded to the scene first and are trying to maintain order. They're all in various states of undress, most in pyjamas, feet hastily shoved into slippers and trainers. The silence from them all is deafening.

The night is starless and a deep blue. The air is thick with smoke and something else that just doesn't smell right.

The location is decidedly public. It's the town square, painted blue and red by the lights of the ambulance and the firefighters who are putting out the last flames eating away at trees, each one in a corner of the square. Opposite the square is a small chapel overlooking the river, its windows dark, the flowers planted along the foot of it in full bloom, white petals striking in the night. An obscene contrast to what they are about to witness.

'What the hell is this,' Isabel mutters as they stride forward.

In the middle of the square there are two paramedics crouched low on the ground, the ambulance shielding them from the spectators. But even as they speed up, Isabel can see someone on the floor, covered, by their feet.

The paramedics look up as they see them coming.

'Jacinta and her team are on their way,' Voronov says, voice low, 'they're about ten minutes out.'

Isabel glances around, eyes searching for anything that might show them how this happened. By the fire engine, she sees Fire

Investigator Cardoso standing to the side, Kuma at his feet waiting with perfect patience. Cardoso's face is set like stone, and his eyes are locked on the firefighting team doing their job.

As if sensing her gaze, he looks their way.

Isabel holds up a finger and thinks she sees him nod in acknowledgement. He's some distance away and she can't be sure.

'Inspectors?' one of the paramedics says, as she rises to her feet.

'Yes,' Isabel says, pulling her ID out of her back pocket and showing it to her and stopping only when she's standing over the body.

'The fire investigator told us to wait for you. We didn't intend to touch her, but when we arrived she was still alive.'

Isabel closes her eyes at that. 'Was she conscious?' she asks.

The paramedic shakes her head. 'I'm afraid not. She had a pulse. We tried to do what we could, I can't say for sure, but we think her heart gave out as we were trying to treat her. We'll have more detail once the coroner takes a look at her but that's our best guess right now.'

'Thanks,' Isabel says, and looks over her shoulder at Voronov, 'do you have any spare gloves in your car?'

'Yes, hold on.' He turns and makes quick work of getting back to his car.

Isabel focuses on the body. She carefully takes the edges of the cover is shielding the victim from head to toe and slowly pulls it back to take a look.

The woman's face is black with soot. Her hair looks dirty and the edges of it look singed. Her eyes are closed. Death doesn't take away the impression of how stunning this woman had been.

There are odd squareish marks bracketing her mouth where her skin is remarkably clean, like her mouth had been taped over. 'Was there something on her mouth when you got her down?' Isabel asks.

The paramedic startles, as if not expecting that Isabel would be asking her any other questions. 'Yes, there was tape over it, my colleague peeled it off and we've placed it in a bag for you.' The paramedic clears her throat, clearly having trouble with this next part. Isabel wonders how new she is to the job. 'It was holding a piece of cloth in her mouth.' She doesn't say it was underwear but going by her expression and what had been done to Carmo, Isabel is willing to bet it was.

Isabel uncovers her down to the waist. She's naked, just like Carmo.

There is no jewellery on her, no earrings on her ears, no rings or bracelets or watch.

The fire was at her long enough to eat away at her skin, splitting it open and leaving it charred all the way up to her stomach and when Isabel looks further, her legs are even worse.

'Could she have survived this?' Isabel asks.

The paramedic glances down at the woman, regret evident on her face. 'The surface area of the burns is severe . . . it would have been touch and go.'

Isabel nods in understanding.

'I'll just be a moment,' the paramedic says, 'I'll bring the bagged tape and cloth for you.'

'Thank you.'

She recognises the sound of Voronov's steps approaching. He drops to his haunches beside her, handing over a clear plastic bag with sealed forensic gloves inside it, his eyes scanning the victim.

Isabel takes them with a murmured thanks and rips into the bag, stuffing the torn plastic into her back pocket and pulling the latex gloves on as she hears Voronov do the same.

'Jacinta should be here soon,' he says, 'the officers who first responded are keeping the others at bay. Fire Investigator Cardoso is examining the scene, the firefighters are finished. Looks like one of them got hurt.'

Isabel glances over at where the firefighters are gathered, clustered around one of the men. He's got his arm held out in front of him but is partially obscured by his team.

'Will he be all right?'

Voronov nods. 'They're looking at it now.'

'Okay.' Isabel stands and walks a few steps over to the victim's feet. 'We'll have to speak to the crowd, see if anyone got a look at her and who called it in.' She bends down to uncover the feet and look at the soles. 'Aleks,' Isabel says, 'look at this.' She points to the skin there and despite the gloves does her best not to touch. The bottoms of her feet are remarkably untouched by fire. The burns start from her calves and up.

Voronov bends down closer, peering at where Isabel is pointing. 'Dirt and stones.'

Isabel nods. They're not big stones, just tiny ones, the kind that are sharp enough to cut and dig into flesh. 'Jacinta will have to confirm but looks like she was made to walk barefoot too.'

'Um,' the paramedic says, as she returns to their side, 'the ones who called this in are with us.' She holds out two clear, sealed plastic bags. In one of them Isabel can see the brown tape and the balled-up black material and the second one has curled up and half-burnt cut-off rope. 'Sorry, I forgot to mention we had this one too.'

Isabel nods in thanks, taking the bags from her. 'What do you mean?' she asks, referring to her earlier comment.

'They're in the ambulance. We're treating them for burns, they're going to need to be taken to the hospital. They tried to get her down and got burned in the process.'

Isabel covers the victim back up and stands. 'Show them to me.'

Voronov stays where he is. 'I'll wait for Jacinta to show up and I'll start speaking with the other witnesses, call me if you need me.'

'Okay.' Isabel motions for the paramedic to lead the way.

The ambulance is facing away from the people surrounding the scene and they have to walk around it. Its back doors are closed, and Isabel waits for the paramedic to open them.

Sitting in the back and in different stages of distress are two guys. Both of them look young, maybe eighteen or nineteen. The medic in the back with them looks at her, surprised.

'Inspector Reis,' Isabel says, briefly flashing her ID, 'are these the two that called it in?'

'Yes, Inspector, we're taking them to the hospital now. The burns are bad and need to be seen to.'

On one of the boys, Isabel can see where his T-shirt caught fire and the burn beneath it. He's got a vacant look on his face. The other though is sitting back, shuddering, eyes barely open. His arms are badly burned all the way up to the elbow.

Both of them are in a state.

She can't talk to them now. They're in no condition to say anything at all. She can feel it, a complete vacuum of emotion where it should be boiling over. She's felt it in others dealing with extreme shock. They'll have to catch them at the hospital.

The one who has his head back doesn't open his eyes and his lips barely move but Isabel hears him speak.

'We couldn't save her. The lady said she died.' His voice is barely there, a painful rasp as he visibly struggles to get the words out.

Isabel glances at the paramedic in question.

'I heard you both tried to save her,' she says, 'that's very brave. You're going to be taken to the hospital, okay? You're both injured. We'll come in to check on you later.'

Neither of them responds, and she doesn't wait for them to. She thanks the medic treating them and steps back so the paramedic who has led her there can close the doors and as she does so, she catches sight of the forensics van making its way to where Voronov is flagging it down.

'Take them in,' Isabel says to the paramedic, 'when you get there, please inform the reception desk that a member of our team will be there to keep an eye on them. We'll be in later to speak with them properly.' She glances over at where the body lies. 'As for the victim, our forensics team is here so they'll take it from here.'

'Yes, Inspector,' she says and doesn't waste time, calling out to her colleague as she hurries to the driver's side that they're heading back now.

Isabel watches the ambulance drive off, the tail-lights a bright red trail that shines ominously in the night.

'Inspector Reis.'

She turns to see Cardoso standing close by, Kuma right beside him, tail wagging excitedly but on his best behaviour. Cardoso looks as unimpressed as the last time she'd seen him at the morgue.

'Didn't expect we'd be meeting at a crime scene again quite so soon,' Isabel says, extending her hand to Cardoso.

'Can't say I disagree. I can walk you through what we've got while your forensics team get started,' Cardoso says.

Over his shoulder she sees Voronov talking with Jacinta, the two of them surveying the space they have to work in while three of her assistants get suited up by the van.

'I'd appreciate that, give me just one moment.' She puts in a quick call to the station, asking them to contact their junior officers, Felipe and Sansão, and get them over to the hospital to watch over the two witnesses until they get there. When she hangs up, she gestures him ahead of her.

'What are your thoughts?' she asks.

'That this person is a sick bastard.' He walks her over to the palm tree in the corner furthest from the chapel. It's the one that anyone coming out of the chapel would see immediately.

Isabel thinks about the victim's feet. Not that that was the main thing that had tipped them off to the possibility that they were dealing with the same person.

'I heard the boys who called it in tried to get her down,' she says. 'She was tied up again?'

'Yes. Like the first one, though I suspect he was more careful this time. No leaking of the accelerant, though Kuma here sniffed it out again. He used it but this time took more care with it. I'm hoping Jacinta may be able to find something that maybe I've missed.'

Isabel glances at the other trees that had also been set alight. 'He set the others on fire as well?'

He looks over at the other trees. 'Yes. They were burning for longer too. It took the two boys longer to deal with those than to deal with the one the young lady was strapped to. They got here quickly.' His face doesn't give much away, but she notices the smaller details, the way he can't quite keep his mouth from trembling at the corners for a moment before he composes himself. It's underscored by a touch of helplessness that hovers around him in the palest of mists. 'She was still alive.'

'I know,' she says. 'The paramedics think her heart gave out. We won't know until the autopsy but they said the likelihood that she would have survived those burns—'

'She wouldn't.'

They reach the tree and he crouches down to point at where unnaturally clear lines divide the bottom of the tree, which is untouched by the fire, from the blackened surface of the tree higher up, the bark flaking and falling off. Debris is all around it, fallen palm leaves from where the fire reached high up. It did enough damage to devastate it, leaving it barren.

The lines themselves are in a squiggly pattern.

She would have expected him to splash the tree with the accelerant but if that had been the case then the accelerant would have sluiced down the tree and the bottom of the tree would have also caught fire.

'I suspect most of it went on her. I took a look at her and the burns start from halfway up her ankles. I think he may have used something to spray the accelerant or perhaps squeeze it out rather than splashing it.'

Isabel thinks about that. 'He would have needed to have enough to use on the other trees but a bottle may have been less conspicuous to carry around . . .' She makes a note that they'll have to check if the victim had any vehicles once they ID'd her. Odds are he'd probably used her car again to transport them over here.

'The patterns on the other trees are different. There the fires started from the ground up. He soaked the bottom of the tree trunks and a little more above that.'

Isabel processes that. 'You said those were burning for longer.' It's almost 2.00 a.m. now.

He looks over at her. 'That's right.'

'How much longer would you say?'

'Five to eight minutes, maybe.'

And it's not like he would have had time to just leisurely go around setting each tree on fire when he had someone with him. That would have been impractical. Although she did have the stones embedded in her feet.

Isabel turns to look at the tree their victim had been tied to again.

Not only was it immediately visible from the chapel, but from this vantage point they'd be able to see everything else too.

'Which one did he start with?' Isabel asks.

Cardoso narrows his eyes on her. Then he points to the tree closest to them on the left.

'And which one was next?'

He points to the centre and then following her train of thought, he points to the one to their right and then jerks his thumb at the one they're standing at.

Isabel takes in the order again.

From where they were, they would have seen each tree being lit one by one.

The bastard had made her watch as he'd come closer and closer to setting her on fire. That's why he'd burned this one last. There's no other practical explanation that Isabel can think of.

She knows the moment Cardoso realises what she's getting at because she hears him mutter a curse under his breath and turn away, rubbing a hand over his mouth as if to get rid of it.

'Isabel.'

At Voronov's call, she sees him standing at the chapel entrance, Jacinta next to him. He gestures her over.

'I'll be right back,' she says and then crosses the distance.

Most of the people who had been there when they arrived have dispersed but there are still a few, as if waiting to see if anything else would happen tonight or if the police would talk to them to tell them what happened.

Isabel recognises the captain of the firefighter team, Horta, whom Cardoso had briefly introduced them to last time, as he heads over to where Cardoso is. He nods a greeting but barely makes eye contact; his jaw looks set in stone. There are bags under his eyes and his overalls are rolled down to mid-waist. Whereas last time Isabel had only sensed exhaustion, this time there's anger too. She doesn't blame him.

'Hey,' she says to Jacinta in greeting, 'what is it?'

Jacinta stands aside so that the door to the chapel is fully visible.

There, on the welcome mat just outside the chapel's door, is a neatly folded dress, a pair of sandals and a ring.

Well. If they didn't know it was the same person before, they definitely do now.

22

Isabel takes a drink of water. They'd managed to find a petrol station not too far away while they waited for Jacinta's team to finish wrapping up and then come back to debrief the officers who had been keeping people from the scene.

The facts they had at this time were as follows: the call had been made at 12.15 a.m.

Somewhere between making the emergency call and the firefighters reaching the scene at 12.30 a.m., the teens attempted to take her down from where she'd been tied to the tree but hadn't been able to. The firefighters were able to get her down from the tree and paramedics were five minutes behind them; they took over from the firefighter teams for first aid. They called her time of death at 12.50 a.m.

Jacinta pulls off her gloves and leans back against the van, her dark skin gleaming with sweat under the heat of the night. She thanks Isabel when Isabel holds out a bottle of water to her too.

They drink in silence for a little while.

Voronov has gone on ahead to the hospital to speak with the witnesses who are still there being treated.

The crime-scene tapes are still up and the last of the officers are there, standing guard. Jacinta's team are taking a final sweep, setting down number plaques next to anything that might be of significance and getting close to document these with the camera.

Isabel joins Jacinta against the side of the van and watches her drink a little more.

'Thoughts?' she asks.

Jacinta shakes her head, still drinking. When she's done she turns to look at Isabel. 'It'll be tougher to get evidence on this one. Paramedics and the firefighters were all over it more than before.'

When the victim is still alive the priority is keeping her that way, not preserving a crime scene.

'But we still have the clothes, we may be able to get something off those, and the evidence the paramedics bagged for us, but if it's anything like the other one, there won't be many opportunities for a print. I'll see what we can find. We might get more when we find out who she is. Take a look at her home.' She looks around. 'Any conspicuous car here?'

Isabel takes in the small sleepy neighbourhood sprawled out from the square.

She can hear the running river from here and despite the horror of what took place, everything is calm. There are people who slept through everything and the ones who returned have probably gone straight to bed. If it weren't for the charred trees and the crime-scene tapes, it would be like nothing had happened.

Unlike in Moita, this is at the centre of the little town; there are houses here rather than apartment blocks, though there are a few of those too. There are cars everywhere, parked right outside the houses, squeezed into some spots from where they would most likely get towed away anywhere else. Even around the square, near the chapel, mopeds have been squeezed in, and small old cars that make Isabel think of her tia's ride which Isabel is really hoping she'll replace eventually. There's no way to tell if there's something here that doesn't belong. Not until they know who she is and get to speak with the locals.

It's looking like another door-to-door job first thing in the morning.

'No,' Isabel says, answering Jacinta, 'nothing that is immediately obvious.' She checks the time on her phone. It's nearing 3.15 a.m. 'I'm just going to take a quick look at what's nearby and then

I'll head over to the hospital, see what Voronov has got from the two boys and then . . . go from there.'

Jacinta nods. 'You need a lift?'

'I'll get one of the officers to drop me off, don't worry about me, you do what you need to do.'

'All right.'

She pats Jacinta's shoulder and pushes off from the van, watching as Jacinta goes to help her team finish off.

Isabel looks around and walks to the edge of the crime-scene area, ducking under the tape.

She looks at the wide streets, lined by large trees, the houses with their white-painted metal gates, the closed shops tucked in between those and traffic lights further ahead. She walks a little way down. The closest buildings to the square are all people's homes. She looks for any cameras. She looks for any open doors.

She does the same with two more streets.

She counts a total of four surveillance cameras, though with one of them she can see it's disconnected. No telling when that was done; the wire dangles down the wall where the camera is mounted. She makes a note of the street name and the house number. Never know.

Eventually she makes her way back, surrounded by the peace of people in restful sleep.

She wonders if the killer is tucked in somewhere himself right now, sleeping too, just like all these people, after committing another murder.

She walks back and sees that Jacinta is standing by the van, looking around as if searching for someone.

Isabel waves an arm to catch her attention, and Jacinta must have been looking for her because Isabel watches her slump.

Taking out her phone she messages Voronov to tell him she's making her way to the hospital now.

She thinks about it again.

No.

She doesn't think this killer is out there somewhere sleeping peacefully.

Someone with this much arrogance wouldn't be resting.

She thinks about how he had made sure that his latest victim would feel every inch of terror as she watched him light up each tree in turn, coming closer and closer to her each time.

He'd enjoyed watching her suffer.

She surveys the square and the houses with their dark windows.

She hears Sara's description in the back of her mind: *hungry*.

No, he wouldn't be resting.

Isabel wonders if he ever left at all.

23

The hospital and the morgue always smell a little too alike for Isabel's liking. Her nose is immediately assaulted by the smell of antiseptic. At least it's cooler as soon as she makes it past the automatic doors into the emergency section.

Unsurprisingly, despite the early hour, it's a hive of activity, with patients slumped in plastic chairs, waiting to be called in and assessed. Isabel heads past them all, following the receptionist's hasty instructions on how to get through to the burns unit.

The walls of the hospital are packed with a mess of emotions and Isabel can already feel how drained she's going to be by the time she walks out of here again. It's harder to ward off the heavy emotions when you're this tightly surrounded by them.

She avoids the lift, not wanting to get trapped inside with more people at the end of such a long day when she's feeling her own tiredness setting in.

When she reaches the burns unit, she sees Voronov's tall figure through one of the doors and thanks God she did because if she hadn't glimpsed him she would have gone in the wrong direction and that could have been the straw that broke the camel's back.

He looks up when he hears her steps echoing in the wide hall. The lighting here is unforgiving and paints him in harsh lines. He's got his arms crossed over his chest and is standing in front of one of the rooms.

'How did it go?' he asks when she reaches him. He indicates the room behind him. 'They're in separate rooms. Their families have been given some time to be with them but the staff have asked them to return during visiting hours.'

'How bad?' Isabel asks.

'One has a second-degree burn, he'll be okay. This one will recover,' he looks in at the people in the room, 'but he will need skin grafts. They're going to try to get him into surgery first thing in the morning. They're going to be removing the dead skin from his hands all the way up the elbows.'

'For it to get that bad he must have tried to get her down for a long time.' She looks at the door, not quite believing it. 'That's a lot, especially for someone so young. Most of us wouldn't be able to stand the pain.'

He sighs. 'He knew her.'

Isabel looks at him. 'The victim?'

'Yes. They both did. She used to be their crèche teacher when they were younger,' he says, 'and according to their parents she was everyone's favourite at the time. But that has changed. She doesn't work at the crèche anymore; last they heard she was working somewhere in Lisbon at some kind of factory. They weren't too sure of the details.'

'What's her name?

'Paz Santiago.' He gives Isabel a sidelong look. 'She was Gifted.'

The name niggles at something. Isabel turns to face him. 'Did they make a point of saying that?'

He indicates with a nod of his head for them to walk a little way down the hallway and away from prying ears and Isabel follows.

They stop at the end of the corridor. The windows there overlook the hospital garden which, despite the hour, is still well illuminated though there's no one sitting on its benches or appreciating the lush flora planted all around it right now. It even has a modest fountain in the middle.

'She had a reputation, according to the parents, for breaking up marriages, so they'd never been too keen on the respect their teenage sons seemed to have for her still. She still lived in the same place but if we believe what they're saying then she'd broken up a number of relationships and men found it difficult to say no to her.'

Isabel crosses her arms over her chest and gives him a look. 'Poor them. Must have been hard.'

He snorts but it's as humourless as Isabel feels. 'That's where her being Gifted seems to be a convenience for them. Apparently, she made them do it.'

'These people,' Isabel shakes her head, 'what do you think?'

He leans his shoulder against the wall, his back to the rest of the corridor. They're keeping their voices quite low, and this side of the ward is silent except for the faraway steady beeping of medical machines. Unlike with the emergency service downstairs, it's much quieter up here.

He gives a one-shouldered shrug. 'I think that we should take what they say with a pinch of salt, it's probably exaggerated to a degree. But there's usually a grain of truth somewhere, even if it's then distorted by a number of mouths that were never involved to begin with.'

'Okay,' Isabel mirrors his pose, leaning against the wall herself and biting into the inside of her lip. There are similarities here. 'This might throw out the idea that this guy had planned the crime but not the victims.'

'I think so,' Voronov agrees, 'both women, one suspected of being Gifted and marketing herself as having some kind power regardless, another confirmed Gifted. Both known to have had or suspected of having had affairs.'

'Or,' Isabel says, 'accused of ruining marriages in general.' She glances up at him. 'Is that why the underwear? Is he trying to say something with that? Gagging them, stopping them from speaking . . . and the use of the underwear itself.'

'There were no hints of any sex crime, but the use of fire could have destroyed that kind of evidence.'

'Both were naked,' she says, 'no fluids on Carmo's clothes or the car. Nothing in her home or shop either. Not recent anyway.' Isabel rubs at her eyes, digging her thumb and index finger to try and grind away at the grittiness that is starting to settle and make them sting. 'What were the boys doing out there at that time?'

'Walking back from a friend's house. They'd both been drinking and smoking too.'

'If it had been just cigarettes, you wouldn't be mentioning it.'

'Weed.'

Okay, that might explain their ability to push past the instinct of self-preservation to try to get their old teacher down.

'Their parents weren't too impressed with that part,' he adds. 'I have the name, number and address of the friend. We can verify that in the morning. They said the walk normally takes them about fifteen minutes and they pass by on their way home. They both live a few houses down so they were still together when they saw the fire.'

'How bad was it?'

'They said it was all over her legs and making it up to her torso. Her mouth was taped. They tried to speak with her and get her down, but she was barely conscious. This one got burned trying to untie the ropes that were binding her to the tree. They'd just about stopped trying when the firefighters arrived on the scene and took over.'

'Anything else?'

'It might be the shock but they didn't see anyone or anything unusual other than the fire itself. I think it's worth talking to them again once they've been treated.'

'Yeah. If we check which direction they came from as well maybe we can see what was in the opposite direction. If he was there watching and then heard two drunk teens coming close he may have run off. I don't think he did all of that to her when there was no one around and just walked away.'

Voronov is silent.

Isabel nudges him. 'What?'

'Both of these places are very public open spaces. The chances of him getting caught keep climbing even if he is carrying out his attacks during in the middle of the night. I think there's a confidence in this we need to look into.'

'You think he's done it before.'

'You don't agree?'

'No, I think you're right. If there had been a major difference then maybe but . . .' She lets out a sharp breath and reaches up to untie and retie her hair, pulling it up so that the strands aren't brushing her neck anymore. 'Let's look into it first thing. See if there are any similar cases here and in surrounding areas.'

She spots Felipe and Sansão making their way down the corridor towards them, no doubt to cover them for the rest of the night.

'We've got the rest of the shift,' Felipe says, stopping in front of them.

Isabel pats him on the shoulder, squeezing. 'Thanks guys. We'll be in the office early.'

'Get some rest, boss.'

Voronov says goodbye and they make their way out together.

'I saw four surveillance cameras on the houses close by. One of them was disconnected; I'm not sure about the others. If luck is on our side they might show us something. There might be some further back, we can speak to the chief and see if we have enough in the bank to get a few more feet on the ground.'

They start down the stairs.

'They should,' Voronov says, 'we have a double murder on our hands. Maybe more.'

24

The coffee nearly scalds her tongue, but it doesn't stop Isabel from chugging it down.

She's going on four hours of sleep, just enough to sharpen her attention a little more before heading back down to Alcochete and to Paz Santiago's home.

It's a small compact apartment with a balcony over a veterinary practice. The staircase leading up to it is an outdoor one on the right side of the building. At the top of the stairs there's a bright yellow shade protecting the open space a little bit from the weather.

Isabel had gone in with Jacinta's team. She wanted to check the situation, and someone also needed to direct the extra people that the chief had assigned to assist them. Bautista hadn't been too happy to be hearing from them at five in the morning but as they now had two women south of Tejo that had been burned alive, she'd let it slide. Isabel is expecting phones to start ringing with press inquiries as soon as it's a more decent time.

While she's standing in front of Paz's house, the early risers start going about their day. Isabel has lost count of the number of times someone has walked past excruciatingly slowly, peering at the house and the van and tape around it.

And here comes another one.

A woman holding a bag of groceries approaches. She has soft brown hair that is moulded to the shape of her head as if she's run her hands over it one too many times or just taken off a bucket hat. It has that slight oily look that indicates it may not have been washed for a while. Her face is pale and she's staring at the house with wide eyes, her steps quick, her shoulders hunched. She looks like she's in her mid- to late thirties. She doesn't feel like the others.

'They're saying she's dead,' she says, heading straight for Isabel, 'but it's not true. It's just another disgusting rumour these people have made up about her, right? Those gossiping bitches, just trying to start another problem for her. They never stop, they never stop!' She makes to tear the tape down, aiming for the stairs. Isabel quickly intercepts her.

'Hey, hey, one moment.' Isabel stays put, preventing her from advancing any further. 'I'm afraid this is a crime scene. I can't allow you to get any closer than this.'

Isabel feels the woman's surge of emotion a moment before the woman shoves her off. Her coffee flies from her hand as Isabel stumbles back. She recovers fast.

The woman is strong and it's not easy to restrain her. Isabel wraps her arms around her from behind, pinning her arms in place. The plastic bag the woman is holding, filled with groceries, drops to the floor. Isabel hears the sound of a glass jar cracking. Pieces of fruit spill out of the bag, oranges roll down the pavement, following the dip of the road.

Isabel grip is positioned low on the woman's arms, making her attempts to elbow Isabel in the stomach awkward. It doesn't stop the woman from struggling and trying again.

Isabel tightens her grip. She plants her feet and spins them both around, letting the momentum carry them forward, bringing them close to the side of the forensic van. Isabel pushes her into it and holds her there with a firm hand on the centre of her back.

The woman is wailing all sorts of things, alternating between yelling for Isabel to let her go and screaming Paz's name. Isabel drags her arms behind her. It takes a couple of tries. She's flailing so hard that Isabel's worried she'll hurt herself. She manages to get her handcuffs out with her other hand and snaps them around the woman's wrists.

Behind her, she hears running steps. A glimpse over her shoulder shows one of the officers who had been upstairs with the forensics team and Jacinta rushing down the stairs towards her. Jacinta's pulling her cap from her head as she runs down, eyes wide in alarm.

Isabel eases back but the woman thrashes again. Isabel pins her again, this time hard enough for it to be audible.

The commotion is drawing attention, and she catches sight of a twitching curtain in a neighbour's window.

'Are you okay?' Jacinta asks and the officer hovers behind her, eyes jumping from Isabel to the woman.

The woman is still struggling, though she's quickly losing her energy. She's breathing hard and Isabel can hear the tell-tale sound of the hitches as she draws in a breath, can see the way her shoulders, even pulled back into the restraining cuffs, begin to tremble.

'Yes, I'm fine,' she says,

'Inspector,' the officer says, coming forward and motioning for Isabel to allow him. Isabel nods and steps back, holding the woman until he takes over.

Isabel notices her hand is dripping with coffee and becomes aware of a stinging sensation on her thigh. When she looks down and notices the dark-brown coffee stain on her thigh, she hisses.

'Here.' Jacinta moves quickly, opening the door to the van and pulling out a bottle of water, handing it over to Isabel.

'Thanks,' Isabel says. She uncaps it and pours it directly on to her thigh. She can't exactly strip off her jeans here.

The cold water soaks into the denim, providing immediate relief but quickly soaking into the rest of the leg of the jeans.

This is great.

Isabel looks back over at the woman. Her cheek is pressed to the van and her eyes are closed, her mouth is open in an agonised shape and she's crying silently, her cheeks slick with tears.

'Who is she?' Jacinta asks.

'No idea,' Isabel mutters, 'came out of nowhere wanting to go inside and lost it when I didn't let her.' Isabel catches the officer's eye. 'Put her in the back of my car. I have to go back to the precinct, and I think a chat there might calm her down.' Isabel tosses him her car keys and turns back to Jacinta. 'Found anything in there?' Isabel asks.

'Not as much as I'd like, but come here.' Jacinta starts up the stairs, motioning for Isabel to follow.

They don't go very far, just to the top of the stairs where Jacinta comes to a stop in front of the apartment entrance. She points down.

'The place is clean, she was a tidy woman. So far, no sign that someone was in there cleaning up. But look at the floor in the front entrance.'

The tiles there are white and gleam under the light. Just inside the door, butting up against the threshold, are scuff marks. They stand out, stark on the otherwise clean floor.

'We're bagging all the shoes we can think of but there's this too,' Jacinta says, indicating one edge of the doorframe. 'It's small and easy to miss, but we picked up skin cells here that I'm sure we'll find belonged to Paz. Do you see it?'

There's a darker red in lines so thin they almost look non-existent. Isabel has to get so close to it that she squints.

'The direction of the lines indicates that someone was gripping on to the inside of the doorframe, and their hands were being pulled in the opposite direction. We've taken prints. I think they'll match Paz too, but I'll confirm once I've tested at the lab,' she says.

Isabel looks at her. 'In other words, she was hanging on and he was dragging her out.'

Jacinta nods, expression sober as she drops her gaze to the scuff marks. 'She must have fought hard for these to be here, hard enough to stall them in this one spot for long enough for this to happen.'

'What kind of shoes do you think did this?'

'I'd guess boots of some kind, possibly some type of working boot. We'll be trying to pick up a print off it. That might help us.'

Isabel stares at the marks for a moment longer. 'Thanks, Jacinta,' she says quietly.

Jacinta doesn't say anything for a little while, and then turns to look at Isabel, face sober. 'He's going to do this again, isn't he.'

It's not a question.

They stand there together for a moment longer, taking it all in, until one of Jacinta's assistants calls her back in.

Isabel slowly makes her way back down the stairs and over to the car.

She sees the woman in the back of her car, face downturned, expression stony.

She's not crying anymore.

Isabel hopes she'll talk.

Isabel sets a cup of water in front of the woman who, upon arrival at the Anjos police station, had given her name as Odette Orestes-Santiago.

She sits with her chair tucked tight to the table in one of the precinct's lower-ground interview rooms. Her gaze is fixed on the table in front of her and she's pulled all her hair over her right shoulder; she keeps running her hands over the ends again and again, squeezing the strands in one hand and then doing the same thing with the other, alternating between each one, over and over.

She doesn't so much as glance up at Isabel when the water is set in front of her.

Isabel wonders if at some point she might end up wearing that water too.

'Odette,' Isabel says quietly, dragging her own chair closer to the table and resting her hands on its surface. She dips her head, peering up at her to try to get her attention. 'Odette. You attacked a law enforcement officer. That's a serious offence. I need you to talk to me, hmm?'

Silence.

It's all outward blankness. Inside her there's a whirlwind of emotion that holds echoes of the explosion of physical madness that had overtaken her outside Paz's house.

'Were you close to Paz Santiago? A family member perhaps?' Isabel asks. 'We've had a tough time finding any family members to notify of her passing. If you can talk to me, tell me what you know about her, then what happened outside her house earlier doesn't have to go any further than this.'

Isabel waits, giving her the space she needs.

They sit there together, neither of them speaking. The sounds of activity in the precinct filter in. Steps outside the room as people walk past. The voices of passers-by outside cursing the fact that they have to work in this heat, uncaring of who might be overhearing. Traffic and faraway honking and a swearword here and there. And woven through all of that are the traces of feelings everywhere, as loud as every other little noise Isabel can pick up. People might think she was crazy if they realised that she actually found this low-level perception peaceful.

'She helped me.' Odette's voice comes out hoarse, like she's strained it. Isabel wouldn't be surprised if she had with the way she had completely lost her senses.

She goes on staring at the table. Her hands still haven't stopped their movement.

'Helped you how?'

'Leave my husband.' She pauses there, then adds, 'He's her brother.'

Isabel doesn't want to break this fragile space that's formed around them, so she doesn't nudge her, hoping that the continued calm and quiet will allow her to keep sharing.

'Getting her as a sister was the only good thing about me marrying that man. She was the only one who sided with me. The rest of that family all thought he was a saint, that he could do no wrong.' The words fall like dead leaves. Light and careful, easily crushed. 'They didn't like her very much. Maybe that's why.'

'Why didn't they like her?' Isabel asks.

'Because she was Gifted. Because people said she was a whore. Because she didn't let any of that stop her, didn't apologise, didn't go and kneel in a church and beg for forgiveness like they all wanted her to.' She speaks faster, picking up speed as she goes. Her hands stop stroking her hair and instead fist it in place. Her eyes begin to redden once more and the lines of her face are rigid, her skin gaining a redness that clearly shows her agitation.

Isabel can feel her getting closer to that loss of control again, can see her heading straight for that edge that will lock her into it and ruin any chances of them being able to progress from here. And with two dead women on her hands, both likely killed by the same person, she doesn't want to mess this up.

'Was she the only one in her family who was Gifted?'

That gives her pause. Odette draws in a shuddering breath and Isabel watches as her shoulders ease up again. 'No. No, she wasn't the only one. Her grandmother was Gifted too. She stayed in touch with Paz but not with anyone else. She didn't come to my and Isauro's wedding.'

'Is Isauro your ex-husband?'

Odette's gaze snaps up then, locking on Isabel without blinking. 'Husband. He's still my husband. Not for lack of me trying.'

'What do you mean?'

'He refuses to give me a divorce. I don't have the money to fight him off in court. Paz . . . Paz was helping me save some money. So that I could do it. Push through the divorce and be free of that man, finally.'

'What ha—'

'He hit me. He liked to hit me. He *enjoyed* hitting me.'

'For how long?' Isabel asks.

'It started as soon as we got married. He at least waited for us to return from our honeymoon.' Her gaze drifts away, landing on the half-open window. 'The first time was because I slept in. Didn't wake up to see him off to work.' She blinks, several times in a row.

Then she pulls her hair over her other shoulder. 'He dragged me out of bed by my hair while I was still sleeping. Some of my hair got torn off. Once I was on the floor he just walked away and left me there, like nothing had happened.'

Tentatively she reaches for the water Isabel had set in front of her earlier. Her hand is trembling. She takes a shaky breath and tips it to her lips in a small sip, and then another. She sets it down just as carefully as she picked it up and leaves the plastic cup cradled between her hands.

'I was with him for five years. Paz would visit me when he wasn't home. Before she'd come to my work, we'd have lunch together and I'd speak to her then. But then he found out and I couldn't see her like that anymore. I thought that was it. I thought I was completely alone.'

Tears start to overflow, running down her face. But Odette's expression doesn't change at all. It's as if she's not even aware of them, like someone who has cried these particular tears too many times and has ceased to feel them.

'She didn't leave me. She never left me.' She lifts her gaze and looks at Isabel. 'She's really gone, isn't she?'

Isabel almost hesitates. Knows what hearing the truth will do to this woman but there's no hiding what has happened and it won't do Odette any favours. She wishes she didn't have to sit here doing this. 'Yes. I'm sorry, Odette,' Isabel says.

Odette grabs the edge of the table with both hands, and she starts breathing through her mouth, big drags of air that fill and lift her chest as she tightens her grip on the table. She doesn't make any other sound, in complete contrast to her earlier meltdown.

'Odette.' Isabel stands and goes around the table and lowers herself next to Odette's chair, looking up at her, 'Odette. You said Paz helped you leave her brother. How did she do that? Can you tell me?'

Odette droops forward, dropping her head into her hands. Her hair falls to cover her face so Isabel can only glimpse the tip of her nose and the curve of her chin.

Teardrops fall on to the table, one after the other, just as silent as the others. Odette makes a deep humming sound, like the sob is trapped in her chest and she's trying her best to keep it in there.

Then she lets out a breath in a rush. 'She came to see me when Isauro was home. She told him that she was taking me away from him and that if he tried to come near me again, she'd make him regret it.'

'How would she do that?'

Odette turns her head, looks at Isabel with red and swollen eyes. 'She said—' Her breath catches and she swallows down a sob, then tries again, her breath hitching over and over again. 'She said, she said that if she wanted to she could kill him and that no one would ever suspect her because she'd make him do it to himself.'

'Did he believe her?'

She nods and reaches for the water again. 'Yes. I left with her that same night, and I stayed in her home up until six weeks ago. I got my own place, just around the corner from her. A small one-bedroom. It's the first space I've had to myself in so long and it was all thanks to her and now, now—' A deep whine starts in her throat and this time she lays her chest and head down on the table and begins sobbing violently, unable to hold back any longer.

Isabel lays a hand on her shoulder and stays with her.

She's not sure how long they stay that way. It's long enough that Isabel's knees start to ache from the unnatural position and Odette's sobs have been reduced to hiccups when there's a quiet knock on the door.

Isabel looks up to see Voronov at the door, waiting.

'Odette, this is my partner, Inspector Voronov. We're both investigating what happened to Paz. He's going to join us for the rest of this interview, but we won't be much longer, and I'll have one of our officers drive you home after.' She'll have to see if they can afford to have someone spend the night outside Odette's place, just to ensure she doesn't get any unwanted visitors.

With Paz gone and the news spreading so fast, it might be enough to have the ex showing up again.

Slowly, Odette sits back up. She dabs at her eyes with the tissues Isabel has given her and blows her nose. 'It's fine,' she says, voice even hoarser than before.

Voronov closes the door quietly behind him and takes the seat Isabel had been occupying before and Isabel stays close to Odette, still keeping that reassuring hand on her shoulder. She can feel the slight sharpening of Odette's focus, like crying it all out has purged the most immediate grief. It wasn't going anywhere any time soon, and not for a very long time to come, but for now, she'd reached a state where she could take in other things around her.

'When Paz threatened Isauro, you said he believed her. Do you recall if he said anything to her? Or to you?'

'He didn't try to stop me from leaving. But he followed us all over the house as Paz helped me pack my things. He refused to leave us alone. He didn't touch either of us but he stayed on us until we left. He called me and her everything under the sun. Whores, devil worshippers . . . frigid,' she looks up at them, 'he didn't lift a finger to touch me though. And he didn't get too close to either of us. He really was scared of her. He said this wasn't right and that God would make her pay for coming between a man and his woman.'

'Did he reach out after you left?'

'Yes. For the first few days he called Paz's house non-stop. He did it often enough that she ended up changing her number just to get the calls to stop.' She closes her eyes. 'It was constant.'

'But he didn't show up in person?'

'No. He didn't. But he opened his big mouth, started spreading it around that she'd made up lies to get me to leave him. That she ruined marriages. And those people, those nasty people that see her every day took to it like fire. There were already rumours about her having had an affair, and now this? People were looking for reasons to hate her, even when she had nothing to do with it at all. Even when she was working they didn't leave her alone.'

'What do you mean?'

'After she stopped working at the crèche, she started her own business making cakes to order and found a small part-time role with the municipality of Moita. She took her course and got her certificate. She was really good too. Most of the time she just worked from home taking orders . . . most of them weren't from here. But she still went to the community fairs and had a stall there because at least there are people from all over the area, those that don't know her, and she made decent money selling on the day. And after all the help she gave me, she really needed the money. Except at the last fair . . . Isauro showed up, caused her trouble. He wanted her to tell him where I was. It got bad enough that the police were called and Paz got hurt. Luckily not too badly. I went and got her from the police station. She was shaken up but mostly okay. I think she was more angry than anything else.'

Isabel straightens. 'This fair, was it in Alhos Vedros?'

Odette looks at her, surprised. 'Yes. It takes place every third Saturday of the month. She was actually one of the organisers for it, which helped her out when she started her stall, because they waived her fee.'

Santiago.

That's where Isabel had heard that name before. It's the name they'd been given by the arsehole at the front desk at the municipal building in Moita. They'd tried calling her but they hadn't had a response.

What were the odds that Paz Santiago was the organiser of the same fair that Carmo attended and the one involved in an altercation at that very same fair?

Voronov's grim expression lets her know he's made the same connection.

'Thank you, Odette, you've been really helpful. Come with me, let's get you home.' Isabel looks at Voronov. 'I'll be right back.'

Isabel looks for Felipe and Sansão to have one of them take her, she'd rather one of their team be the ones to escort her home – she trusts them to handle Odette with care – but remembers as she approaches their team desks that they won't be in until later after helping them secure the scene in Alcochete in the early hours of the morning.

Carla though, who'd been in bright and early and who had seen Isabel approaching from behind her desk, stands up with a serious but warm smile.

Like Isabel, she'd probably sensed the weight of Odette's emotion as they'd approached the desk area. 'I'm happy to take her, Isabel. If that's okay with Odette?'

Relieved, Isabel thanks her. 'Great, thank you, Carla, I appreciate it. Odette, this is Inspector Moniz.' Then, after a pause and because she thinks it might help in this situation. 'Inspector Moniz and I are Gifted, like Paz.'

That seems to have an impact as she sees some of Odette's numbness clear a little bit, that heavy greyness of grief lightening for a moment as Isabel's words sink in. Because behind the grief and settling in with as much speed as the grief had done, is fear, inky-black and insidious. It had been steadily twining itself around Odette as they had left the interview room. As she had begun to think beyond the loss of a loved one and realised through her conversation with Isabel that she had also lost the one person who had kept her safe.

Hearing Isabel say that they were both Gifted loosens a touch of that fear, even if only momentarily. For once, revealing themselves as Gifted causes not fear but relief.

Odette looks from Isabel to Carla and then back again. 'Thank you both,' she says, voice barely audible.

She stays with Odette until she's tucked in the back of the car. Resting a hand on the roof, she leans down so Odette can hear her properly.

'Listen,' Isabel says, and holds out her card, 'take this. If you need anything, call me right away. If he shows up, don't open the door. Call me or the police right away and we'll be there as soon as we can.' Odette looks at the card, unsure, but then takes it with a small thank-you. 'And, if at any stage, you feel you want to formalise this and file any charges against him, I will help you. Whatever you need, okay? I promise we'll keep you updated on the case.'

When she gets a nod from her, Isabel stands back and closes the door before heading back inside.

'We need to get back in touch with the municipality, confirm that she's the same person who worked for them.' She rests her hands on her hips and shakes her head. 'It can't be a coincidence that both Carmo and Paz were at that fair and were both targeted.'

'As someone who attends those fairs, Lopes would have known who she was, surely? Especially if he intervened in the argument,' Voronov points out. 'Why didn't he mention she was the event organiser?'

'Bastard. We've wanted to speak with him again anyway, this is one more thing we can grill him on. Okay,' she rubs a hand over her eyes, 'Odette gave us the names, numbers and the addresses of Paz Santiago's family. I'm thinking we speak to all of them but I want to prioritise the brother, Isauro Santiago, and once we have confirmation that she was the organiser for the fairs, we should get access to her office or desk or whatever she had, so let's make sure no one touches anything before we get to go through it,' Isabel says.

She's at her desk staring at the details Odette had scribbled down for them, forehead wrinkled in a frown.

Voronov pushes back from his laptop to twist in his chair to face her. 'We can head over to him this morning. It'll be better if we speak with him before the news reaches him.'

Isabel agrees. 'It might be possible, according to Odette he lives in Sines.' That's outside the Setúbal district and crosses over into Alentejo. 'I'd say about an hour and a half away from Alcochete by car.' That might come in handy when checking his whereabouts last night.

'I'll ask Daniel and Carla to go and speak to the rest of the family and Sansão and Felipe to go over to the municipality,' Voronov says.

'Sorry, what are you asking us?'

Daniel approaches them and leans over the partition.

'What did you do with my partner?' he asks.

'Aw, can't survive without her for two minutes? I understand it's tough, she's clearly the brains of the operation.'

He smirks but doesn't say anything. He's got bags under his eyes and his stubble is coming through.

'And we were talking about getting you both to go and speak with Paz Santiago's Gifted-hating family. Up for it? You look like you've had a late night.'

'Not as late as yours,' he says, 'we can cover it. We were finishing up the door-to-door with Carmo's neighbours and getting the statements on the system.'

'Got anything else useful?' Isabel asks.

'No, not that immediately comes to mind, though a lot of people seemed to think João Frade was a creep. Decisions were split on whether Carmo was at fault or not for what went down with him and Thelma. Most people seemed to think she wasn't blameless but were surprisingly willing not to condemn her for it.'

Isabel rests back on her chair. 'That *is* surprising. Usually everyone is always happy to throw the woman under the bus, especially if it's the other woman. I guess when they said she was really valued by the community, they weren't exaggerating.'

'They weren't,' he agreed, 'there's going to be a gathering on Saturday, to celebrate her life. A number of local cafés are contributing food and there are some big donations coming in to fund the whole thing. Apparently even some big names will be attending. Might be a good place for us to be, see if anyone slips up.'

Isabel looks at Voronov. 'What do you think?'

'I agree. If it's the kind of gathering it sounds like it will be, there might be a lot of people with loosened tongues.'

'What time is it starting?' Isabel asks Daniel. 'Do you know if the son will be there?'

'Yes, he should be there. It's going to be from eight p.m. They're going to start at the café closest to her shop, and I think they're erecting a tent behind there.'

'Okay, thanks.' She taps her notepad with the pen, leaving some deep points of ink in between the lines. 'I need to check in with Jacinta, see if anything else has come up for either of them. Both Carmo and Paz were at the last community fair together. I don't think they knew each other personally, but definitely at the business level if Paz was the main organiser for the fair. Maybe Paz's colleagues at the municipality might be able to tell us, or the other attendees.' She stands up and looks to Daniel. 'Leaving the family with you?'

He rubs a hand over his shaved head, nodding. 'We'll get to it today, get on the road as soon as Carla gets back.'

'Okay. We'll see the abusive ex and speak with the municipality about the fair, catch up with Lopes first thing in the morning. We'll make sure we're all at that gathering on Friday, all hands and eyes on deck. Let's see if we can get something today that can put us ahead in the case. Two murders on our hands and nothing to show for it doesn't sit well with me and it won't sit well with the chief either. Especially when I get the feeling this sick bastard is very much planning on doing it again.'

Daniel mock-salutes.

Voronov stands as well, ready to go.

'And let's pick something up on the way,' Isabel mutters, 'I'm starving.'

25

Sines is a picturesque port-town known for its beaches, all very pretty and always packed. Although it belongs to the district of Setúbal, it actually forms part of the Alentejo region. In the heat of spring, although it's not entirely the beach season, they spot some people lying down on towels with a book or having a snack with friends as they drive in. It's not crowded like it would be in the summer but there are people making the best of the hot weather they're riding out at the moment.

By the time they reach Isauro's home in the old quarter, it's edging towards 3.00 p.m. His house is a little flat one-storey building, painted brilliant white with windows outlined in a happy blue that is also used as a border on the face of the building.

There's a small bench out front and a single plant pot. There's also a small, old-looking car that has seen better days, that is parked questionably right up against the side of the house, lopsided with one side up on the cobbled pavement and the other side on the road.

They take the registration number down to check later if it belongs to him, in case he refuses to share that information.

Voronov knocks on the door. 'Isauro Santiago? Polícia Judiciária.'

Isabel can't hear any sounds from inside and can't sense anyone either. She looks at Voronov with a slight shake of her head and a shrug, then walks a little away from him to peer in through the window. There are gauzy curtains in place that make it difficult to see into the house but she's able to make out the outline of a sofa set and a TV. It's switched off and there is no one that she can see.

'Don't think he's home, Aleks,' she says.

The sun is out in full force at this time of day and she can feel its heat beating down on her head, cursing herself for not bringing her hat with her.

Nudging the sunglasses back up on her face, she's about to turn back to Voronov to suggest they try the neighbours when the door of the house to the left of Santiago's opens and a neighbour leaves the property, bag over her shoulder, keys in hand ready to lock up as she brings the door closed behind her.

When she sees them both standing there, she looks startled, then nods at them. 'Boa tarde.'

'Boa tarde,' Isabel greets her, 'do you know where we can find Isauro Santiago?'

The woman quickly locks up, obviously in a hurry to get to where she needs to be but she still answers them. 'And you are?'

'We're with the Polícia Judiciária and need to speak with him. It's quite important.'

That makes her freeze and her mouth forms a small O of surprise. 'Ah, sorry, sorry. Well,' she unzips her bag and drops her keys inside before shifting it to the other side, 'you won't find him here at this time, he'll probably be at work. He's doing a small job two streets over.' She points down the road. 'Just go to the end of this road and turn left, it's two streets down, you won't be able to miss it. There's a large skip outside that they've been using for the renovation. He'll be there probably until six.'

'Thank you.'

'Sure, you're welcome.' With that she wishes them a good day and is off, doing the half-walk, half-run of someone who is late.

They follow her directions and she's right. The street she directed them to isn't a particularly big one. It's quite short with only a handful of houses in a small cul-de-sac. The cobbled pavements are skinny things that people can barely fit a foot on and look more like decoration than anything else. A tree sits in the middle of the road, acting as a natural roundabout within the cul-de-sac, and not too far away from it is the skip she mentioned.

Even from the street entrance, Isabel hears the sound of drilling and sawing taking place. It echoes in a way that it usually only does when the building is completely empty.

When Isabel and Voronov reach the house in question, it's missing an entire front door and there are two men in the front garden, one of them skilfully cutting tiles and setting each one down carefully as he works his way through them and the other sitting on the front step of the house, protective mask pushed up to rest on his head and a cigarette between his lips. There's staticky music playing from somewhere Isabel can't quite see but the melody is drowned out by the sound of the work going on inside the property, where heavy hammering can be heard.

The guy smoking his cigarette is the first to notice their presence. He squints at them under the brightness of the sun. He lifts a hand to shade his eyes.

'Boa tarde,' Isabel says, 'we're looking for Isauro Santiago. We were told by his neighbour that he was working on this property?'

The guy looks her up and down and then his gaze slides over her shoulder to take in Voronov behind her. He doesn't respond to her but twists around to call into the house. 'Isauro! Some people are here looking for you.' He's got a good set of lungs on him. The bellow temporarily drowns out the rest of the noise just before it stops altogether.

The worker who has been cutting the tiles shuts off the machine and tugs down the white protective mask and the goggles he's been wearing, eyeing them both with curiosity, He doesn't say anything, but does nothing to pretend he isn't watching them.

Isabel sees someone approaching the doorway, mostly in shadow. She sees his feet first. Sturdy boots with black soles, camel-coloured but stained with paint here and there. The jeans he's wearing are much the same. Like his colleagues, aside from goggles and a mask that hangs at his neck, he's not wearing any other protective gear. He's in a worn red T-shirt that is most likely used only for work, like the rest of what he's wearing. The sleeves have a couple of holes in them.

Isauro Santiago bears a striking resemblance to his sister. He's a very good-looking man, with sharp, flinty eyes a brilliant green. His form is tall and obviously very fit. It's evident that its strength and muscle are more from the work he does daily than from a gym. His lower face is covered in a neatly trimmed beard. In one of his gloved hands, he's still holding a hammer.

He glances at Isabel and Voronov but doesn't say anything, looking instead at the smoking guy. 'You need something?'

'Not me,' the guy says, finishing off his cigarette and dropping it to the floor. He crushes it with his boot and then points at Isabel and Voronov. 'These two are looking for you.'

Santiago frowns and looks at Isabel and Voronov. 'Looking for me? Why?'

Voronov steps forward, calm and controlled, firm. 'We're inspectors with the Polícia Judiciária. We'd appreciate it if you could join us for a moment. We'll try not to take too much of your time.'

'Polícia Judiciária?' he asks, his eyebrows shooting up towards his hairline. 'Why?'

'It's a serious situation, Senhor Santiago,' Voronov says as he gestures with his arm for him to step outside and join them further away from the house, 'please.' His tone is polite but brooking no refusal. He isn't asking and it's obvious.

After a moment, Santiago nods, acquiescing, and makes to start walking in the direction that Voronov has suggested.

'Senhor Santiago,' Isabel says. He stops and looks at her with a startled expression, like he wasn't expecting her to speak. 'Let's leave the hammer here with your colleagues, hmm?'

He glances down at the hammer. Then back up at her.

'Health and safety, yes?' she says.

His co-worker slaps him on the back. 'Just give it to me.' He takes it from him and sets it next to his seat. 'Don't take too long, we have to start putting those tiles down before the day is finished, okay.'

'Yes, boss,' he says and then motions for Isabel and Voronov to follow.

They don't walk too far from where they were, just putting enough distance between themselves and his co-worker and boss that they won't overhear the conversation.

The house they stop in front of is quiet. Its windows are closed and the shutters behind them down. A small plant pot hangs from the pretty exterior light that is fitted to the wall next to the door.

Santiago folds his arms over his chest, feet set wide apart, and gives them an expectant look. 'Well? How can I help you, officers?'

'Actually, we're inspectors. Reis,' Isabel says as she takes out her ID and gestures to herself, and then Voronov. 'Voronov. Senhor Santiago, have you heard from your sister, Paz Santiago, lately?'

The scowl is immediate, and tension immediately crowds in, bunching his shoulders closer to his neck. 'We don't speak.'

'What about the rest of your family? Your mother and father? Do you know if they've been in contact with her.'

'Look.' He pulls the goggles all the way off and slicks his hair back from his face a couple of times. 'She's not considered family. We don't talk to her.'

Isabel gives an understanding hum. 'I see. Is that because of being Gifted or because she took your wife away?'

His head jerks around and he's taken half a step towards her, all rigid and barely restrained rage before he catches himself. He eases back under Isabel's cool gaze and looks back at his colleagues, probably to check if they'd seen him step up to an officer of the law.

'It's none of your business.'

'Yes, it is,' Isabel corrects him, 'Senhor Santiago I'm very sorry to tell you that your sister was found dead in the early hours of this morning. Her death was determined to be the result of foul play. Inspector Voronov and I are here to speak with you as part of our case.'

He freezes and stares at them, unblinking. 'My sister was killed?'

Interesting that he's now referring to her as his sister when just two seconds ago he'd refused to acknowledge her as part of his family.

'Yes, I'm afraid so,' Isabel says. 'When was the last time you spoke to Paz, Senhor Santiago?'

He presses a hand to his mouth and paces away from them, only stopping when he reaches the end of the road and then he stands there for a moment, hands on his hips and head down.

Isabel looks at Voronov.

Voronov gives a subtle nod and follows in Santiago's footsteps, Isabel close behind him. He rounds Santiago to stand in front of him. Santiago is a tall man and the two of them are pretty much eye to eye. The quiet confidence in Voronov's stance makes it clear where the power lies, however.

'Senhor Santiago,' he says, 'we need to know the last time you spoke with Paz.'

Deliberately staring over Voronov's shoulder, he finally responds. 'The last time I spoke to her was when she showed up, threatened to kill me and took my wife,' he grinds out.

'We're not going to find out that you spoke to her during one of the many calls you made to her residence, are we?' Voronov asks. 'Paz Santiago had to change her house number because of those calls. Are you sure you didn't speak to her at any other point? Please understand that as part of our investigation we will be checking phone records, Senhor Santiago.'

He clenches his jaw. 'I said I didn't. I wanted to speak to my wife.' He glares at them. 'A man has the right to speak with his wife.'

'Senhor Santiago, would you say that you felt that your sister was standing in the way of you seeing Odette?' Isabel asks.

'She was.' He says it simply, doesn't need to embellish it. Like he knows it to be absolute truth.

'I see,' she says. 'We'll need an account of your whereabouts from yesterday evening to the early hours of this morning.'

He narrows his eyes on her. 'Why? You're not going to pin this on me.'

'It's a natural part of the investigation to question people close to the victim, Senhor Santiago, particularly if there was conflict prior to the death in question, like the one that took place at the community fair between you and your sister. But this is just procedure. No one is accusing you of anything.' Yet. 'You say you haven't spoken to her so there shouldn't be any issue cooperating with our investigation. The sooner we get what we need then the sooner we're out of your hair.'

There hasn't been one speck of grief from him since the moment they told him Paz was dead.

He readjusts his stance, chest opening and chin tilting up as he looks from Isabel to Voronov with an edge of taunting.

Isabel remembers Odette, breaking down in the interview room, lashing out trying to make her way to Paz's home, needing to reassure herself that Paz was okay. A stark contrast to Paz's actual brother, who is showing no feeling whatsoever.

This man is a nasty piece of work.

'We finished work here just after six, grabbed a couple of beers before dinner. Went home, ate, went out to the local café around nine. Stayed there until closing time. Then I went back home and I went to bed. We started working at five thirty in the morning. You can check with them.' He jerks a thumb over at his colleagues.

Voronov is jotting down the details. 'Name of the place you went for drinks last night and the café after.'

Santiago reels them off, glaring at them the entire time.

'What about the rest of your family? Have they been in touch with Paz?'

He shrugs and crosses his arms. 'You'd have to ask them.'

'Thank you.' They'll have to get access to his phone records too, check into any calls that follow after this particular investigation. 'We'll let you get back to work. If we have any other questions we will be in touch.'

Without bothering to reply, he turns on his heel and heads back to the house. His co-worker and boss are standing together having watched their interaction from a distance with undisguised curiosity.

'What do you think?' Isabel asks Voronov, still watching Santiago.

'He's a dangerous man who we already know isn't a stranger to getting violent with women – and she was holding something back from him. Motive is there for Paz,' he says, 'but I'm not sure about Carmo.'

'We have him at the same community fair,' Isabel says, 'he could have been there more times than we know.'

Voronov inclines his head, conceding. 'It will depend on his alibi.'

They're still waiting for Jacinta's report to come through and corroborate Cardoso's findings.

It's pretty much all but confirmed that the crime was committed by the same person; the MO is the same. But there's the very slim chance that some psycho had got wind of what happened in Moita and copied it. There are always opportunists around.

Looking at Paz's brother, it would be very convenient for him for his sister to disappear right now. She took his control of his wife away from him. He's clearly not even thought of giving up on Odette. Perfect time to pass off the murder of his sister as someone else's handiwork.

'Did you get anything from him?'

Isabel shakes her head. 'There was nothing there but arrogance. He doesn't care that she's dead. He must have really hated her. The only emotion that spiked then was when Odette was mentioned.'

Voronov turns to look at her. 'What was it?' he asks.

'Hunger.'

26

'The parents haven't heard from her.' Carla's voice fills the interior of the car as they drive back from Sines.

Unlike their son, the Santiagos live in Alcochete, just like their daughter about a half-hour's walk away.

Isabel's leaning back in the passenger seat. The window is opened by a sliver and sending her hair flying all over the place as Voronov makes swift work of getting them back.

'By the time we got there they had already heard what happened,' Carla continues.

'How did they seem?' Isabel asks.

'It was pretty cold. They wanted nothing to do with it. According to them they haven't spoken to her in years and blamed her for the breakdown of their son's marriage. They were very much of the opinion that she shouldn't have got involved.'

Isabel stares at the dashboard where Carla's name is displayed, as if by doing that Carla would be able to see her incredulity through the speaker. 'Are they aware that their son was abusing his wife?'

'They think Paz convinced her to tell lies,' Carla pauses there, 'they say she used her Gift to do it.'

Isabel falls silent.

She believes Odette. But there's also precedent for what the parents are saying, though Isabel is sure their assertion that Paz made her do it stems more from their intolerance than it does from actual research into cases where Gifts have been used in the past to coerce others into doing something they never would have done otherwise.

She sighs. 'Sounds like they're all as bad as each other,' Isabel mutters.

'They say they cut off contact with her after it got out that she was with a married man. That was before she took in Odette, and apparently the man she was having an affair with moved abroad with his family. We'll double-check it just in case. In any case they made it clear that they considered her a nuisance and that she dragged the family name through the mud. They had enough, apparently.'

'Did she ever try to get in touch with them again?'

'According to them she never reached out.'

'Yeah. Don't blame her.' Who would want to stay in touch with people who clearly didn't give a crap about them? 'The affair apparently took place around the time when she worked at the crèche, have Sansão and Felipe see if they can track down her old co-workers. See what happened. Maybe there's something in it. Is there anything else?'

'Yes, Sansão and Felipe confirmed Paz Santiago was the organiser from the municipality. They secured her desk over there and are bringing everything over, including the work laptop.'

'Okay, good. Thanks, Carla.'

They end the call.

Isabel tucks her hair back, locking it down with her fist.

'João Frade works in construction,' she says, 'Jacinta said the scuff mark was likely from a work boot. Both João and Isauro might have that type of shoe, both of them would have access to rope too. Then there's Padre Lopes at the community fair and his weird obsession with the first victim, within distance of the first murder scene. With no report on file about the altercation at the fair we can't be sure of his contact with Paz during the incident.'

'All of it is circumstantial,' Voronov says.

'I know.' She leans her head back against the headrest, turning to look at him. 'We have the partial print. We can try and test against it. If Jacinta determines enough information can be pulled from it maybe we can match their prints against it.' She taps her fingers on the door handle. 'Both killed near rivers, both walked to their death, stripped naked, clothes preserved, tied up and burned to death. Both women Gifted, both with a history of extra-marital affairs and a notorious reputation, occupying similar spaces . . .'

'But our suspects don't entirely cross over.'

Isabel shakes her head. 'João Frade is too fixated on Carmo, I wouldn't put it past him to resort to violence to keep her. You know, "If I can't have her no one else can." We know that happens all too often, but I don't think he'd be so deliberate in the way he murdered her – I can see him wanting control but those crime scenes speak of a need to humiliate, to make them pay for something.'

'And Santiago and Lopes . . .' Voronov nods. 'I can see it.'

'The fire, the removal of clothes, the choice of victim: is this being done as punishment of some kind? Because of their perceived transgressions?'

'Could be. Choosing to burn them alive could just be a fetish, a taste for arson, or . . . maybe they could be using it as a tool.'

'A tool for what?'

Voronov shrugs, still thinking it through. 'If it's a need to punish then that would mean the killer views them as having done something wrong or committed a sin. Fire also has ties to purification.'

Purification. The word sits wrong with her. It makes her think of overzealous religious nuts.

'If that's what they're trying to do, then how many sinners are they planning to go through?'

They make the rest of the drive in silence.

27

The next morning, Isabel lets the team know she'll be in a little later than usual with the promise of bringing breakfast with her.

The café she heads to is a little further from the precinct than the one she usually goes for, about a twenty-minute walk through the narrower streets.

The tourists are already out in droves despite the early hour, eager to enjoy the warmer than usual early spring weather. Everyone is in short sleeves and shorts or skirts and dresses, climbing the intricate cobbled streets that run up and down the hills of Lisbon.

Isabel works her way up a zig-zagging road that climbs up into a square overlooking a section of the city. It's a far cry from one of the city's miradouros but still gives anyone with an appreciation of a lovely view something nice to look at.

The majestic tree in the square provides some shade over a small drinking fountain and the two benches beneath it.

Tucked towards the back of the square is a hole-in-the-wall type of café with just a couple of tables outside in the building's shadow.

The square itself is empty aside from the two elderly men sitting side by side on one of the benches, one with his cane in hand, both with their flat caps in place, short sleeves for the hot weather and a newspaper out. It's a quieter place, more of a stop for the locals than the tourists who stick to the more well-known streets. Isabel has been here a couple of times, but it's rare for her to come here when it's neither on her way to work nor on her way back home. They have some of her favourite tostas mixtas though.

Isabel greets them as she walks past them to the café. It has one of those entrances with steps immediately inside leading down into the establishment.

Bracing her hand on the top of the narrow entryway, she ducks her head to peer inside and her face is immediately bathed in the cool air of the café. Her T-shirt is sticking lightly to her upper back.

The interior is quite small, enough for the food counters and coffee machines and the cash register, an ice-cream refrigerator and six tables with two chairs each.

There are two people sitting inside, each at their own table, one with their eye on the news channel playing on the TV mounted up high in the other corner of the café, the other a younger patron, slouched low and scrolling through their phone. The young man at the counter is putting more pasteis de bacalhau on to a paper-covered silver tray with the ease of someone who has done it a million times. He looks at Isabel when she greets him.

'Boa tarde,' she says. 'Can I get a carioca de limão and a tosta mixta please? I'll be out here.'

He nods. 'Take a seat, I'll be right with you.'

'Thanks.'

She takes one of the two tables outside, sinking into the hard plastic chair with a sigh and surveying the peaceful scene around her that is such a contrast to what she deals with in her work.

Tia Simone is right: her work is grim.

She hasn't tired of it yet though.

The thought makes her reach for her phone and open up the message from Matthews. Isabel hasn't replied to it yet.

To think she'd even reached out to Bautista.

She would be lying to herself if she didn't acknowledge that it was a definite ego boost.

'Your carioca de limão,' the guy says, setting the tiny white teacup and saucer, lemon peel swaying gently in the water, on the table, 'would you like more sugar?' He points to to the one packet he's put down next to the teacup.

'No, thank you, this is fine,' she says.

'I'll bring out the tosta in a few minutes.'

Isabel nods her thanks and reaches for the packet of sugar, tearing the corner before pouring it into the hot drink. As she stirs it in, she hears the approaching footsteps.

She doesn't immediately look up, not until those steps come to a stop right in front of her table.

'It's been a while, Inspector Reis.'

Isabel glances up then.

Dr Nazaré Alves is smiling at her, dimples showing as she adjusts her glasses. She doesn't look like she's changed at all since their last meeting outside Isabel's house, when Nazaré had come to warn her that Monitoring were keeping a close eye on her.

She's dressed in a fitted white T-shirt and flowy powder-blue wide-leg trousers, her Converses peeking out from below them. She's got a cloth bag hanging off her shoulder and a thick blue plastic bangle on her left wrist.

'Thanks for coming,' Isabel says, by way of greeting.

They hadn't parted on the best of terms, although Isabel had contacted her since for her thoughts on the London case.

Nazaré worked closely with NTI, guides and Gifted. Her primary role was with Monitoring and she was also the expert that the police would use when dealing with a case revolving around Gifted individuals. That was how she and Isabel had met a couple of years ago.

The smile Nazaré now gives her has a wry edge to it as she pulls out the other chair at Isabel's table and takes a seat.

'I have to say I wasn't expecting this,' she says as she sets her bag on her lap and leans back in her chair. 'If someone had told me you'd be requesting me as your Monitor I would have laughed in their face.'

Isabel lifts her teacup. 'Hmm.' She takes a sip.

The guy comes back out with the tosta mixta and sets it in front of Isabel, taking note of the new customer and asking what she'll have.

'Just a lemonade and do you have any queijadas?'

He lists off the kind they have and she orders one too. Isabel waits for him to go.

'It wasn't my number one plan, no,' she admits.

Nazaré tucks a stray wavy strand behind her ear. 'What changed?'

Isabel looks out at the square. 'I'm sure you've received my file by now. You should know, right?' She picks up one half of the tosta and takes a satisfying bite.

'That you're a nine bordering on a ten?' Nazaré asks.

Isabel shrugs. 'More like the bit where evidence of erosion has presented itself.'

Nazaré's amusement dies down then. 'Yes. I saw. I'm sorry, Isabel.'

Isabel finishes chewing, takes another bite before setting the bread down and dusting her hands. She looks at Nazaré. 'The moment I got retested and learned I was a higher-level Gifted I've been expecting it. And I'm luckier than most.'

Nazaré nods and forestalls her response when the guy comes back with her order. She thanks him, picking up her glass and looking at Isabel. 'That's true. Many Gifted at your level and at your age, the erosion would be a lot more advanced.'

'A polite way of saying they'd already be locked up in a room and incapacitated.'

Nazaré sighs. 'It's not quite like that.'

'Don't worry, I didn't ask for you to become my Monitor so you could reassure me that people like me don't just get spirited away to somewhere no one will find them.' Isabel gives her a sardonic smile. 'I wouldn't believe you anyway.' There is just too much evidence out there to the contrary.

Nazaré sighs, like she hadn't expected to hear otherwise. She probably hadn't. She's known Isabel long enough to know better.

'For real, this time,' Nazaré says, 'why did you ask for me? I barely ever get assigned Monitoring cases, they like throwing me at the consultancy aspect of things. And how did you even get Monitoring to agree? I've never heard of someone requesting their Monitor.'

What goes unsaid is that most people aren't in a fit state to make any requests by the time Monitoring gets involved.

Isabel, in that regard, really has proven to be an anomaly.

That's easy enough to answer though. 'There's a research team in America doing some work on erosion, slowing it down. They successfully trialled a new drug to prevent it and they're at their next stage. I've agreed to be a part of their next phase.'

Behind her glasses, Nazaré's eyes grow comically wide. 'What? Why would you agree to that?'

Isabel thinks about the person who had led on the research for the drug she's currently got stashed away in her own bag. A very talented researcher who had put her everything into a drug that could save her high-level Gifted sister who really hadn't had much time left.

In the end, Isabel had watched them both die in London.

It had left a deep impact on her.

'I trust the intentions of the person behind it,' she says simply. 'And their first rounds of trial phases were positive. So it's a calculated risk. But the reason why this matters here is because they needed additional, willing test subjects, and because of the way my Gift's level changed so drastically from how I originally tested, I more than hold their interest. The reason why I was able to request you, and get what I want from Monitoring, is because I only agreed to play along if they could get Monitoring to play nice with me. In return . . . Monitoring get access to the research results. It's a win for everyone involved.'

'I see,' Nazaré says. There's a rare seriousness to her expression. Then she tilts her head, not looking away from Isabel. 'And why did you choose me?'

'Better the devil you know,' Isabel says.

'Ah.' Nazaré shakes her head and picks up her drink, her gaze slipping away.

'And because,' Isabel concedes, 'I trust you not to let them spirit me away to a place where no one will find me.' She holds up her little teacup.

Nazaré watches her quietly for a moment, eyes sober.

Then she nods.

She lifts her own glass and clinks it against Isabel's.

She's about five minutes from the precinct when she gets a call from Jacinta.

'Hey,' she says, dodging around a group of tourists crowded on to the pavement, paying close attention to the tour guide standing in the middle of the road.

'Bom dia,' Jacinta says, 'heard you were going in a little later today.'

'Yeah, I'm on my way back now, though I was tempted to go back home for a second shower to be honest with you.' She frowns up at the sunlight streaming down on her without mercy. 'Feel like I'll be needing another one by mid-morning. It's already so hot out.'

'Not for me,' Jacinta says, sounding smug, 'nice and cool for me over here.'

Isabel snorts. 'You mean with all the lovely dead bodies?'

'Don't knock it until you try it.'

Isabel shakes her head and crosses over on to the other side of the street and into the shade offered by the buildings on that side. 'Did you call me this early so you could gloat to me about literally chilling out with all your dead friends?'

'No, I called you this early to make your day.'

That definitely gets her attention. 'Make my day how?'

'Finally finished the other case yesterday so I spent the afternoon wrapping up the evidence we gathered from Carmo's apartment.'

'And?' She slows down, keeping out of the way of people going the opposite way, not wanting to miss what Jacinta has to say.

'We pulled three different set of prints. We got a match to Carmo Vilar, another match to her son, and the third to one Zé Lopes. Your favourite priest.'

Isabel's grip on the phone tightens. 'Jacinta. I love you.'

Jacinta's cackle comes through the speaker. 'Yeah, you owe me a drink.'

'Done.'

28

Isabel and Voronov meet Daniel outside one of the lower-floor interview rooms at the precinct.

The precinct is in full swing with phones ringing, papers being filed and conversations happening on every floor. The sound of whirring fans all over the building adds a constant low-level buzz over all the other noise, as if a gauze has been draped over each and every room, forcing everything else beneath it.

Daniel is leaning back against the wall, arms folded.

'Senhor Padre isn't too happy with us,' Daniel says, indicating the closed door to the interview room with an unimpressed nod of his head.

Isabel shoves her quarter-length sleeves further up her arms. 'What did he say?'

'Told us he wasn't going to cancel his service because of us, and I told him he'd probably prefer coming with me and getting in the car in a calm and compliant manner to me cuffing him outside his church.'

'Hmm. I'm sure he wasn't very happy about that,' Voronov says, walking around Daniel to the door.

'Oh he loved it,' Daniel says.

'Thanks,' Isabel says, eyes on the door and itching to get in there, 'I'm impressed you held back from kicking things off yourself.'

Daniel shrugs. 'Just seeing the look on his face when we turned up outside his house was enough. Besides, Carla's already helping Sansão and Felipe go through Paz Santiago's belongings that they pulled from the office and if I'm not there soon to help out she's going to be pissed.'

Isabel nods. 'Okay, once we wrap up in here, we're coming to pitch in too.'

Daniel nods and then heads upstairs to their floor.

Isabel glances at Voronov. 'Shall we?'

'Yes, I'm looking forward to what he has to say for himself.'

Voronov opens the door and walks into the room, waits until Isabel is in as well before closing the door behind her.

'Padre Lopes,' Voronov says, 'thank you for coming in.'

Despite the surprise summons to the precinct while he'd still been at home, Lopes is neatly dressed in his clerical shirt, hair neatly combed. He sits ramrod-straight at the table; his fingers are locked together where they rest on the table and the cup of water set there for him is full and untouched.

He watches passively as Voronov takes a seat opposite him at the table and Isabel walks over to the window where she leans back against the windowsill.

The sunlight is pouring in through it and when she settles with her back against it, Lopes squints and eventually glances away, turning his attention to Voronov instead.

'You've already disrupted my day, Inspectors; I'd appreciate it if we could move this along.'

'We understand this isn't the most convenient of times, but I hope you understand the seriousness of the case we're investigating, Padre,' Voronov says, 'I'm sure people will understand your absence seeing as you're here assisting us.'

If word gets out that they've brought him in for questioning, the gossip will spread; it won't reflect any story resembling the positive spin Voronov is putting on this and Lopes is only too aware of that fact.

'How can I help?' Padre Lopes asks. His tone is calm, impatience carefully filtered out of it.

'If you could explain why we found your prints on a glass inside Carmo Vilar's apartment, that would be very helpful to us,' Voronov replies.

Outwardly, Lopes only flicks a glance Isabel's way before he refocuses on Voronov.

Clearing his throat, he shifts in his seat.

'Padre Lopes?' Voronov prompts.

He licks his lips and reaches for the water.

Isabel glances at Voronov, catching his look.

'Well, Padre?' she says. 'It can't be difficult to remember since you barely ever interacted with her, according to you, no? Why were you at her house? Was it for her services? Too ashamed to go to her shop like everyone else in case people called you a hypocrite?'

He keeps his eyes on the water in front of him.

'Or,' she says, 'were you there for her? Hmm?'

That gets a reaction, and he snaps his head around to look at her only to wince at the sunlight.

'Because I'm getting the sense that your interest in Carmo Vilar was more than whatever righteous crap you've been spouting.'

'No,' he finally says, and this time the calm tone he uses is clearly forced, 'no, it wasn't like that.'

Voronov sits back in his seat. 'Then what was it like? The sooner we can clear this up then the sooner you can go back to your day, Padre.'

Lopes takes a deep breath, eyes closing for a second before he folds his hands together again. 'I heard that she was going through a difficult time because her relationship had come to an end.'

Isabel's eyebrows fly up.

Voronov's stare bores into him, an echo of that first meeting in the church and Voronov standing over him, his presence dwarfing that of Padre Lopes. That same subtle balance of power swells in the room.

'And how did you know about her relationship, Padre?'

'People talk.'

'To you, specifically, about Carmo Vilar?'

'No, no, in general.'

Isabel gives a low whistle. 'Just how obsessed were you, Padre?'

'I was not—' he catches himself, stopping the sudden snap of words. 'You're wrong.'

'I don't think I am,' Isabel says. 'At first you were keeping tabs on her because you were concerned about her business being inappropriate, not in line with your own beliefs. You even cast her out for it. You've been checking in with people who have been to speak to her. And now we find out you were at her house, which you conveniently neglected to tell us. I don't have to tell you this doesn't paint you in a good light, Padre. And on top of that you were also getting information about her relationship. What business was it of yours?'

'I was not obsessed!' He spreads his hands, lifting and jerking them down in a decisive motion. 'I wasn't. I was concerned. Everyone was speaking about it after the incident with the car. I was just doing my part as a leader within the community. Senhora Vilar never stopped being a Catholic. It's my duty to help.'

Well, where had this energy been the first time they'd spoken to him?

'When were you in her apartment?' Voronov asks; he doesn't comment on Lopes's nonsense excuse.

Nerves sprout, sharp and sudden, and Lopes looks between Isabel and Voronov.

'If you withhold information from us again or lie, Padre,' Voronov says, 'I think you know there will be consequences for you. I can guarantee you they won't paint you in a good light with your community.'

Lopes licks his lips. 'I visited her on Tuesday.'

The day before she was killed.

Isabel moves away from the window and pulls out the chair next to Voronov. She sits.

'Padre,' Isabel says, leaning her arms on the table, 'this isn't a good look. You saw her the day before she was found dead. Your prints are in her apartment. You didn't tell us this when we first spoke to you.'

'I didn't hurt Carmo.'

Ah, and it's Carmo now.

'Padre,' Isabel says, 'her relationship with Senhor Frade ended months ago. If what you say is true, why did you wait so long to go and check on Carmo?'

'Because he wasn't leaving her alone. I thought she might be distraught.'

So he was sticking to it. Fine. 'Okay. What did you talk about? If you were there long enough for her to offer you a drink then you must have talked.'

He tightens his jaw. 'I told you. I was there to offer her my support.'

'Which was what? Did you invite her back to your church? Or were you hoping to be a shoulder to cry on?'

'I offered to *listen*. To *pray* with her. And I told her that if she would just listen to reason, abandon that – that immoral business of hers, that she might be able to find peace.'

Isabel waves that away. 'So, you went there to tell her you thought she was being borderline-stalked by her ex because of her business?'

'No. I was honest in my guidance.'

'Guidance? Is that what you were doing?' Isabel asks. 'And? So? Did she want your guidance?'

'She asked me to leave.'

'And you left? Just like that?' She lets her doubt come out loud and clear in her tone.

'Yes. Of course.'

'Of course.' Isabel locks her gaze on him. 'Prove it.'

At her side, Voronov stills, but he masks his surprise well, his attention not wavering from Lopes.

'Excuse me?' Lopes says.

'You're aware I'm a Gifted individual, Padre,' she says, 'if you consent to me looking at your memories of that day then everything you've told me is easy enough to verify, no?'

His mouth snaps shut.

On his face is barely hidden disgust.

And fear.

There's fear too.

Isabel leans forward, extending her hand over the table. She doesn't need to touch him to look. But she wants him to feel the pressure of it.

'It would take a few seconds,' she says, her voice gentle, 'nothing more.'

His eyes drop to her hand, stay there.

He drags his eyes back up to hers.

'No. Thank you.'

Isabel draws back. She pointedly leaves her hand resting on the table. 'What about Paz Santiago?'

'What?'

'The woman from the community fair who you said was involved in an altercation. Her name was Paz Santiago. But you probably lied to us about not knowing her either, hmm Padre?'

'What are you—'

'Padre,' Isabel says, 'Paz Santiago is dead too.'

He slides his hands off the table. Maybe he's worried she'll be able to pick up his thoughts just by touching the same surface he is.

It wouldn't work of course.

In reality she doesn't need to touch him at all.

'For a priest, your relationship with the truth fascinates me, Padre.'

29

They might have got nothing from Lopes but the prints in Carmo's home and his history with her is enough to get them a search warrant for his house and car. Nothing is found but it doesn't change the fact that this shoots him up to the top of their list.

On Saturday evening, despite having understood how people seemed to genuinely care for Carmo, it still takes Isabel by surprise when they reach her home neighbourhood and encounter the sheer number of people present. And it's clear that there are more still arriving.

There's music playing in the background, someone has set up a speaker and Isabel can hear the haunting notes of a fadista singing.

There are cars parked everywhere, squeezed into every available space there is.

'Not what I expected,' Isabel says to Voronov.

They have to park closer to the roundabout and walk over to the café where the gathering is being held.

They spot the people from the café, busy, their pace fast as they carry platters of food and drink around to the back.

'They did say she cared for her community,' Voronov says.

Despite the hour, the sun hasn't set just yet. The sky is a bright landscape of blue, red, yellow and purple, all melding together with just wisps of cloud here and there. The heat has dropped by a couple of degrees, making it a little more tolerable.

Isabel and Voronov fall behind a group of people also heading to the back of the café and when they get there Isabel has to stop to appreciate the sight before her.

There are so many people, filling the recreational square at the centre of the apartment buildings, with so many candles at the centre of each cluster of people, some on the grass, some at the chairs and tables that have been laid out.

There is a young woman standing at the back, against the wall of Carmo's building. Wires make their way from the front of the building to the back, connecting to the bright lights trained on the wall. Paint and brushes take up space on a white cloth sheet on the ground as she stands on a short ladder and continues adding to the large-scale portrait of Carmo.

Isabel can see the outline of some letters at the bottom, though they haven't been properly painted just yet.

With us, always.

'They really went all out for her,' Isabel murmurs and despite herself feels moved.

It's hard not to when she can literally see their love for this woman, the soft but sad colours of grief, mixed in with bright spots here and there as these people share their stories and memories of someone who was a pillar of their community.

'If this is really how they all felt about Carmo,' Voronov says, taking it all in, 'no wonder Lopes had a chip on his shoulder about her.'

Just then, at the opposite end, closer to the other accessway into the area, she sees Tiago and his wife Eugénia walking together, holding hands.

The low murmur of conversation that had been uninterrupted until then quietens for a moment as people register their arrival.

And then people are pushing back from their chairs, one group at a time going over to greet them and give their condolences.

Isabel thinks of Paz.

She wonders if anyone other than Odette is going to mourn her like this and feels a sadness for her. Carmo is someone who had denied her Gift but used it to make a life for herself. Paz is someone who had acknowledged what she was and even weaponised it, to save someone from a dangerous situation at a potential cost to herself. And yet the deaths of the two women couldn't have been received more differently.

The music is turned down and Tiago is led to the front, closer to the mural of his mother. He stops to look at it as the artist stands back to let him see, compassion on her face.

Eugénia follows closely behind him, her hands on his shoulder, supportive, eyes downturned. Someone gives him a microphone.

An uncomfortable, needle-sharp whistle cuts through, the feedback making everyone wince before he moves the microphone back a bit from his mouth before trying again to speak.

'Sorry,' he says, 'sorry everyone.' Then he stops and looks around, and seems to gather himself.

Behind him, Eugénia gives him an encouraging squeeze.

'Thank you for organising this. I know . . . I know my mother was a big part of this community.'

Isabel looks up at Voronov. 'Split up? See what people are saying and then meet back here?'

'Sounds good.'

Voronov drifts to the right side of the crowd, badge out.

There are more people here than they'd already spoken to. Eugénia and Tiago had said that Carmo's clients weren't just from this area and that people came a long way to see her. They've been going through her books, but money pays for secrecy too. There are a lot of people who might have paid Carmo to stay off the record when it came to her services. Especially if she was supporting someone from a more affluent side of the fence. Someone she might have met through her ex-lover, for instance.

More than anything else, Isabel wanted them to be here for the whispers. The things people can't help but say to each other, to their next-door neighbour, but not to the police.

But now everyone is silent. She looks at the multitude of people and allows herself to see entirely through her Gift, letting it reach out from inside her to taste the emotion-laden air and capture the emotions.

She's never quite dismissed what Sara, the little girl from Carmo's crime scene, had said. And now she searches for the same markers.

What emotions are here that don't fit? That aren't grief, that aren't sadness, that aren't sympathy. There are spikes of other emotions. There's the melancholy of relived shared moments and, growing in number, the mellow warmth of inebriation.

But nothing resembling hunger.

Isabel wonders if it's her, if she's the one who's unable to see it because her lens is different from Sara's.

In the background, Tiago is still speaking, stuttering, talking about his mother and what these people meant to her. There's an increasing hardness to his tone that prompts her to pay more attention to his words.

Voronov catches her eye as he starts cutting a path through the tables and the people standing to come back to her.

The emotions Tiago is exuding have changed. They've gone from the shakiness of nerves, maybe from facing a big crowd in this way, and a slate-grey grief still engulfed in shock, to a deep-rooted red that stinks of self-blame, resentment and fear.

Then she feels the softest sensation of something unfurling in her mind. Like a flower, tucked away in the recesses of it, that has been curled in on itself for some time, and now its petals begin to open up one by one, soft but greedy. It only ever wants one thing.

Her attention.

It's been a while.

She turns, looking over her shoulder.

It's as if there's a rope linking her directly to him. Maybe it's that. Or maybe it's that he's become so seared into her mind he could be standing in a crowd of hundreds, and she'd still be able to zero in on him.

He stands far away, all the way at the other end of the recreational space, by the short, square tunnel that leads from the block's centre and out to the back in the direction of the river. She can't make out his features, just his silhouette.

Voronov reaches her side. 'Did you get anything useful?'

'Aleks,' Isabel says, as her eyes lock on a single shadow, 'I'll be right back. Keep an eye on Tiago, I feel like he's about to lose it any second.'

Voronov takes in the look on her face and follows her line of sight. When he doesn't see anything, he stiffens.

They've spoken about this before and he understands what this means.

'Is it him?' he asks.

'Yes.' She peels her eyes away from where *he* awaits and lays a hand on Voronov's arm. 'It's fine. Don't worry. Stay here.'

She watches as his jaw tightens, a muscle jumping in his cheek.

'Aleks,' she says, quickly touching a hand to his face, 'he can't do anything to me.'

He stares down at her. 'You're sure?'

'I'm sure.' And she is. Especially now.

He gives her a curt nod and goes back to watching as Tiago continues to speak.

Isabel pats his arm once and then waves her way through the clusters of people and tables. The figure stays still, not shifting one bit.

Soon she's far enough away that Tiago's voice, although still echoing within the barriers of the surrounding apartments, fades with the buzz of activity. It's quieter down here. Separate, like she's entering a different location.

Maybe it's because it's an underpass, but a rush of air blows her hair back from her face as she approaches it.

She can see him clearly now.

He's got his back to her, staring out at the wide expanse of land between them and the river. The sun has left the sky now. Evening is settling in properly with only the lighter blue slowly being swallowed by midnight.

She stops there, at the entrance of the tunnel.

'It's been a while, Isabel.'

'Has it?' Isabel says. 'You're a lot more present in my everyday life than I like.'

She sees his head turn. He doesn't turn all the way. Just enough that she can see the outline of his nose, mouth and chin.

Despite their proximity, he remains largely in shadow.

She's sure it's his doing. A way to keep her from seeing him completely. A way to stay in her head, stay in her thoughts but keep her from seeing just enough that she might have an easier time finding him.

'Did the Americans help you?'

Isabel looks beyond him. She can see the wide line of the river. 'You weren't able to see for yourself?' she asks. 'You're slipping, Gabriel.'

She doesn't have to ask. That's one thing that had changed whilst she'd been in America. The fear of having him in her head had changed. It had started changing before she'd even arrived. It's amazing how much changed when she stopped viewing her Gift as her enemy. Once she understood exactly how much she could do with it, even if using it was to her own detriment.

Keeping Gabriel firmly tucked into a corner of her mind had become as easy as breathing. Showing him just enough to keep him thinking he still had the upper hand and keeping enough back that he didn't even have a chance to realise she could rip their connection to shreds and he'd never be able to touch her mind again.

The only problem with that plan is that, if the connection she has with him is dissolved, then the last lead they have for finding him and putting him back in prison is also gone.

She doesn't want to take that chance. Especially when he'd taken such care to make this as personal as it could be.

‘I notice you don’t spend much time with your mother,’ he says, ‘I’m surprised. I went through a lot of trouble to give you what you wanted.’

‘You’re bored and you like power games,’ Isabel says, unperturbed; he doesn’t think too deeply about the mess he’s left on her hands and the constant calls on her phone from a parent who hasn’t given a crap about her for the better part of her life wanting to check in on her. ‘You don’t do things for other people, Gabriel. You do things for yourself.’

She hears him sigh. ‘No, I don’t. One day you’ll see that. I’m sorry you didn’t like my gift.’

‘I’d say you should feel free to take it back whenever you want, except I don’t want you to go near any of my family or my friends again,’ she says. ‘Do you understand?’

She stares at the strip of his neck that she can just about see.

His being here is nothing but his own projection of himself. That’s how he’s able to fudge details of his appearance like this, allowing her to see only what he wants her to see.

‘I won’t forget what you did,’ she says.

‘You won’t be able to find me,’ he says.

‘Yes, I will.’

She leaves then and slaps up a barrier fast and hard enough that his presence dissipates as if he’d never been there to begin with.

Tiago is rounding off the end of his speech.

Voronov is where she left him but it’s clear he’s been keeping watch for her return.

‘Okay?’ he asks as she rejoins him.

‘Hmm.’

She hears the vibrating of a phone, touches her hand to her own pocket instinctively even though she knows it isn’t hers. Voronov digs into his own pocket, glancing at the screen.

Tiago surrenders the mic to another man who must be a friend. Isabel can see Tiago’s shoulders shaking from where she stands and hears the first stifled sobs before his friend switches off the mic and calls out for someone to grab him a beer.

He allows himself to be taken to one of the tables where he sits down. Eugénia doesn't return to sit with him; Isabel sees her standing to the side, arms wrapped around herself, tucked away from prying eyes.

'Isabel.'

'What?' she looks over at Voronov. He's putting his phone away as he comes back to her side. There's a change in his demeanour, a gravity that hadn't been there earlier in the depths of his stare.

'Daniel and Carla are on their way, about five minutes out. They found something.'

Isabel stares at him. 'I'm guessing it's bad?'

An odd quiet falls over the crowd.

Isabel and Voronov follow the gaze of everyone who seems to be staring in the direction of where Isabel had spotted Eugénia.

This idiot.

Standing there, defiant and looking like nothing or no one can move him, is João Frade. Isabel has no idea how long he's been there. He stands there surveying the crowd of mourners; he's unapologetic, dressed completely in black. The hush that has fallen over everyone is unnatural and the two men who have just guided Tiago to a seat have their hands on his shoulders. His eyes are pinned to the newcomer and the rage that has only just started to calm down Isabel can now feel ramping back up even from this distance.

'Great,' she says, 'this isn't going to turn ugly at all. Think we should interfere now?'

'I'll go speak to Tiago,' Voronov says.

'I guess I've got the creepy ex.' She sighs.

He's got a beer in his hand that he's already taken a few sips from. He ignores Isabel walking towards him. He's looking straight at Tiago, as if he has something to prove.

Isabel grabs his arm. 'Maybe people would be more likely to believe that you're not here to start trouble if you weren't trying to stare down Carmo's son. Come with me and *don't* make me have to put you in cuffs.'

'I'm here to mourn too,' he says, but allows himself to be dragged away, 'am I not allowed to do that?'

'You are. But there are plenty of ways you could have joined this gathering that would have created less of a dramatic entrance. The way you walked in here just now is like someone trying to prove a point.' Once they're back out in front of the shops, she lets him go and turns to face him.

He's still looking over his shoulder. Where they're standing now, they can still see the area behind the shops where the gathering is taking place.

Someone has put the music on again, filling the silence that lingered after Isabel dragged João away.

'Look,' Isabel says, 'I can't stop you from being here, but think this through. You're adding fuel to the fire. Her son is already upset about what people used to say behind his mother's back. You being here isn't going to help any of this. Particularly when her relationship with you was part of what caused a lot of the rumours going around about her. So, if you want to stay, why don't you go and drink your beer quietly in a corner and do your best not to antagonise her grieving son.'

'I'm grieving too. Why is his grief more important than mine?'

'Because he's her son. Because he's not a relationship that had already ended but he was refusing to accept it. I understand your grief. But this isn't about you. I'm sorry.'

He scoffs and drinks half of the bottle in one go, spinning away from her to walk off a few steps, his back to her.

Isabel sees Voronov returning, catches the look he gives her.

She nods to tell him she's got it under control.

'You've spoken to him, haven't you?' João says, facing her once more. 'Do you know he was ashamed of his mother? That he left her, barely kept in touch with her. But now he's here, acting like the dedicated son. Maybe you should be asking him where he was at the time that she died. Why are the two of you here? Aren't you supposed to be out there doing your jobs and finding out who burned her alive?'

His voice is starting to rise with each passing word.

There is that edge of self-blame Isabel had seen just a little earlier in Tiago. She wants to know why it's there. What he blames himself for. But she's not going to entertain this attitude from this man.

Isabel steps up to him, close enough that it startles him into retreating a step. Likely he'd been expecting his size and attitude to scare her into backing down.

'You might want to reconsider your actions right now,' she says, calm, 'do you know statistically speaking how many women are murdered by their significant other? Most women are in the most danger when they decide to leave their partners. And you, in particular, are one that wouldn't let go. So. Trust me when I'm saying we *are* doing our jobs, and it would be very good for you if I don't show up in front of you again. Understand?'

Never mind that they now have a second murder on their hands. Doesn't rule him out but it does mean that their immediate reason to suspect him won't apply to both women, unless there's something else they don't know about.

Her words seem to have a sobering effect. João backs up a couple more steps, eyes drilling into her.

'João. Where were you last night between midnight and three in the morning?' she asks. She's got him here; it'll save her a trip.

The question seems to throw him and the resentment that had been brewing in him dissipates. He blinks at her a couple of times. 'I spent the night at my brother's,' he says.

'Where does your brother live?'

'Lisbon. Why?'

'Can your brother confirm that you were there?'

'I think so.'

'You think so?'

'No, yes. Yes. He can confirm.' He shakes his head, frowning at her. 'Why are you asking me these questions?'

Isabel doesn't respond.

He takes a step closer but thinks better of it when Isabel levels him with a look. 'Has something happened again?'

'Are you familiar with a woman named Paz Santiago?'

He shakes his head. 'No . . . but the name sounds familiar.' There's genuine confusion there.

'She was the organiser of the community fairs, usually there at each one. Did Carmo ever mention her?'

'Carmo kept her business dealings to herself. She never wanted any help.'

'So that's a no?'

'No,' he says, 'I didn't know her. I'm getting another drink.' He turns away from her.

He doesn't return to the back to join the gathering; instead he heads into the café, under the watchful eyes of the owner, who doesn't look too happy to see him there, taking a swig of his drink as he goes.

When Voronov approaches, Isabel peers around him. 'I take it Tiago isn't on his way over to take issue with Frade being here.'

'The others managed to talk him down,' he says.

Isabel rubs at her temples. 'This was a waste of our time. Unless you got anything?'

'Nothing we haven't heard already through the interviews.'

Voronov steps closer to her, lowering his voice. 'What about you?'

'Me?' She's confused by the question until she sees that he's looking at her calmly, patient.

He's asking about Gabriel.

'I'm okay.'

'Does he appear often?' he asks, a hard note in his voice.

She doesn't blame him. The last time he'd dealt with her after an encounter with Gabriel, he'd barely stopped Isabel from going over a balcony.

She reaches for him, rubs his arm lightly. 'No. It's the first time he's appeared since London.'

Voronov's eyes roam over her face, gauging her, taking in her calmness. 'You don't seem worried.'

'I'm not,' she says, 'don't you worry either. I can promise you he's not in control here.' She holds his gaze as she says it, so he knows she's not making it up and that she means every word.

Under her hand, she feels his arm relax and eventually he nods.

Isabel's attention is drawn away when she spots Daniel's car heading down towards them. Isabel can see him at the wheel and Carla next to him in the front passenger seat. She lifts a hand to signal their presence there. A moment later, Daniel's slowing to a stop in the middle of the road. He doesn't have much of an option considering how packed the road is with cars parked every which way.

Daniel lowers the window and sticks his shaved head out. Carla leans forward to be able to see around him. She's got an open laptop on her lap and the light from it paints her face in an eerie blue-white light.

Isabel knows it's serious when she and Voronov reach the car, peering inside, and he doesn't even crack a joke.

'Sorry, we would have been here earlier, but we found something.'

Daniel makes a motion for them to get in, closing his window back up.

Voronov rounds the car to get in on the other side and both of them slide into the back. They slam the doors shut, sealing the car in silence.

'What's going on?'

Daniel turns to Carla. 'Show them.'

Carla carefully passes over her laptop to them.

'First when I was searching for recent deaths similar to our cases, I was getting a lot of accidental fires, often involving more than one person, but they didn't include the other things we encountered,' Carla says, 'like the clothes being set aside or victims being made to walk to their deaths. No one had been tied up and no accelerants used. But then I went back further.'

Isabel stares at the logs. These are case numbers, five of them, logged between the years 2005 and 2007.

'These are almost twenty years old,' she says.

Daniel nods. 'Five victims, causes of death vary but there were a lot of similarities. They were tied up, set on fire and all of them were women and known or suspected to be Gifted.'

She clicks on one of the case numbers, zeroing in on the location. 'Same municipality.'

'That's right. All committed in towns in Setúbal. It was well documented, I found a couple of blogs online talking about it and small columns written in the newspapers covering the story.'

Voronov reaches over to scroll through the details. 'The murders were linked at the time, same investigator.' Isabel spots the name: Vitorino Guerra.

'I called the precinct to speak to him, but they say he's retired.'

Isabel hands the laptop back over and sinks back into her seat, rubbing at her eyes. 'That's a long time ago but we can't ignore the similarities. What do you guys think?'

Carla shimmies closer to the edge of her seat so she can ease the awkward posture when trying to look at them directly. She pushes her hair back, tucking it behind her ear. 'I called the precinct listed, as a courtesy, told them we'd be visiting them first thing in the morning in relation to one of their old cases.'

'And the chief?'

'We cleared it with her first.'

'Good. Good.' She leans her head back on the seat and closes her eyes. 'All right. Seems like we have a long day ahead tomorrow. Might as well call it a night, get some rest.' She opens the door to get out. 'Good find, guys.'

Daniel, still seated to watch them as they get out, remarks: 'Imagine. It's almost like we're real inspectors too.'

And there it is.

'Fuck off.'

30

Isabel and Voronov arrive at the precinct in Barreiro at nine in the morning on the dot. Maybe because it's Sunday, the main road is even busier than on a working morning. It's situated at the top of the incline and surrounded by lush greenery, from the various tall trees hanging over it to the flower-studded shrubbery that looks like it's cradling it. The sign has seen better days, the blue worn down from the whims of the weather over the years and the white lettering yellowing slightly.

Isabel would feel a little jealous that it looks so much nicer than their headquarters in Anjos, if it weren't for the fact that it's pouring down with rain and she wasn't preoccupied with just getting past it.

Thunder rolls through the skies, still far off, when Voronov hurries on ahead of her. His navy T-shirt is clinging to his back even though they had made a run for it as soon as they had got out of the car, splashing up water with every single step.

'How are you feeling about tomorrow?' Voronov asks. He holds the door open for her to pass through, arm up over his head to protect himself from the rain that is coming down on them hard.

Isabel ducks down. 'To be honest I'll be glad to have it behind me.'

Tomorrow is her sister's wedding. They have already cleared being out of work with the chief, though they've agreed that if there's a significant development in the case then they'll be called in right away.

Now out of the rain, she glances at him as he comes in after her. 'And you'll be there to distract me so.'

He huffs out an amused breath.

The run from the car over to the entrance has left both of them with clothes plastered to their bodies.

Isabel slicks her hair back from her face, holding in the swear-words trying to escape and the two of them stand just at the entrance for a moment, getting their bearings, trying, and failing to wipe away the rain from their faces.

The interior is a little less impressive than the outside and that makes Isabel feel a little better. It's nice to see the government budget is a menace to all precincts, not just theirs. Glaring overhead lights, benches for seats, no air-con to speak of going by how they're immediately enveloped in warmth.

It might be raining but the temperature hasn't let up one bit. They're probably looking at a prolonged storm today.

'You both really got hit by the rain, huh?'

A portly man in uniform stands next to the reception desk drinking from a bottle of water. His small eyes are crinkled at the corners, and he chuckles at the sight of them.

'A bit of rainwater won't kill you,' he says. 'We've been due a good downpour with all this heat.'

'True,' Isabel says, wry. Well. Not like they're going to manage to look decent now anyway, so she fishes out her ID to show him. 'Inspector Reis.'

'I'm Inspector Voronov,' Voronov says, and somehow manages to sound dignified and as if being soaked from head to toe is just a part of his routine. 'Our colleague, Inspector Carla Moniz, called yesterday evening to say we would be coming this morning with regard to one of your old cases.'

'Oh, so it's you two? Yes, she did.' He gestures them over and takes a seat behind the desk. 'You can call me Carlinhos. I'm one of the officers who is based here at the precinct. What's your interest?'

Isabel presses her hand to her hairline, trying to keep the rivulets of water from continuing to run down her face. She's wearing a short-sleeved top so it's not as if she can use a sleeve to soak up any of the moisture. She's careful not to touch the desk because she'll leave it a mess of rainwater.

'We're from the Anjos precinct—'

'Lisbon? Aren't you both a little far away from your area?'

Isabel doesn't speak right away, instead watches him with a quizzical expression, waiting to see if he wants to keep talking or if he's ready for her to speak.

He catches her meaning and holds his hands up in apology, motioning for her to continue.

'Thank you,' she says, 'as I was saying, my partner and I are from the Anjos precinct. We were given a case from this side of the river. Our one murder has turned into two and our colleague—'

'Who called yesterday.'

'Yes,' Isabel says, giving him a pointed look, 'who called yesterday. She saw a case on your records yesterday, spanning 2005 to 2007. Five murders in total. Based on the case notes there are more similarities than we'd like and we want to take a look at the files and logged evidence. Our chief's sign-off should have come in late last night.'

'One moment, I'll see if that's come through.'

This potential connection to an old case could bring them back to square one, though Isabel admits they're not in a strong place in terms of evidence, but it felt like every door they looked behind had a potential suspect.

'We got the sign-off, buuuut . . .' He purses his mouth together and gives his head a little shake.

'Is there a problem?' Voronov asks. He leans his forearms on the desk, doing his best to keep the rest of him from touching it.

Carlinhos darts a quick look back down at the computer. 'Well. You see, we had a flood a couple of years ago. It got our entire basement level which houses our old case files and our cold-case evidence. This case is one of the ones that was impacted.'

Isabel looks at him in disbelief. 'You're joking. What's left?'

Carlinhos leans back, scratching at his chin. 'Not much. According to our logs we've got one useable box of evidence.'

Merda. 'Right. Okay. We'll be taking that with us. What about the inspector who led the case at the time? Is he around? I believe his name was Vitorino Guerra.'

'Guerra? No, no, he's not around anymore. He retired in 2008. Had a stroke.' He leans forward, lowering his tone. 'A lot of people around here think the case got to him. He fought to keep it open but higher-ups were telling him to move on.'

'Why were they telling him to move on? Not enough results?' Voronov asks.

'That too, but you know how the higher-ups are,' he says and gets up, 'need to justify the money being spent on all the man hours. Just kept pulling people out of the task force. Then the trail went cold. No new crimes committed and, well, that was it. Come with me, let's sign out the box for you. I'm sure you've got things to do.'

They follow him, hanging back a little.

'Think maybe Guerra is still around somewhere?' Isabel asks Voronov. If the evidence is gone then they could speak to the person who had lived and breathed the case until they couldn't anymore.

Carlinhos must have ears the size of a satellite dish because before Voronov can respond, he says: 'Oh, Guerra? He hasn't gone too far. He lives in the old historic district in Setúbal. He's lived there all his life, never moved. If you want to speak with him, you can find him there.'

Isabel looks at Voronov.

'Carlinhos,' Voronov says, 'we'd appreciate it if you could share his address.

31

The woman who opens the door is short, stocky, and has a mean face as she looks both Isabel and Voronov up and down. She's standing, fully in the way, broom in hand, having come out to glare at them like she's hoping they'll disappear and not come back. She's maybe in her sixties, with brown age spots gathered around the corners of her eyes.

The rain has eased up but has left puddles here and there, the water glimmering in the cracks between the cobblestones. The storm isn't over. The clouds remain, heavy, grey and crowded. A wind is picking up that means any more oncoming rain will be an onslaught and that anyone caught in it outside won't get away with just getting soaked.

'Good morning, we're looking for Vitorino Guerra?'

'And who's asking?' she asks. Her voice is loud and unapologetic, she doesn't even pretend to be polite.

Hah. Isabel steps back. This is not a job for her.

Voronov steps up, face calm and unfailingly polite. 'We're from the Anjos precinct, we're hoping to speak with Senhor Guerra in relation to a case we're currently working on. My name is Inspector—'

'He's retired.'

Wow. This is the first time Isabel has seen Voronov's charm fail. Normally they take one look at those big blue eyes and they're a melting pot of helpfulness. Not this woman.

Isabel kind of respects it.

She takes another step outside, broom still clutched in her hand as she wags her finger at them both. 'Do you have any idea what that job did to him? He had a stroke because of you people! Get out of here.'

'Senhora . . .' Isabel hesitates, unsure of her name.

'I'm his wife,' she states.

'May I call you Senhora Guerra?' Isabel asks.

Senhora Guerra doesn't shut her down, but she doesn't encourage her either.

'We promise we just want to have a quick word with him and then we'll be out of your hair and you won't see us again.'

'I told you, he's *retired*—'

'Woman, what is with all this racket?'

Isabel hears the tap-tap of a walking stick on the floor before she sees a man who she assumes is Vitorino Guerra appear at the end of the entry hallway over his wife's shoulder.

His hand grips the curve of his cane tightly. He's in a button-down short-sleeved shirt, dark-grey slacks and sandals. His hair is all white but thick. His features are hawkish, with heavy, dark eyebrows over deep-set black eyes.

His body shows his age, but his face, and the sharpness of his eyes, show a fierce intelligence and reveal his ability for quick assessment.

They made the right choice coming here.

'Amalia, come out of the way, woman, why are you holding the broom like that? Want to be arrested for hitting officers of the law?'

She turns on him, shaking said broom. 'You – you're a fool! Have another stroke, go on. Who has to deal with the fallout? Crazy, all of you! Don't say I didn't warn you!'

She turns away with a huff, not even glancing their way, like she's wiped their existence from her immediate memory, and disappears back into the house, leaving Isabel and Voronov standing, bewildered, on the front step.

Guerra is looking in the direction his wife stalked off in and then he looks at them both, still standing outside.

'Well? You pissed her off already. You might as well come in. Unless you want to stay outside for the next rain.'

Right. 'Excuse me,' Isabel says, stepping inside and wiping her feet as best as she can. Should she take her shoes off?

As if he's the one who's Gifted, he waves it off. 'Leave them on. I'm sure she hopes you won't stay long enough to warrant removing them.' He looks at the box Voronov is carrying, curious. 'And what's that? She'll have your balls if you bring anything dangerous into her house.'

Voronov comes in and Isabel shuts the door behind him.

'This is what's left of one of your old cases,' Voronov says.

Guerra, in the process of leading them into another room, stops and looks again. Isabel feels the weight in the room shift.

He knows exactly what case they're referring to.

He sighs and turns away. 'Come on, through here.'

Isabel follows him through an arch in the wall, no door here, and into the dining room with double doors leading out to a patio.

It's an old-fashioned space, decorated with dark mahogany pieces: cupboards, the oval dining table, the glass cabinets showing off the finest china. One of the chairs isn't tucked in and there are two knitting needles, both still tucked into the baby-yellow yarn of an unfinished project that has been left there, next to a glass of water carefully resting on a coaster. On the far end of the table sits an old, grey television, playing a telenovela, the sound on loud enough to make Isabel wince.

There's a feeling here. One of long-lived familiarity and contentment.

'Take a seat,' Guerra says, gesturing to the other chairs at the table, and taking a seat next to the chair where the knitting is resting. 'You can set that down on the table.' He eases himself carefully into the seat. He can't quite tear his eyes away from the box that Voronov is holding on to.

'Thank you for speaking with us,' Voronov says.

Guerra leans over to grab the old-looking remote and mutes the TV.

The open patio doors allow for the wind to sneak in, ballooning the curtains covering them.

Guerra reaches into the front pocket of his shirt and takes out a squashed packet of cigarettes and a red lighter.

'I've had these for three months,' Guerra says, taking one out and balancing it on his lips. 'I promised Amalia I'd be more careful after the stroke. I haven't quit completely, and I have one every now and then, only when I really need it. Some people may find it odd but I find it comforting to have them on me, even when I'm not planning on smoking.' He holds the flame to the tip until it flares red and then tucks everything back away as he takes a deep drag and lets the smoke escape out of the side of his mouth. 'Mostly I smoke when I get itchy.' He takes the cigarette and points it at the box sitting in front of Voronov. 'That,' he says, 'makes me itchy.'

'You know it just by looking at it?' Isabel says.

'Of course. That case . . . my wife isn't wrong when she says it gave me a stroke. It certainly didn't help me.'

The clinking of glasses and fast, clipped steps interrupt Isabel from asking her next question.

To her surprise, Amalia is walking into the dining-room space, shoulders back, no-nonsense face. She's balancing four glasses on a tray, all of them with ice already in the glasses. There's a pitcher of what looks like lemonade and a sweating glass of beer. She's also included a small plate of biscuits.

She sweeps up to the table and puts a beer in front of her husband and then divides up the glasses between Isabel, Voronov and herself.

'Since you're both here in your capacity as inspectors, I won't offer you alcohol.'

Guerra, reaching for his beer, laughs. 'I drank.'

'These two are young and healthy. Stop trying to corrupt them.' Then she quickly pours them all a lemonade and places the plate of biscuits at the centre. 'Help yourselves.' She takes her own lemonade glass, sits back on her chair and stays there.

'Amalia was with me for the worst of that case. There's nothing you can say here that will be news to her.'

'That's right,' she agrees, 'sat with him until six in the morning sometimes, watching that thing drive him crazy. He had so many cases but none of them got to him like that one. Is that why you're both here?'

Voronov glances at Isabel.

She shrugs in response.

It's one thing for Amalia Guerra to know what her husband shared with her. That was a past case and well, people turned a blind eye to a lot of things back then. This does involve newer incidents though and that's something they have to consider. If they share details here of two ongoing homicides and they get leaked, then there won't be anything left of either Isabel or Voronov by the time the chief's through with them.

'We wanted to look into the Setúbal fire deaths case files but when we went to your old precinct this morning we were told there was a flood a few years ago. Almost all of the files and evidence were destroyed.' Voronov touches the box. 'This is the only remaining evidence and there isn't much of it. We were hoping you might be able to tell us what you remember about the case.'

'And why would you need me to do that?' Guerra asks. 'Have they decided to reopen a cold case? Didn't think they had that kind of fortune in their coffers.'

'I'm afraid they haven't,' Voronov says. 'As we mentioned to Senhora Guerra, we're actually here about our case.'

Guerra pauses mid-cigarette drag, eyes flicking up to them. 'Go on.'

'Over the past two weeks we've had two women murdered in the Setúbal municipality,' Voronov says, 'both were tied up and set alight.'

'I presume you have more to link them together?'

'We do.'

He nods to himself. 'My case was almost twenty years ago.'

'We know.'

'But I knew someone like that wouldn't just stop.'

'Senhor Guerra,' Isabel says, 'it might not be the same person. That case was a long time ago, just like you said. But it could be a copycat, maybe. But we want to make sure we consider all the possibilities. Is there anything you can tell us about what you remember from that case? Specific places, anything you noticed was a part of his routine.'

Guerra considers them for a moment. He takes a drag of his cigarette and doesn't stop until it's down to a short little stick and then he stubs it out on the clean ashtray on the table. He picks up his beer, takes a swig and sets it back down with a decisive thud.

'I can do better than that.'

He gets up and Amalia immediately stands too. 'Let me—'

'Ah, I'm fine, woman, you worry too much.'

'Maybe if you stopped smoking those things,' she mutters, 'I wouldn't have to worry so much. Now the whole room stinks of smoke.' Out of nowhere, she produces an air purifier spray and proceeds to spray here and there, steadily diminishing the strong smell.

Isabel leans over the table to see what he's doing as he goes around the table without his cane. He goes to the lower cabinets of the huge shelving unit in the corner.

She hears his bones click and the grunt of exertion he makes when he lowers himself to the bottom cabinet.

'Young man,' Amalia says, slapping Voronov's arm, 'go and help him before he breaks a hip. That's all I need.'

Voronov murmurs an assent and quickly goes around the other side of the table.

'Don't need any help,' Guerra grumbles, but still directs Voronov on the cabinet he needs to open and what to do.

When Voronov stands up, he's holding a hefty-looking cardboard box that he sets on the table between them.

Isabel stands to take a closer look as Guerra returns to his seat as if he's been winded.

Inside, she sees folders held closed by rubber bands, papers grouped and held together by thick paperclips.

She realises what she's looking at. 'Senhor Guerra, are these . . . documents from your case?'

'That's right. They made a mistake closing that case. And I wasn't doing too well. But I never planned on letting go of it. Not after everything it cost me. They took me off it, fine. But all they did was stick it on a shelf. No one out there was trying to get justice for those women.' He's sinking backwards, looking at his past self and remembering. The frustration and darkness of that time is coming back into being around them, muting the colours of a warm home. 'So I made copies, of every log, of every report and statement I had and when I retired and that case was still there as a cold case, I brought all this home with me.'

Isabel looks back down.

'What's left in the evidence box?' Guerra asks.

Voronov takes the lid off and tilts it for Guerra to see three small plastic bags inside. One contains a piece of burnt rope, another contains a torn piece of fabric, and the last one contains a charred rosary.

He tsks and Isabel feels the disgust rising in him. 'Those useless . . . they lost so much.'

'How much?' Isabel asks.

He slaps his box. 'Once you see in here you'll know.' He shoves it across the table at them. 'Go on, you can take it.'

'Thank you,' Isabel says.

'But you have to give me something too,' Guerra says.

'Like what?' Isabel says.

'You're not telling me everything.'

'Senhor Guerra, you know we can't do that – especially with an active investigation,' Isabel says.

That doesn't move him though and he just keeps staring at her, hard.

Isabel sets the box he pushed at them aside and rests her arms on the table, leaning closer. 'Here's what we can do. We'll take this back with us and we'll look through every last page. And if we see that there is a genuine connection between our cases and your case, we'll let you know exactly what we're doing.'

He considers this. 'Have you got anything on your perp?'

'A couple of things. A partial print and scuff marks. Nothing on the prints but our forensics lead is working on the scuff marks. They think they were made by work boots. Both of the victims were grabbed from places known to them, that they would have considered safe.'

Amalia darts a look at her husband and Isabel feels her worry spike.

'Anything else?' Guerra asks, very measured.

'They were both burned alive in very public places. Easily discovered. We don't like what that says about his confidence.'

'Public, you say?' He sighs and reaches back into his pocket for that same packet of cigarettes, ignores the sharp look he gets from his wife, and lights another one up. It's telling how much Amalia actually knows about the case, knows how it affected her husband, knows how hearing this will affect him now. Otherwise, there's no way she wouldn't drag him over the coals for that second cigarette.

Isabel is surprised she doesn't turn around and kick them both right out of the house.

'Then if it's the same person, you should be worried, Inspectors. His balls have got bigger. And he never killed this quickly. You said a couple of weeks? He killed one in 2005 and one in 2007. But 2006 was his most prolific year.'

'That year,' Amalia says, shaking her head. 'I'm surprised the stroke didn't happen then and there.'

'There were three that year,' he pauses, 'that we know of. He wasn't as brave then. Used to do it in tucked-away places. An abandoned factory, a garage, little shacks in the woods. The back of a car.'

'When did he kill them?'

'At night. Always at night. The reports weren't made until the morning for most of them. The victim he left in the car was found earlier than the others, it was left in a supermarket parking lot and one of the staff called it in at the start of their shift, not that it did us much good.'

'Supermarket?' Voronov asks. 'Did they have any footage?'

'No, they didn't. But the petrol station across the road did. It caught the car driving past before it entered the car park.'

Isabel sighs. 'But that was the victim's car, wasn't it?'

He nods. 'Yes. Her name was Milagre. She was number four. Mother of three. Went to work and never came back. Colleagues didn't see anything. Nothing was odd. She stayed behind to finish off the inventory at the clothes shop she worked at in Baixa da Banheira. And that was it. Not one soul saw anything after that.'

Which is tough to do. Baixa da Banheira is a small but tightly packed area. That no one would see anything near a shop is unusual.

It makes her wonder what kind of person this is. Is he someone who is perceived as non-threatening? Maybe even well known to his neighbours, colleagues? Someone people wouldn't think twice about seeing down the street. Someone who is part of the fabric? Or is he so good that he can just show up, take his victims, and disappear like the bogeyman? Like someone who never existed.

'Was there anything that you noticed connected the victims? Any similarities?' Voronov asks.

'Yeah. All of them were Gifted. Poor girls. It was already a bad time for anyone tested by the NTI getting out of there with a Gifted designation. You remember what it was like, don't you, Amalia?'

Amalia nods, picking at the knitting wool on the table, slowly pulling out a thread. 'Those were bad times.'

'Did you ever get a profiler in?' Isabel asks.

'Hah. Why? Is that your next move? Those guys just spout out nonsense. Don't make me lose respect for you, Inspectors.'

'Should I take that as a no?' Isabel asks.

He plucks the cigarette from his mouth as he makes a rolling motion with his hand. 'Time was getting on. I questioned a few people but it never got anywhere so they brought someone in.' He indicates the box. 'His report is in there. Sounds like just common sense, anyone working the case could have worked it out.'

'Any prints?'

'No. Nothing. We even held on to a match hoping there would be something on it.'

'A match?'

He nods. 'In the last one. He used alcohol. Doused her in it.' Guerra's gaze goes dark.

'She was only fifteen.'

32

'Close the door,' Chief Bautista says.

It's a little after one in the afternoon and Isabel and Voronov had made a beeline for the chief's office.

The box they'd picked up from the other precinct earlier in the day and the one they'd been given by Vitorino Guerra sit on a chair on the other side of the chief's desk. Voronov stands over them like a sentinel. Isabel stands next to him, hands curled around the back of the other chair. There's a tightness around her shoulders that she's trying to ease out but no amount of rolling them back is loosening it up.

Chief Bautista is by one of her windows, leaning on the window balustrade and smoking.

'You spoke to the inspector? Guerra, you said it was?'

'Yes, Chief, we just came straight from there.'

There's a plant on the chief's desk, which is a new development. She's never really been into decorating her office with things she needs to keep alive.

Bautista catches her looking at it. 'It was a gift.'

'Oh.' Isabel doesn't comment further.

'Well?' she asks. She finishes her cigarette, closes the window and returns to her desk. She switches on the fan.

Outside, the thunder that Isabel has been expecting for most of the day rolls through the skies.

'He's given us his files, but we think that we should bring the whole team together. Get Jacinta in too. Lock ourselves in a room and work through what he's given us and see what we can come up with.'

'You both think they're connected?'

'We do, the similarities are there. At the very least, it could be someone who knew of the crimes and has decided to reenact them. Chief,' Isabel says, 'I don't think this killer is going to stay quiet for long and we've got a couple of people we're looking at but no hard evidence. This killer moved on from Carmo Vilar to Paz Santiago very quickly and he's not afraid of going for big public displays. I don't think he plans to stop there.'

'All right. Get the team in. Do what you have to do, but I want regular updates.'

'Yes, Chief, thank you.'

'All right. Out.'

Isabel is almost to the door when something else occurs to her. Voronov notices that she isn't behind him and looks over his shoulder.

She holds up one finger to tell him she'll be right there and turns back into the room, pulling the door ajar.

'Chief?'

Bautista, who had gone back to the work on her desk, glances up.

'I have an odd request.'

'What do you want?' She sits back and folds her hands together on her stomach.

Isabel goes and perches on the arm of one of the chairs. 'Remember the two girls at the first crime scene?'

'The ones who called in Carmo Vilar's death? Yes.'

'If we're able to get some suspects in here, would you okay bringing the younger one in? Sara.'

'Why? She didn't see him. Unless you neglected to tell me a vital piece of information.'

'No, she didn't see him.' It's surprising how hard this still is, even though Chief Bautista has always been someone who had her back. Even despite the way she feels about her Gift at the moment. The way she's able to comfortably work with it as and when she needs to without feeling like she's scrambling for control. And yet, she still hesitates here. 'She's a telepathic Gifted. High-level.'

Bautista waits, patiently, to hear where Isabel is going with this.

'At the crime scene she saw something that I'm hoping she can recognise again.'

'Like what?'

Isabel sighs. 'It's hard to explain, but it has to do with the emotions people have and how they manifest. I'm hoping she can recognise it again or the markers of it if she's in the same building as them.'

Bautista digests that. 'Can't you or Carla do that? Why are you asking me to bring in a little girl to do it for you?'

'It's . . . not quite the same, Chief.' Isabel tries to find the best way to explain it. 'We all perceive these things differently. I could have been standing there right next to Sara and maybe she would have seen red and I would have seen blue. It's different for each of us. Sometimes, if you're high-level enough, you'll recognise the essence of that person in the emotion you saw, even when that emotion is no longer present. Maybe I'd be able to see the emotion, but I could be seeing that in anyone. I wouldn't be able to tell if it was the same one as at the scene because I didn't witness it myself.'

'I don't like bringing in a child to do our work for us.'

'She wouldn't,' Isabel says, quickly, 'and would it really be any different from getting a child in here who said she'd seen the culprit and getting them to identify them in a line-up? It's the same thing, Chief. And of course I'd get permission from her mother first before we did anything. She wouldn't be in the room with anyone we might ask her to look at. The nature of our Gift and her level means that just being close might be enough.'

'I'll consider it,' Bautista says, 'but first, I want that suspect pool firmed up.'

'On it, Chief.'

33

They all pack into the case room, Isabel, Voronov, Carla, Daniel, Jacinta, and they also drag in Felipe and Sansão who have been doing quite a lot of the slower work for them. They've got food and coffee and water and have even taken a few of the fans that were out on the desk floor and brought them in.

Isabel walks over to where they've set up a makeshift tea and coffee station and pours herself the first of what she's sure will be many coffees. 'I want us to lay out what we have. Jacinta, any updates you have for us? We could start with that before we dig into Guerra's files.'

Jacinta stands up. Isabel feels like since she's been back she's only seen Jacinta in her protective gear. It's almost odd to see her friend again in regular clothes. She's the picture of classy simplicity, her voluminous hair pulled back in a neat ponytail, a fitted white top and dark-blue jeans, comfortable trainers.

'Thanks.' She looks around at everyone who's seated and gives a self-deprecating smile. 'I'm feeling a little bit like I'm a class president or something.' She quickly sobers. 'Here's what we have.'

She walks them through the gathered forensic evidence that is listed on the file Carla has meticulously put together.

Forensic Evidence summary:

Murder 1: Carmo Vilar

- Prints from the home
- Rope used to tie victim
- Car
- Victim's clothes

Murder 2: Paz Santiago

- Scuff marks in the home
- Victim's clothes

'I'm not sure we'll be able to use the partial prints we lifted from Carmo's car,' Jacinta says, and accepts the coffee Isabel hands over to her with a thanks. 'I don't think they hold enough information, but we can try. No DNA other than the victim's DNA on the underwear used to silence them. The tapes used to seal their mouths were completely burnt and there was nothing we could lift off that.'

She takes them through Cardoso's findings too.

'An accelerant was used to start both fires. Both times, the point of origin of the fire was on the lower half of the victim's body. With the first one, it was from the feet up. Our killer used gasoline.'

'Which,' Isabel steps in, 'has helped give us some type of time frame for how long our killer was on the scene, which in turn might help us spot when he left. He took his time, in both crime scenes,' Isabel continues, 'with Paz he even took the time to snatch her from her home and take her to the site of the murder where he burned each of the surrounding trees, presumably whilst Paz watched, before setting fire to Paz herself.'

'That's some arrogance,' Daniel mutters. 'No urgency when committing a crime like that in a public place? Nothing to stop anyone wandering over.'

'Which tells us he's becoming reckless,' Isabel says. She looks down at Guerra's documents. 'And I think you only get to the reckless stage when you've had a few practice rounds.'

'His playing around is what meant that Paz was still alive when emergency services arrived,' Jacinta adds, 'autopsy results confirm she died of a heart attack in the end. It's likely that the ordeal was too much for her. She sustained severe burns. Even if she had made it to the hospital I'm not entirely sure she would have survived. Too much of her skin was gone. That's the bad news. However I do have a win for us.'

That gets everyone's attention.

'Look at you all, so well behaved,' she says. She goes to her bag and pulls out a blue plastic document wallet. She removes two pictures and a flimsy paper that looks like a lab report.

One picture is a close-up of the scuff marks in Paz's entryway, and the other is of the footwell of the driver's side of Carmo's car, the pedals to be specific. Voronov pulls the report closer to read through as Isabel leans closer to examine the picture of the pedals to understand what she's looking at. She doesn't see it.

'What is it?' Isabel asks.

'Footwear trace evidence,' Voronov says, 'the same shoes that caused the scuff marks inside Paz's home match the matter Jacinta found on the pedals of Carmo's car.'

'Placing the same killer at both scenes.' Isabel looks at Jacinta. 'Paz's brother. Have you had a chance to examine his boots?'

'I have,' Jacinta says, 'and the work boots weren't a match. But it may be another pair.'

Isabel shakes her head. 'No, those we got voluntarily, but I doubt that he'll give us any more without a warrant. Which we won't be able to get without something more substantial. I want us to walk out of this room with a direction. The chief is expecting it and we need to move this investigation along, not least because we have no idea when he's going to go out there to grab another woman and burn her alive. Let's go, team.'

Jacinta wraps an arm around her and pulls her close. 'Glad to be back and have your favourite team again?'

Isabel lets out a chuckle. 'Would have been happier if we could have just caught up over food or something first.'

'When all this is over,' Jacinta sighs. 'Come on.'

It's probably the first time they've had so many people in here and it makes for a tighter than usual fit but they make it work.

They have a map of the Setúbal area projected on to the wall with the two murders. Carla goes in and, nose down in the map Guerra had worked with during his case, she adds five blue dots to the wall and the ghost of the map on it. Their own murders are represented by two crosses on the same map, one over Moita and one over Alcochete.

Grabbing on to a file they each go over the crime scenes, looking over the pictures Guerra had managed to include. The statements from witnesses and when the victims were last seen.

Silently they start adding to the information around the room. On one of the mobile whiteboards, Voronov adds the names of the victims from 2005, 2006 and 2007.

2005 – 06 Mar	Inês Roberto, 34, stay-at-home mother and wife, Gifted, Setúbal, home garage, severe burns
2006 – 01 Jan	Barbara Nascimento, 45, fitness instructor, Gifted, Setúbal, home, suffocation
2006 – 24 May	Katia Ludovico, 24, midwife, Gifted, Palmela, abandoned factory, immolation
2006 – 15 Oct	Milagre de Amada, 38, boutique sales assistant, Gifted, Baixa da Banheira, Supermarket parking lot, set alight inside car, immolation
2007 – 21 Feb	Anita Gascon, 15, student, Gifted, Parque Natural da Arrabida, shack, smoke inhalation

'All the victims were stripped naked in this case too,' Daniel says, 'though he wasn't as neat about it. Some clothes were found at the scene and others weren't. All jewellery removed but again, some found at the scene and others not.'

Jacinta frowns, scooting forward and pulling the bag with the rosary closer to her to look at it and Isabel locates the file containing the profile that Guerra had been so disdainful of. It was tucked into the back of a case overview file.

'Assuming these two are connected,' Carla says, tapping her pencil on her open notebook, 'then it has to be someone who could have been strong enough to be a threat to fully grown women. Or benign enough to be able to get close to them without frightening them. Now with the last two crimes, he managed to get Carmo in her car and Paz, going by Jacinta's report, walked all the way from her home to the square. Threatening them with a weapon?'

Something that scared them enough – or at least Paz, enough – that she didn't attempt to make a run for it on the walk over.

Just like picking public places to commit his crimes. Another display of arrogance. Or insanity. Probably both.

'My point is,' Carla says, as if brushing that aside for the moment, 'it's been nineteen years. Carrying the gasoline, getting away from the crime scene quickly enough not to be noticed – he'd still have to maintain a good level of fitness, but also the likelihood of him being very young in 2005 would work against him.'

It's not unheard of for teenage killers to exist. If it had been just the fifteen-year-old victim then maybe Isabel could buy him being younger, but the fifteen-year-old had been his last murder before he disappeared. Up until then they'd all been over their twenties. Most women wouldn't be intimidated by one teenager. But it becomes a different story if they're armed or look older than their age. But even in 2005 he was already showing signs of greater sophistication in his crimes.

'What are you thinking?' Isabel asks, absently flicking through the report, about to start reading it.

'I'd put him at late thirties, early forties, maybe? In the present?'

That would match up.

Isabel sits down and drags her coffee over and opens up the profiler's report on Guerra's killer. It's a lengthy one.

Criminal Profile Report: *Subject A (Unidentified Male)*
Offence Type: *Serial Murder (Pyromania, Femicide, Ritualistic Elements)*
Victimology: *Female, Perceived as 'Promiscuous' or 'Morally Corrupt', Gifted*
Crime Scene Locations: *Vicinity of Churches, Symbolic Spaces of Religious Significance*
Method of Murder: *Immolation, Victims Found Naked, Burned Post-Mortem or Alive*

Isabel pauses there.

Vicinity of churches.

Carmo had been murdered near the church in Moita and there had also been a small chapel that looked directly on to the square where Paz was murdered. How had they missed that detail?

Isabel sets the report down on her lap. She looks up at the map.

'The report mentions that the locations of the 2005–07 murders were all near religious places. Can we pull the map up on a laptop or something? I want to see what's around.'

Isabel relaxes her grip on the pages when she realises the pages are crinkling under her fingers.

> *Subject A is a highly organised and methodical killer with deep-seated psychological motivations. His choice of victims, modus operandi, and crime scene locations suggest a blend of religious fanaticism, misogyny, and personal trauma. His murders display both symbolic and ritualistic elements, with each killing being a reflection of his complex internal belief system.*
>
> *Subject A's crime scenes are focused near churches or religious sites. The subject may have a conflicted or obsessive relationship with religion. Churches serve as symbolic spaces of purity, judgement, and salvation in his mind. He could be performing what he perceives as a form of divine justice or cleansing. This individual is likely to be outwardly religious, possibly quiet and controlled, but harbouring intense inner conflict and resentment.*

Like Voronov had said. Punishment and purification.

> *There may be a history of trauma involving a female figure in his life, possibly a mother or romantic partner who he believed was unfaithful or corrupt. This trauma likely triggered his obsessive fixation on women who he believes are immoral or sexually dangerous. His inability to control the*

actions of this female figure may have led to a broader desire to punish women he views as similar.

Isabel lowers the report.

Lopes fits those final definitions. But to have been inactive for almost two decades? Another question is why now? Whoever this is, why such a lull between the murders?

'Guerra said there was a little coverage on the murders back then,' Isabel says, 'there should be clippings in the box.' She stands and looks over the remaining folders that people haven't grabbed on to yet. 'He said they kept any details that only the killer would know out of the press. So a copycat wouldn't have known about the proximity to churches,' she muses.

She sees a sepia-toned corner sticking out from a white folder that has become yellowed with time and drags it closer.

'Aleks,' she says, 'have a read of the profiler's report.' She taps it before sliding it across the table to him. 'It's not looking good for our favourite priest.'

She leafs through the photocopied newspaper cuttings, wondering if there's more online—

Isabel slides one page the rest of the way out, eyes glued to it.

'Aleks,' she says.

He glances up from where he's perusing the report she's just shoved his way. 'What is it?'

'Look at this.' She takes the page over to him and lays it out flat.

It's a press photo at the scene of Inês Roberto's murder. It's a wide shot and shows the open garage door, the blackened walls of the garage and neighbours crowding around the house being kept back by the firefighters and the police entering the scene.

She taps her finger on the picture of one person in particular.

'Is it me or is that a young Investigator Cardoso?' she asks.

There, in a fireman's protective gear and looking several years younger, is Investigator Cardoso with a team of firefighters.

34

It's just after nine in the morning on Monday when Isabel and Carla walk into the fire station. Her sister's wedding is taking place in four hours but there's no way they'd be leaving this to another day. Speaking with Cardoso as soon as possible takes precedence over attending a wedding she wouldn't even be going to if it weren't for family pressure.

Her sister's lucky. Although the rain from yesterday continued through the night, this morning arrived with only a few clouds and with predictions of a slightly overcast sky, but no more rain.

Last night they'd agreed before heading home that Lopes is still one of their main persons of interest. But what about the boots? Isauro definitely had a pair that could have made those scuffs, and also exhibited some of the traits in the report. A hatred for women, need for control . . . He'd been in a shared space with both the victims, would have had access to rope. But there was nothing connecting him to Carmo.

Jacinta's interest had been piqued by the match that Guerra had bagged, and she'd taken that away with her along with the report on it. Voronov and Daniel were heading into the station to finish up with Paz's work files. They'd finally managed to get into her laptop.

'Hello?' Isabel calls out. 'Anybody in?'

Carla is sweeping her eyes over the giant space as Isabel's voice echoes. 'There are definitely people in here,' she says.

Isabel nods. 'Hmm, I can sense them too. But where?'

The fire engine takes up a huge chunk of space in the middle of the garage floor and there's a door to their left.

Despite working in emergency services, this is the first time Isabel can remember being inside a fire station. The closest she'd got to this was when she was a little kid, and the firefighters had come to the school to talk to them all.

'Through here, maybe,' Isabel says and without checking she pushes the door open only to jump half a step back with a hissed-out 'Merda' at the loud bark that greets her.

'What's going on, boy?' The call comes from further inside the fire station and Isabel can hear the steps rushing closer.

Carla clasps a hand over Isabel's shoulder. 'Are you okay?' she asks, peering around her at Kuma who has gone from barking to wagging his tail the second he realises he's met these people before.

Heart still going a mile a minute, Isabel presses a hand to her chest and breathes out in relief. 'Yes, sorry, that startled me.' She drops down to her haunches and reaches out a careful hand to Kuma. 'Sorry, gorgeous,' she says, 'I think we both scared each other.' She smiles when Kuma tucks his huge head under her palm, happily panting and doing full-body wriggles that remind Isabel of her own babies at home.

Then the captain comes into view. He's got his phone in his hand and is red-cheeked.

He blinks at them both. 'Inspectors, sorry. I heard Kuma barking.'

Isabel gives Kuma's head one pat. 'No, no, we're sorry. We did call out but I don't think you heard us. We don't want to disturb you for very long but is Investigator Cardoso around? We need to speak with him.'

He nods and then seems to remember he's still holding a phone. 'Sorry, my wife—' He puts the phone back to his ear to tell his wife he'll just be a second, covers the mouthpiece on his phone.

'He should be in soon, we're just having breakfast. Why don't you both join us?'

Carla glances sideways at Isabel.

Isabel shrugs and smiles at Horta. 'As long as we're not disturbing you?'

'Not at all, come this way.'

They follow him through the fire station and despite herself, Isabel can't help but peer around as they go, taking in the fireman's poles and the fire engines and suppressing the little spark of childlike fascination.

Kuma trots after them.

They take a noisy set of stairs up to the first floor, single file behind Horta, Kuma's tail wagging excitedly the entire time.

Horta stops at the last door at the end of the corridor and laughter and jeering can be heard coming from inside. He holds the door open for them and there's a pause in the liveliness inside. 'I've got to finish this call but go ahead, the team will make you coffee.'

They say their thanks again and step inside to find the five other members of the squad clustered around two tables in the small but serviceable kitchen. Kuma obediently trots over to his bed in the corner of the room. One of the guys is sitting across from one of the female firefighters, the two of them in the middle of a card game. The other three, two more guys and another woman with thick, plaited hair all the way down her back, are eating their breakfast.

'It's the inspectors!' one of the guys eating says, way louder than necessary.

Amused, Isabel comes the rest of the way inside, Carla following suit. 'Your captain said you'd make us coffee.'

'Of course, of course, take a seat.'

The team introduce themselves to Isabel and Carla properly whilst getting them a coffee and making space for them at the table.

'How's the case going?' one of them asks.

'It's going,' Isabel says, 'but seeing as we're here bothering you on a Monday it could be going better.'

'Yeah. That last one was a little . . . we knew the victim.'

Isabel blinks in surprise and glances at Carla, sees that she's also looking at him in shock. 'Paz Santiago?' Isabel asks.

He nods, his mouth closed tightly for a moment and his chin dimpling; earlier he'd introduced himself as Ivo. 'We rotate with the other squads on the fair. We didn't know her well or anything, but we'd see her around because she organised the whole thing. She was there for every fair. She seemed like a nice lady. We weren't at the last one – kind of wish we had been now.' The edges of his mouth wobble a bit before he manages to control himself.

Isabel exchanges a look with Carla.

In his bed Kuma perks up, sitting up straight, and his tail starts swinging fast in excitement.

'Ah, Cardoso must have arrived.'

Cardoso, having just reached the top of the stairs, stops in surprise when he sees them sitting comfortably with the rest of the team.

'Inspectors,' he says. 'You've started out early.' He's got his hands tucked into his pockets and glasses perched on his nose.

'We wanted to speak with you if that's all right.'

He narrows his eyes at them as if trying to figure out what they want. Then he motions them over. 'My office is over here.'

Cardoso is quiet as he stares down at the photo Isabel has set in front of him. Carla stands by the door, observing, and Isabel is in the seat next to his.

'Why didn't you say anything to us?' Isabel asks.

'I didn't even know this had been taken,' he says, pulling it closer to him. The lines of his face look grave under the fire-station lighting.

'Cardoso,' Isabel prompts, leaning forward and peering at him. 'Why didn't you tell us?'

He crosses one leg over the other and leans an arm over the back of his chair, looking from Isabel to Carla. 'It was a long time ago. A very long time ago.'

'Nineteen years to be exact.'

'Yes, exactly. And the case was closed.'

'Because the deaths stopped, not because the culprit was caught. You must have seen the similarities when you showed up at that first scene.'

'I did my job.'

'And you could have helped us do ours better if you had just told us about the similarities. What was it? Were you worried about something?'

'No,' Cardoso narrows his eyes on her, 'why? Are you thinking just because I was there that I had something to do with it?'

Isabel doesn't respond.

He stares at her, incredulous. Then he laughs. 'I don't believe this. A little girl like you having the nerve to speak to me like this.'

'I think we already established that calling me Inspector will do. What about the others? Were you present at the other fires between 2005 and 2007?'

'No. I attended the garage fire. That was the only one.'

'Are you sure about that? Or will you only confirm it if we find another picture of you at the scene?'

'That was the only one.'

'All right.' Isabel folds her hands on her lap. 'Then tell me what happened.'

He looks back down at the picture, like he's oddly fascinated by it.

'It was the first fire I attended as a captain.'

So definitely memorable.

'I'd already seen enough. We'd lost people before.' He's going back in time, thinking it through. 'This was a new one to me. Bastard tied her up. They put her there on purpose and lit her on fire. Her three children were in the living room, watching cartoons. The smoke had started spreading and they were all passed out after they'd inhaled it long enough. Lucky. I like to think they didn't hear their mother scream.'

He drags over his mug of coffee, a wide sturdy thing that looks closer to a soup mug than a coffee mug, and takes a gulp of it. He meets Isabel's eyes before he continues to speak. He doesn't look away once.

'I didn't deal with it very well,' he says, 'had a few too many drinks that night. Broke down in front of my colleagues. They sent me to the doctor to get myself checked, make sure I had no screws loose. They put me on medical leave for a month. Left my team without me for a long while. Almost didn't get the captaincy back.'

She doesn't see any lies, can't feel anything embellished or fake about what he's saying.

'That's all I did. I wasn't associated with the rest of that case. I heard about it after. That there were more girls killed in the same manner. Then they closed the case. But there was none of this, none of the clothes being taken off and set aside, or them being taken and displayed in public like that.'

'Do you understand how this looks?' Isabel asks him. 'You've withheld information from us regarding an active investigation. You were at the scene.'

He stands up. 'Young lady, I am too old for this. Are you really suggesting I had something to do with it?'

'No, I'm not. But there's a connection that I can't just ignore so I'm going to ask you to come into the precinct to answer a couple of questions. If you could give us access to your home, I'd appreciate that too. Do everything voluntarily, sir,' Isabel says, 'it will just look like you're coming in to give us additional information if everything checks out and there's no suspicion. Your team won't have to know, neither will anyone else. You're just assisting us with the investigation.'

'You make it sound like you're doing me a favour.'

'Right now,' Isabel says, 'we are.'

35

The wedding ceremony is well attended, the church packed with people from both the bride's side and the groom's.

Isabel opted out of sitting at the front with the rest of the family. It's not something she would have felt comfortable with, so she'd sat further back, with Voronov looking even more attractive than usual in his suit.

The only highlight for her had been watching her brother preside over the ceremony, even if she could pick up the bitter-sweetness he was feeling right then. She doesn't think marrying a younger sibling to someone you don't respect is an easy thing to do. Still, Sebastião does it all with a smile on his face and no one can tell a thing.

At the front, she'd glimpsed her mother sitting with her aunty, their hands clasped together and tears in their eyes that hadn't stopped as they'd both watched Rita walking up the aisle.

Isabel listened to their vows with her head held high.

People often compliment the bride, tell her that she's glowing. The term would've fitted Rita perfectly. Happiness gathered around her frame where she stood at the front of the church before all the people in her life. It manifested in a halo of brightness around her that, despite everything, had made Isabel's eyes prickle with the threat of tears.

'You okay?' Voronov asks now.

The bride and groom had their first dance long ago and now that everyone has been well fed, the dancefloor at the centre of the small venue is packed with guests dancing under the strobe lighting.

From their table tucked into a corner of the room, Isabel can see her mother and aunty at the centre of it all with Rita. All three of them are smiling.

She hasn't seen her mother and aunty smiling like that in a long time.

'Yeah,' she says, and shifts in her seat to face him. 'We were in such a rush earlier I didn't even get to tell you how good you look.' She reaches out and smooths her fingers over the lapel of his suit jacket. 'Very nice.'

'I didn't forget to tell you,' he points out and drinks the rest of the champagne in his flute, reaching for her with his free hand and sliding his fingers through hers.

Her smile widens. 'No, you didn't.'

He'd been very appreciative of the view when she'd pulled the gate closed behind her and stepped down in the satiny-soft yellow dress with its halter neck and skirt that fell all the way to her feet.

She'd like it better if they were all dressed up to head out on their own date instead of being here.

The song changes to something mellow, prompting some people to return to their table.

'How about one dance,' she says, 'and then we'll have done our duty and we head out?' She stands, tugging on his hand, eyebrows raised in challenge.

He allows her to pull him on to the dance floor. 'Don't complain if I ruin your shoes.'

Isabel turns to face him and winds her arms around his neck. 'You can just sway,' she says, pleased when he pulls her close and does as she says.

Pressed close she relaxes against him as they move together.

Over his shoulder she sees her brother dancing with their aunty. He catches her eye and smiles, raising a smile from her too.

'What do you want to do when we leave?' Voronov murmurs against her temple.

'What we didn't get to do the other night.'

He chuckles. 'Is now too soon?'

Grinning, Isabel steps back. 'As I'm sure you're already very aware, I don't need convincing here.'

Wrapping her hand around his wrist, she leads the way off the dance floor and to their table to collect their things. She signals to Sebastião as she goes, to let him know she's heading off and gets a thumbs-up in understanding.

He'll let her mother and aunty know she's left.

Outside, the air is still tinged with the green scent of freshly mowed grass. The venue is surrounded by well-tended flowers and trees, whimsical paths paving the way from the domed glass building of the venue out to the main gate that leads to the parking lot.

They walk to their car, passing a few guests that have gathered to smoke outside. Isabel's heels click and the murmur of outdoor conversations follows them, with the music from the reception muted.

Voronov unlocks the car and Isabel gets in. She's looking forward to getting the heels off.

She reaches into the back for the bag she'd tossed on to the back seats at the start of the evening with her trainers inside it.

'Yours or mine?' Voronov asks as he starts the car.

'Yours,' Isabel says, 'you're closer.'

She's just slipped off her heels when the sound of someone shouting her name filters in through the closed windows of the car.

She jerks her head up, leaning forward to look through the windshield.

Sebastião is running towards the car, waving an arm.

Voronov cuts the engine.

Isabel opens the door, and comes out, uncaring that she's barefoot on the gravel of the parking lot.

The look on Sebastião's face has her hurrying over to him even as he skids to a stop in front of her.

She grabs on to his arm. 'What's wrong?'

'It's tia Maria,' he pants as he drags in air, chest heaving from having run over to reach her, 'Rita found her in the bathroom, she was huddled in a corner screaming. Michael's checking her now.' He drops his voice lower. 'She was tearing at her hair and crying for us to get him out.'

Isabel feels a chill down her spine. She grabs her trainers and shoves her dirty feet into them. 'Let's go.'

When they walk into the lounge room outside of the bathroom proper, it's been cleared and they're greeted by Michael. They'd passed tia Simone on their way in; she'd been assuring guests that all was well.

They must have overheard something.

Michael glances over her shoulder at where Voronov is standing behind her with her brother. He turns his attention back to her. 'She's calmed down,' he tells them, looking a little pale in his wedding suit but otherwise in perfect control. 'Rita is sitting with her. She wanted to get back out there but we managed to convince her to rest for a little. She was asking for you though.'

Isabel nods. 'All right.'

Inside, her mother is sitting on a burgundy velvet seat with Rita as close to her as the large white skirts of her wedding dress will allow. She has a glass of water in her hands and is telling Rita she's fine.

Her mother looks up as Isabel walks in. 'Ah, you're here.'

'How are you feeling, mãe?' She gathers the skirt of her dress in one hand and lowers herself in front of her.

She reaches a hand out to Isabel and the small gesture makes Isabel's chest squeeze tight.

'I'm fine,' she says, 'but your brother and sister don't believe me and are making me rest for a little while.'

'Ai, tia,' Sebastião says, 'it's just for a little bit.'

She shakes her head. 'But I'm fine! Michael checked me over and said I'm all right.'

'Mãe,' Rita says, her voice a little choked but calm for the most part, 'you couldn't stand up, we had to help you up off the floor.'

Maria just huffs but doesn't deny it.

Isabel takes advantage of the moment and in the blink of an eye, she's surrounded by walls and walls of her mother's thoughts and memories, all wrapped up in her essence. She looks past it all, searching instead for that hole, the one he made, the one he used to get into her mind just like he did Isabel's.

Even though she'd known what had happened, what Gabriel had done, she'd never looked for herself. Hadn't wanted to cross that line. But if she's going to try to solve this, she needs to understand how bad it is.

It's hidden so well that she almost glances right past it. But it's there. A small, furled thing, just like the one in Isabel's head. The only difference is Isabel has been able to isolate the one in her mind, corner it and monitor every move it makes. It does mean that sometimes she doesn't get as good a sleep as she'd like to but she can manage that for now.

But she doesn't know how to do that for someone else, hasn't been able to fine-tune her Gift that way.

So when she sees that little ball of malice, dormant right now, nothing but a speck in someone else's mind, she has to hold back sheer rage at seeing it touch someone who is a part of her life, someone she deeply loves, despite how much that love hurts her. It makes her skin crawl seeing it there and the visceral need to rip it out rises up in her so fast she has to shut her eyes and cut herself off.

'Isabel?'

She blinks her eyes open and finds everyone's eyes trained on her. 'Sorry.' She squeezes her mother's hand. 'I think they're right. Let's just sit here and rest for a bit, okay?'

Her mother closes her eyes and rests her head in her hands. 'Sorry. My head . . .'

'I'll get her something for her head,' Michael says, 'I think she'll be okay.' He flicks a look at Isabel. 'I know you were on your way out, we can keep an eye on her and we'll make sure we get her home.'

Next to their mother, Rita stiffens for a moment but then plasters a reassuring smile on her face. 'Yes. Don't worry. We'll keep an eye on her.'

Isabel's gaze drifts back to her mother's face. Her eyes are still closed.

She reaches out a hand and gently cups her cheek.

Her mother looks at her then, holds Isabel's palm to her cheek and pats it gently.

'Both of my girls looked beautiful tonight. It's been a good day.'

She seems oblivious to the sombreness that has swept over the room.

It's an hour later when Sebastião walks both Isabel and Voronov back to their car.

The reception is still in full swing with both Michael and Rita in the middle of their guests. Tia Simone had stayed with her mother.

'Don't worry,' he says, 'I'm going to take her home. We'll keep an eye on her.'

Isabel nods. 'All right.' Her voice comes out tight.

Voronov tugs her into his side, wrapping his arm around her.

'I know someone who can help her,' Isabel forces the words out, 'they helped out in an old case of mine. The one that started all this. And then . . . she really will be back to normal.'

He doesn't ask her why she hadn't shared this information earlier. There's no judgement in the silence he allows her.

It makes Isabel sigh and turn to look at him. He has their dad's eyes and his kindness too. She feels the trembling of her smile but pretends she doesn't. It's not there if she doesn't allow it to be. 'You're a good brother. I should tell you that more often.'

Sebastião picks up her hand and squeezes it. 'You'll make the choice that's right for you, maninha. I'm not going to judge you for it. No matter what you decide.' He glances at Voronov, a question in his eyes.

'I've got her.'

Isabel sighs and leans in to kiss her brother's cheek. 'Stop, you two. I can look after myself. Call me if anything else happens, okay?'

Sebastião nods. 'I will.'

They say goodnight and Isabel watches him walk back to the venue, the music still playing and the laughter ringing out like nothing had happened.

Voronov presses his mouth to her temple. 'Let's go.'

She nods and for once doesn't roll her eyes when he helps her into the car.

36

They roll into work a little later than usual on the next day.

She'd woken up to a text from her brother saying her mother had gone to sleep right away and everything was okay and that had made her feel a little better after the restless night she'd spent.

She'd been quiet as Voronov had driven them both to work that morning and he'd let her be, which she appreciates.

They're still quiet as they make their way to their desks when Carla pops her head out of their case room.

'You're here,' she says and beckons them over; there's a note of urgency in her voice. 'You got here just in time. We found something.'

Isabel pulls off her sunglasses and they bypass their desks altogether.

Inside the room, cardboard boxes have been neatly lined up and labelled, proof of the work the team had been doing the past couple of days as they'd sifted through Paz's things.

Daniel glances up from the table where he's sitting with a laptop open in front of him. It isn't his so it must be Paz's work laptop.

His expression is serious.

He doesn't even greet them before he stands and turns the laptop to face them.

'What is it?' Isabel drops her bag on the floor as both she and Voronov lean forward to look.

It's a very simple email exchange.

One email is dated last month, from Carmo Vilar to Paz Santiago. The email details her request to Paz for an amendment of the usual fair floor plan. In it she's asking the fair organisers to change her usual spot next to the church stall. It goes on to detail personal reasons for the change.

Paz's response followed a day later telling her not to worry and that the change has been made and Padre Lopes has been notified and there had been no issues.

That's all. Both the emails are short and to the point, revealing no particular hint of a personal relationship between the two women. But . . .

Isabel straightens up and looks at them.

'This proves Lopes knew exactly who Paz Santiago was,' Daniel says.

'And not only that,' Carla says, gesturing to the laptop, 'I checked the plans from previous fairs.' She heads to a pile of papers set aside and clipped together. 'I printed them off. Paz had them stored in her organisation folder, the plans for each of the fairs, the ones in Alhos Vedros and the ones in Moita. The layout is a little different for each one but in every single one, the church's stall is always next to Carmo's.'

Voronov steps forward and takes the offered papers, leafing through them. When he finishes, he glances back at the laptop.

'So Carmo wasn't the only one who said no to him,' Voronov says.

'Most likely,' Carla says. 'He'd established a pattern of inserting himself into Carmo's life. He definitely would have protested and tried to maintain the status quo.'

Isabel sinks on to the corner of the table, bracing herself with a hand on the surface for balance. 'He said he broke up the altercation that day,' she says. 'But if he's already pissed at Paz for her interference, then how much did he actually try to interfere when he saw Isauro getting violent with Paz?'

And then Paz shows up dead.

It's a thin connection between the two women but it's still a connection. And potentially a connection between two very controlling and resentful men. At least one of whom has an – alleged – history of violence.

Both are from the area and with a historical dislike for Gifted and the correct age group to align with the 2005, 2006 and 2007 timeline for Guerra.

Old enough that they could be copycats.

Old enough that one of them could be the original killer.

Isabel glances up. 'I think we bring the two of them in here, both at the same time, and we'll bring Sara in too. This might be it.'

37

In the precinct, they have a room that's kept especially for when they have to interview children. It's one of the nicer rooms in a building that hasn't had a lick of paint in years and where complaints are always being made about the equipment available.

Sara walks in with her sister, hand in hand, eyes wide as she takes in the ceiling, painted with a fantastical theme of dragons, unicorns and mermaids. There are bean bag chairs and tables with games and Lego, even an entire section with dolls on another side of the room which almost immediately grabs her attention.

Carla stays back outside with their mother.

'Do you like the room, Sara?' Isabel asks, crouching down to her level.

'Yes, this is fun! Can we play with anything we like?'

Isabel smiles. 'You can. And like I said, you won't have to leave this room. I just want you to pay attention to the emotions all around you, okay? But not right away, I'll let you know when. And then, once you're done, I get you and Savana and your mum some ice cream as a thank-you. How does that sound?'

'Yes, that's fine,' she says, clearly bestowing her approval on Isabel.

Cute. Isabel pats her head and stands. 'All right. Then you guys make yourself comfortable and I'll be by to check on you in a little bit, okay?'

'Okay!' Sara says and takes off after the dolls she's been eyeing up since they entered the room.

Savana watches her sister. She's moved to sit down on a bright red squat chair in the corner and has her arms wrapped around herself. On the walk from the entrance to the precinct to this room, her face had lost colour, and Isabel can see the circles under her eyes from the lack of sleep she too has been dealing with.

'Savana?' Isabel says, softly.

Savana glances at her. Her dark eyes are serious, and she doesn't say anything.

'Nothing will happen to you both, I promise. Your mum is outside, and she'll come in with you guys too. She's just speaking with my colleague so she understands what will happen next. Is that okay?'

Savana gives her a sharp nod and then returns to watching her sister.

Shit.

Isabel leaves the room.

Like she'd said, the girl's mother is right outside the one-way mirror and watching both her children, speaking with Carla. When Isabel steps out and closes the door behind her, she walks over immediately. Worry is pouring off her in waves. Isabel doesn't blame her.

'Are they okay?'

'They're fine.' Isabel smiles reassuringly. 'Sara is happy with the toys, but Savana is feeling quite apprehensive. Are you all right to sit inside with them both? I'm going to go and check if my colleagues are ready. Is that okay?'

'Yes. Thank you, I'll sit inside with them.'

'All right.'

Carla nods at Isabel to give her the go-ahead and then takes the mum inside with her.

They bring in Padre Lopes and Isauro Santiago. They don't have enough evidence to bring them in under any charges, so they get them to come in for further interviewing.

Voronov gives her a nod before going into the interview room himself to interrogate Lopes. Carla has already headed into her designated interrogation room with Santiago when Isabel returns to the quiet room.

The girls are sitting together, working on building a Lego house when Isabel lets herself back in, and their mother is sitting quietly in a corner.

Sara's glossy head of hair pops up when she hears the door close and she smiles when she sees Isabel coming in. 'You're back!'

'Was I gone too long?' Isabel smiles and goes to sit beside them.

'Nope.' She shakes her head, making her ponytail swing hard enough that the end bounces off her cheeks.

'Good. So.' Isabel reaches out and gently closes her hands over Sara's. 'We're ready now. Would you be willing to take a look around now and see if you recognise that red, hunger feeling you felt the night we met?'

'I just have to see if I recognise it?' Sara asks.

'Yes. Just try and look hard for me.'

'What about if I don't find it?'

'Then that's okay. We finish here, go and get ice cream with your mum and sister and then you go home.'

Sara dips her head. 'You promise you won't be upset?'

Isabel nudges her chin back up. 'How about you look at how I'm feeling right now? Can you tell if I'm telling the truth when I say I won't be upset?'

Sara looks at her and squints. Savana has walked over to stand next to her mum who is holding her close; both of them look startled at Isabel inviting Sara to use her Gift to see how she's feeling, to gauge the truth of her words.

Isabel hopes that seeing what Sara is capable of doing for real won't change the way they feel about their daughter and sibling.

It's one thing being told your child is Gifted, but especially with telepathy, it's hard to accept it because you don't see anything really change. In this situation neither Savana nor their mother is allowed to look away and pretend it's not there.

After a second Sara is smiling up at Isabel. 'Truth.'

'That's right,' she says and brushes the little girl's hair back from her face, 'so you don't have to worry. Are you ready?'

'Yes!'

'Okay. Take a look now.'

It's an odd feeling seeing this from the perspective of an outsider.

Isabel knows how this feels, like static raising the hairs on your arms when you allow your senses to expand and capture something not yours. An emotion, a thought, a memory. She's never really been on the other side of it. At least not knowingly.

Sara doesn't close her eyes. But one second, she's looking right at Isabel and the next second she's looking through her. Seeing with her Gift and looking beyond them all.

A second later she scrunches her face in concentration and does a slow turn, eyes looking up at the ceiling and then back down, as if sweeping the floor. Then she pauses and looks back to one spot. She lifts her hand and points.

Isabel feels her heart thud in her chest, hard.

'Sara?' she says, keeping her tone quiet. 'Do you see something?'

'It's there. But it's angrier.'

Isabel licks her lips and swallows. 'Sara, if I hold your hand and stay with you the whole way, will you guide me to where you can see it?'

Sara, eyes still spaced out, like she's not in the room, nods.

'Right, I'm going to hold your hand now, sweetie, and we're going to walk together. You just focus on guiding me to where you see it, okay?'

'Okay, Isabel. And then ice cream?' she says.

'And then ice cream.'

Isabel takes her hand and motions for Sara's mother and sister to stay put as she slowly guides them to the door and leads them out into the corridor.

'Do you still see it, Sara?'

'Yes, he's moving.'

‘Can you still follow?’

‘I think so.’

Isabel gives her hand a gentle squeeze. ‘Lead the way.’

Sara begins to walk, eyes locked on the trace of emotion she’s found. Isabel motions for people to move out of their way as they go; she doesn’t want them to impede their progress.

Unexpectedly though, when they reach the turn in the corridor that would take them in the direction of the interview rooms, Sara turns in the opposite direction.

Isabel stoops so that she can speak a little closer to Sara, not wanting to startle her, walking awkwardly alongside her. ‘Are you still following it, Sara?’

‘Yes.’

‘You said it’s moving?’

‘Hm-hm.’ She takes them to the stairs leading down to the main reception and Isabel’s heart speeds up. She looks around to see the faces of those around them. The station is busy as always, with officers walking in with people they’ve picked up doing something they shouldn’t, with others arriving and hounding the front desk to make a complaint or file a report. It’s filled to the brim with police officers, especially at this time of day. But Sara keeps going right down the stairs until they’re walking out on to the pavement and the busy road outside.

That’s where she stops, on the steps of the precinct. This time she’s looking around and around her, and the focus that had kept her eyes vacant begins to dissipate. When she looks up at Isabel, she blinks a couple of times.

‘Sorry, Isabel. I lost him.’

Isabel wraps an arm around her shoulders. ‘That’s okay,’ she says, ‘are you sure he came this way, Sara?’

Sara nods. ‘Yes. I walked towards it like you said I should. But it was moving.’

‘And he wasn’t closer to where we were inside?’ Isabel asks.

‘No, this is where it was.’

Isabel gets down to Sara's eye level. 'You did very well, Sara. Thank you. How about we go and get your mum and your sister and I buy you all ice cream now?'

Sara grins.

'It's not a total loss,' Isabel says, 'we're pulling footage of the reception area and the front of the precinct as we speak. So we might still find something.'

She's throwing a bottle from hand to hand, sitting on one of the desks in the case room which has filled out in terms of information since their emergency session the other night.

'Did we get any more out of those two in the interview rooms?' she asks.

Everyone is on their best behaviour and trying to pretend Chief Bautista isn't standing there, back to the closed door, hands in her pockets and puffing out cigarette smoke like a chimney.

'Not much,' Carla says, 'but Santiago really resented being brought in like that. Even worse, he really hated that he was being grilled by a Gifted woman on top of it all.' She touches her hand to the front of her throat and rubs there, as if attempting to get rid of a phantom sensation. 'He says he doesn't know Carmo Vilar, was there for his sister and that he doesn't remember Padre Lopes. He denies he got physical with Paz at the fair.'

That last part is easy enough to disprove when an entire fair of people had seen it.

'Nothing new from Lopes,' Voronov says, 'he admits to getting the call from Paz but says he accepted the new arrangements without any issues.'

'So why didn't he tell us?' Isabel asks.

'He didn't remember it,' Voronov says.

Daniel scoffs. 'Yeah right. For someone who preaches to others for a living he seems to like lying a little too much for his own good.'

Chief Bautista, seemingly having heard enough, straightens away from the door. 'Sounds like you all have more work to do.'

She opens the door but stops before walking through it. 'How's the little girl?'

Isabel sighs and folds her arms. 'She's fine. She enjoyed her ice cream.'

Bautista nods. 'Good.'

'Chief, can we free someone up to keep eyes on her house?'

Bautista scoffs. 'Reis, I'm sure your time away hasn't made you forget that my department is *not* swimming in money.'

'How could I forget,' Isabel asks, 'when the ceiling is still looking like it's going to cave in on our heads at any moment.'

Bautista narrows her eyes. 'Make your case.'

'She did sense the killer nearby.'

'Which we can't be sure is accurate.'

'And we can't be sure it isn't. What if he's aware of what we're doing here? Or aware that she can potentially lead us to him? This is someone who has proven that he is not afraid of risk. And Sara is Gifted. Let's not forget that he murdered a fifteen year old.'

'And who exactly do you think is free to be on babysitting duty, Isabel?'

'No one. I know we're all busy but—'

'We can do it,' Felipe says from the back, putting his hand up, 'I agree with Isabel, Chief. And if he does show up and we're there, it might even be a good thing. We might have something we can take forward.'

Bautista looks at Felipe's determined face and at Isabel. 'Fine. But get this thing moving,' she says, looking at them all, 'and that's for all of you.'

She leaves the room, closing the door behind her, and it's like the room empties of all the tension.

'Thanks, Felipe,' Isabel says.

'No problem,' he says, 'don't really want another kid getting hurt on our watch if we can help it, you know?' The first case they'd worked for the team had ended badly for both Felipe and Sansão, who'd got seriously hurt whilst on duty looking after a runaway teen helping them with a case. It had been gruesome and left a deep impression on them all.

'All right.' Isabel groans and rubs her hands over her eyes. 'It's been a long day and we haven't really stopped for a while. I vote we take an earlier one today, rest up, get back at it tomorrow.'

38

Isabel jerks awake so hard that she tumbles off the sofa.

Her elbow bangs into something sharp and the pain robs her of her breath. As she purses her lips to breathe through the pain and sits back on her knees on the floor, her head is nudged as her two dogs immediately start snuffling at her, big heads bumping at her as they seek reassurance that she's okay.

'I'm fine,' she groans, even as she cradles her elbow, 'I'm fine.'

Her living room is dark as she scans it for a sign of her phone. That's what had woken her up.

She'd got home, just had enough energy to heat up leftovers and then she'd sat on her sofa like a lifeless body, eyes unseeing on the TV as she'd slowly made her way through her meal. Something about the day had left her drained. In the end she'd ended up starfishing as much as her sofa would allow and falling asleep right there and then.

There's a ghostly light coming from beneath her sofa and she dips her head to peer beneath it, the vibrations of her phone and the ring tone immediately becoming louder. She sees her phone there, sliding across the floor a little bit more with each ring.

Shaking her arm in hopes of getting rid of the pain faster, she grabs her phone and manoeuvres herself back on to the sofa, not bothering to check the number as she picks up.

'Reis,' she says, plopping her head in her hands and rubbing her eyes. What time is it even?

'Isabel?'

The whisper that comes across the phone line surprises her.

Sara.

'Sara?' She sits up, bracing her hand on the sofa. 'Is everything okay?'

'There's a man outside our door.'

Isabel feels a cold wave roll over her body. 'Sweetheart, are you sure?'

'Yes,' Sara's whisper is loud.

Isabel pulls the phone away. Five past midnight. 'Sara, where's your sister?'

'She's by the door. She told me to call you.' She falls silent and Isabel can hear the little quick breaths she's taking. 'We're scared. Can you come?'

She's already standing and hurrying into her bedroom, slapping the light on and scanning the floor for where she'd kicked her trainers off earlier in the evening. 'Of course, sweetheart, I'm coming. Don't open the door, okay? Is the chain on the door?'

'Mm-hm.'

'Good.' She finds one trainer, then the other one on the other side of the bed. The heat feels suffocating.

She doesn't bother throwing on jeans, grabs her keys and her bag and with a quick 'stay' to the dogs rushes out of the house in her old worn T-shirt and loose shorts she'd stolen from her brother years ago.

'Did either you or your sister see the man's face?' Her keys jingle in her hands as she makes her way down the slope.

The tram sits at the bottom, looking hollowed-out with all the lights inside turned off.

Isabel hurries as much as she can without risking tripping up and rolling down the steep hill.

Her car is parked near the café at the bottom of her street.

'Savana peeked a little through the peephole.'

That makes Isabel's heart thud hard against her chest, but she pushes the alarm down. 'Did she recognise him?'

'No.'

'All right. Stay away from the door. My colleagues, two really nice men called Felipe and Sansão, are near your house. They're there just in case you need help. I'm going to hang up but for only a moment so I can call them and get them to come and see the man, okay?'

She reaches her car and unlocks it.

Sara doesn't answer right away.

Isabel switches the phone to speaker and sets it on the seat. She starts the car.

'Sara, did you understand me, linda?' Isabel asks. She drags the seatbelt across her chest and clips it into place.

'Do you have to?' Sara's voice comes through, sounding smaller than before.

Isabel closes her eyes briefly. 'Yes, but I promise, I'll be quick, and I will call right back. Okay, Sara? I promise.'

Isabel starts the car and starts backing it up.

For a few seconds all that she hears are those soft sounds of Sara's rushed breathing. 'Okay.'

'Right. Just stay really quiet, I'm coming. I'm going to call you back and I'll stay on the phone with you the entire time until I get there, yes?'

'Okay. Isabel?'

'I'm here, Sara. What is it?'

A pause. 'I see it. It's red, like hunger.'

Fuck. *Fuck*. Isabel resists the urge to hit her hand on the steering wheel.

'Sara. I am coming.' She takes a deep breath. 'I'm going to hang up now. I will call you right back. Ask Savana to put the phone on silent.'

'I will.'

'You're being very brave, Sara. Hold on to the phone and pick up as soon as I call back.'

She gets another small okay from her and then, with everything in her protesting against hanging up, she cuts the connection. She rubs at her eyes as she speeds through the roads that are thankfully quieter than usual. She turns on the sirens just as Felipe picks up the phone.

'Isabel?' his voice echoes in the interior of the car. 'Is everything all right?'

'I need you to get to the girls now. He's up there, Felipe. He's in the building.'

She hears him swear loud and clear through the line and the instant clacking open of the car door. She hears Sansão's voice in the background but doesn't know what he's saying.

'We're on our way, Isabel.'

'I'm already on the road. Alert the others. I'll be there soon. And be careful.'

She hangs up. Slams her hand on the wheel, then grits her teeth. Heart in her throat, she calls Sara back.

She feels her pulse throbbing in her throat as the phone rings once, twice.

The line clicks. 'Isabel?'

Relief rushes through her. 'Yes Sara, it's me, I'm not going anywhere now.'

39

By the time Isabel gets there twenty-five minutes later, Sansão and Felipe are already posted outside the door to the girls' home.

Isabel is still on the phone to them as she speedwalks down the corridor towards Sansão and Felipe's familiar faces.

'I'm here, I'm going to knock on the door now.' Sansão and Felipe move out of the way. 'Can you guys open the door for me?' She knocks quietly.

'That's you?' Isabel hears Savana's voice through the door, the sound of it overlapping with the voice coming through her phone.

'It's me Savana, see? I'm going to knock one more time,' she says, keeping her voice gentle. Before she can though, she hears the sound of a door chain rattling and a lock clicking. Two arms wrap tightly against her waist as Sara pushes into her space, her shoulders hitching.

Isabel hangs up, wrapping an arm around the little girl, and looks over her head at her sister Savana who looks back at Isabel for a full moment. She's standing tightly, the veins on her neck visible, and there's a fine tremble all over her. Slowly, her eyes take on a sheen and then she's stumbling back against the wall of the corridor and covering her face with her hands. She begins to cry.

Bringing Sara with her, Isabel steps inside and lays a tentative hand on Savana's shoulder.

'Savana? You're safe, okay?'

Savana doesn't uncover her face, continues to sob quietly into her hands. After a second she nods her head.

'Let's all go inside and sit down. My colleagues are here and they're keeping watch. We've called your mother and some more of my colleagues that you met at the station are on their way too.'

She wraps her other arm around Savana's slim shoulders and gently guides both girls back into the living room of the apartment where she sits them both down together and kneels in front of them.

They stay like that, talking quietly, until Voronov and Carla come hurrying in through the door.

Voronov's hair is all over the place and his jawline is darkened with the beginning of stubble. Aside from that, he looks more put together than she does. Carla is miles away from her usual attire in an oversized T-shirt, jeans and trainers. Her hair is pinned up.

'Carla,' Isabel calls out, 'can you do me a favour? Can I ask you to keep Sara and Savana company for a few minutes?'

'Of course,' Carla smiles at the girls as she takes Isabel's place on the floor in front of them.

Isabel motions for Voronov to follow her back out.

'Okay, tell me what happened when you got up here,' Isabel says as they come to a stop outside the door, turning back to Sansão and Felipe who she hadn't been able to debrief, not while looking after one distraught girl and a teenager who wouldn't have dealt well with her leaving their side in that vulnerable state. She rubs at her aching eyes.

Felipe looks like he's expecting her to rip into him. 'He'd already left by the time we reached the floor.'

'We think he heard the lift doors,' Sansão offers, not looking much better than Felipe.

That makes sense. The lift isn't too far away. 'So he either took the main stairs down or a fire exit?'

Felipe shakes his head. 'Main stairs, they serve as the fire exit too.'

Isabel curses. They had him in the same building. They had officers right here and yet he managed to get in and out without being seen by either one of them.

'What happened, Isabel?' Voronov asks.

She looks up at him. 'Got a call just after midnight. It was Sara, she said there was a man standing outside their apartment, staring at the door. I told Sara and Savana to stay quiet and wait for us. Said I'd hang up and call Felipe and Sansão so they could come up and that I'd immediately call them back. By the time I got them back on the phone the girls said he wasn't there anymore.'

Voronov glances at the inside of the apartment. 'Did he ring the bell or knock or try to get them to open the door?'

Isabel shakes her head, resting her hands on her hips. 'No.' She lifts her head, which feels way too heavy right now. 'It was Sara. She sensed he was there. She told Savana and when Savana looked out through the peephole, she saw him standing outside and staring at the door.'

'He must have known about their visit to the precinct,' Voronov murmurs, 'either that or he knows about them from the first victim.'

She'd been the one to take Sara into the precinct.

Isabel takes a deep breath and paces away.

'We have extra people searching the nearby area,' Voronov says.

Sansão takes a step forward. 'There's a security room on the ground floor, opposite the utilities cupboard. They don't have security at the entrance, but they have cameras in the building. I've already called the building manager, she's on her way so we can view the security footage.'

'Thanks, Sansão.'

At least there's that.

40

With Carla minding the girls, they head to the security room.

Luckily for them the building manager only lives a ten-minute walk away.

She's clearly unimpressed by the number of people waiting for her, and grumbles about people making her come out of bed at this hour of the morning looking indecent. She has a robe wrapped tightly around her, an odd match for the trainers on her feet.

She leads Isabel, Voronov and Felipe into the room, Sansão having stayed upstairs with Carla and Daniel outside, directing the search to see if the killer is hiding anywhere nearby. Though Isabel suspects he is long gone.

She remembers the long but isolated walk from Lopes's house from Gaio-Rosário to the centre of Moita.

The building manager ushers them into a small windowless room that's barely big enough for four people. There's one computer with a screensaver appearing and disappearing on the screen. The walls are covered in pinboards that have a mix of pamphlets and notices pinned to their grey surface.

She tells them they can do whatever they want and that she's going to get a coffee and come back, and they'd better be done by then.

They close the door behind her and Voronov slides into the one chair available to access the computer.

Isabel steps up behind him, gripping the back of the chair as she watches him find the correct folder on the desktop. He finds the folder for today and clicks it open.

There are two files. One is a shortcut to a feed, presumably for when the building manager wants to check in throughout the day. The other seems to be the recording.

Voronov clicks it open.

The video camera's angle is from the left corner of the corridor from the direction of the lift and stairs. It captures the length of the corridor. The angle of the camera messes with its perception, making it seem like the corridor thins out towards the end. There is no sound to the video and the image isn't very clean.

Voronov speeds up the footage, and the day speeds by on the screen. People zip into the frame, their walk turned into a caricature. There are no windows looking on to the corridor so the lighting stays consistent throughout, only the people coming and going marking the time.

As the hours of the past day flash by, Isabel catches sight of Savana, Sara and their mother exiting and returning to the apartment too.

Voronov keeps going.

Although the speed remains the same, the activity they see on the screen lowers significantly until eventually after a few beats of no movement, nearing 23.57 p.m. a tall man enters the frame.

Voronov returns the speed to normal and leans forward.

The three of them watch the silent surveillance video with only the hum of the desktop and the sound of their quiet breathing to accompany it.

He's wearing a heavy-looking black coat that makes Isabel think of protective gear. He has a hood over his head.

When he appears within the scope of the camera, he's coming from the direction of the stairs so his back is to the camera.

Isabel clutches the back of the chair in frustration, her nails digging into the cheap upholstery.

The man reaches Sara and Savana's door.

It has already happened but Isabel has to consciously slow her breathing as she thinks of the two people inside. Defenceless.

How had he got into the building?

'Is there a camera in the lobby as well?' Isabel asks.

On screen they watch as the man steps close enough to the door that the toes of his boots must be butting up against it. Isabel can't tell because of the poor quality of the recording.

The man reaches forward around the same height as where the keyhole and doorknob are. Isabel squints. Is he holding something?

'Is there something in his hand?' she asks, frustrated.

Voronov gives a slow shake of the head. 'I don't know. The image quality is too poor.' Frustration bleeds through his voice too.

The time ticks into 00.05 a.m. and the man steps back. He doesn't leave right away but remains there, facing the door.

'I don't understand,' Isabel says, 'anyone could walk out at any time. But he's just standing there . . .'

At 00.08 a.m. he turns his head, facing the camera.

A glimpse of what looks to be a white chin is visible. Then he begins walking fast, back in the direction he'd come from, his head ducked all the way.

Just like that, he's gone.

Isabel rocks back on her feet, covers her face with her hands and just breathes for a moment. 'Any chance we can get someone to zoom in on his face and clean up that image?'

'I think all we'll get is pixels,' Voronov says, 'but we can try.'

'Let's see if there's one for the lobby—'

A knock sounds on the door. Definitely not the building manager because that woman did not give the impression that she would be knocking to get anywhere inside this building.

It's Sansão.

'Isabel, the mother just arrived.'

'Okay, okay.' Isabel sighs. 'Aleks,' she says, looking over her shoulder, 'I have to go and speak with their mother.'

He nods. 'Go ahead. We'll stay and see if there's something on the lobby.'

Isabel makes her way back upstairs, dreading the moment she has to face the mother of the two girls she's endangered.

In the end, she feels the slap she gets across the face is more than justified.

41

As expected, the search of the area turns up nothing and after arguing with the building manager Isabel is able to take the tapes from the day as evidence.

Chief Bautista calls as they're wrapping up and Isabel goes outside to take the call and bring her up to speed.

'I heard you took one to the face,' Bautista says, after she's finished, 'are you all right?'

Isabel tongues the cut on the inside of her cheek. She'd cut it on her tooth when Sara and Savana's mother hit her. 'I'll live.'

'It's been a rough few hours. Get yourself home and rest up. The others can hold the fort for a little while.'

'I'm fine—'

'I'm not asking you, Isabel. I'm telling you. Understand?'

Isabel grinds her teeth together and leans her head back, pressing it hard against the wall behind her.

In her head, she can still hear Sara's voice, so small over the phone, and Savana's soft crying into her hands. She feels the phantom squeeze of fear that had been with her every second of the race to the girls' home, waiting for the sound of the door breaking down to sound through the phone at any moment. Fear that she wasn't going to make it in time.

'This isn't on you.'

Isn't it? 'I fucked up, Chief,' Isabel says, 'I put those girls in danger.'

'This isn't. On. You. So go home. Get some rest, clear your head so we can pin this bastard down.'

Isabel takes a deep breath, nods to herself. 'Yes, Chief.'

After hanging up, she approaches where Voronov, Daniel and Carla are speaking with another police officer near the surveillance room and lets them know what the chief said.

'Want me to drive you?' Voronov asks.

She shakes her head. 'No, stay here. I'll be fine.'

His mouth thins but in the end he nods. 'Message me when you get home?'

'I will.' She pats him on the arm and nods at Daniel and Carla before leaving.

In the end, she allows one of the police officers who arrived later on the scene to drive her and her car back to her place.

By the time she gets home and grabs a bag of peas out of the freezer for her face it's nearing four in the morning. She returns to the sofa, dropping on to it and pressing the peas to her cheek. The dogs, who haven't stopped whining since she walked back in, clamber on to the sofa trying to get her to pet them. The mother's slap had felt closer to a punch.

She drops her head back on the sofa, her dogs nestled against her, and when she closes her eyes, she feels the burn of emotion against her eyelids.

Curling into her dogs, she stays there and only falls asleep as the first rays of light begin to touch the sky.

42

She wakes up with the sunlight bright and unforgiving on her face and her phone going off somewhere on the floor. The bag of peas has become a slushy lump wedged between her shoulder and the sofa, a big damp spot beneath it where it has melted on to the sofa cushion.

At some point after she'd fallen asleep, the dogs had migrated to their beds and they peer up now as she starts to move.

'Merda,' she mutters, and then winces, pressing a hand to her jaw and stretching it experimentally, before pancaking back on the sofa on her front and fumbling for her phone on the floor.

She flips on to her back.

It's 6.13 a.m. and it's the chief.

'Yes, Chief?' Her voice is rough from sleep.

'Isabel.'

That's all she says. Not her surname, not barking out orders.

That's all Bautista says and Isabel knows something has gone wrong.

Isabel shoves herself upright, suddenly wide awake. 'Chief?'

'Voronov is in the hospital and Carla is missing.'

The Hospital de Barreiro is a big structure in a pastel pink, mostly surrounded by big roads and trees. By the time she reaches it, the heat is peaking, and the clouds are back, heavy and darker than before. There's a flash of lightning in the far distance. The sound of thunder reaches her a few seconds later as she gets out of the car.

Isabel leaves it in the parking lot, doesn't even remember to take a ticket, and rushes to the reception but before she can make a beeline for the reception desk, she sees Daniel standing there, face white, running his hand over and over his shaved head and walking back and forth.

'Daniel!'

He jerks his head up and it takes him a few seconds to spot her coming towards him because there is so much traffic in the corridor.

People are queueing up at the reception to be seen and doctors are hurrying by, some alongside gurneys, others with their heads buried in charts. The emergency waiting room is filled with people and a child is wailing, their cries drowning out the other sounds.

'Good, you're here, come on.' He takes them straight to the lift, pressing the call button.

'What happened?' she asks. Chief was going to bust her if she got clocked for speeding, which Isabel is pretty sure happened at a couple of intersections. She stopped short of running red lights but had been pushing the speed limit and sometimes gone beyond it in her rush to get here. All she remembers from the car ride over are honking drivers and the sound of her own heart, drumming a ceaseless fast beat in her ears that corresponded with the thudding in her chest. She'd had to blink several times to get rid of the tunnel vision that had been closing around the edges of her visual field.

She shouldn't have been driving herself.

She'll have that conversation with herself some other time.

The doors open and they stand aside to let people out before rushing in. Daniel presses the button for the sixth floor and the lift holds while they wait for a few more people to get on, enough that the two of them are pushed into a corner of the lift.

It's like someone is mocking them. The lift stops off at every floor on the way up.

'What the hell happened, Daniel?' she asks again.

Daniel's mouth flattens and he digs his teeth into his lower lip. 'There was a call after you left. Isauro Santiago and Odette Orestes-Santiago were found dead in his residence in Sines.'

Isabel turns to look at him, eyes wide. 'What?'

Daniel stares straight ahead. A muscle ticks in his jaw. 'They were in his car inside the garage. She was tied up. He wasn't. Garage was sealed and the car was running.'

Isabel pushes her fingers through her hair and fists the strands, letting the sharp sting of the pull ground her. 'Who found them?'

'Santiago's colleague. He didn't show up at work and wasn't answering calls so he went to check.'

Isabel shakes her head and presses a hand to her mouth.

'I told her he wouldn't find her,' she says.

Daniel looks at her and reaches for her shoulder, squeezing it gently.

The lift reaches the sixth floor and the doors ding open.

'At the end,' he says.

She follows him out and down the corridor.

'The local police were first on the scene and they found a couple of things in the boot of the car.'

'What did they find?'

'Working boots. Rope. Accelerant. They've already been handed over to Jacinta for her to test them.'

No. No way. This . . . this doesn't make any sense. 'How do Voronov and Carla come into this?'

'Chief sent them down there to meet the local police,' he says. 'Voronov offered to go and Chief wanted a Gifted on scene.' His voice sounds tight, and he stares ahead. Isabel can feel the emotions he's struggling to hold back.

He stops in front of the last door on the corridor and glances over his shoulder at her. 'Come on.'

Voronov is sitting on the last bed on the left side of the room, closest to the windows. The other beds in the room are empty.

He's got a blanket up to his lap and is wearing a hospital gown. The bed has been adjusted so that it's in that half-seated, half-reclining position. He's so tall his legs reach almost all the way down the length of the bed. There's bandaging around his head and his left arm is in a sling, held closely to his chest. It's in a cast. There's bruising and swelling on the left side of his face too, and the skin over his nose is split.

At the end of his bed, Chief Bautista is standing with a doctor, speaking in low tones.

'Chief,' Isabel says, walking over.

She doesn't expect Voronov to open his eyes at the sound of her voice and he turns his head, the movement careful and painstakingly slow. 'Hey,' he says.

And ah, it's not her day today because her eyes start smarting and she has to ruthlessly blink it away.

'Chief Bautista, these people—' the doctor starts.

'They're his team,' she says. 'And that's his partner,' she says, nodding at Isabel. Isabel doesn't know if she means that in the professional or in the personal sense. She doesn't care either.

Isabel approaches the bed, checking him from head to toe.

'Hey,' Voronov says again. His voice is hoarse, but he doesn't need to say much else. She looks at his face.

'How bad?' she asks quietly and carefully fits her hand to the right side of his face. It looks like that side of his face is fine, but her fingers still tremble a little, scared of causing more damage before she finally moulds her palm to his cheek and strokes it gently with her thumb.

'Four stitches on the side of the head, minor concussion,' he says quietly, leaning his face against her hand with a quiet exhalation, his eyes shutting, 'a few hits to the face. Broken arm, they're going to take me in for surgery later. Broken ribs.'

'Okay,' Isabel breathes out, 'okay.' She slides her hand down, cradling the side of his neck. 'Your pretty face doesn't get you enough attention so you thought you'd go out and get more?' she asks.

His mouth quirks at the corner but it's quickly extinguished. 'I lost Carla.'

'Tell me what happened.'

'Wait, hold it, Reis,' Chief says from the back.

It's a testament to her worry that Isabel had forgotten the chief's presence. She looks over her shoulder at her. She doesn't withdraw her hand though. Too late anyway.

At Isabel's blank look, Bautista elaborates. 'I think Voronov isn't up to telling things multiple times and we're going to have to move fast on this. Felipe, Sansão and Jacinta are on their way over and should be here inside of ten minutes. He can tell it then.'

Jacinta is the first to arrive and she winces when she sees Voronov on the bed. 'Looking a little worse for wear there, Inspector.' She goes to join Daniel by the window, wrapping an arm around his shoulder. She doesn't offer anything, doesn't need to.

Felipe and Sansão come in about ten minutes later. Bautista, who was outside still talking to the doctor, follows them both in and shuts the door behind them.

'All right. I want everyone to listen properly. Voronov is going to be telling this once and then he's going into surgery. So we won't be able to double-check anything with him until he's up from that.'

Voronov groans as he tries to face Bautista. 'We can delay it. I want to make sure Carla is safe.'

'No, we can't. The doctor says you have a bad break, the sooner they sort it out, the better the chances of it not having a long-term impact.' Her tone is absolute, leaving no room for discussion.

Voronov clears his throat a couple of times and Isabel tells him to hold on and gets the water next to his bed. He takes a few sips of that, wincing as the left side of his mouth comes into contact with the cup. He takes a couple of sips and Isabel returns the cup to the bedside table.

'We were on our way back from the crime scene when we got a call from one of the fire squad team, Ivo. He wanted to speak to one of the team urgently, regarding the case. He was clearly agitated, and asked us not to say anything to anyone else, including Cardoso. We said we'd be there.'

Isabel forces her breathing to remain even.

'When we arrived we couldn't find anyone. We started looking – at first we thought maybe they'd been called out to a fire but the fire engine was still there. Then Carla sensed something. Someone came at me from behind. They used a weapon, metal, maybe a pipe. Hit me in the arm and then on the head, hard enough to send me down. I lost sight temporarily. I heard Carla yell but I couldn't see her.' His Adam's apple bobs as he swallows. 'At this point, I blacked out. When I came to the place was on fire. I couldn't hear Carla anymore. I was on the ground floor and managed to crawl out through the emergency door in the back. That's when I called the team. I'm not sure if I blacked out again but what I remember clearly next was the paramedic talking to me.'

'We have the car on the way to our forensics,' Jacinta says, 'and our team are there, looking for any traces he may have left behind.'

'Is there anything else you remember? Any smells? Noises? Anyone you passed by?' Isabel asks.

'There might be,' Voronov says, 'but right now there are parts that I'm finding hard to remember.' Isabel can hear the tightly leashed frustration in his voice.

'This is someone who is familiar with the investigating team. Enough to have a decent idea of who would show up if he called,' Daniel says and looks at Isabel. 'They would have known we have two Gifted individuals on the team. We ID ourselves to every person we speak with during the course of an investigation.'

'They would have known Carla is Gifted.'

'And that you're Gifted,' Voronov adds. 'They knew the probability was high that there would be at least one Gifted woman at the scene.'

'He baited us,' Isabel murmurs.

But why? Going for a police officer is too risky. Before, they would have had to evade their team alone, but now the scrutiny will just increase. They'll have less room for making mistakes.

No. No. That isn't it.

The only reason to make a move on a police officer when there were probably other victims that they could have got to a lot more easily, was that somewhere in the last day or so, they must have made a move that spooked them. Something that they felt pushed them into a corner.

'There's more. We followed up with Cardoso this morning, couldn't reach him. We sent someone over to the station. The members of the squad were there in their bunks . . . but no sign of Cardoso.'

Isabel blinks. 'What do you mean?'

'Their throats were cut,' Voronov says.

That team? Isabel was speaking to them just a few days ago. They were a young and strong team. There's no way one man could have taken them all on and won. It's just—

'He probably drugged them.'

The horror of the situation sinks in.

She rubs a hand over her mouth. 'And now he has Carla, a Gifted woman. His favourite type of victim. And he always strikes in the early hours.'

'We have all eyes on the highways, and I've called in a couple of favours to get more boots on the ground,' Bautista says, 'they're canvassing as we speak.'

'Cardoso is the only one with links to the old crime scenes,' Isabel says, 'the others . . . and we talked about how our culprit was able to subdue our victims into going with him with minimal fuss.' She rests her hands on her hips. 'A firefighter is usually someone who is trusted without question by the public.'

'Barking.'

Isabel looks at Voronov. 'What?'

'I think I heard barking. After I went down the first time.'

A knock sounds on the door.

'Carry on,' Bautista says, 'but if it's the doctor here ready to take Voronov to surgery then you're heading there immediately, Voronov. No arguments.'

His expression closes off. 'Yes, Chief.'

But then when she opens the door all they hear is silence and they turn to look.

Standing there is Cardoso. He's out of breath and braces his hand on the doorframe, trying to get his breathing under control. There's a fine sheen of sweat on his forehead and the sides of his hair are damp and darker than the rest.

'It's Horta. The man you're looking for is Horta.'

43

Cardoso takes a seat. They're all still, waiting for him to elaborate on his assertion.

He takes a drink of water. 'Horta's mother died in a fire. She burned alive, to be exact, inside a church. He was five or six at the time I believe. His father was the priest at that church. It was a terrible accident – it's the reason he wanted to become a firefighter. He joined as a volunteer under my time as captain. That picture you have of me at the murder scene of Inês Roberto, he was already volunteering then. He would have been twenty-one or twenty-two at the time. He trained for the fire service right after he came out of the military. He wasn't on shift that night. You'd have to look into shift records for the others. He was there for the Carmo murder. That one was close to our station. The second one, he was supposed to be on sick leave. He turned up late to check on the team after he heard they were called out to another woman set on fire.'

He pauses there for another drink of water. 'He married his wife in 2007. Had his daughter shortly after.'

'That could account for the break,' Isabel says. 'But why start back up?'

'She initiated divorce proceedings earlier this year and is suing for custody of their fifteen-year-old daughter.'

That could do it.

'Do you know if his mother was Gifted?' Isabel asks. 'Or if there was infidelity in his parents' marriage?'

'That I don't know.'

'This didn't all spring out of the blue. What made it occur to you that it could be him?'

'It didn't,' he admits. 'It was Ivo. He overheard your conversation with me the day you and your colleague came to the station. He put two and two together. Horta has been taking some personal time but kept tabs on the team as the captain.'

'Why is that an issue?'

'It wasn't,' Cardoso says, 'except he was getting to the scenes too quickly. He was there for them both. Always in a hurry even when there was no need for him to be there. And then there was the community fair.'

'What about it?' Isabel asks.

'The community fair. Our department is there every month. The kids . . .' He stops there and shakes his head, almost as if shoving away any doubts trying to make him take his words back, 'the kids love the fire engine, it's always a hit. We're the only emergency services representatives that attend every fair. We man the stall in shifts throughout the day. Usually two teams to a day. I remember I saw him walking away from Carmo's stall. He had a charm from her. Said it might give him luck in winning back his wife and he always stopped to speak with Paz, always. But there was no reaction from him at all when we were called to the scene and found out she was the victim of that second fire.'

Isabel looks at Bautista.

'I'll go back to the office; I'll pull some strings to get a quick warrant for his house. Jacinta, come with me, as soon as I have it I want your team to go in immediately.'

'Yes, Chief.' Jacinta gets up.

Isabel turns back to Cardoso. 'Does he know that you're on to him?'

Cardoso nods. He pulls a note out of his pocket. 'I went to the station to speak to him before coming here and the entire place was up in flames. Thought I could, I don't know, talk some sense into him. I've known him since he was a kid. I just . . .'

'You should have come straight to us.'

He hands over the note.

Isabel unfolds it.

Look after Kuma for me. He'll listen to you.
It's been an honour working with you.

'Where could he have taken her? You know him. You said it yourself. You've known him since he was a kid. Where might he go? He'll try and stick as close to his rituals as possible but make it hard for us to catch up, especially if he suspects you'd come to us.'

Where would he go if this was his last stand? If he'd taken the ultimate risk for this final kill? No wife, no kid. Nothing but this to live for and now even that was up. He was going to make this one count. He wouldn't let this one be like all the others. That would go against the arrogance he'd displayed, killing Carmo and Paz so publicly, leaving them for the world to see.

Churches.

He always burns them near religious buildings.

Isabel snaps her gaze up. 'The church where his mother died, the one where his father was the priest. Where is it?'

44

Evening is starting to fall.

Horta's car is confirmed to be heading in the direction of a small, isolated neighbourhood near Parque Natural da Arrábida.

The church where his father had been the head priest had been one of the more traditional-looking churches, a single-floor building with a triangular roof and painted white on the outside. That was the picture supplied by the internet.

Nothing fancy. Something erected to cater to the people of the small neighbourhood was all it had been.

In its place now is an elevated cemented floor that still bears hallmarks of having once belonged to something grander. Now it's a large, pock-marked area, the floor tiles that had been a part of it either picked off entirely, broken or cracked. The structure of the building itself had been removed long ago. The flooring is the only thing that remains of it. A trio of goats graze nearby unattended. Their black eyes stare at the newcomers but they continue to eat, mouths working the heat-dried grass.

The trees loom behind it, tall and dense. Sunset is still a while away but the clouds don't make it any easier. The storm that has been threatening is kept at bay, stuck in the thick, menacing clouds. The wind has picked up, a warm air current that has anxiety beating in Isabel's chest.

Horta's car is parked there, neat as can be. It stands out in the otherwise deserted surroundings.

Daniel rounds the car. He has his bulletproof vest on and he's adjusting the gun holster strapped around his hips.

'Chief says the helicopter is on the way and Cardoso confirmed there's a firefighter team five minutes out.'

Isabel nods and turns to face the group of twenty or so officers that have joined them, most of them from nearby precincts.

'Okay, we don't have much time left. The suspect is most likely armed with an accelerant. He is unstable and a serious risk to all here and our surroundings. He has with him Inspector Carla Muniz of the Anjos precinct. We believe that she is still alive. *She* is the priority here. We want to find her alive. And we want him alive too so that he can be held accountable for his crimes. We have a fire engine on the way. Be careful. Take bottles of water with you and split up into teams of two or three. We should all—'

Isabel stops.

The smell is distinctive.

Fire.

It's fire.

'He jumped the gun,' she says in disbelief.

'Isabel – I have to—' Daniel is already starting towards the treeline.

'We're not leaving her.' She turns to Sansão. 'Sansão, call it in. Tell the firefighters to step on it, the bastard has lit up earlier than we expected. And call one-one-two. Tell them there's a potentially wide-spreading fire on the outskirts of Arrábida. We'll need medical assistance.'

And God help them if the fire gets out of control.

Isabel grabs her backpack and throws it on, feels the weight of the water hit her back.

'Let's go.'

45

They enter the forest line.

'Don't split up. Twos and threes. We'll find her.'

Daniel barely acknowledges her; the nod he gives is absent-minded, which doesn't bode well.

Around her she hears the echoes of the other officers calling out Carla's name as they advance through the trees.

He ties them up and covers their mouth. She most likely won't be able to respond but she'll know they're coming. She'll hang on. She will.

The trees loom over them. The grass beneath her feet is a faded green. Not quite as dry as what the goats had been eating, but dry enough that if a lick of fire touches it, the whole land will be burning in the blink of an eye. And there they are. Trapped in the middle of it all.

She's always heard that fire moves faster than people expect. She's never expected to be in a position to learn just how fast it can move herself.

'Keep a sharp eye out,' Isabel says, 'I'm going to see if I can find her trail.'

Daniel doesn't ask what she means. He's worked with Carla for long enough to know at least some of what a telepathic Gifted can do.

Above their heads, the tree branches start to bend under the force of the wind.

The smell of smoke is becoming thicker.

They've been walking for about five minutes. She can't see her way back to the church anymore. She prays the fire engine is close by.

Drawing air into her lungs, Isabel lets it out in a bellow. 'CARLA!' She projects it, pushing the same echo that her voice sends vibrating through the trees into the air, throwing her Gift out like a net, high and wide, but searching for only one key signature. Just Carla.

She waits. For anything. Even a ripple. Nothing.

'Isabel?' Daniel asks.

Isabel shakes her head. They speed up. Isabel drops her barriers entirely and the voices of several people at once rise as one, their words abstract, their colours painting the forest around them in multicolours, each leading back to a different person. But she can't spot the one with the signature she knows well.

And then she sees it. Faint.

Here . . . I'm here. I'm here. I'm . . . I'm here. Find . . . find. Me.

Each word is weighed down, sinking lower with each one even as Carla pushes them out, reaching for Isabel like Isabel's reaching for her.

'Found her,' Isabel whispers. She grabs on to them, just like Sara had held on to her hand and guided her towards the hunger.

She doesn't see the hunger here. Even though it's here somewhere.

'This way, she's this way.' She picks up her pace – doesn't run. Too afraid that if she runs she'll make a mistake, move too fast in one direction and it won't be the right one. They have to be more careful than this. She speeds up.

Daniel is right on her heels.

Ahead in the distance, Isabel sees a glow. A yellow-red glow and she knows exactly what it is. Fire.

It's one of the most terrifying things she has ever seen.

'Daniel,' she says, holding on to the faint call, still there, still weakened, like it could slip through her fingers at any time, 'this is bad.'

'I know. I'm not leaving here without my partner.'

They move quicker, sticks breaking under their feet.

And then that hunger explodes. Red, just like Sara said. Like a plume to their left and Isabel only has a split second to react – she shoves Daniel just as a blast of heat comes at them fast. Isabel hits the ground, already recoiling.

She hears Daniel cursing and scrambles up to see Horta standing over them both, holding a blowtorch. He's in his fireman's gear, protected.

He's been trained to do this. Trained to run, to carry twice his weight in uniform. In this situation, he's the one with the advantage over them.

'She's my final one,' he says, 'you're not touching her.'

Isabel . . .

Around them the smoke is rising. The distant red glow is becoming a blaze.

Daniel launches himself at Horta, driving them both into the ground.

'Go!' he yells over his shoulder.

Isabel doesn't waste time. She springs to her feet and takes off.

She follows that disappearing thread. She pulls the radio from her back pocket.

'This is Inspector Reis! Horta has been found; he's armed with a blowtorch. Inspector Verde has engaged him, backup needed, and make sure medics are on standby! Inspector Muniz is alive!'

She releases the button even as people respond, confirming receipt of her message.

The smoke here is thicker. A glance up shows the flames starting to catch on tree branches.

The next inhalation has her coughing.

I'm coming, Carla, I'm coming.

The heat is rising, and she can feel her clothes beginning to stick to her body.

They don't have much time left.

She looks around. The radio is still going. Messages about the ambulance arriving but she doesn't hear any confirmation that the firefighters are on the scene.

One will no longer be enough. This is a forest fire now.

They have to get out of here.

Here . . .

Isabel follows that dying word to a huddled figure at the base of a tree. It's Carla tucked in on herself, her hair a tangled mess, her skin exposed.

Isabel runs over to her.

'Carla,' Isabel coughs again, the smoke working its way into her throat, 'I'm here. I'm here.' She slides a hand under Carla's chin, tilting her head back to get a good look at her face.

Carla's eyes are a mere glitter, they're low-lidded and they don't focus on Isabel even when Isabel holds her head up. It's like she's been drugged. There's a rope tied around her wrist and nothing else.

Gritting her teeth she yanks off her T-shirt, leaving herself in just her sports bra. It's baggy enough that at least it should cover Carla up to some degree. It takes longer than Isabel would like to get Carla into the T-shirt. She takes the water out of her bag, tries to keep her hands steady as she opens one bottle. Leaning Carla against the tree, she slaps her lightly on the cheek. 'Come on, Carla, drink a little bit, okay, and then we have to get going.'

She doesn't know how long Carla's been here, exposed to the smoke and God knows what else.

She manages to coax her into drinking a little, takes it slow. Most of the water dribbles out. There's a bad-looking bruise at her temple and her lips are chapped.

Isabel chugs some water down herself, packs everything away and braces herself for the next part.

'Carla, he set the fire and it's spreading fast, you're going to have to hold on to me, okay?'

She doesn't wait for her response, just hauls her up, grunting as she takes on her weight. Carla's head lolls against her shoulder. The T-shirt reaches a little lower on Carla than it does on Isabel. Isabel looks around. She doesn't have the luxury of time and she needs to make sure she finds the right way back.

Carla is an unsteady weight against her but there's some strength in her still as they begin the trip back.

Isabel's throat and eyes sting and with each step, every lungful of air begins to hurt. They have nothing to breathe through.

Isabel keeps her eyes focused forward. Takes one step. Then another. Then another.

'This is disappointing. Isabel, is this how you die?'

The voice, so close to her ear, almost freezes her on the spot.

Isabel looks to her side and finds Gabriel standing next to her, looking perfectly calm, perfectly neat and untouched by all the smoke. Because he's not really there.

She'd slipped up and he'd been waiting for the right moment to slip into her mind again.

Isabel grits her teeth and readjusts her grip on Carla. She powers forward.

'You need to move faster,' Gabriel says, walking calmly alongside them like he's out for a stroll.

'You're doing just fine, Carla, one step after the other, stay with me, hmm?' Isabel says; she doesn't acknowledge his presence. She focuses on Carla instead.

Carla tries, but they're always at risk of toppling over as she tries to keep up with Isabel. 'I . . .' she croaks, her cheek jostling against Isabel's shoulder.

'Shh, shh. We shouldn't talk.' Isabel readjusts her grip around Carla's waist and brings Carla's arm more firmly over her shoulders.

'I ran,' Carla chokes out. 'He . . . he . . .' Carla tries to strengthen her grip, but her fingers slide over Isabel's sweat-slicked shoulder, no strength in them no matter how she tries.

'You're not leaving.'

Horta's voice comes from behind them.

She overrides the instinct to freeze. Instead, she grits her teeth and keeps walking, moving in the direction of the fire.

A sharp sensation on her scalp winds her before the force of the yank on her hair sends her tumbling back and down, elbows scraping the ground.

She watches as Carla crumples to the ground too, just about managing to keep her face from hitting it.

Isabel spins, scrambling to her feet.

Horta stands above her, his blowtorch still in hand and right at his side, looking down on her too, Gabriel shakes his head.

'Goodbye, Isabel.'

46

Slowly, she stands, facing Horta. Her throat feels like it's burning and she coughs again.

'I expected you all to come after her, you know?' His voice is distorted behind his mask. 'But I didn't think I'd be this lucky. I get two of you today. That's one thing I never managed.' He starts a slow walk around her, not even looking at where Carla is on the ground. His eyes are only on Isabel now.

'You're surrounded,' Isabel says, 'you know that. You won't be able to walk out of here.'

He bends his head to the side, a curious gesture like he doesn't understand what she's saying. 'But neither will you. And that's what matters. I'm tired and I've been found out now. I'm glad it was José. He's always kept watch over me. That feels right. Fair.'

Isabel mirrors his steps, circling as he circles her so that her back is to Carla and so that she can back up slowly.

'You want to ask me why?' he asks.

Isabel keeps backing up until she feels Carla's hand clutch on to her ankle and relief courses through her. She's still alert enough that they can do this.

'No.' Isabel says. 'I don't care why you did it. I'm not a priest. If you want to unburden yourself of all the evil you've done then I'm not the person for it.'

He laughs behind his breathing apparatus mask, the sound odd and distorted.

Isabel holds a hand down to Carla, grits her teeth when she feels Carla grab on and pull herself up.

'Will you be laughing when your wife and your child ask you why?' Isabel asks. She doesn't dare take her eyes off him. 'Do you think you'll be laughing when they're walking down the street and people start talking behind their backs, spreading rumours about them, just like they did with the women you killed? Except they'll be calling her the wife of a murderer. They'll be calling your little girl the murderer's daughter. Will you be laughing then?'

That stops his laughter right there. 'Shut your filthy mouth. You aren't fit to speak about them. You'll drag them down with you into hell.'

'No. That would be your doing. You're the one doing that. Dragging them down with you. You've ruined their lives. You might as well have killed them too.'

He starts walking towards Isabel, full of intent.

'There's a power imbalance here,' Isabel says. 'But you're wrong about who is short-changed.'

She focuses, feels the easy bend of her Gift under her will, feels the hair rising on the back of her arms and neck as she slips, like a hot knife through butter, into his mind. She stops him in his tracks.

'You meant to die here. Because you're a coward,' Isabel says, and now she feels like she's able to take her eyes off him. She looks down at Carla, who has dragged herself back up to standing using Isabel as support. 'Well,' she continues as if she's just talking about the weather, 'right now that's not something you can do without my permission.' She begins walking. He follows. 'You're going to face your family. And you're going to face the families of all your victims. You're coming with me one step at a time.'

She pauses to look over her shoulder at him.

'Surrounded by fire, I really must look like the devil to you now, hmm?'

It takes concentration, more than she has in her right now, to half-carry Carla and make a strong-willed man come with them, and take them out of the danger zone. It means that she's tied up enough that she can't even try to feel out Daniel.

The fire is raging now. Her legs are tired and her arms are hurting. She's not sure how long they've been walking for. Her ribs and upper chest hurt from the coughing and Carla is like lead beside her.

But his steps, under Isabel's influence, never falter. Not once.

They've been walking for so long that Isabel almost thinks she's hallucinating when hands grab her and she's swung into someone's arms. Her instinct to hang on to Carla is so kneejerk she almost falls out of the strong hold and on to the ground.

'It's okay, Inspector, I've got you.'

Felipe.

Isabel slumps in his hold. 'Thank God,' she croaks. 'Carla—'

'Sansão has her.'

'What about Daniel?'

'Bad head wound and severe burns to his hands. That fucker burned them with a blowtorch. He's in pain. But medics say he'll be okay.'

'Good.' Exhaustion overcomes her and the pain of her throat and stinging in her eyes becomes acute. She lets her eyes close. 'Felipe?'

'Yes, Isabel?'

'Is Horta still following?'

She feels the shift of his body as he turns to check. 'Is that your doing?' His voice comes out oddly strained.

'I take it that he is.'

'Yes, he is.'

'Yes, that's my doing. And someone better get him in cuffs soon before I pass out.'

Isabel climbs on to the back of the ambulance, wraps the blanket tighter around Carla, careful not to jostle the oxygen mask, and then takes a seat next to her, arm wrapped around her shoulder.

She accepts the mask the paramedic pulls into place over her own face, only adjusting slightly before she slumps back against the inside of the ambulance. The medics had agreed to let them ride with Daniel and he's alert, watching to make sure they get in, from his place strapped down on the bed and mask in place. She gets the sense that even strapped down, he wouldn't have let the ambulance take him anywhere without knowing that Carla made it out.

She feels him finally let go when he sees them settling down next to him. He lets his eyes close.

Through the back window, she watches as Felipe and Sansão shove Horta into the back of the police car, Cardoso at his side, looking on solemnly.

Isabel hugs Carla a little tighter. 'You're safe. You're safe.'

The paramedics close the doors to the ambulance. Carla settles into her side.

The rain begins to fall as it takes them away.

47

'Are you both all right?' Bautista asks.

Isabel smooths her hair back with wet hands and takes a deep breath; the smell of smoke is still strong despite the change of clothes and the hours spent at the hospital.

It was nearing the early hours of the morning by the time Isabel and Daniel made it back to the precinct. Carla was still in the hospital, being monitored. She'd been exposed to the smoke for longer than the rest of them and her symptoms were concerning, so they'd wanted to monitor her for longer. They'd wanted to monitor the two of them for longer too but there was no way either of them would have stayed put knowing Horta was now in custody.

As she'd sat on the hospital bed, her answers to the doctor's questions had come out in a flat monotone. The smell of the burning forest seemed so alive to her still, and that final moment in the forest, with Carla, a heavyweight in her arms and Horta, determined to make sure all of them died together, felt carved into her memory.

'I'm good, Chief,' Daniel says. He's standing ramrod-straight by the door. His entire body is tense, running on reserves most likely, just like Isabel. His hands are wrapped in gauze and there's a bandage around his head too but Isabel sees the same sharp determination stamped on to his face that she knows is showing on her own.

'Same.'

Bautista looks at both of them, assessing them.

Isabel's aware that her appearance doesn't add much credence to her words. First thing she'd done when they'd set foot back in the precinct had been to try to clean herself up as much as possible, wiping the stickiness and soot from the fire off her face, neck and arms and changing into a spare set of clothes.

She feels marginally better. It doesn't quite tamp down the anger simmering under her skin.

Daniel has changed too, and his face is carefully neutral but it's clear he won't budge from this.

They both want to get in the room with Horta. There are too many people who have lost their lives at the hands of this man. Too many Gifted lives. None with any closure for over twenty years. They can't afford to mess up here.

And he'd hit them all too close to home.

A retired inspector who still keeps his case tucked away, like a sin he'll take with him into death, an entire team betrayed by their leader, their friend, their colleague and an investigator who hadn't noticed the killer who committed the crimes he'd been tasked to investigate had been right under his nose for twenty years.

And then there's Voronov and Carla.

Their partners.

Isabel wipes at her forehead. The heat that she'd experienced in the forest feels like it hasn't left her, feels like it's still right there, surrounding her, trapping her – singeing and inescapable.

'We need to get in there and speak to him, Chief. We need to get as many answers as possible from him now. We don't know when he'll clam up.'

'Please, Chief.'

There's a peculiar kind of quiet on their floor that comes with the winding-down of the work day, even though for them, it never really stops.

The desks outside the chief's office are mostly empty, only one person focused on their laptop. Downstairs is busier; Isabel can sense the presence of other personnel dotted throughout that floor.

Horta is down there, with officers posted outside the room.

She can pinpoint him by his emotions alone.

His emotions are like bubbling tar, spilling out and smothering whatever it touches.

Chief Bautista drags a thumbnail over the arch of her brow, mouth tense, an unlit cigarette in between the fingers of the hand resting on her hip. Maybe it's the time of day or having two – almost four – injured and hospitalised inspectors from her team, but the lines of her face look as if they've been etched deeper into her skin; they spread outwards from the corners of her eyes and bracket her mouth that is pressed into a thin line as she considers their request.

'With the kidnapping and Carla's witness statement and mine, we have enough, but Chief,' Isabel says, 'this guy has evaded us for well over a decade and we have families that will need closure. And reassurance. We need to get in there and we need to get him to talk.'

'And you think you can make him do that? He's been tight-lipped since he arrived. Hasn't even asked for a lawyer.'

Isabel lifts her hand before dropping it again. 'Yes. I think we can. Believe it or not, even a monster like that has a weakness.'

Bautista arcs an eyebrow in question.

Daniel looks across at Isabel. After a moment he says: 'His daughter.'

'All right,' she says.

When they enter the room, Horta is cuffed to the other end of the table in the interview room and his face is turned away from the door, his gaze fixed on the window looking out on to the street and the night beyond it.

He's been stripped of his gear and is in a black T-shirt and black Nomex trousers. His hair is unkempt, black strands sticking up every which way.

His hands are cuffed together in front of him, linked to the shackles on his feet. There's enough give in both for him that if he wants to drink from the plastic cup of water placed in front of him, he can do so without any difficulty.

Daniel walks in ahead of Isabel. Isabel doesn't need her Gift to be able to see the tight control he's exerting over himself, tamping down on the anger. His hands are tucked into his pockets, and his muscles are corded with tension.

Isabel closes the door behind her and carries the mug filled to the brim with black coffee – she doesn't want to think about the amount of sugar she added to it, she's desperate for the energy – as she walks calmly to pull out the chair next to Daniel's. The legs gently scrape the floor, the sound scraping her already over-sensitised senses. She holds back a flinch and sits down with barely a ripple to her expression.

She sets the mug down on the table, crosses her legs and leans back in her chair. She stares at the side of Horta's profile.

He hasn't moved an inch from the time when they opened the door to when they sit down, remaining statue-still.

Outside, the rain continues to come down, a deluge masking the sounds of the city night, but the heat inside feels worse, the humidity clinging to each breath taken.

Waiting on the other side of the interview room walls is Bautista, observing.

'You should know,' Isabel starts, 'that right now we have officers at both of your homes. They've already started searching both properties. Maybe you were hoping the fire you set would get rid of the evidence in the second one.' She keeps her eyes trained on his face, ready to catch the smallest twitch. 'But the firefighters got to the scene in time to prevent that. They're going to go over every inch of it.'

Still nothing. Not on the surface.

Sara had been right when she'd said this man was surrounded by hunger. She can feel it now, yawning open like a maw.

And it's directed at her, she realises. She can feel the concentration from him, the way his attention, his thoughts, his focus, all lap in her direction in the same waves of red smoke the young girl had described.

Just having her in this room is like having an unbearable itch he can't scratch.

In his mind she's like all the others, Gifted, an evil he must get rid of – he had the chance to do so but didn't quite make it.

That he came so close and lost is eating at him.

'We've called your ex-wife. She'll be here first thing in the morning.' Isabel picks up her coffee and drinks, the caffeine strong and hot, knocking her back into full control, 'whether we talk to your daughter too is up to you.'

That gets his attention.

Slowly he turns his head. His gaze locks on Isabel.

'She's fifteen, right?' Isabel puts the mug back down and leans forward, folding her arms on the table. 'Old enough to understand when I explain to her why her dad is a murderer.'

Next to the plastic cup of water, Horta's hands curl into thick fists.

Beside her, Daniel shifts in his chair, readjusting. He shifts his feet further apart, one arm over the back of his chair; he looks relaxed. Mocking even. 'Oh,' he says, 'I don't think he likes that.'

Horta's eyes slide from Isabel to Daniel. He stares.

It's as if his eyes are dead.

That hunger in him intensifies, the red surrounding him deepening to almost black. Leashed violence.

'I think you're being too nice,' Daniel says; he turns his head just enough to make it clear he's addressing Isabel, but he keeps looking at Horta. 'I say we go and get his daughter and bring her here right now. Maybe she can sit in here with us, ask Daddy why he's a murderer. Except maybe she won't want to see you, hmm? Because her dad is a monster.'

The sound of the rain fills the room. Just under it, the clock ticks the seconds of silence away.

'You knew everything was going to come out and you were willing to die just so you wouldn't have to see the look on your daughter's face,' Isabel says, voice low. 'It's shocking,' she says, 'that there's any sense of shame in you. How does shame coexist with murder?'

Horta's eyelashes sweep down, and he picks up his water. He takes his time drinking from it. He does it in small, individual sips, as if he's taking the time to savour each one. When he finishes, he sets the cup down carefully, adjusts it just so and then rests his hands on the table.

'Sergio,' Isabel says and waits until his eyes lift up to hers again.

He looks at her.

'What if I promise to protect your daughter?'

On his face, she registers a small flicker, a twitch that briefly pinches together the skin between his eyebrows before his expression smooths out again.

'My daughter isn't in danger.' His voice is devoid of emotion, monotone.

But they have his attention. That blackened red smoke of hunger has receded; a different emotion, a different need, is forcing its way to the surface.

'She is,' Isabel says. She keeps her tone matter-of-fact. This isn't someone who will respond well to gentleness, to cajoling, not from someone like her. 'This – what you've done, the people you've hurt – is all going to come out. There is nowhere your ex-wife will be able to go where this won't follow.' She paints him the picture. 'Fifteen. At school. No friends. Kids are cruel, Sergio. Their parents will say things about her, about you, behind closed doors and that will all come out. Her teachers won't look at her the same. Neither will her neighbours. She's the child of a murderer. She won't be able to hide from that. Your ex-wife won't be able to protect her. She can't be with her twenty-four/seven. And you won't be there, because you're going to be in jail for the rest of your life.'

His mouth curls into an ugly smile that does nothing to ease the deadness of his gaze. 'Is this where you tell me you can protect her?'

Isabel shakes her head. 'No. We're giving you a chance here. You tell us everything, from the beginning. There are families out there who need to know why you killed their daughters.'

'What? You want to give them justifications?' His expression shutters and his gaze finds its way back to the window.

'Personally, I don't care about justifications,' she says bluntly, 'that's between you and your God. But the families of your victims might. Your daughter and your ex-wife might. Your friends, the ones you betrayed, might. Cardoso. They'll want to know. And if you tell us everything, then in return, we'll do everything in our power to ensure that your daughter and ex-wife are shielded from all of this.'

The words taste like ash in her mouth.

She wants his name out there. She wants everyone to know who this man is and what he did. But his ex-wife did nothing wrong. Neither did his daughter. They can protect them both, at least, from being the final victims of his actions.

His eyes narrow on her. 'What does that mean, exactly?'

'We can't guarantee we can keep your name out of the press. But we'll try our best to. In the event that it does get out, we'll step in,' Isabel explains, 'we'll help your ex-wife and your daughter. Relocate them. New identities, if need be. So maybe at the very least they can live a life free of persecution for crimes they had no part of.'

They let him sit with it, not pushing any further.

The seconds drag on. Isabel sits back in her chair and picks up her mug again. Settling in to wait.

There's a knock on the door.

Daniel scoots his chair back, touches her shoulder briefly before going to the door. It opens with a squeak of its hinges.

Horta's eyes shift from Isabel's face once.

Behind her, she hears the baritone of Daniel's voice in a hushed tone and what sounds like Bautista's typical rasp.

The exchange lasts only about thirty seconds. She hears Daniel's shuffle of steps but not the door closing.

She glances over her shoulder then.

Daniel is standing, new tension pulsing off him. He keeps it from showing on his face. 'Senhor Horta,' he says, 'your lawyer is here.'

Isabel slides a hand into her pocket and eyes him over her mug as she continues to drink her coffee.

The door squeaks again and this time there is a new set of steps. Professional. The shoes clack on the floor as they make their way to Horta's side of the table.

'Are the cuffs really necessary when my client is in a building surrounded by officers?'

The door is closed behind them again. Daniel slides back into his seat next to Isabel.

Isabel spares the lawyer a brief glimpse. He's in a sharp grey suit that doesn't distract from the puffy skin beneath his eyes. Overnight court-appointed duty. Isabel is familiar with most of the government-appointed officials. This guy is probably a new addition to the roster. They need it.

The lawyer turns to Horta. 'Senhor Horta I'd advise you not to—'

'My mother died when I was five,' Horta says.

The lawyer twists in his seat to face his client. 'Senhor—'

Horta turns to him. 'Shut up. I'm speaking.'

The lawyer blinks at him but when Horta's unwavering stare stays pinned to him he doesn't protest.

He shakes his head but doesn't interfere again.

When Horta sees the lawyer isn't going to interrupt, he returns his attention to Isabel.

'You said your mother died when you were five,' Isabel says.

'That's right.' He nods. Then he pauses. 'It was a fire in my father's church.' His eyes become glazed, distance growing in them.

He's looking in Isabel's direction but not *at* her.

'She screamed throughout the whole thing,' he says, 'but he didn't let her out.' He pauses. 'Divine punishment,' he says slowly. 'My dad later told me she was going to leave us.'

Is he saying what she thinks he's saying?

'I remember the flames. I could see them through the windows. I remember thinking that they looked like they were trying to come out. I thought it was my mother using them to escape.'

He pulls himself back into the room.

'She didn't escape. I don't remember the rest, but I remember that.' This time when he reaches for his cup of water he drinks the rest in one go and lets the cup drop to the table. It bounces, toppling and rolling halfway across the table where it stops.

He scoots forward in his chair until he can rest his arms on the table, leaning forward until his chest is almost touching its surface. His eyes are alive.

'You want to know everything?' he asks. 'Down to my very first one?'

The lawyer stiffens and tries to intervene again. 'Senhor Horta, I advise you not to say anything further.'

Horta ignores him completely. 'You'll protect my daughter?'

'We will,' Isabel says.

Horta turns to the lawyer. 'Then your only job here is to make sure they do as they've promised.' He turns to look at Isabel and the smile he gives her makes Isabel think of being stuck in that forest, Carla a near dead weight in her arms and understanding that this man would do everything in his power to make sure that they burned together. 'I'll make sure you get everything down to the very last detail.'

Daniel leans forward, steepling his fingers. 'Then—'

'I consent.'

Daniel blinks. 'Excuse me?'

Isabel feels her stomach roll as she comprehends his intention.

'To Inspector Reis here accessing my mind and my memories. Isn't that how it works? I consent. You even have the lawyer here to corroborate that I gave permission.'

Daniel shoves himself back.

'What's wrong, Inspector?' Horta asks, mocking him. 'Isn't this what you wanted?' He relaxes back into his chair, and he turns his attention back to Isabel. 'You can have what you asked for. And your colleague here will have a front-row seat for everything. Down to how each and every one of her kind sobbed and screamed.'

He extends his arms further across the table, his hands knocking against the empty cup in the middle, fingers outstretched towards Isabel.

The smile stays on his face, making a grotesque shape of his lips.

Isabel's gaze drops to the hands he's offering her.

'Whenever you're ready, Inspector.'

She'll never be able to unsee. He knows it.

This is his way of ensuring she still burns with him.

'Well?'

Isabel lifts her eyes to meet his.

Then she leans across the table and touches his hand.

48

Isabel, Daniel and Chief Bautista watch as the two uniform officers shuffle Horta to the door, his lawyer beside him.

Isabel keeps her eyes on him. The smile hasn't left his face since she'd pulled herself out of his mind. There's a bruise on her wrist and four deep nail impressions from where he'd grabbed her at some point while she'd been inside his head. She'd had enough presence of mind to throw a hand out to keep Daniel from intervening even as she'd transitioned into the next memory.

The next death.

The next torture.

Until he'd shoved the final one at her, different from all the others, where his hands were not involved and the view was from a low vantage point and in the memory hard fingers dug into his small shoulder as fire licked out of the windows and a woman screamed and screamed as the church, imposing and towering over her, went up in flames.

By the time she'd slipped back out of his mind, there had been a film of sweat on her that had nothing to do with the heat of the room, nor with using her Gift. The sound of rain had slowly filtered back into her senses, like a dial slowly turning the sound back to life.

She'd seen a lot of things in her line of work.

As the chief and Daniel walk with them to the door, she takes advantage of the fact that they're not looking to clench her hands together, temporarily stilling the tremors that have been threatening to make themselves known.

She doesn't want them to see.

Doesn't want *him* to see.

Once she feels certain in her composure, she follows them out into the hallway.

Horta catches sight of her coming back out and digs his feet in to put a stop to the officers trying to get him moving.

'You think I'll burn in hell, don't you?' he says, like he doesn't even feel the officers pulling on him. He stands his ground, barely budging, his eyes on her face.

'It doesn't matter what I think,' Isabel says.

'I worked in the service for over twenty years. I saved more lives than I can count,' he says. 'I saved many more than I took. Some of those lives . . . were even the lives of things like you.' His gaze travels from her head down to her toes and there's disgust there. And a fever.

It wasn't enough for him to have made her experience it all first hand. It would never be enough until he got to do to her and others like her exactly what he did to the others.

He wants to burn her down to her very bones.

Isabel walks closer to him and stops. She doesn't make any effort to put distance between them. Let him feel the proximity. Of how, if his hands weren't handcuffed, he could reach right out and wrap his hands around her throat.

This is the closest he'll ever get and she wants him to feel it. His powerlessness.

'You think your God won't judge you?' she asks.

Slowly, he shakes his head. 'No. You'll all burn eventually. I was just his messenger.'

Then he looks away from her and gives in to the guards' tugs.

They disappear into the hallway, the sound of his chains loud in the hall.

Isabel steps back. She looks at Daniel. His eyes and mouth are tense around the edges as he stares back at her. The chief is also looking at her.

'Reis,' she says.

'I'll be all right, Chief,' she says. There's no point in lying to Bautista. But there's no point in telling her that she can still taste the smoke in the back of her throat, that she can still smell burning skin, that she can still feel skin under her fingernails and the struggle of limbs under her hands. And hear muffled screams and screams and screams.

'Get your statement down,' Bautista says, 'then I want you both to get out of here. The rest can wait until tomorrow.' She gives them both a sober look, then leaves.

Daniel shuffles over and wraps an arm around Isabel's shoulder. Frustration and anger roll off of him, infused with guilt.

'Come on,' she says, patting his back lightly. 'So we can get properly cleaned up and go and check on our partners.' Isabel pauses. 'And get a drink.'

He doesn't snort or crack a joke, like he normally would. But the arm around her relaxes a little.

They begin to make their own way back together.

49

This time when Vitorino Guerra's wife opens the door she doesn't give Isabel a piece of her mind, which Isabel appreciates.

She doesn't immediately move out of the doorway either though. Instead, her gaze shifts over Isabel's shoulder to take in Cardoso, who is standing just behind her, and then drops to Kuma sitting perfectly quiet at his feet.

'So now you're bringing dogs over too? What do you think my house is, Inspector?' she says.

Isabel shakes her head and steps back. 'No, I'm not coming in this time, Senhora Guerra.' She gestures to Cardoso. 'This is Investigator Cardoso. I brought him here because I think it would be good for him and your husband to talk.' She meets Senhora Guerra's eyes. 'I think it'll do them both a lot of good. Maybe allow them to move on from that nightmare.' She glances at Cardoso, who meets her gaze unflinchingly. Then he gives her a subtle nod.

Isabel feels rather than sees Senhora Guerra's eyes soften. 'What?' she asks. 'Is it over then?'

Isabel bends down to stroke Kuma's head, smiling when the dog gives her hand a small lick. 'Yes. But I'll let Cardoso here explain.' She stands up again and offers him her hand.

He takes it and gives it a firm shake. In his eyes there's a respect that hadn't been there when they met.

Isabel says her goodbyes and starts making her way back to her car.

When she looks again, the door to the house is already closed and there's no one else there.

The sun has been hiding for a while now, the sky clouded, though all around the birdsong is plentiful, injecting a touch of the whimsical into the morning. Isabel thinks there'll be rain in the afternoon.

As she gets in the car, she takes out her phone and calls her brother.

Sebastião answers on the second ring. 'Hey maninha, are you done?'

'Yeah. I'm headed back to the precinct now. Are you with mãe right now?'

'Yes, we just arrived. They've already got her signed in,' he says, and then lowers his voice. 'Are you sure you don't want to be here? I think tia would be really happy if you were here.'

'Is Rita there?'

'Yes, she's here too.'

She nods, even though he can't see, and sits back in the car seat, her gaze drifting back over to the Guerras' house. 'That's good.'

After the incident her mother had suffered under Gabriel's influence, Isabel had reached out to NTI and Monitoring. They were in part responsible for this and had, in the past, reversed Gabriel's hold on his then-partner, a young woman on whom he had used his Gift to help him commit his crimes. They'd agreed to examine her mother and begin the process of reversing what he had done.

'No,' Isabel says, 'she'll be back to normal soon. I don't want to spend time with something that isn't real.'

'Isabel . . .'

She knows he wants to say something to contradict her, but can't. She leans her head on the car window. 'It's all right, maninho, hmm? I'll be fine. I've got you and tia, remember? I've got people in my life who want me. But—' She opens her mouth, closes it, seals her lips together.

'But what, Isabel?' Sebastião prompts, his voice soft.

'Tell her that if after . . . after. If she still wants to see me, I'll see her then.' She pretends to herself that there was no tremble to those words, that they had come out of her mouth flawless and that it doesn't feel like her chest is being compressed and her lungs are too tight.

Sebastião will understand anyway.

'Okay maninha, I will.'

She hangs up and stares at her phone for a moment.

Then she gets in her car.

Voronov is waiting for her.

50

Isabel opens her eyes to the most beautiful view of a lake.

The briny scent of it dances under her nose. Her arms rest on a railing in front of her and her gaze is trained on the not-too-distant mountain, lush with green and small, brightly lit colourful houses climbing its face, charming in the evening light.

It looks like something out of a fairy tale.

Behind her she hears the voices and leisurely steps of people out for an evening stroll, she recognises the rapid-fire speech and its rhythm as Italian.

She doesn't speak it but there are enough similarities with the Portuguese language that she understands some. She'd understand more if it wasn't so fast.

'So, this is where you are,' she says.

The body she's in flinches and she feels the shock that reverberates through him, the complete surrealism of feeling your mouth open, hearing the sound of your own voice but knowing the words are not yours.

'I told you, Gabriel, that I would find you,' she murmurs, even as he pushes away from the railing and spins away from the view. He drops his gaze to the ground, limiting his field of vision and hers. 'A bit late for that, you already let your guard down.'

She feels the beating of his heart, the way it feels exactly like her own, nestled beneath her ribcage. The panic dries his mouth.

'You don't need to run away. I was only saying hello.'

Outside of him, of their connection, she hears the familiar sound of someone saying her name. Her team. Aleks.

She's done here. For now.

'Next time, I'll be saying hello in person.'

ACKNOWLEDGEMENTS

Just a few months ago, getting to this moment felt almost impossible, but we did it – we've reached the final instalment of the Inspector Reis series. And I do mean *we*.

To the Hodder team, a huge thank you to Kate who has helped me see the series through to its end, to Jo and Sorcha, and to the one who started it all, Eve. Without you, Inspector Reis never would have found a home in someone else's bookshelf.

Very grateful for my wonderful agent Oli Munson at A.M. Heath who has always been so supportive and calm and a voice of reason. Thank you, Oli!

To my group of wonderful friends who have kept me sane throughout the entire process: Lori, Audrey, Lyn, Imaan, Myra, Emily, Nadine, Sade, Richard, Melissa and Deanne. I love you all, thank you for believing in me.

A massive thank you also to all the lovely authors who took the time to read my proofs, giving me time out of their busy lives to lend their enthusiastic voices in support of the Inspector Reis series and a nervous debut author. My appreciation is heartfelt.

To my mum, Fernanda, and my sister Helena. Thank you for listening to my rants, for staying up late with me, for all the cups of tea, all the hugs and the reality checks. I love you both very much.

Lastly, to everyone who gave Inspector Isabel Reis a chance and spent time in this little world of mine, it has meant so much to me. Thank you for sticking with us and I hope to introduce you to other worlds and other characters again in the not-too-distant future.

All the love,
Patricia x

'Patricia Marques takes the classic crime novel and transforms it with a fascinating speculative twist. Pacy, immersive and brain-shiveringly clever' **Philippa East**

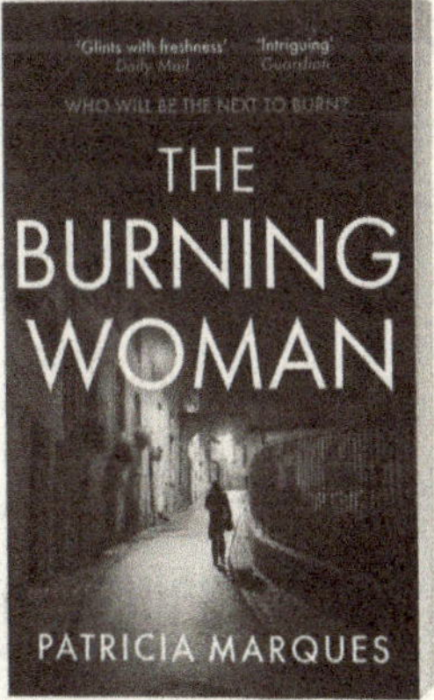

Follow Isabel Reis and Patricia Marques
to wherever they go next at
www.patricia-marques.com